Anya sighed."Even if you don't understand why things have happened the way they have, God does care."

"He has a rotten way of showing it." Nick turned away from her. Then something occurred to him. "So why didn't you go ahead and adopt me anyway?"

Anya touched his chin tenderly and turned his face toward her. "You needed a father, Nick. I couldn't give that to you."

"A father like that one?" Nick jerked his chin from her touch, pointing it toward the trailer where J.D. lived.

The Fatherless

The Fatherless

A novel by

Erin Inman

BAAL HAMON PUBLISHERS,
Akure, Nigeria.

Copyright © Erin Inman, 2008.

www.baalhamon.com/publishers/

publishers@baalhamon.com

ISBN-10: 978-075-691-4
ISBN-13: 978-978-075-691-8
EAN: 9789780756918

For Dustin

Part 1

Prologue

May 30th. His twenty-first birthday. For most, the milestone represented a beginning. For him, it meant one day closer to the inevitable victory of the enemy that stalked his body. Unless by some miracle someone else died who could give him life, his number of days left on earth equaled his peers' probable number of years.

He stared at the translucent skin that stretched over the bones in his hand. The pulsing of his blood, easily apparent in the purple lines fanning across the back of his hand, gave evidence of lingering life.

He wondered what the flesh would look like when the blood behind it coagulated and congealed; when he could no longer command his fingers to move.

His hands quivered uncontrollably at the thought and his stomach met their pattern. It would not be long. He knew it, the hospital personnel knew it, and Les knew it, though Les had chosen for him to cease to exist already.

But Anya… Anya did not know, and somehow he regretted that most of all.

He reached for the notepad and pen beside his hospital bed and drew them toward him. The smallest efforts caused his emaciated body to tremble with fatigue. He leaned his head back on the pillow, seeing a myriad of dancing white circles behind his eyelids.

After a long moment, he opened his eyes, raised his head, and grasped the pen between bony fingers. Part of him argued that to write was futile. This letter would simply add to the growing pile he had not sent.

Ever since he had found out about his illness, he had felt God's judgment upon him. He knew Anya would mother him, explain his wounds away, but he wanted to bear them. He deserved to bear them. Maybe then he could somehow atone for the damage he had done both to himself and to the name of Christ.

But still he wrote. He had found comfort in releasing his apprehension to ink and paper, as though leaving it there could relieve his mind.

And so one last time he began to write even though she would never receive the letter, even though he would die alone and soon.

"Dear Mrs. Martin..."

Chapter 1

Western Kansas
18 years earlier)

Anya Martin had turned 36 the same day her first child came into the world. Several minutes later, her second child was born. At the time, she found it amusing to think of the twins as being her first children since she had five stepchildren waiting eagerly for them to come home from the hospital.

Now, only a breath later, those twins were eighteen and away at college, which made her 54 and well past the halfway mark to a century. The five stepchildren had grown and been away from home longer than she cared to think about, getting married and producing grandchildren.

Anya sighed and reached for the head of lettuce on her kitchen counter. As she shredded it into a large bowl, she thought of those years of young children with crumbly play dough littering the linoleum. She missed the late night talks and ice cream runs during the teen years. Their big farmhouse held many memories.

Two arms slid around her from behind.

"Hello, Annie."

"Russell!" She turned in his arms to face him. "You're home early."

He nuzzled her cheek and ear. "I thought I'd quit early so we could do some painting over at the new house."

"Actually, Nell and her crew came over and helped me this afternoon," she said, referring to their daughter-in-law and grandchildren. "We got the bedrooms and closets finished. The painting is caught up as much as it can be for now."

"That's wonderful news." He sighed in relief.

Anya rubbed at the perpetual crease on Russell's forehead from his farmer's cap. "You look tired."

He lowered his head onto her shoulder. "I'm worn out. Trying to build a house and keep down my job at the same time is for a much younger man than me."

"Since when did you get so old?" she teased.

He smiled wryly. "I'm only a few years away from 70."

She brushed dirt from his flannel shirt. "I don't think you have to worry about losing your job, Russell. You know the boys will never fire you."

Two of their sons had taken over the farming operation and although Russell was still basically in charge, all the legal paperwork listed the sons as the owners.

Russell smiled. "No, they'll just start hinting that we move to Florida soon."

Their old rotary phone interrupted them and Russell pulled away to answer it. Anya moved back to the sink.

"So much for being finished early," Russell said, dropping the receiver into its cradle. "Karl has a heifer having trouble."

Anya set down the head of lettuce. "Do you have to go?"

He came and kissed her once more. "I'll be back as soon as I can, Annie," he said. "Thanks for doing the painting today."

She curled her fingers through his belt loops, holding him to her. "Things will slow down once we can get moved."

"The sooner, the better," he said.

Wichita, Kansas

"Nick Pierce, please report to the office," the disembodied voice sounded over the school intercom.

"Hey, Nick, you get in trouble?" A student jostled Nick from behind.

"Naw." Another student snickered. "The only thing Nick ever does wrong is act like a girl."

Nick bit the inside of his bottom lip and scooped his piano books from his desk.

"Pretty Boy can't even go to the principal's office without his music books," the first student sneered.

Nick tucked his books under one arm and walked down the narrow aisle, avoiding protruding legs and shoes.

"Come back as soon as you're finished," his teacher told him. "We will be going over the final review for the test."

Nick didn't respond. He knew he wouldn't be back.

In the office, the secretary directed him to a plastic chair with the order to wait. He sat stiff and straight, listening to the secretary hammer on her ancient typewriter.

"I'm sorry you had to wait."

Nick turned to see the principal.

"I'm afraid I have some bad news for you, son. We got a phone call just a few minutes ago."

"She died."

The principal cleared his throat. "Yes, son. I'm sorry."

Nick looked down at his ragged tennis shoes and let the air run out of his lungs.

"Someone will be here to pick you up," said the principal. "I'd suggest you get your things."

"I already have them," said Nick.

On cue, the door opened and Mrs. Anderson, Nick's social worker, entered on a wave of cheap perfume.

As he stood, several loose pages of sheet music slid out from his books onto the floor. He picked them up.

"How are you doing, Nicholas?" Her voice sounded neither sympathetic nor interested.

Nick did not answer. She did not ask again.

After signing several papers for the secretary, Mrs. Anderson herded Nick out to her Buick.

"It's not as though it's unexpected, but that doesn't make it easier," she said. "But don't worry, Nicholas. Time heals all wounds and you will always have memories of your grandmother."

The woman spouted the clichés as though quoting from a grieving manual. He didn't care to hold on to his memories, memories of playing alone, memories of countless failed attempts to please an old woman who made no secret of despising children and dirt, memories of futilely watching out the front window for his mother to come back.

Mrs. Anderson drove him into the hospital parking lot and cut the engine.

"You no doubt already know that your grandma did not wish to have a burial service. The hospital will take care of the proper arrangements with the... er... body."

He nodded. Grandma Bates had no money for hospital bills or burial. Now her burial would be paid for out of the goodwill account at the hospital. Charity. The truth was that Grandma Bates didn't have friends to come to a service anyway. A priest had been called in to administer the last rites.

The hospital had become a familiar place for Nick. He'd spent many evenings by Grandma Bates' bed, unsure what else to do, until a nurse had followed him home one night after visiting hours were over and reported him to social services. They had placed him in foster care after that. He would have preferred to continue living alone at Grandma Bates'. He was accustomed to fending for himself. He had done so for most of his twelve years.

Mrs. Anderson ushered Nick into the hospital. An empty gurney sat by the bed that Grandma Bates lay in, ready to carry her away.

Seeing her body, Nick hung back. It was one thing to visit Grandma Bates when she was hooked up to machines that made strange bleeping and whooshing noises. With all the equipment turned off, the silence pressed into him.

"Go," Mrs. Anderson urged. "You need to pay your last respects. It brings closure." She stayed by the doorway.

Nick edged closer. Grandmother's thin skin seemed pasted onto cardboard bones and painted watery blue. Her sunken chest did not rise with breath. So this was death.

"Ma'am," a stranger's voice spoke quietly. "I hate to take away from your good-byes, but we need to remove the body."

"Please, the boy just got here from school. Give him some time."

Nick looked away from his grandmother's body. He had said goodbye months ago, when Grandma Bates became so sick that she no longer recognized him. And how could he truly say goodbye to someone who never wanted him in the first place?

Grandma Bates was dead. His mother had disappeared out of his life years before.

"I'm finished," he said. He wasn't sure if he referred to looking at the body or to his future.

"Hello, boy."

Two words. The first words Nick heard his father speak. He hated being called boy as though he were a little kid.

Mrs. Anderson stood nearby, pleased with her own efficiency in locating J.D. Dobbs, Nick's birth father. She had visited Nick at his foster home last week and explained that the instant he was placed in foster care, the agency began searching for his parents. They found his father in western Kansas and references showed him to be the hard-working hired man of a farmer. They were unable to find his mother.

Mrs. Anderson brought Nick to Grandma Bates' empty house so that he could pack the last of his belongings and wait to meet the man who now stood before him. Nick had only been allowed an hour until his birth father came. He tried his best to pack all he thought he might need and quell his rising nerves.

He peeked in the doorway of Grandma Bates' bedroom, thinking to pick out a memento of her, but after years of never being allowed in her inner sanctum, he closed the door. As to what would happen to her house and her things, he had no idea.

Nick placed his palm against the man's outstretched hand. Feeling the rough calluses, he pulled away and tucked his hands into the pockets of his jeans.

"Well," said Mrs. Anderson, rubbing her hands together. "Are you ready to go, Nicholas?"

Nick looked down. Two suitcases, Grandma Bates' hardback green luggage, lay at his feet, holding all twelve of his years. He nodded without looking back up at the stranger who shared his last name.

His father lifted the larger suitcase easily.

"Off you go, then." Mrs. Anderson made a shooing motion with her hands, no doubt eager to reduce her caseload.

Nick grasped the handle of the smaller suitcase and watched his father's muddy cowboy boots tromp back to the front door. Grandma Bates would fuss at the mess if she could see it. The house already smelled musty and stale just in the two weeks since her death.

Nick paused to look around the tiny entryway with the tiled floor, remembering when he had driven matchbox cars along the grout lines, trying not to bother Grandma while her favorite game shows were on. Many tiles had cracked or popped out completely and created an intricate map for his vehicles to traverse. Grandma had always said she might not be able to afford replacing anything, but at least things would be clean.

"You coming?" His father stood holding the screen door open.

Nick lifted the suitcase in front of him like a shield and edged out of the doorway. He walked stiff-legged down the sidewalk to the battered pickup truck at the curb, aware of the man behind him. His father hefted the luggage into the back of the pickup and tightened a bright blue tarp over the top.

Initially, Nick had wondered if he would stay in foster care, or if maybe his mother would come for him. Never once had he considered his father taking him, a man he had never even met or heard about.

The sky rumbled fair warning of rain. Nick reached for the door handle and climbed inside. It took two tries before the door stayed shut without bouncing back open.

He stared out the mud-flecked pickup window at Grandma Bates' house. Once beautiful and stately, the house had fallen into disrepair and ruin like all the other homes in the inner-city neighborhood. Life there had not been happy but at least it was familiar and consistent, every crocheted doily and plastic flower arrangement.

They pulled away from the curb with a lurch. Several beer bottles rolled out from under the seat. Nick kicked at them with his foot.

He peeked at his father, trying to see a glimpse of himself in the sun-baked lines of the man's face. Alone in the cramped cab with this stranger of a father, he wished he were anywhere else, even if that anywhere meant foster care.

"Be glad once we're out of this traffic," his father said. "Never was much for city driving."

Nick watched in silence as they rounded the corner and passed the music store where he had taken piano lessons for free from the storeowner until Grandma's illness.

His father turned the truck up the interstate ramp and turned north. Neither made any pretense of small talk as miles and minutes took them away from Wichita.

As rain started down, the windshield wipers beat out in steady 4/4 time, in keeping with the country music station that his father switched on. Nick gritted his teeth at the nasal voices and predictable melodies. Tchaikovsky would have cried in outrage.

They turned west on Interstate 70, driving out from under an umbrella of clouds and into the sunshine. The sun dipped below the visor and glared into the pickup cab, finally relenting and falling under the horizon, casting pink and orange hues onto the lingering clouds.

Nick's neck protested after hours of facing the passenger window, but he kept his face turned away from the man at the wheel. Huge expanses of fields and pastures swept by, broken only by occasional farmhouses, grain silos and Quonsets. The interstate exits grew further and further apart, the towns smaller and smaller.

"We're getting close. We'll be at the farm soon."

Nick jumped. A farm seemed as remote and foreign as the Antarctic. Nick stared out at the miles of flat yellow grass. He supposed he could survive anywhere as long as he had access to a piano.

Anya stood in the middle of her new living room. She felt somewhat like a tropical island surrounded by cardboard boxes instead of water. However, the only tropical thing about her was the humid sweat trickling down her back. This April had dished out warmer weather than normal and Anya could only hope that the new air conditioning unit worked.

Two of her stepsons, Mitch and Karl, grunted as they muscled a couch through the doorway.

"Where do you want it, Mom?" panted Karl. Sweat poured down the sides of his face.

"A little out of shape, Karl?" teased Mitch. "You know, that's what happens when you're an old man in your thirties."

Mitch's last word ended with an oomph as Karl shoved the couch toward him.

"Watch it, squirt," he warned. Karl was the eldest, while Mitch had been not much more than a baby when she married their father.

Anya shook her head in amusement and pointed to the only empty space in the room.

"Put the couch over there for now. We'll move it later. There are too many boxes in the way right now."

She watched her boys, men really. Karl loved farming. He claimed that during fall harvest the corn kernels in his combine looked like gold nuggets, no matter what the market price was. He also raised cattle and horses for breeding stock, a side business that had grown to the point that Karl now paid a full time hired man.

Although barely 20, Mitch had not shown any interest in college other than one year of trade school. He preferred working on any type of motor and reading mechanic manuals. He had cleaned out an abandoned shed on the farm site to use as a repair shop. Russell bragged that Mitch's expertise saved time and money in repairs. Others in the area had begun bringing their vehicles and machinery to Mitch for repairs as well and he worked many long evening hours after his share of the farm work was done. Anya knew that he dreamed of opening his own repair shop someday. He was glad to farm with Karl but Anya figured his first love would win out as soon as he had saved up enough money for his own building.

Despite Anya's insistence that he could continue living at home as long as he liked, Mitch liked his independence and lived in an apartment in town.

A sudden cry and crash came from the kitchen.

"It's okay, nobody's hurt," Russell hollered. "But we sort of need a broom."

Anya rushed to the kitchen to see her granddaughter Sara standing in the midst of shattered pottery.

Sara turned agonized eyes toward her grandmother. "I'm sorry, Grandma. I didn't mean to drop it. Really. I was trying to open the door at the same time and it slipped out of my hands and I couldn't catch it in time."

"Sara, honey, it's okay." Russell comforted her.

"Are you hurt? Did you get cut anywhere?" Anya fussed. She inspected Sara's hands, face and legs.

"No, but I broke your lamp. I'm so sorry, Grandma. I know you've had it for just forever and now I broke it."

Russell picked up a large shard. "Never liked this old lamp anyway," he said.

"Neither did I," Anya said in amazement. "I only kept it because I thought you liked it. Goodness knows I threw away so much accumulated junk when we packed. And to think I could have parted with this monstrosity as well."

Russell suddenly laughed. "Sara, girl, it looks like you done did your grandma and me a favor."

"Let's get this mess cleaned up," Nell said, throwing her in-laws a grateful smile.

Karl poked his head in and addressed Nell. "Honey, Mitch and I are going to pick up the pizzas for supper." He looked at the broken shards. "Don't tell me. I don't want to know."

Their youngest child, Avery, skidded into the room. Karl collared him by his shirt. "Whoa there. Be careful, Avery."

"Would you take him with you?" Nell asked her husband. "I don't want him getting into this glass."

"Yes, ma'am." Karl pecked Nell on the lips and turned to go, only to bump into Russell, who was on his way back with the broom and dustpan. The broom clattered to the floor. Avery shrieked.

"Just think, Mom," Nell said with a grin. "We get to go through this all over again when Karl and I move into your old farmhouse."

Anya grinned back. "What makes you think I'll help?"

Nell laughed as she handed the broom to Sara, who began sweeping up the pieces of broken lamp. "Go ahead with whatever you were doing, Mom. We can finish this here."

"I'm not sure I was doing anything." Anya opened the top flaps of a cardboard box to reveal glass bowls sheltered in plastic bags. "I feel like I'm just puttering around without any real progress."

She had taken so many loads to the dump and thrift store as she sorted and packed that she wondered if they'd have anything left, yet their belongings seemed to multiply like rabbits. She was thankful for a smaller home to take care of but wondered where on earth she would put everything.

Anya unwrapped several bowls and set them in her new cupboards. She pictured the empty and lonely cabinet she had moved them from. It had been hard to strip the old farmhouse bare. She and Russell had spent so many years together in that house, surrounded with children, laughter, and contentment.

Yet, Karl's family would fill it soon enough and give the walls new memories to hold.

As soon as Karl and Mitch returned with the pizza, they all sat down on the living room floor to feast.

"Where's Michele?" asked Nell, referring to her oldest daughter.

"Probably on the phone." Sara rolled her eyes. The girl turned to Anya. "She's always on the phone."

"Can't be. Our phone's not hooked up yet," said Russell. "Sara, why don't you go and find her. Tell her we're ready to pray for our food."

"Michele!" Sara hollered.

"Sara, go get her," Karl admonished.

"I'm coming." Michele appeared from the hallway.

"Where were you?" asked Sara. "We're hungry."

"I was in the bathroom," said Michele defensively. She rolled her eyes at her little sister and sank to the floor.

Russell thanked the Lord for their food and the tremendous amount of work they had accomplished as a family, then Nell opened the pizza boxes on the floor and everyone dug in.

Anya bit the tip of her slice of pepperoni pizza, catching a string of cheese with her finger. The crust tasted like the cardboard box.

At the sound of a motor, Russell looked out the window. "J.D.'s here."

Anya never ceased to be astounded at Russell's ability to recognize vehicles in the dark by their headlights or the sound of their engine.

"I gave J.D. the rest of the week off," said Karl taking a swig of his soda. "I wonder why he's back so soon."

Russell chewed on his toothpick. "You told me this is the first vacation time he's asked for in two years."

Karl nodded. "Always before I've had to practically force him to take time off. He said some kind of emergency had come up and he had to go to Wichita."

A vehicle door slammed, echoed by another.

"It sounds like he has someone with him," said Anya.

"Maybe he went and got a wife," Karl teased.

"Pity the woman who'd marry him," retorted Nell.

"He's a little rough around the edges, I'll grant you. But he is a good worker," defended Karl.

"When he's not drinking," Nell retorted under her breath.

A loud knock rattled the newly installed front screen. Russell opened the door.

"Hello, J.D., come on in."

J.D. stepped in followed by a tall, skinny boy. Anya stood up in greeting. The rest of the family stared.

"My son," J.D. said, gesturing toward the boy. "Went to Wichita to pick him up."

"Your son?" Russell failed at hiding his shock. "Well, I'm glad to meet you. The name's Russell Martin. J.D., uh... your Dad works for us."

Russell held out his hand to the boy. Anya noticed the nervous way the boy drew one shoulder higher than the other.

"What's your name?" Russell asked.

"Nick." The boy spoke under his breath, without meeting Russell's eyes.

Russell released Nick's hand. "Nick, I'd like you to meet my wife, Anya, and some of our children and grandchildren. They came to help us move in today, as you can no doubt see for yourself."

A chorus of hellos echoed around the room. The boy's ears reddened.

"Welcome, Nick," Anya said warmly. "Sorry about the mess. As you can see, we still have a long ways to go."

Nick glanced up and nodded before looking down again.

J.D. spoke. "Saw lights down this way as we drove up. Knew you were moving today so we thought we'd stop by."

"Well, J.D., that makes you and Nick are our first official visitors," said Russell. "We'd have you sign our guest book, but we have absolutely no clue where it is at the moment."

"Figured you needed to know about the kid," said J.D. with a shrug.

"So, is Nick visiting?" Anya asked hesitantly.

"He'll be living with me from now on. Been living with his grandma. She died last week."

"I'm sorry to hear that," Anya said. She reached out to touch the boy's arm in sympathy. He jerked in surprise, as though unfamiliar with touch.

"Would you like some pizza?" Nell asked. "We have plenty left."

The boy looked longingly at the open pizza box.

"No thanks," said J.D.

"It's no problem," said Nell. "You must be hungry after your trip."

"Already said no thanks." J.D. crossed his arms over his chest and turned to Karl. "I won't be in to work until tomorrow afternoon. Probably take me a good part of the morning just to get the kid to school and enrolled."

"That's fine. You don't have to work at all, you know," said Karl. "You still have the next two days off. Maybe you could wait to enroll Nick. Take those few days to get to know each other."

"Yeah, well," J.D. cleared his throat. "Don't want to get behind on anything."

"Oh, you wouldn't be," Russell assured him. "End of March is a slower time of year. After we get into April and planting season, then it'll get busy."

J.D. tightened his mouth.

"Whatever you decide will be fine, I'm sure," Karl capitulated, ever the peacemaker. Anya knew that although J.D. worked hard, he rarely took advice or suggestions gracefully.

"Truly, J.D., you'd be helping us out if you take this. We ordered too much." Nell held out several slices of pizza wrapped in a napkin.

J.D. jerked his head toward his son, indicating for him to take it. Nick took the bundle from her with a grateful smile. His eyes landed on Anya's upright piano and lingered. Anya read his interest.

"Do you play, Nick?" she asked.

He glanced at his father before answering with a jerky nod.

"Social worker told me about that. Won't have time for that no more," said J.D. gruffly.

Nick looked back at the floor.

"Many world-class pianists are male, J.D.," Anya said.

"Not my kid. He ain't gonna be no pansy." J.D. curtly opened the door and walked out.

Nick's eyes met Anya's, both pleading and resigned, and then he followed his father, carefully latching the screen door behind him.

The family waited until the sound of J.D.'s pickup faded down the road.

Russell sighed. "So J.D. has a son. I can't exactly picture him knowing how to be a father."

"That poor boy," said Anya. "I wonder if his mother is still living. How old do you suppose he is?"

"Maybe ten, maybe twelve," said Nell. "What do you think, Sara? Did he look about your age?"

"I suppose," Sara answered. "Maybe he'll be in my class at school."

"If he is, you'll have to make an extra effort to be nice to him," her mother told her.

Anya consolidated the leftover pizza slices into one box. "I know that J.D.'s a responsible worker, but he makes me nervous. With his drinking, I don't like to think about him caring for that young boy."

"What does he drink?" asked Avery.

"Never mind, sweetie." Nell rubbed at pizza sauce on the boy's chin.

"I don't particularly like it either, Annie," said Russell. "But it sounds like J.D.'s all the boy's got. And to give him credit, he has been good hired help. Not only that, but with us in our new house, we live within a half mile of J.D.'s trailer. We can keep an eye on him. In fact, I can't help but think God had us build right here, close to that trailer, for a reason. I think we have a God-given responsibility with that boy."

"Hear, hear." Karl applauded.

Anya took her husband's hand, feeling unaccountably scared. "Let's pray, Russell."

He rubbed his thumb over her knuckles. "And act," he said.

Anya opened her eyes and blinked at the glowing green hands on the clock. 2:53 am. She squinted to make sure. She couldn't see clearly without her glasses.

Moonlight streamed in uninvited and lay across the foot of the bed, the same bed Russell had bought three weeks after their wedding.

"Didn't want you to ever think you had to take Elin's place," he had said as he carried in the headboard, referring to his first wife who had died shortly after Mitch's birth.

Anya rolled over to find Russell's empty pillow. Fumbling out from under the covers, she padded into the dark hallway, skirting around several boxes stacked along the wall.

She stopped in the doorway and surveyed him. He sat in his oversized tan recliner, the chair that bore permanent contours of his body. A worn Bible lay open on his lap. His wide hands rested reverently on the creased pages, his eyes closed, his lips moved soundlessly.

How much this man meant to her, had become part of her very being. Somehow, the sight of him praying in the familiar recliner caused the alien walls and windows of the new room to become intimate and homey.

He opened his eyes. "I didn't mean to wake you," he said.

"You didn't," she assured him. "I never sleep well on the first night in a different place."

When he held out one hand to her, she crossed the room and settled on the arm of his chair. He rested his hand on her hip; she laid her fingers on the back of his head where his hair still grew thick and wiry. They sat without speaking, each feeling the other's warmth, at ease with the stillness.

Finally Russell spoke. "I woke up thinking about our new neighbors."

She waited for him to continue.

"I felt led to come and pray." He sighed. "I have this urgency. I can't quite explain it, Annie. Almost as if there's not much time."

She smoothed his hair without speaking. She felt it too.

Chapter 2

Nick awoke the next morning with a jolt of confusion. He rolled over and buried his face, remembering where he was.

"Time to get up," someone said on the other side of the small room's door. His father. There was a pause. "You awake in there?"

"Yes," Nick answered. He sat up in bed.

The night before, J.D. had shown Nick up rickety metal stairs into a singlewide trailer. Nick had waited for his eyes to adjust to the dimness inside from the poor lighting before inspecting his new home.

Dark paneling covered the walls, buckling in various places. The carpeting had not been vacuumed for an indeterminate amount of time; mud clods and stains spotted its shaggy surface. The main living area consisted of a chipped Formica table, 2 mismatched chairs, a sagging brown couch and well-worn recliner. In contrast to the sad furniture, an expensive large screen television dominated the far wall, perched precariously on a cheap entertainment center that had veneer peeling off the corners of its particleboard. A tired bed sheet had been tacked over the room's only window.

"Kitchen's over here." His father had jerked his head sideways to indicate the location.

Nick had peeked through the opening to see a tiny square kitchen. Age-old grease splattered the cupboards and crusty dishes vied for countertop space. Nick suppressed a shudder.

"I don't cook much," said J.D. "I eat out some, pack sandwiches for lunch at work. Whenever you're hungry, help yourself. I try to go to the grocery store couple times a week, so let me know if you need anything."

Nick couldn't quite imagine asking this stranger for anything, but neither could he fathom finding edible food in that kitchen.

J.D. moved on to a long, cramped hallway. He held Nick's large suitcase in front of him in order to fit through.

"This here's the bathroom," he said as they passed a narrow door. Nick wondered if the bathroom was in the same condition as the rest of the house and if his father owned any bleach.

"This'll be your room." J.D. stopped at the second door. "Got my desk in there right now and been using it for storage but I'll move most of that into my room or out to the shed. Meant to already have that done."

Nick carried his smaller suitcase and set it down on the floor. J.D. followed him into the room and dropped the larger case on a sagging twin bed.

"Made up the bed for you with clean sheets," he said, obviously proud. "You can put your stuff on this shelf and in the closet."

Nick tried to say thank you but the words stuck in his throat.

"Well." His father pulled on his shirt collar. "Guess I'll turn in. Been a long day. For both of us I'd imagine."

He turned back to Nick at the door. "You'll be all right?"

"Sure," Nick said.

"Holler if you need anything." J.D.'s ill-at-ease expression implied that he hoped Nick would not.

"I'll be fine," Nick said.

The floor creaked as his father left him. Several moments later, he heard the canned sound of television voices coming from the bedroom on the other side of the wall.

Nick looked around the small room dubiously. J.D.'s desk and chair took up most of the space, spilling over with paperwork and junk mail. The shelf J.D. had indicated earlier had been emptied but not cleaned. Nick refused to put any of his belongings on top of the layers of dust and grime.

He hoped the closet had space for most of his clothing. He had no intention of leaving his underwear exposed in the open where that man might see them.

The closet door screeched when Nick started to pull it open. He winced and tried without luck to be quiet. To his relief, the closet stood relatively empty with the exception of several large taped boxes.

He took shorts and a t-shirt out of his larger suitcase before putting both cases into the closet, still unpacked. He would look for cleaning supplies and try to make things more habitable. Until then he could live out of his suitcases. He had done it during his months of foster care. He could do it for a while longer. If he were honest, Nick felt reluctant to admit his permanence in this hovel with this stranger by unpacking.

He started to unbutton his shirt but the silence and darkness outside the bare window made him nervous. He was accustomed to streetlights and traffic noise. Somehow the blankness of the window threatened him. What if his father were out there, looking into the lighted room? His skin shivered even though the thought was hardly realistic. Nick tiptoed to the bathroom and found a rumpled bath towel that looked relatively clean. Going back to his room, he tacked the towel over the glass using thumbtacks he found scattered on his father's desk.

He changed quickly and huddled under the covers, worrying about whether or not he could sleep in this strange place.

"Nick, time to get up for school." J.D. rapped on the door again.

Nick looked around. The grime had not disappeared with the morning light. If anything, the more persistent rays that made their way through the thin towel only made it look worse.

Nick shook himself. "I'm coming."

He yanked on a pair of pants and a clean, albeit wrinkled, shirt.

After a quick trip to the bathroom, in which he tried to accommodate his needs without touching anything more than necessary, Nick ventured into the kitchen.

His father stood in the front of the open refrigerator. "Don't know if the milk's still good. If it is, there's cereal in the cupboard."

"No thanks," Nick said, his appetite fading. From his vantage point, the refrigerator seemed to be stocked with white bread and cases of Busch beer.

"You can make yourself some toast." J.D. slung a loaf of bread toward Nick. "Toaster's on the counter by the sink."

Nick looked doubtfully at the overflowing counter. Sure enough, a toaster sat by the sink, surrounded by dishes and wadded paper towels.

"Do you mind if I, uh… do any dishes later, after school or something?" Nick asked.

J.D. blinked at him, a crease between his eyebrows as though he thought the question odd. "I guess not. Go ahead, long as you don't move anything around. I like to be able to find things where I put them."

This time, Nick blinked. How could he clean up without moving things? And anyway, how could his father find anything in this pit the way it was?

"Your toast," J.D. reminded him. "Best keep moving. I don't know what time school starts."

Nick put two slices of bread into the toaster and pressed down. He tried to ignore the myriad of crumbs already around and on the toaster. He could easily picture an army of ants coming to carry off the payload.

J.D. unscrewed the cap on the milk carton and sniffed the opening. Without a word, he poured the liquid into the sink.

Nick covertly studied his father, searching for any facial clues to link them. Possibly the nose and chin, definitely not the eyes or forehead.

"How did you meet my mom?" he asked.

J.D. slowly set down the empty carton. "Why do you ask?"

Nick wished he hadn't.

J.D. handed Nick a butter knife. "You'll need this. Margarine's in the fridge." He left the kitchen and once again, Nick heard the television click on.

"Hey, B...b...brenna!" a voice taunted behind her. Brenna did not need to turn around to identify it. Her tormentor. Tate Mason.

Her first two classes of the day were Tate-free, but once third hour rolled around, she faced a constant barrage of insults.

She closed her eyes. She'd been unable to eat breakfast that morning, dunking each piece of cereal in the milk and watching it bob back up again, wishing she could fake being sick.

Brenna's brother, Bradley, had looked disgusted and stood up from the table, his bowl polished clean.

"Just ignore them if they tease you, Brenna. But whatever you do, don't talk. Don't give them even more reasons to make fun of you."

She had made a face at him. Bold Bradley. No one would dare make fun of him to his face. She wished, just once, she could be as bold as her brother.

Brenna clenched her jaw and pulled her homework out of her book bag and laid it on her desk.

"T...t...too bad the r...r...rich kid can't pay to learn how to t...t...talk." When Tate laughed, several others joined in.

Not for the first time, Brenna wished she could stay at home and do her schoolwork. Her house may be stifling and sad, but she had a large bookshelf in her bedroom where she kept all her favorite books. With them, she could disappear into foreign lands and eras any time she wished, places where no Tates existed to taunt her.

Tate bumped into Brenna. His boot landed squarely on her sandal. "Hey, rich girl. Are you deaf as well as dumb?"

"Knock it off, Tate."

Brenna looked up to see Sara Martin. She knew Sara had a reputation for sticking up for the underdog. To have evoked Sara's public sympathy embarrassed her.

"Class, it's time to get started," said the science teacher.

Sara smiled at Brenna and found her seat.

"Class, I'd like to introduce a new student to you," the teacher said. "This is Nicholas Pierce."

Desks creaked and clothes rustled as the students turned to gawk at the new student.

"Welcome to the seventh grade class. I understand you prefer to be called Nick," the teacher said.

The boy nodded.

"Tell us a little about yourself, Nick."

Nick shrugged and traced his finger over his desktop. He sat with one leg crossed over the other knee, girlish-like and swung his foot back and forth.

"Start with where you moved from."

"I moved here from Wichita." Nick spoke with precise enunciation.

Tate snickered. "Well, if it isn't Saint Nick," he said, mimicking his tone and posture.

"That's enough, Tate," said the teacher. She turned her attention back to Nick. "Tell us what your interests are, what you like to do?"

Nick pursed his lips together and glanced at Tate. "Nothing special, I guess."

Brenna couldn't help but hope that maybe Tate would move on to new bait, even if it wasn't fair to the new kid.

"Well," said the teacher. "Maybe we can let you get to know us first. Students, why don't each of you take a turn, stand up, and tell the class your name and something you enjoy doing."

Brenna's heart dropped down into her stomach. Stand before the whole class and talk? The teacher might as well have asked her to do cartwheels on a trampoline.

"Now then, let's start right here." The teacher pointed to a girl in the front row.

"This is stupid," Tate whispered. "We've all known each other since kindergarten."

For once, Brenna agreed with him.

"Very good." The teacher beamed after the girl spoke, then pointed to the boy in front of Brenna. "You next," she said.

Brenna felt bile rise from her stomach. The teacher wasn't even choosing the students in order. How would she have time to prepare anything to say, much less practice it in her mind?

She pressed her ice-cold hands against her stomach. Her anxiety increased as student after student stood up and spoke. Then the teacher's finger pointed at her. The class broke into giggles, mocking Brenna before she had even stood. Tate made stuttering noises above the laughter.

Brenna stood but kept one hand on her desk. The teacher tapped on her clipboard with her red pen. Brenna stared at the pen, watching it turn into a red blur as the teacher's tapping sped up. She opened her mouth, but no sound came out. For one terrifying instant, blackness closed in on either side of her face, as though she wore blinders like the ones they had put over the horses' eyes in the book "Black Beauty". Abruptly, she sat down without saying a word and hung her head.

More titters erupted but the teacher made a quick motion with her pen, cutting them off and pointed to another student.

Brenna studied the scratched wooden surface of her desk. Tears prickled behind her nose. She sensed eyes on her and looked sideways, only to see the new boy watching her intently. She looked away.

Nick accepted the lunch tray the school cook handed him, eyeing its contents. Corndog, green beans, applesauce and a brownie. Not too bad. Better than his old school's food and definitely better than having to fix his own.

He shuffled down the lunch line behind the rest of the class. A new school. Nick felt nervous and angry, nervous at the changes, angry at his nervousness. His last school had to be four times the size of this one. Anonymity seemed less possible here. He had survived by staying in the shadows before. It would be harder here. Already, he had felt cowed by the other kids in the first class. He knew he could have said that he played the piano when the teacher asked what he enjoyed. But he hadn't. He hated that he felt he had to hide the fact that he loved the piano and was good at it too. Why was that such a stigma? Most composers were men – and concert pianists as well, just like that older woman down the road had told his father last night.

Nick grabbed a chocolate milk carton out of the open chest-style refrigerator and made his way through the crowded tables toward the far end of the lunchroom.

"Hey," a boy called to him. "You can sit here with us if you like."

"No thanks," he mumbled and steered to a spot where he could sit alone. He had never tried to make friends. He wouldn't start now.

The shy girl with dark bangs sat alone at the table to his left. He had seen her obvious terror as she stood by her desk unable to speak. He knew her feeling of wishing to disappear. He knew it all too well.

Brenna stabbed greasy green beans with her fork.

"Hi, Brenna. Mind if I sit here?"

Brenna looked up to see Sara Martin. She shrugged.

Sara dropped into the seat opposite her.

"I guess I'll be riding your bus soon," Sara said. She reached for the ketchup and squirted a dollop beside her corndog. "My grandparents built a new house and we're moving into their old farmhouse. It's close to yours, I think."

Brenna took a bite of green beans so she wouldn't have to answer.

"You live by the highway, right? In that big brick house with the swimming pool?"

Brenna nodded. She didn't bother to tell Sara that the pool hadn't been filled for two summers.

"You know," Sara said, "the new kid, that Nick guy, lives in the trailer house on that road, too." Sara dipped her corndog in ketchup and took a large bite.

Brenna knew the trailer Sara spoke of. Stuck back in an old tree row, with branches littering the ground and rusty farm implements nearly hidden in tall grass, it looked deserted. Her house sat at the intersection so she often saw the owner roar around the corner in his rusty pickup truck.

She also knew which house belonged to Sara's grandparents. She had ridden her bike down the sandy road several times to watch the construction.

Once, an older man had offered her a cookie from his sack lunch. He had seemed nice enough but Brenna had been trained well. She had quickly ridden her bike back home without speaking to him.

"There's Nick over there." Sara pointed with her remaining corndog.

Brenna looked. He sat at the end of a table, alone.

"He looks kinda lonely, don't you think? Maybe I should ask him to come sit with us," suggested Sara.

The boy looked up from his tray.   His eyes met Brenna's. Flustered, Brenna looked away.

"I guess he came during second hour this morning," Sara continued, not seeming to mind that Brenna had not said anything. "His dad, J.D., works for my dad and grandpa. Only we didn't even know that J.D. was a dad until he brought Nick to my grandparents' house last night."

Brenna was curious. "Y...y...you m...m...met him already?"

"Well, sort of," Sara told her. "It's not like we were introduced or anything. I mean I didn't talk to him. Boy, were we all surprised when he came in with J.D., though. I feel bad for him, sitting all alone. It must be hard to have to start at a new school at the end of March. Everybody else knows the routine, has their friends and cliques already."

Sara finished her corndog and stood up. "I'd better hurry. I'm supposed to meet some other girls in the band room to practice our flute trio."

Brenna felt empty when Sara walked away. She thought of Sara's words, "everyone else has their friends already". Sara was only being nice because she felt sorry for her.

Brenna sneaked another look at the new student. He was a loner, like her. She wondered why.

J.D. stared at the pickup dash in front of him. His sandwich lay on the seat beside him, wrapped in a leftover plastic bread bag, but he was uninterested in food. His thoughts centered on his son. And his son's mother.

He shook his head with a rueful sigh. He and Julienne were just two kids having a good time in the proverbial back seat. He hadn't liked her decision to give the baby up for adoption, had pressed her to have an abortion, but she had been adamant.

"I'm well aware that I don't know how to be a mother," she had said. "And you won't stick around long enough to be a father. I know that too. We just messed up, J.D., messed up big time. But a baby is a baby and this kid's going to have a chance at life."

Julienne had dropped out of school and moved away to live with her grandmother until the baby was born. He hadn't heard from her again, hadn't tried to contact her.

J.D. had quit school as well, taking up a job offer at a cattle ranch across the state. He had dated women off and on over the years, usually women from the bar who weren't interested in more than a few good nights.

At times, he had blamed Julienne for making him "marriage shy", but he knew that was unfair. He simply didn't know how to be a husband or a father just as she hadn't known how to be a mother. He didn't know how to love.

Off and on, he had wondered what ever happened to Julienne's baby, mentally giving her ownership as though that somehow distanced him. Up until the social worker from Wichita had called to inform him that he now had legal guardianship of the boy, he had not known that she had never given the baby up for adoption after all. Instead she had taken off for parts unknown on his third birthday and left him with his grandmother. They had tried to contact her with no success, he was told. Would he come sign the papers and take the boy?

Now that child lived under his care, under his protection. The boy, nearly a teenager, was a real-live person that he could no longer ignore. He was suddenly expected to be a father.

He wanted to make Nick feel comfortable in his home, wanted to be friendly, meet his needs. But so much seemed beyond his comprehension. Nick eyed him like a distrustful dog backed in a corner. He knew they needed to establish trust in each other same as he worked on building up trust with each of Karl's horses that he trained. Truth be told, J.D. had long ago given up trusting anyone, not with the sort of intimacy that comes from building a family.   Animals you could predict. People, no.

Not to mention the fact that the boy's feministic mannerisms and affectations irked him to no end. How any self respecting boy on the planet could mince his steps and speak with such girlish precision and still maintain any sense of ego was beyond J.D.'s comprehension. He knew he should teach the boy how to be a man, but where was a body to start? His boy needed more than he could give, that much was clear.

J.D. thumped the steering wheel with the heel of his hand and cursed Julienne for deserting their son, cursed himself for the knowledge that he would do the same in an instant if he could.

Nick walked cautiously into the boys' locker room. He hated gym class to begin with, but the locker room only made it worse. Much worse.

Every locker room seemed to contain the same components – the athletic jock, the fat kid, the underdeveloped, the overdeveloped, and the kid who'd raided his father's stash of porn.

Male virility oozed from every corner of the room, a maleness that Nick had rarely been exposed to and did not comprehend. Boys shoved at each other, gave high fives, told dirty jokes and walked around in various stages of nudity.

Nick tried to blend in with the nobodies, but as before in Wichita, the bully sniffed him out.

"Hey, you." Tate Mason, the same kid that had teased the dark-haired girl in first class, stopped in front of Nick, wearing nothing but cowboy boots and underwear. His seventh-grade chest was already covered with a mat of fine hair. "You new here?"

Nick's hands froze on his jean zipper. "Yes," he said warily. Tate already knew that. Why was he asking now?

"I can tell. You know how I can tell?" The boy paused for effect and pushed his face close to Nick's. "Because the girl's locker room is down the hall."

A burst of laughter rounded the room and landed on Nick's red face.

Tate held out his arms and turned around in a slow circle, as though he accepted accolades from an adoring crowd.

Nick wondered what it was about his body that singled him out, made him the butt of gender jokes. Wasn't it obvious that he was a boy? None of the other boys in the room had facial hair yet. Many still had skinny bodies and childish faces. Nick was even taller than most of them.

"Come on, Nick. That is your name, isn't it? Nick? Or should I call you Nicky? Let me guess. Short for Nicole, right?"

Nick swallowed but kept steady eye contact. The bully narrowed his eyes.

"Come on, Nicky, let's see you drop your pants. Prove to me that you have the right stuff." The boy cupped his hand provocatively around the large bulge in his own shorts.

Nick stepped backwards. His spine collided with the lockers behind him.

"Hey cut it out, Tate," someone said. "That's disgusting."

"Me, I'd rather see the hooters on Amanda Ketting than the equipment I see on myself every day," said someone else.

Another round of laughter circled the room. This time it bypassed Nick. He forced himself to relax.

"All right, men, hurry it up in here." The coach strode into the room, every bit a drill sergeant, shouting out instructions. He fit the stereotype of a P.E. instructor with his lean, fit muscles, crew cut and whistle.

Tate swaggered away from Nick. Nick willed his fingers not to tremble as he gathered up his gym clothes and headed for the bathroom stall.

"Pierce," the coach barked.

Nick turned.

"What are you doing?"

"Uh, using the bathroom?"

"No you're not. You may be new here, Pierce, but you may as well get used to undressing in front of everyone. Toughen up." The coach motioned Nick back to the lockers. Nick's face turned from red to white.

"Andrew, Eric," the coach ordered. "You two come with me and help set up. And Tate, get out of those cowboy boots and come too."

Nick stalled until Tate left the room.

*   *   *

Nick sat on the metal steps of his father's trailer, where he had come outside to eat his supper of bologna on dry white bread. After the first week of school, he had settled into a sort of routine – school, clean the trailer, scrounge for food, and wait for his father to come home. He wondered what he would do all day on the weekends.

He watched as a pickup truck drove by, slowed to a stop and backed up to turn in the drive. An older man climbed out and walked up to him.

"Hello, Nick," the man said. "I'm Russell Martin, your dad's boss. We met the other night when you first got here, if you remember. It's good to see you again. Would your dad happen to be home yet?"

"No, not yet," Nick answered.

Russell hooked his thumb through his belt loop. "How are things going for you, Nick? Are you getting settled in?"

"I guess." Life wasn't that different from Wichita where he had ridden the city bus to and from school and filled his time alone so he wouldn't bother Grandma Bates. Only the location had changed. He still rode a bus to and from school, still spent hours alone so he wouldn't bother his father.

He had noticed that the girl with bangs and a painful stutter rode his bus. He felt a kinship to her. They both had marked differences that invited ridicule from their peers; neither had a close family – he had watched the way Brenna's brother treated her.

"Your dad tends to work pretty late in the evening," Russell commented. "That leaves you with a lot of time to yourself."

"I'm used to it." Nick took a bite of sandwich. He hadn't had that much spare time on his hands. Cleaning the bathroom had been his first self-assignment. Even though he had cleaned it with hot water and dish soap, the only cleaning supplies on hand, he had been pleased with the results. J.D. either hadn't noticed or didn't care. Emboldened, Nick had begun to attack other rooms as well.

"Actually, I've been thinking," Russell went on. "I still have a great deal of work to do at our new house, mostly yard work now that spring is nearly here. I was wondering if you would care to help me out with a few things. I'd pay you, of course, and we'd have to check with your father to make sure it's all right with him, but what do you think, Nick?"

Nick swallowed his bite of sandwich. "What kind of work?"

Russell sat down next to Nick on the steps. He took off his farmer's cap and scratched his scalp. "Well, we need to plant grass. Maybe you can help with mowing later if we get a good stand started. I'd also appreciate some help with putting up a fence and building plant beds along the front of the house. Annie also loves to have a garden. She's got a green thumb but it'll no doubt take more babying this year and she could use your help as well with weeding and watering."

"The only plants my Grandma had were plastic," Nick said. "And I've never been outdoors much."

Russell laughed. "Did I mention that training comes as part of the job? By the way, how old are you, Nick?"

"Twelve."

Russell slapped his cap against his pant leg and put it back on. Dust rose from the cap and floated away in the wind. "I suppose it's not legal for me to hire you full time and take you out of school, now, is it?"

Nick shook his head, not sure if the man joked or not. "When would I start?" He tossed his last bit of bread crust into the patch of weeds by the steps.

"I'd probably have you start next week if you could. It's still too early to plant anything for fear of frost but we need to get started on that sprinkler system and some raised beds for Annie's garden. As for hours, you might want to work some evenings after school, maybe a few Saturdays a month." Russell looked down at the dry bread on the ground. "You could eat meals with us too. Consider it a job benefit."

Nick's ears reddened. Had the older man guessed how hungry Nick had been throughout the week? Nick had always eaten much more than his skinny body testified. Grandma Bates had complained about the grocery bills but had at least kept the cupboards and refrigerator well stocked.

J.D. did not keep much on hand or seem to eat much himself, Nick had noticed. Years of bologna and canned pork and beans no doubt stunted one's appetite. Nick had been grateful for his school lunches, despite the general complaining he overheard in the cafeteria.

"My wife's a great cook," Russell said. "Raised seven children, four of them boys and my goodness, how they could eat, especially once they hit those teen years."

Nick felt his face redden even more. Yes, this Russell Martin knew. Or at least suspected. He wondered if Russell offered him this job out of a genuine need for help or out of charity. Grandma Bates would have said a few choice words about accepting charity.

"So what do you say, Nick? Does it sound like anything you're interested in? Should I talk to your dad about it?"

Nick shrugged. "Whatever."

Chapter 3

Brenna dragged the stool over to the cupboard above the refrigerator where her mother stashed the cookbooks. Saturday seemed as good as any day to teach herself how to cook.

Her mother had not cooked for nearly a month, unless macaroni and cheese from a box counted. Bradley claimed that if he had to eat another bowl of cold cereal, he would keel over and die. Even Brenna's father had begun to show irritation with the daily fare. He had spent good money to have a cow butchered at the locker and they had a freezer full of good meat – why weren't they eating it?

Even that small criticism had sent Brenna's mother to the bedroom in tears. Lately it seemed that she took any excuse she could to distance herself from the family. Brenna and Bradley rarely saw her in the mornings before school since she slept late and she often retired to bed early in the evenings, claiming exhaustion. Brenna wouldn't have believed that anyone who slept that much could be exhausted, but her mother looked the part. She refused to go to the doctor whenever Brenna would plead with her to get well. She would just say that she would get better, it would just take time - she'd done it before.

Brenna hoped that her mother would recover soon. She remembered one other time that her mother had been so sick. Well, maybe not sick, just tired and distant. Brenna had been six years old and in first grade. Her teacher had given her the assignment to take home little beginner books and practice reading to her parents. Prizes were to be awarded to the students who read to their parents the most. With her mother's mysterious illness and her father's workaholic answer to anything difficult, she had not been able to read to either of them. Instead, she had read to the farm cats and Bradley, if he would listen.

She had discovered a world that existed in books that took her far away from the sadness and problems in her home and soon found that she was reading at faster speeds and higher comprehension levels than most of her peers at school.

Brenna had gotten the lowest number of points in the contest. Her low score on the contest chart for all to see had not been an accurate portrayal of her skills and she had felt it grossly unfair.

Bradley had told Brenna that their mother had gone through a spell like this when she was two or three years old as well.

Brenna was every bit as much as tired of prepackaged foods as her father and brother. Earlier that morning, Brenna had dug through the chest freezer in the garage and read the labels on the packages of meat wrapped in white butcher paper. She had taken out several and tried to put them in the microwave on defrost before her father stopped her and told her to give them time to thaw in the sink. She had no idea how to fix either kind of meat, but both packages looked fairly small so she had decided she'd better fix both.

Cooking can't be that hard, she thought to herself. She pulled down a red and white cookbook and carried it to the bar.

She read the labels on the meat packages once again. Muttering the names of the meat cuts under her breath, she opened the Betty Crocker cookbook to the index pages and looked under beef. The pages about beef showed a diagram of a cow, divided into sections with the names of different cuts of meat from each area.

Brenna wrinkled her nose. She would prefer not knowing where her food came from. She ran her finger along the page searching for chuck roast or sirloin steak. That's what the labels on the meat packages said anyway.

Chuck eye roast. Hopefully that was the same as a simple chuck roast, like the package said. She looked across the page at the roast cooking directions. It seemed simple enough, so long as she could find the right kind of pan. She had no idea what a roasting pan looked like.

The directions referred her to a timetable for cooking meat. It stated to cook the roast for 25 minutes. Good. That gave her plenty of time before she had to put the roast in the oven.

With satisfaction, Brenna went back to the diagram to look for a sirloin steak. An entire section was devoted to sirloin cuts: the flat bone sirloin steak, a round bone sirloin steak, and the top sirloin steak. The package in the freezer simply said "sirloin steak". Underneath each picture of steak, cooking directions were given to broil or panfry. What on earth was broiling?

Brenna wondered if she should just pull out another box of macaroni and cheese. She knew how to make that well enough. Maybe with the chuck roast, they would have enough to eat.

But, panfry? Surely that simply meant put the meat into a pan and fry it. And frying usually involved grease – at least it did with French fries.

Brenna took out her mother's large skillet and poured a liberal amount of vegetable oil into it. She unwrapped the package of sirloin steak and realized that the small bundle actually contained four large steaks. She laid them in the skillet and poured more oil over the tops of them for good measure. Brenna turned the burner on high and went on to the package of chuck roast.

Again, she was surprised at the amount of meat inside the package. She lined a cookie sheet with foil, as the directions in the cookbook advised, and laid the chunk of meat in the center.

The cookbook said to season the meat with herbs or spices. Brenna did not know what to choose from so she opened the spice cabinet and took down cinnamon and ground cumin. She sprinkled the seasonings on the roast and covered the cookie sheet with foil. She would put it in the oven later.

Next, Brenna tackled a salad. She felt more confident with that. They did not have much in the refrigerator for her to work with, but she tore up a head of lettuce and chopped baby carrots and added them to the lettuce.

A loud pop startled her. Brenna looked at the stove and realized with horror that oil spat angrily out of the pan of steaks. She somehow managed to turn off the burner and move the pan without getting hit by flying grease.

Brenna looked at the stovetop with dismay. Grease had splattered everywhere. She wiped at the mess with the dishrag, which only smeared the grease around.

"What's going on in here?" Bradley walked in. He wrinkled his face in distaste.

Brenna scrubbed at the grease harder. "I...I'm c...c...cooking s...supper."

Bradley laughed. "You? I'd rather eat another bowl of cereal. It smells awful in here."

Brenna stuck out her tongue childishly at him.

Bradley came closer. "What are you trying to cook? He eyed the skillet with suspicion.

"I...it's a s...s...surprise," she said stubbornly. "G...go aw...way."

"It's a surprise, all right," Bradley said. "A surprise if you survive after eating it."

"B...Bradley!" Brenna pushed at him.

"B...Bradley!" He mimicked her and pushed back.

Brenna glared at him. "If y...you're n...not going to h...h...help, then l...leave."

"I'm going, I'm going." As Bradley turned, his hip rammed against the table. The salad scattered over the floor.

"Bradley," she wailed. "L…look wh…what you j…just d…did."

"I didn't mean to." He glared at her as he rubbed his hip. "You think I intentionally wanted to give myself a bruise?"

Bradley stalked from the kitchen, leaving Brenna with the mess of splattered grease, lettuce and chopped carrots.

At least the chuck roast was still unscathed. Brenna jumped. The chuck roast! She needed to get it into the oven immediately if she wanted it to have the full 25 minutes to cook. Brenna hoped it, at least, would turn out.

Later, as her brother and father sat down at the table, Brenna proudly pulled the roast out of the oven and placed it on the table. Her father lifted the edge of the tinfoil.

"Brenna?" His eyes squinted at the meat. "How long did you let this thing cook in the oven?"

Brenna's heart plummeted. "W…Why?"

He took the foil off. "This is why."

The roast sat innocently in the center of the pan, still pink, still raw.

"I'll fix some macaroni and cheese," her father said. "You put this back in the oven and let it cook longer. We can eat it tomorrow."

"B…b…but the b…b…book s…said t…t…twenty-f…five m…minutes," protested Brenna. She fetched the book and pointed, her stammering increased by her failure. "S…s…s…see?"

Her father read the page. "Twenty-five minutes per pound. That roast is probably four pounds. It still needs another hour and 15 minutes in the oven." He tucked the tinfoil back over the meat.

"From now on Brenna, don't try anything new," he said over his shoulder as he opened the pantry door.

Brenna dropped her head.

J.D. dumped a laundry basket onto the folding table at the Laundromat. He and Nick stood before the mound of dirty clothing with washing machines and dryers whirring around them, the scent of fabric softener heavy in the air.

"You say you already know how to sort clothes?"

Nick nodded.

"Not surprised," J.D. grunted. "You know how to do every other woman's job."

Nick flinched. He knew he displeased his father, but didn't know how to correct it. At first, he had figured J.D. didn't want his life interrupted by responsibility. Now, he sensed that his actions and personality annoyed his father as well.

"Here," J.D. said. He dumped a fistful of heavy coins onto the table. "Get the laundry started. I'll be back later."

"Where are you going?"

J.D. picked up his cowboy hat. "Got a few errands."

"Can't I come with you once we get the clothes in the washers?"

J.D. narrowed his eyes. "Best if you stay here. Earn your keep."

The bell on the Laundromat door jangled as his father left. Nick glared at it.

Earn his keep? That's all Nick had been doing since he arrived. What did his father think he was? His personal slave? Not only had Nick cooked and cleaned for J.D. as well as himself, now J.D. expected him to complete nearly two weeks worth of dirty laundry – the first visit to the Laundromat since Nick had moved in. The trailer didn't even have washer and dryer hookups. Nick had not owned enough clothing and had been rinsing out his shirts and underwear in the bathtub. He had been afraid that J.D. never did laundry.

Nick yanked a pair of J.D.'s jeans off the top of the stack. Grease stained the knees. He had no extra change to buy stain remover from the dispenser on the wall. He shoved the jeans into the ready and open mouth of a washing machine.

"Serves him right if they're still dirty," he muttered. Not that it mattered. Appearance was not on J.D.'s top list of priorities.

Nick went down the line of washers, stuffing in whites, darks, and denims, the way Grandma Bates had shown him. No delicates this time. He started to measure partial cups of soap powder, accustomed to Grandma's stinginess, but thought better of it and added more to each load. Still angry, Nick shoved quarters into the slots and rammed them into the machines, only slightly mollified by his violence.

As the washers filled with water, Nick found himself with nothing to do. The Laundromat was small, only seven washers and five dryers. Several hard plastic chairs huddled in a corner next to an ancient small screen television. Nick clicked on the heavy knob. Nothing. The plug hung down onto the floor, unattached to the outlet. He plugged it in and clicked the knob again. Still nothing.

Nick slumped into one of the chairs and stared at his feet. He wondered if Russell Martin had talked with J.D. about giving him after-school work. J.D. had not mentioned it. Nick wanted the job. He wanted to be away from the trailer as much as possible, wanted the money.

He had changed his class schedule to include music after J.D. had left the school. The music teacher had offered to give him lessons during the lunch period once she heard him play the piano, saying he could bring his lunch tray to her room. But lessons cost money, money that he could earn if J.D. would agree.

The doorbell jangled. A middle-aged housewife came in. She gave Nick a curious glance and went to the dryers. Folding with the precision of a military officer, she slapped the folded items into her basket, balanced the basket on her hip, gave him another curious glance, and left.

Nick sighed and inspected his feet again. After what seemed forever, the washers began to screech to a halt one by one. Nick put the damp clothing into the dryers and wandered to the window to watch down the street.

Main Street consisted of a short three blocks of old brick buildings, some with new awnings and hand-painted signs in the windows, others with facades most likely installed in the late fifties, a few abandoned and empty with boards nailed over the windows.

The cars that were parked along both sides of the street gradually emptied out as the shadows lengthened across the pavement and the streetlights came on.

Nick wondered if the Laundromat had a closing time. He walked out the door to inspect the sign. Nine o'clock. He consulted the wall clock inside - only half an hour away.

The growing darkness outside made him nervous. Anyone driving past could easily see a young boy alone in the brightly lit Laundromat windows. He would have felt safer in the city with more people and open stores around.

Surely his father would be back soon. What kind of stores would be open this late in a small town like this anyway? How long would the errands take his father?

The dryers buzzed. Nick started folding the clothes, putting J.D's into one basket, his own in the other. He hurried, wanting to be finished as soon as J.D. came in.

With relief, he heard the door jangle. Nick turned to see a short, fat man holding a ring of keys.

"I don't usually find anyone still in here," the man said. "I'm Max, the owner."

"I'm just about done. My dad's supposed to come pick me up any minute now," Nick said.

"Do you want me to wait here with you?" asked Max. "It's getting dark outside, you know."

Nick pulled his shoulder up nervously. He imagined what J.D. might say if he came back and found him with a babysitter. "No, thanks. I'll be fine. Like I said, he'll be back in just a little bit."

"Well," Max rubbed the fleshy skin underneath his chin. "How about if I lock the door anyway, so I don't have to come back. When your dad gets here, you can let him in. Just make sure the door is shut tight behind you and turn off the light. Would that be a problem?"

"No, not at all," Nick said. He folded a towel in half and snapped it like he had seen the housewife do.

Max went to each machine and used his key to open the coin slots. He emptied the change into a zippered bank bag.

"You sure you'll be okay in here?" Max shifted from one swollen foot to the other.

"I'll be fine." How many years had Nick been saying that to adults who only asked to be polite?

"Make sure your dad is the only person you let in," Max warned. He left, locking the door behind him.

Nick finished the folding and paced the floor, uncomfortable whenever headlights swept by. His stomach growled from missing supper. He eyed the vending machine hungrily, wondering how easy he could break into it.

Finally Nick sat again. He pulled his feet up under him, padded his head with his arm, and closed his eyes.

A pounding on the Laundromat door awakened him. J.D. cursed him when he opened it.

"What'd you lock me out for?"

"I didn't." Nick defended himself. "The owner locked it."

"You talking back to me?" J.D. stuck his face close to Nick's. A sour odor assaulted Nick and he suddenly understood the belligerence in his father's demeanor. Alcohol. His father had spent the past hours at the bar.

"J.D., is there a problem?" a strange voice came from behind his father.

J.D. turned to face the newcomer and nearly lost his balance. "Mitch?"

The young man, Mitch, stood with his legs slightly apart, his hands clenched as though ready for a fight.

The man addressed him. "Is everything okay, Nick?"

Nick blinked. How did the man know his name?

"Listen, Mitch," J.D. protested. "Everything's fine here. Me and the boy, we're just getting ready to take the laundry home."

"The Laundromat closed hours ago. Did you leave Nick here alone all this time while you went off to get drunk?"

"Oh, come on, Mitch, I just had a few beers with the buddies. You know what it's like."

"Actually, no, I don't." Mitch took several long breaths as though attempting to gain control. When he spoke, his voice was soft. "Go get in my truck, Nick. I'll take care of this."

Nick hesitated.

"Go. I'll handle your dad."

J.D. grabbed Nick's shirt collar. "You stay right here, Nick."

Without warning, Mitch knocked J.D.'s hand away from Nick. J.D. fell into the open doorway and cursed. His heart pounding, Nick backed to the newcomer's truck and shut himself inside. He watched through the windshield as his father took several ineffectual swings at the younger man and fell to his knees.

Mitch pressed his face close to J.D.'s and spoke. After a long moment, J.D. nodded.

Mitch went into the Laundromat and came out with the clean clothing. He put the baskets in the back of his truck and helped J.D. to his feet.

They left J.D.'s pickup parked in front of the Laundromat and headed out into the country. Nick sat between his father and Mitch, afraid to face his drunken father or the stranger on his left, trying to avoid touching either of them and to stay out of the way whenever Mitch needed to shift. The green digital numbers on Mitch's watch glowed in the darkness. Nick twisted his head to read them. Eleven twenty-four.

J.D. slumped over against the passenger door and mumbled incoherently.

"Does he do this often, Nick?"

"No, at least I don't think so. This is the only time, at least since I came here."

Mitch's hands tightened on the wheel. "You've only been here a few weeks. I'd have thought…"

Mitch braked, the taillights glowing red behind them. J.D. slid further down in the seat, still mumbling.

"It's a good thing I happened to drive down Main Street," Mitch said. "How long did you wait for him at the Laundromat?"

"A while. It's no big deal." Nick stared straight ahead.

Mitch frowned. "I happen to think it is."

J.D.'s head lolled against the window and he snored.

Mitch glanced at him, concerned lines in his forehead. "If your dad gets drunk like this again, or acts aggressive toward you, I want you to walk down to my parents' house, okay?"

His parents' house. The house just down the road. Now Nick knew how the stranger knew his name.

Mitch pulled up alongside the trailer and helped J.D. inside. When he came out of J.D.'s bedroom put his hand on Nick's shoulder.

"I meant what I said about going to Mom and Dad's if there's trouble again, Nick," Mitch said. "In fact, I'd be glad to take you home with me for the night."

Truth be told, Mitch intimidated him as much or more than his father. Nick had never been around many younger men. Mitch clearly worked out. His pectoral muscles bulged under his shirt. Beard stubble shadowed his lower face and his dark hair fell over his forehead. Nick felt a strange curiosity and attraction to his manliness. He stood straighter in an effort to show off his height, painfully aware of his pale skin and puny muscles.

"I'll be fine," he said. "He won't bother me. He'll probably sleep till morning. My foster mom in Wichita would sleep for hours when she came home drunk."

Mitch frowned. "I can take you over to Mom and Dad's instead. You can come back here early in the morning before he wakes up if you're worried about that."

"No, really I'll be fine. Thanks for bringing us home and all that."

Still frowning, Mitch took a notepad and pen from his shirt pocket. He scribbled something down, tore off the page and handed it to Nick.

"Here's my phone number," he said. "Call me if you need anything. And I mean anything, any time of the night. Don't worry about waking me up. I put Mom and Dad's number on there too. The same applies to them."

Nick took the paper.

Mitch took several steps toward the door and stopped. He turned back. "I can't do this. I can't just leave. See if you can find an extra blanket somewhere and I'll sleep on the couch."

Nick swallowed. "You don't need to…"

"Yes, I do."

Afraid to argue, Nick procured a blanket for Mitch and sequestered himself in his own room. He heard the couch creak as Mitch settled in.

Nick slid the phone numbers into his music book in case his father saw it and became upset. He pulled the covers to his chin and wondered what motivated Mitch and Russell. Why were they so eager to help him? What did they expect from him?

"He's so talented. I mean, have you heard him play the piano?"

"I'll bet he'll be somebody famous someday."

From her desk, Brenna watched the tight circle of girls giggle over their latest crush. She rolled her eyes.

"It's so dumb, don't you think?" Sara sat down beside Brenna. "Those girls thinking they're in love or something."

The girls went on. "And he's polite - not at all like most of the boys in our class."

"And so tall. It's such a pain when we're taller than most of the boys our age."

Now Sara rolled her eyes. "My parents won't let us date until we're sixteen and even then it has to be double dating. My sister Michele just turned sixteen but she said she isn't going to date yet. She thinks it's stupid to go out with someone that you aren't interested in getting married to. As for me, I'm only twelve. Who wants to think about being married?"

Brenna smiled. The more Sara sought her out, the more she appreciated the other girl. Sara didn't seem to care what others thought of her, yet clearly cared about others. Her life seemed an oxymoron, yet everything about Sara appeared sincere. Brenna wanted to know what made her different.

The girls' giggling increased when Nick Pierce came in. He glanced around the room before coming toward the empty desk beside Brenna and Sara.

"Mind if I sit here?" he asked. His expression implied that he had prepared for a negative answer.

"Of course." Sara patted the empty seat. "You're welcome to sit here."

Nick slid into the seat, oblivious of the flurry of whispers and glances in his direction from the group of girls.

"You ride the same bus as Brenna, don't you?" Sara asked him. Brenna envied her ease at friendliness even as she blushed at the sound of her name.

Nick's eyes flitted toward Brenna and he nodded. He laid his notebook on his desk and pulled a ballpoint pen from the spiral.

"Isn't that neat?" Sara enthused. "All three of us will be riding the same bus soon. My family is moving next week into my grandparent's old farmhouse. You know them already, Nick. My grandpa, Russell Martin, is your dad's boss. You can't imagine how surprised we all were to find out J.D. had a son."

"Not as surprised as I was," Nick muttered. He uncapped his pen and scribbled in the corner of the front cover of his notebook until the ink flowed.

"Who knows," Sara said cheerfully. "We may all get to know each other pretty well. My Uncle Mitch says you're a real trooper."

Nick's face flushed. He shifted in his seat to angle his shoulder away from them in what seemed a deliberate snub to Sara's friendliness. Sara's smile faltered as she met Brenna's eyes. Brenna shrugged her shoulders in mute reply.

At the end of class, Nick tore a paper from his notebook and folded it into a small square. To Brenna's surprise and consternation, he dropped it onto her textbook as he left.

Ignoring Sara's questioning expression, Brenna waited until she got to her locker before unfolding the paper.

It read, "I'd like to see you smile sometime."

Nick sat at the rickety kitchen table to write his history report. He pressed his knee against the table leg to steady it but found himself thinking, not of Winston Churchill, but of the note he had rashly given to Brenna. Why had he reached out to her? She seemed shyer than ever now, avoiding him on the bus and in the hallways. He regretted his impulsive action.

The smell of baked beans and boiling hot dogs filtered through the trailer. Nick hoped that by cooking supper, his father would be willing to listen to what he wanted to ask.

Nick stole a glance at his father. J.D. sat in his recliner in front of the T.V., the ever-present beer in his hand. After the Laundromat incident, J.D. had not hidden his drinking from

Nick, but neither had he gotten drunk again like that night. Still, Nick felt insecure.

Nick flipped his notebook shut and stood to stir the beans. "I think the food is ready," he said.

J.D. did not turn. "Just bring it here."

Nick spooned the beans onto a plate and speared a hot dog.

"Don't forget the ketchup."

Nick took the plate to him and stood beside the recliner.

"You gonna stand there and watch me eat?"

Nick shook his head. He folded his arms across his stomach. "I wanted to ask you something," he said.

J.D. waved the spoon. "So ask me."

Nick wet his lips. "Did Mr. Martin talk to you about me working for him after school?"

J.D. looked up. "Yeah. I meant to tell you, it's fine by me."

"Did he say when I should start?"

J.D. shrugged and plunged his spoon into the beans. "Whenever."

Nick took a deep breath. "I was thinking, that since I'd be earning some money, maybe I could take some lessons from Mrs. Collins at school. She said she'd be willing to give them over the lunch hour since we live so far from town. That way I wouldn't miss the bus and you wouldn't have to make a special trip to town."

"What kind of lessons? You flunking a class or something?"

"No, sir." Nick shifted from one foot to the other. "Music lessons. Piano lessons."

J.D. nearly spilled his plate of beans. "Look here, I thought I made myself clear on that. You act like a girl enough already and I ain't raisin' no limp wristed sissy."

Nick clenched his teeth together. Although connected through DNA, he and his father seemed to own no commonalities, no comprehension of the other's thought processes.

"Most famous pianists are men," Nick plunged on. "Anya Martin said so."

"Real men?" J.D. snorted. "Fags, that's what."

Nick flinched at the word. Boys at his old school had called him names like that. He knew he exhibited feminine qualities. He didn't know why, or how to change.

"You ain't taking no lessons from that Collins teacher and that's final. You hear me? You wanna learn how to do something, learn how to go hunting or fishing. Besides, any money you earn can go toward paying for necessities."

J.D. picked up the T.V. remote and punched the volume button, drowning out any attempt at protest, although Nick would not have dared anyway.

Nick sighed and went back to the stove for his own plate.

"Necessities," he muttered. "You probably just want it for your beer, that's what."

He looked at the pile of dirty dishes and congealed grease on the stovetop and considered leaving the mess. Wasn't his father acting hypocritical by letting him do all the women's work around the house, yet not wanting him to be womanly? Yet Nick could not bear to live in filth. At least Grandma Bates had taught him that much.

Resignedly, Nick ate his food and filled the sink with soapy water. He supposed it was for the best. Summer vacation was only five weeks away, not long enough to truly get started on piano lessons. Yet his fingers itched for a piano and the stolen moments in the music room between classes was never enough.

"Nick." Anya Martin greeted him from where she stood at her mailbox at the side of the road. "You didn't have to walk, you know. I can come pick you up or you could have the bus drop you off here."

Nick looked over his shoulder at the trailer house sitting down the road amidst its grove of straggly elms. "It's not that far," he said. "Walking won't hurt me."

Anya shut the mailbox with a snap. "Well you're right about that. I need more exercise myself."

She started up the gravel driveway. Nick fell in step beside her.

"Russell wanted to come home and help you get started since it's your first day but he called a little bit ago to say that he'd be late. Cattle got out of the pasture next to the highway so he and Mitch are rounding them up and fixing fence."

Anya stopped to open the front door for him. Nick stepped inside, feeling guilty for not holding the door for her.

"Mitch said he drove you home the other night."

Nick stopped. "He did?"

"I wanted to reiterate Mitch's offer for you to call us anytime. I mean that, Nick." She met his eyes earnestly. "I'm sorry that you even had to deal with a situation like that and I pray that you won't again."

What was with this family and their concern for a nobody like him? Nick's heart clenched with a delightful sort of pain. He could get used to it.

"Come on in the kitchen." Anya led the way and laid the mail down on the countertop.

"Now." She opened the refrigerator. "No doubt you're hungry. Our children always came home from school ravenous. I have leftover biscuits from breakfast that you can have with jelly or honey, if you like."

"You don't need to feed me, Mrs. Martin," Nick protested feebly.

Anya fetched a butter knife and napkin and laid them on the table. "Yes I do. I'm a mother and a grandmother, Nick. It's in my nature. Now sit."

He sat, though he did not believe her. If fussing over him were second nature to mothers and grandmother, as Anya implied, then why hadn't his own mother stayed with him, cared for him? Why had Grandma Bates treated him with no emotion other than tolerance?

"How many biscuits would you like?"

"One is fine," Nick said.

Anya put two biscuits on a plate and set the plate in the microwave. Nick wondered if she would have put three on the plate if he had asked for two. As soon as the timer dinged, she set the steaming biscuits before him, along with a honey bear, butter dish, and a jar of homemade jam.

Nick buttered the flaky insides and relished the aroma of melted butter. Anya poured him a glass of milk and sat across the table to watch him eat. Strangely, he didn't mind.

"Have you ever had a job before, Nick?"

"No."

"Well, I hope this will be a good experience for you. I was so glad that J.D., er, your father agreed. Hopefully Russell and I can get a head start on some of our summer projects."

Nick started on his second biscuit, thankful that she had given him the extra one.

"I assume Russell told you some of the things we'd like for you to do." She waited for his nod and continued. "For starters today, there's quite a bit of junk lying around from the construction, scraps of wood, bricks, twigs, nails, screws and what not. Would you mind going around outside and picking up any trash you see? The leftover bricks can be stacked against the west side of the house. Russell said he'd use them to build a planter, even the broken ones. He usually can't stand to throw anything away. He always tells me it may come in handy some day."

Nick savored the flavor of his last bite before washing it down with milk. "I'm ready now," he said.

"Good. Let me get you a trash bag and a pair of gloves."

Nick put on the gloves and walked the outside perimeter. He scoured the bare dirt surface scarred from heavy equipment for debris and stooped frequently to add to his bag. The plastic bulged before long. Nick tied the top shut and leaned it against the house. He began moving bricks and cinder blocks, stacking them where Anya had directed.

His back ached from bending over. Other than housework, he had never done any kind of manual labor. Just as the cinder blocks seemed to be getting heavier, Russell Martin stepped around the side of the house, his cowboy boots leaving impressions in the dirt.

"Hey there, Nick. Glad to see you hard at work. Are you about finished?"

"About." Nick swiped at the sweat that dampened the edges of his hair, despite the chilly bite of April's wind.

"It looks good." Russell nodded with approval. "You did a very thorough job. Thanks for making a pile of the broken bricks as well. I can use some of the larger pieces."

Nick ducked his head. "Thanks," he mumbled. He wondered if he should tell the older man that Anya had asked him to do so.

"While you finish up, I'll tell Annie that I'm taking you home. Your dad asked if I could get you home in ten minutes or so. He's on his way there now. I guess some state worker is coming out to meet with the two of you and check on how things are going."

If Nick hadn't wanted to please Russell, he would have dawdled to delay having to go back to the trailer. He hoped that the social worker would not be Mrs. Anderson.

Oscillating fans in each classroom waged a poor defense against the summer heat. Contrary to cooling things off, the fans seemed to merely circulate the hot air from one side of the room to the other. Brenna figured that the bricks on the building soaked in the sun's rays and turned the school building into an oven, baking the students inside. She was glad to be free from the building and on her way home toward central air even though the dusty air that slapped through the open bus windows wasn't much cooler. Bradley complained that the school system should either fork out the money for air conditioning or cancel school as soon as the temperatures rose above 80 degrees.

Sara sat with her little brother Avery across the aisle from Brenna. Avery read to her from his beginning reader, his finger pointing to each word. Sara's head was bent close to his so that she could hear him over the noise of the engine and other students.

She seemed to feel Brenna's gaze and turned to smile. She opened her mouth as if to say something but Brenna turned back to the window after a brief returning smile. Usually she discouraged Sara or others from talking to her by burying her face in a book, although her stomach felt sick when she tried to read with all the bouncing, but she had accidentally left her library book in her locker.

Her ears picked up the sound of her name. Bradley and his friend were laughing in the seat behind Sara and Avery. Her face burned. She knew they mocked her in some way. She pretended not to hear, although she strained her ears. Bradley was talking about her cooking fiasco. She felt angry. At least she had tried, which was more than anyone else in their house could say.

The bus ground to a stop in front of Brenna's house. Dust clouded up and filtered in the windows.

Brenna filed down the narrow aisle and her bulging bag bumped up against someone. She turned to apologize. It was Nick.

"It's okay," he said. His smile was guarded.

"Hurry up, Brenna," Bradley ordered from behind her. She quickly obeyed.

The school bus closed its doors behind her with an exhausted puff and continued down the road, churning up more dirt.

Bradley ran up the circular drive, anxious to be away from the bus, which he viewed as too demeaning to ride. Brenna had heard him proclaim more than once that the bus would be a relic of his past when he got his driver's permit in the fall. Brenna wondered what he planned on driving but didn't really care. She knew he would not haul her along anyway.

She looked up at the open Kansas sky, a pale blue bowl inverted over their brick farmhouse. The house was built as a wedding present by her grandparents when her parents married. From listening to conversations and hints over the years Brenna knew that it brought contention between her parents.

Her mother had grown up very rich and pampered. She met Brenna's father at a ski resort, which she frequented often. Her father had barely scrapped together money for a one-day pass. A flurried romance and later elopement ensued. Resigned to the fact that his daughter had married a poor farmer, her grandfather had built the house so that her mother would not have to sacrifice every comfort she had grown up with.

Brenna's father, however, viewed the house as charity, not giving him a chance to prove his ability to provide for a wife. He complained that the large house was a money hog and took too much of their profits to keep repairs done and pay the utilities. Brenna knew that her grandfather often slipped large amounts of cash to her mother when they went to visit them.

She wondered what her dad had been like when he first met her mother. Their wedding pictures looked happy. Now his face was drawn and he stayed out in the fields as much as possible. She couldn't blame him for withdrawing. When her mother went through her spells, the house became a sepulcher.

Brenna let herself into the house through the sliding glass door into the family room. Bradley already sat at the breakfast bar with a bowl of cereal. She made a face at the box.

The sugar content alone made her go to the refrigerator and dig out an apple.

"You are sick, sick, sick," Bradley announced, his words muffled and cheeks full. "Here you are, almost an eighth grader, and you choose a healthy snack."

Brenna washed the apple in the sink and crunched down on the crisp skin. She savored the juices in her mouth.

"W…w…where's M…Mother?"

Bradley shrugged. "Probably in bed, as usual."

Brenna climbed onto a stool to sit beside him. "W…why does she al…al…always…"

"Always stay in bed?" Bradley finished for her. "Tate Mason's mom says she's got clinical depression."

"Y…you told T…Tate?"

"Didn't have to. Everybody knows. People talk about us. The family that shouldn't have been."

"What d…do you m…m…mean?"

"You know Mother and Dad had to get married."

Brenna looked confused. Had to. What did he mean by that?

"Because she was pregnant, stupid," Bradley said with impatience.

Brenna frowned. She was sure that her parents had been married for several years before Bradley was born.

"That baby died, okay? Gaw, are you really as dumb as everybody says you are?"

Brenna ignored his statement. She had long given up on receiving any words of affirmation from him or anyone else. She most likely didn't deserve them anyway.

"Is th…that why Mother s…stays in b…b…bed?"

Bradley shrugged and shoved a large bite of cereal into his mouth. He wiped a dribble of milk off his chin with his sleeve.

They sat in silence for a minute.

Brenna digested the revelation. "W...was it a b...boy or a...a g...g...girl?"

Bradley shrugged. "Don't know. Don't care."

At a sound in the hallway, they both turned to see their mother tottering back to the master bedroom, her hands over her face.

Bradley grimaced. "Nice going, dumbo."

"Wh...what d...did I do?"

"She heard you asking about it. Dad told me once to never bring it up." Anger flared on Bradley's face and he spoke with true bitterness, more than his normal sarcasm. "We never talk about it but it's still always there. I guess Mother loved that first baby more than she loves us."

"B...Bradley," Brenna hissed, horrified.

"Yeah, well, I don't really care. She don't love me, well, I don't love her, either." He spat out the last word and pushed off his stool. He yanked open the glass door and stomped outside.

Brenna sat in silence, terrified that Mother had heard Bradley's outburst. Then she heard low, stifled sobbing coming from the bedroom.

Brenna cleaned up Bradley's messy cereal bowl and spoon and put the milk in the refrigerator before slipping out the still-open door. She knew better than to try to comfort her mother. Maybe Bradley was right. Maybe her mother didn't love them. The times she had tried to go in the bedroom before, her mother had rolled over and left Brenna staring at her back.

Brenna sank down on the back patio step, taking a half-hearted bite out of her apple. The juices didn't taste as crisp now. One of the many farm cats came to wind around her bare legs, its fur warm from the sun.

If she looked out across the road, she could just make out the row of sickly elms that bordered Nick's trailer house. He kept to himself despite Sara's attempts at friendliness on the bus, much like herself. She wondered if he was as unhappy as she.

You couldn't live in such a small town without knowing something about everybody and she had heard stories about J.D. Dobbs.

Brenna tossed her apple out onto the grass. The cat leaped after it and batted at it with her paw. Brenna buried her face on her knees. She listened to the dull thump, thump of Bradley's basketball on the slab of concrete by the garage.

The ringing of the telephone roused her. Brenna hurried inside to pick it up before it disturbed her mother.

"H...h...hello?"

"Hi, is this Brenna?"

"Y...yes."

"Brenna, hi! This is Sara. My mom gave me permission to call you. She says I can have a friend over this evening. We're having brown cows."

"B...brown what?"

Sara giggled. "Brown cows. That's what Dad calls root beer floats."

"Oh."

"Can you ask your mom or dad if you can come? We'll come pick you up and bring you home."

"J...just a m...minute." Brenna laid the receiver next to the phone and tiptoed to her mother's room.

"M...Mother?" Her mother lay on the bed in the semi-darkness, with her back to the door. Brenna knew she was awake by the stiffness in her body.

"S...Sara M...Martin w...w...wants me t...to come ov...over. I...is it okay?"

Her mother took a long time to answer. When she did, her voice wavered.

"Be back by 9."

Brenna lingered in the doorway. "I...I'm sorry, M...Mother. About the b...b...baby. I...I wish I'd kn...known."

Then she fled.

Chapter 4

"Come on, Brenna. Let me show you my new room." Sara tugged on Brenna's sleeve. Together they ran up the steep stairway.

The ceiling in Sara's room followed the roofline of the old farmhouse with several sharp slants.

"Really, this should be called the attic," Sara explained. "Grandma told me that when she married Grandpa, the only way into the attic was through a little cut-out place in the ceiling of the pantry. One time a squirrel got trapped in here and Grandpa had to get a ladder and crawl up here to get it out. Grandma said that she had to move lots of canned stuff out of the pantry first and then she was scared that he would get stuck in the opening. In the end, the squirrel ran back out the hole it had come in so Grandpa patched it up. I wish I could have been there. I bet it was funny."

Brenna smiled. Sara's talkativeness made her an easy companion.

Sara continued. "Then they built the stairs and made the attic into bedrooms because they had so many kids. My Dad has seven brothers and sisters altogether in his family. He's the oldest. I'm glad that we moved here because now I get my own room. I think I got the best room in the whole house."

Brenna wondered what it would be like to share a room. She thought about the brother or sister she would never know. Sadness washed over her.

"Brenna, are you okay?"

Brenna looked at the other girl. She wanted to talk. She needed to talk and she couldn't talk to anyone at home. Her mind always raced with words, phrases, sentences but her mouth refused to produce them.

"Let's sit down on the floor," said Sara. "You can tell me if you want to. I don't mind if you stutter."

Brenna winced at the last word. Sara looked alarmed. "I don't mean to hurt your feelings, Brenna. My mom tells me that sometimes I'm too blunt."

"I...It's okay." Oddly, Sara's frankness emboldened Brenna.

They dropped to the soft rug beside Sara's bed. Brenna buried her fingers in it. "M...m...my m...mother l...lost a b...b...baby," Brenna told her, so softly that Sara instinctively leaned closer.

"I didn't know your mom was going to have a baby."

Brenna shook her head, frustrated at her inability to communicate. "B...bef...fore B...Bradley."

"Did you just found out or did you already know?"

"J...just f...found..." Brenna found it easier to only speak key words. "T...t...today."

Sara sat with her eyes on Brenna, patiently waiting for her to continue. Brenna felt a wash of respect for her new friend. Most people tried to fill in her sentences for her.

"My b...brother s...s...says that's wh...why she's d...d...depressed. I feel..." Brenna paused, wondering if she even knew how she felt, how to share it, how to get all the sounds out correctly. "It hurts. N...not just finding out th...that I h...had a b...big br...brother or s...s...sister that died. Th...they didn't t...tell me. And M...Mother acts l...like we're not th...there, l...like she's only s...s...sorry about the other b...baby. Sh...she sleeps all the t...time and..." Brenna lowered her head, appalled at the tears in her eyes, at her openness. She stiffened in surprise at Sara's hug.

"Can I pray for you, Brenna? I mean, would that be okay with you?" Without waiting for an answer, Sara began to pray. "Dear Jesus, thank you for my new friend, Brenna. Thank you that we are in the same classes at school and that we ride the same bus. Forgive me for not trying to be a friend to her sooner.

Brenna is very special to you, Lord, but she doesn't feel like she's very special to her mom. Help her mom to get better. Help Brenna to know how much you care about her. Say hi to her brother or sister for us. In Jesus' name, Amen."

Sara paused. "Do you want to pray, Brenna?"

Brenna wiped her cheeks with the heels of her hands. "I d...don't kn...know how," she whispered without looking up.

"Telling Jesus about stuff always helps me feel better," said Sara. "He already knows about what I tell him, but it still helps. That's all you have to do when you pray. Just talk to Jesus."

Talk. The one thing Brenna struggled with.

Sara's mother called up the stairs, "Sara, your grandparents are here."

"Do you want to go downstairs?"

Brenna shrugged and tried to smile. She didn't care for the idea of being around so many people. She hadn't known Sara's grandparents were going to be there. But she could tell Sara was excited about it so she followed her back down the stairs and they entered the spacious farm kitchen.

"Hello, girls. As soon as Dad and Avery get here, we'll have the brown cows. Grandma and Grandpa are already in the living room with Michele." Sara's mother transferred glasses and spoons to the large kitchen table.

"Michele's my big sister," Sara explained. "And Avery's my little brother. You probably knew that already from seeing them on the bus."

An unexpected roar caused both girls to jump and screech as an older man leaped around the corner toward them. Sara threw her arms around the "bear's" neck.

"Grandpa!"

He laughed, giving her a quick hug before nodding to Brenna. "You wouldn't happen to be the Williams girl from down the road a bit?"

Brenna nodded shyly. She recognized him as the older man who had offered her a cookie at the building site.

"I'm Russell Martin. Your dad has helped me out with a few projects before. He's a hard worker," he said. "How's your mother doing?"

She stiffened. Her father had made it clear that neither she nor Bradley should discuss home issues with outsiders. She'd already broken the rule once tonight.

After an awkward pause, the man patted her shoulder. "It's all right. It's really none of my business anyway."

Sara bounced past them to hug the woman sitting on the piano bench. "Grandma, do you think the house looks different now that we live in it?"

"Oh, yes and no," the woman answered. "Same house, different furniture. It's starting to look more like a home now that you're getting unpacked."

Brenna perched on the edge of the couch.

"Oh, Brenna." Sara clapped her hands. "You've never heard my grandma play the piano. Play something, Grandma."

"Maybe we should wait until everyone is here," said Sara's grandfather.

"Oh, no. You aren't going to make a big production out of this every time." The older woman shook her finger at him with a smile.

"Please, Grandma," Sara pleaded. "Play that song that you played for offering at church on Sunday. I loved that song."

The woman adjusted the bench and brought her hands up to the keys. Brenna watched her fingers as she played, the peaceful melody flowing over her. She heard the emotions transferred from the woman's fingers to the sounds, feelings of quiet joy and tranquility. She longed to communicate in such a way – through music rather than the hateful consonant sounds required in speech. A sacred silence clung to the air after the last chord.

Sara turned to Brenna. "I'm taking lessons from Grandma but I'm only in book three. Michele's been taking lessons for forever and she can play really good, but not like Grandma yet. I think Grandma's the best piano player in the world."

Her grandma laughed. "Thank you for your vote, Sara, although many could prove otherwise. What about you, Brenna? Do you play?"

Brenna shook her head.

"She could take lessons, too, Grandma. Brenna has a piano at her house," said Sara. "I saw it when we picked her up."

"Maybe she doesn't want lessons."

Brenna looked away. She wished she could explain how she wasn't allowed to touch the piano in the formal living room because of her mother's headaches.

"Have you ever considered taking lessons, Brenna?" asked the older woman.

Brenna made a noncommittal gesture with her head.

"I would be honored to teach you, if you ever decide you want to learn."

"Where's the food, woman? You've got some hungry men here." A teasing voice accompanied the slamming of the back door.

Brenna turned with relief. Through the open doorway, she saw Sara's father and little brother.

"Let's go eat before we starve." Sara bounded away. Brenna followed shyly.

"Welcome, Brenna. I'm Sara's dad," Karl Martin greeted her. "Are you sure you want to put up with us?"

Brenna smiled.

"Let's eat before the ice cream gets too soft," Nell fussed.

The family tumbled into the kitchen. Their chairs scraped on the linoleum floor as they jostled into their places at the table. Karl scooped vanilla ice cream into tall clear glasses while Avery passed them out with importance.

"Here, we can share this," Sara said. She handed Brenna an open can of root beer. Brenna poured it over her ice cream and watched the foam rise above the rim of her glass.

Just as she lifted the first sweet, sticky bite of fluff to her mouth, the screen door in the mudroom next to the kitchen banged shut and a young man appeared in the window of the adjoining door. He lifted his fist to knock when Karl called out, "Come on in, Mitch."

The young man walked in, sniffing exaggeratedly. "I thought I smelled something good as I was driving by."

"Uncle Mitch!" Avery laughed. "You can't smell brown cows from the road."

"Some brown cows you can." Mitch winked at Karl who laughed in response.

"Mitch, you seem to have a sixth sense for when we're eating," Nell teased him. "Your bachelor cooking not all that great?"

Mitch shrugged good-naturedly and accepted the glass she handed him. He pulled out a chair and sat down across from Brenna.

"Hi, there," he said. "You must be Sara's friend."

"This is Brenna Williams," Sara said. She draped her arm around Brenna.

"Hello, Brenna Williams," Mitch said. "Are you enjoying your ice cream, Brenna Williams?"

Brenna blushed.

"Of course she is, silly," Sara answered for her. "Who wouldn't like ice cream, Uncle Mitch?"

Mitch reached for a can of root beer and popped the top. Brenna peeked at him over her float. His dark hair had been flattened to his head from a farmer's cap while the bottom edge of his bangs stuck out comically. She liked the way his eyes crinkled at the corners.

She ate her ice cream while the stories and laughter began. Brenna listened in amazement. She wondered if normal families talked to each other so easily, so naturally.

All too soon, Nell looked up at the wall clock and exclaimed, "Oh my goodness, it's nearly nine o'clock. We'd better get you home, Brenna."

"I can take her," Mitch offered. "No sense in you getting out. Sara can ride along."

"But then you'll have to drive extra to bring Sara back," Nell said.

"Who says I'll bring her back? Maybe I'll keep her for a few days and make her do my mounds of laundry and dirty dishes."

Sara wrinkled her nose at him. "Somebody needs to, Uncle Mitch. Mom said your house is a mess. She said it looks like you just go buy more dishes when yours get all dirty."

"Sara!" Nell shook her finger.

"How did you know?" Mitch feigned astonishment, then lowered his voice conspiratorially. "I do the same thing with my underwear, you know."

"You do?" asked Avery, his eyes wide.

Mitch ruffled his hair. "I'm just kidding, Sport."

"You'd better be," said Nell. "I may feed you but I'm not going to offer to do your laundry, or your dishes for that matter."

Mitch drained the last melted bit of ice cream out of his glass and stood up. "Ready to go, Sara B'garra?"

"Yep!" Sara bounced out of her chair.

"Ready to go, Brenna Williams?"

Brenna nodded and carried her dirty glass and spoon to the sink before following them to the back door. Recalling her manners, she turned around. "Th...th...thank y...you," she stammered.

"Thanks for coming, Brenna," Karl said.

Sara's grandma came over and gave her a hug. "It was wonderful to meet you. I meant what I said about if you ever want lessons," she said before releasing her. Brenna couldn't remember ever receiving as much physical affection as she had in the last few hours.

She followed Sara and Mitch out to an old farm truck. Mitch opened the passenger door.

"Here you go, Princess Number One," he said as he lifted Sara inside. Brenna held back.

Mitch held out his hand. "Princess Number Two, may I escort you into your carriage?"

She giggled and placed her hand in his. It felt warm and rough. He hoisted her onto the dusty seat.

The pickup was no elegant carriage, but the young man driving it fit Brenna's girlish dreams of a Prince Charming.

Russell came out of the house, pulling a John Deere cap on his head, his face showing surprise when he saw Nick standing in front of the garage waiting for him.

"Good morning, Nick," the older man greeted him. "I didn't realize you were here already. You should have rung the doorbell."

Nick shifted his weight. J.D. had dropped him off a half hour earlier on his way to work. "I got here early and I didn't want to bother you."

Russell squinted in the morning sunlight. "Have you waited long?"

Nick shrugged.

"You wouldn't have bothered us. We don't bite, you know."

Nick did know. He often lay in bed and replayed the encouragement and praise that Russell and Anya gave him even though he knew his lack of strength and skill. In the darkness of night, he couldn't withhold the secret wish that he could move in with the Martins. He looked forward to the days he could work with Russell.

"Grandpa! You forgot your keys," a voice called.

They turned to see Avery bounding down the front steps.

Russell took the keys and explained, "One of my grandkids. He spent the night at our house last night for something special."

"I know. I ride the bus with him."

Avery bounced back into the house as quickly as he had spilled out the door.

"Sara told me you were in her class at school."

Nick cringed, wondering what else Sara might have said. He was not well liked at school, though he supposed he brought much of that on himself with his standoffish behavior. Nick shook himself. No, Sara would not speak negatively. He had never heard Sara speak disparagingly about anyone. Not only that, but Sara was one of the few students in their class who went out of her way to befriend Brenna.

"Shall we get to work?" asked Russell. He walked to his truck and pulled down the tailgate. "I need some help unloading these landscaping timbers."

"What are we going to do with them?"

"We're going to build planters along the front of the house." He scratched his head and replaced his cap. "I guess there weren't enough leftover bricks. Annie teases me about trying to reuse everything but this time I couldn't make it work. I'll have to think up something else for them."

Russell pulled a small notepad out of his front shirt pocket and held it out to Nick. The pages were curled from carrying it around.

"Here's a diagram of what we'll build. The large rectangle is the house. Where it juts down here is the garage and here's the sidewalk." Russell pointed with the pen from his pocket.

Nick saw how the beds started at the front steps and wrapped around the side of the house.

"We'll plant some large bushes throughout this section. Annie will plant herbs and flowers in between. She loves to grow fresh oregano and parsley. Nothing beats Annie's home canned spaghetti sauce with her own spices. She'll take starters and transplants from her old garden and leave the rest for Nell."

Russell walked around to the side of the house. "We'll put a narrower planter along here so Annie can start a new patch of iris. We have bulbs from her mother's garden that are still producing some of the largest yellow iris you ever saw. Annie loves peonies too, the fat pale pink ones, but they attract ants so she'll plant them along the edge of the yard away from the house."

Nick enjoyed listening to Russell describe the different types of bushes and flowers. He supposed his interest in flowers would only fuel the scorn of his peers at school if they were to find out but Russell was a man's man and seemed to know a great deal.

He followed Russell back to the loaded truck and began to help pull the timbers off the truck bed and stack them in the middle of the yard.

By the time they had unloaded the heavy timbers, the muscles in Nick's arms and shoulders warned him of impending soreness. Anya brought out tall glasses of lemonade with liberal amounts of ice cubes despite the morning coolness that still hung in the air, and Nick was glad for the excuse to sit and rest. She and Russell discussed the final placement of the flowerbeds while Nick lay back on the hardened dirt and watched puffy clouds gliding across the sky, tugged by an invisible higher wind stream.

Russell looked up as well. "Rain in the forecast for this afternoon. Let's get a move on."

They went into the garage to gather the tools that they would need. Nick looked around. The Martins' car was parked in one stall, the other taken up with the large unfamiliar shapes of woodworking machinery.

Nick wandered around as Russell rummaged through a stash of tools. Russell had built a waist-high work shelf along the back wall of the garage with shelves and peg boards above it. Even though the Martins had not lived in their new home long, sawdust already clung to nearly everything, attesting to the amount of time Russell spent in his workshop.

Russell handed him a brown paper sack full of long spikes. He nodded toward the equipment. "I'll tell you what I tell all my grandkids, Nick. Don't ever touch any of my tools, especially the machinery, without my permission and if I'm not here to watch you. I don't want you to get hurt and these blades can be extremely dangerous. Understand?"

"Yes, sir." Russell had not used a stern tone of voice with him before. He had no wish to make Russell unhappy with him. With blades baring their fierce teeth at Nick, the promise came easily.

"I know I can trust you," said Russell. He held out a rubber mallet. "Careful. This is heavy."

Nick took the mallet and Russell hefted an electric miter saw.

"I'll put this on a work table I already set up in the back yard with saw horses. Ready to roll?" he asked.

Nick nodded.

"What were saw horses?" he wondered. But before he could ask, Russell nodded his head toward a bright orange extension cord hanging on the wall.

"Grab that thing, too, will you?" he asked Nick.

They went back outside. Russell began to measure the timbers, marking on the wood with the pen from his pocket.

"Hold this steady while I cut it," he said.

Nick obeyed. He disliked the rough feel of the wood on his already tender hands.

"A little closer," directed Russell. "I won't cut you."

Russell powered up the saw and lined up the blade with his mark. Wood chips flew into Nick's face. He flinched but dared not take his eyes off the spinning blade. No wonder Russell had given him a stern warning.

They soon developed a system of Russell measuring and cutting while Nick fetched and held the timbers steady while they were being cut.

"Would you like to run the saw?" Russell offered.

Nick looked at the fanged circular blade, its cord plugged into the long orange extension to form a long wicked tail. He stepped back. "No thanks."

He felt the familiar sense of shame for not trying new things, pulled in his head waiting for scorn but none came. Russell motioned for Nick to hold the wood and grasped the handle of the saw himself.

They continued measuring and cutting, measuring and cutting until hot sunrays poked through Nick's shirt and drew sweat. They measured out the plots and shoveled dirt to level the ground and tamped where the beams would lay with a heavy block-like tool on the end of a long wooden handle. The longer Nick worked, the more he forgot about his sore muscles and felt a sort of invigoration from the labor.

After a lunch of turkey sandwiches, fried apples, and cottage cheese drizzled with honey, they went back outside and began stacking the timbers in place, Russell drilling the holes, Nick taking the long nails and pounding them in with a hammer.

He tried to imitate the forceful, straight strikes Russell had made when he had demonstrated, but the heavy end of the hammer did not obey and his blows often only nicked the nails or went sideways. He bit his lip in concentration, aware of Russell's watchful eye.

Dirt ground into the knees of Nick's jeans. He swiped at the sweat that dribbled into his ears and down his chin, leaving a muddy streak on his arm. His arm trembled with fatigue but he kept on.

"Sometime next week, we'll use the rest of the timbers to make a raised bed for Annie's strawberry patch in the back," Russell said. "Ever had homemade strawberry jam?"

Nick shook his head.

"Best thing this side of heaven." Russell licked his lips.

Nick thought of the small jam packets his grandmother had received with her meals-on-wheels for lunch. She didn't care for jams or jellies so she would save the packets for him, which he would spread over Saltine crackers for a snack after school. Saltines were reasonably affordable, she would say, which meant cheap.

"This is the time of the year when we've ran out of nearly everything Annie put up the summer before," said Russell. "My taste buds have a real hankering for more pickles. We ran out of those clear back in February. Annie makes the best pickles around. She doesn't use that quick mix stuff from the store. She soaks her cucumbers in brine for several weeks and uses her own fresh dill. You'll have to taste some of her pickles in the fall."

"What else will Mrs. Martin plant?"

"Tomatoes, green beans, lettuce, onions, some peppers. Mitch loves hot peppers so she always grows at least one chile pepper plant for him."

Gradually the planter began to take shape.

"How did you learn so much about building?" Nick knew from Anya that Russell had basically built the house himself, hiring out only for the foundation work, electrical wiring and plumbing. Russell handled the tape measure, T-square and saws comfortably, every bit as at ease with them as Nick was with piano keys.

"I used to work for a construction company years ago, to supplement the farm income." Russell leaned back on the heels of his worn cowboy boots. "I've always enjoyed building, creating, watching something grow under my hands. Truth to tell, I think God gave me a love for building so I could understand Him better."

Nick frowned. He still had not become accustomed to the Martins' "God-talk".

Russell handed Nick a nail. "You see Nick, God is a Creator – He created everything that we see and know, including ourselves - and He gave us the ability to create as well. So when I build and create things, I think about God."

Russell laughed. "And, I think about how much easier it is for God to create. He just speaks whatever He's making into existence. Me, well, I have to start out with His materials and take quite a bit of time."

"You really believe that?" Nick squinted in skepticism.

"With all my being. How else do you explain everything?"

Nick shifted his jaw. "I don't know. I never thought about it much."

"Have you ever attended church or Sunday School, Nick?" Russell held the drill perpendicular to the wood and pushed down to bore the hole. Nick watched Russell's arm muscles bunch. He looked at his own skinny arm, wishing that he had more strength. Russell pulled the bit out of the hole and brushed at the sawdust with his thick fingers. Nick watched him before answering.

"We went to Mass a couple of times, but I never heard much about God there, just a lot of mumbling and reciting. Some priest guy kept swinging this lantern around."

"What I'm talking about isn't religion, Nick. I'm talking about learning to know a God who is real, a God who wants to be your friend and your Father."

Nick frowned again. He had no reason to believe that another father was desirable, God-Father or not.

"You see, Nick, a lot of people assume that only the churchgoers think God exists. That simply isn't true. Whether you go to church or not, whether you believe it or not, God is real."

"How do you know that for sure?" Nick challenged.

"Because the Bible says it and every word of the Bible is true."

"How do you know that?"

Russell held the drill out towards Nick. "Take this," he said.

Nick shook his head. "I'd rather you used it."

"I'm not asking you to use it. Touch it. Is the drill real?"

"Of course." Nick laughed but Russell remained serious.

"How do you know that?"

"Because I can see it."

"Now look at the trees."

Nick blew air from his nostrils, impatient with the older man's game.

Russell smiled. "Can you see the leaves moving?"

Nick watched the treetops dip and sway in the light breeze that had kept the day's heat bearable.

"What's making them move, Nick?"

"Wind."

"Can you see the wind?"

"No."

"It's the same with God, Nick. We may not be able to see Him yet, but I know, just as certain as I am of the wind, that God is everything He says He is."

Nick rubbed his nose where flecks of sawdust tickled his nose hairs. "That doesn't make sense."

Russell smiled. "No, I suppose not totally. That's where faith has to come in. But if God was smart enough to create the whole world, including me, can I expect to understand Him? Obviously not. Besides, I can't think up a more reasonable explanation for the earth and creation. Too much evidence points to the Bible and the existence of a Creator."

Nick pounded at a nail. His hammer missed several strokes.

"I've made you angry."

Nick shook his head, almost irritably. "No, just confused. I've never heard this stuff before. To me, it just sounds like the Greek myths about gods and goddesses who make lightning and thunder. I read about them in my old school." He glanced at Russell, afraid he had offended the older man.

"Those stories are man's invention to explain things without God. But I've preached enough. Give yourself time, Nick. Learn as much as you can about God. Test what I've told you."

Nick picked at a splinter that had embedded itself in the side of his hand.

"Here," Russell held out the drill once again. "We only have a few holes left to drill. Why don't you try it? I'll hammer the rest."

"I'd rather you…"

"Did it myself. I know. You said that. But to tell the truth, my arm's getting tired. I need some of your youthful energy."

Nick narrowed his eyes. Russell had shown very little, if any, signs of fatigue whereas Nick's muscles and ligaments had protested to having unfamiliar demands put upon them.

Without comment, Nick allowed Russell to poise the drill and take his hand, clasping it around the drill. Nick kept his arm pliable and limp and watched with detachment as Russell's large knuckles tightened over his own narrow hand, almost as though neither hand belonged to him. He couldn't remember the last time someone intentionally touched him other than the jostles he sometimes received in the hallway from sneering athletic types.

"Put some muscle into it," Russell said.   He lifted his hand away from Nick's.

Nick's hand cooled with Russell's hand gone.   He complied by pressing the drill bit harder into the timber.

""That's it, push on it. Now give it some power."

Nick squeezed the trigger and the drill responded, like a kitchen mixer on high speed.

"That's it."

The power surged sporadically as Nick struggled to force the drill bit deeper into the wood, his fingers slipping on the throttle.

"Keep it steady."   Once more, Russell's hand closed over his. The drill bit sank easily into the timber.

Russell pointed to the next spot, releasing his hand. Nick poked the bit at the spot.

"Hold it at a ninety degree angle. That's it. Now you've got it," the older man encouraged him.

Nick applied the bit to the wood with more confidence.

"Good job, Nick. It just takes a little practice, that's all. There's something about men and power tools, Annie always says."

Nick lay the drill down on the pretext of searching for another nail. He swallowed against the burning in his throat. What was it about him that made everyone assume that he needed help figuring out that he was male?

Sara came up the stairs with a jar of home canned green beans from her grandma's cooling shelves. Grandma Anya and Brenna stood at the stove.

"You'll want to keep the burner on fairly low heat so the grease doesn't spit out and burn you," Anya told Brenna. "Just lay the bacon strips down like this in the skillet."

Brenna complied.

"Good. Sara, why don't you put those green beans in a saucepan? We can add the bacon once it is cooked."

When her grandma had invited Sara to come over and bake cookies, Sara sensed an opportunity and asked if she could bring Brenna with her and if they could learn how to make an entire meal instead. She told Grandma Anya about Bradley's comments that she had overheard.

"They were making fun of her, Grandma, but I could tell that she really didn't know anything about cooking and that her mom probably can't teach her. You know how everyone says her mom is sick. If she wants to learn, maybe you can teach her."

Anya had hesitated. "I don't want her to feel like she's a project, Sara. Besides, no one can learn to cook just like that. Think of how much more practice Michele has had over you, and she still has a great deal to learn."

But Sara had begged until Grandma had come up with the idea of the girls fixing a mystery dinner and inviting their families over for the meal.

"With a mystery dinner, we can fix several main dishes and many other kinds of foods," Anya had told Sara. "That way Brenna can learn how to fix several dishes, but it will still be fun and not seem too obvious that we are trying to help her."

Earlier that week, the girls had met at Anya's to make invitations. They read, "You are invited to a crazy mystery dinner. Wear your best clothes if you haven't any. We have one or two plates so we'll put out many. Admission is free, but you can pay at the door. We'll save you a seat so you can sit on the floor." The invitation went on to give details about when and where. The girls had giggled over the wording and Sara had kicked herself for waiting to get to know Brenna.

"So who all will be here tonight?" Anya asked the girls.

"My whole family is coming," Sara said with an excited little bounce. "And I invited Uncle Mitch, too."

Brenna looked down, letting her hair hide her face, but not before Sara saw it redden. Maybe she had better warn Uncle Mitch not to tease Brenna tonight. She didn't want her new friend to feel uncomfortable.

"What about your family, Brenna?" Sara asked.

Brenna did not raise her head. "B...B...Bradley is c...coming."

"Your parents can't come?" Sara asked.

Brenna turned over a slice of bacon with her fork and did not answer. Sara looked at her grandmother, who shook her head. Sara wondered if Bradley only planned on coming because he hoped to see more cooking mistakes to tease Brenna about.

"I invited J.D. and Nick as well," Anya said. She popped open the seal on her home-canned jar of green beans and handed the jar to Sara. "I hope that's all right. Your grandpa and I figured the more the merrier."

"Oh, that's good," Sara enthused. "Nick is in our class at school. Tell us more about this mystery meal, Grandma Anya. Where did you get the idea?"

"I don't know when I first heard about it," answered Anya. She paused to turn on the faucet and wash the celery stalks in her hand. "Some of my friends and I put one on for our husbands when the children were younger. The general idea of a mystery dinner is to have the guests order from a menu, only the menu doesn't say what they're going to get. It only gives clues."

"And you give them strange dishes and cups and stuff to eat with, right?" asked Sara.

"That's right." Anya began slicing the celery into sticks. "If I remember correctly, Grandpa had to drink out of a gallon jug for his glass and used a toothpick as a fork."

Brenna giggled.

"Part of the fun was setting the table, but then we made every couple draw numbers to see where they would sit."

"We can do that too, can't we Grandma?"

"Yes, we can." Anya smiled.

Sara set her bowl of green beans in the refrigerator until closer to dinnertime when they would warm them on the stove. Grandma Anya helped Brenna put the finished bacon slices on a paper towel covered plate.

"Let's get the cake and pudding finished, then we can take a break from cooking and write up the menus and set the table," Anya directed.

"It's a good thing we have all afternoon," said Sara. "Do you want to make the cake or the pudding, Brenna?"

"I...I d...don't c...c...care." Brenna tucked her head.

"Why don't you both help with both," suggested Anya. "You girls need to learn how to make things from scratch. We're not using mixes for either one."

"I thought the only way to make pudding was to buy one of those packets and add milk," said Sara.

Anya laughed. "No, Sara girl. You're going to get a lesson on how not to scorch milk on the stovetop."

"Grandma, what should we call everything?" asked Sara.

"That's something we need to decide. The name has to give a clue as to what the food is, but it can't be too obvious. We don't want our guests to guess."

"That way we keep it a mystery," said Sara. "You know, Grandma, some of those combinations of food might not be too appetizing."

"I thought of that already," said Anya and handed Brenna the milk jug and a measuring cup. "I figured that we would let people go into the kitchen and serve themselves for seconds. That way no one goes hungry."

"Th...that's g...good," said Brenna. "B...Bradley d...d...doesn't l...like c...c...celery."

"And Avery doesn't like corn," said Sara.

"Here," Anya directed Brenna. "Pour in two cups of milk for the pudding. It will come up to this line."

Sara giggled. "We could call the corn 'Avery's favorite'."

"Or, 'spots of sunshine'," said Anya. "We wouldn't want to trick Avery into ordering something he doesn't like."

"The g...green b...beans could b...be 'green l...logs'," suggested Brenna.

"That's a good idea," said Sara. "Maybe we could call them 'mossy logs' so they're not so easy to guess."

Brenna stirred the milk into the dry ingredients in a saucepan on the stove, enjoying the scent of chocolate that rose from the 2 Tablespoons of cocoa Sara had mixed in with the cornstarch.

"You'd better turn the burner down a bit," Anya warned. "Let the milk warm up slowly or it will burn on the bottom."

"Here. Y...You c...can stir." Brenna offered the spoon to Sara who stirred designs into the brown liquid. Both girls watched anxiously for the mixture to boil, ready to push the timer for exactly one minute.

"Grandma, it's taking forever," Sara exclaimed.

Grandma Anya smiled. "Patience, child." She handed Brenna a bowl and 2 eggs. "Watch me separate the yolk from the white of the first egg, then you can do the next."

Brenna copied Anya's motions, a pleased smile crossing her face when the egg white dropped neatly into the bowl and left the yolk nestled in one half of the shell. Sara smiled as well, glad that her friend seemed to enjoy herself.

The pudding began to bubble and Grandma Anya deftly folded the egg yolks in. After helping the girls put the finished pudding into a decorative bowl to cool, they mixed the cake and slid it into the oven. Then Grandma Anya rubbed her hands together. "Come on, girls, it's time to set the table."

"Oh, good," Sara enthused. "This is going to be great."

Anya brushed her fingers over Sara's nose. "I don't think I've ever heard you get excited about setting the table before."

"Grandma!"

"Maybe I should call up your mother and tell her that since you love to set the table so much, she should let you do it every day for the next month," Anya teased.

Sara wrinkled her nose. Brenna was watching them curiously with a bit of loneliness mixed in. Sara wondered if Brenna was feeling left out and stepped away from Grandma Anya.

"Can we really use any dish that we find?" Sara asked.

"Within reason, of course, but by all means, be creative."

Sara reached for Brenna's hand and pulled her into the kitchen. "Let's look in this cupboard first. I think there are some Cool Whip containers in there that we can use for bowls."

"Draw numbers? You got to be kidding." Bradley moaned when he saw the table. "Not that it makes a difference. No matter where we sit, we're sunk."

"Don't whine, Bradley," Sara said. "We have to draw numbers too and we're the ones that set the table."

"Girls," Bradley shook his head in disgust as he reached into Russell's cap for a slip of paper. Brenna knew he had only come with the promise of food.

"What number did you get?" asked Sara.

"Three."

"You sit by me," little Avery crowed with pleasure. "I have a two."

Brenna hoped that Bradley would be patient with Sara's little brother.

Karl opened his slip of paper. "I'm a ten."

"I already gave you that score years ago." His wife Nell slid her hand around his neck and pecked his lips with her own.

Bradley looked at Brenna with skepticism as if to say, "These people are crazy."

Brenna smiled. Crazy or not, she liked them. Sara's family and grandparents made her feel special and wanted.

"Okay, I think everyone has their numbers. Sit up to the table," Russell ordered.

They scurried to obey. Russell, sitting at spot six rather than his habitual head of the table, held out his hands to Nick Pierce and Michele who sat on either side of him. Michele readily put her hand in his, Nick with reluctance. Gradually, everyone around the table grabbed each other's hands although J.D. looked less than pleased and Brenna had to admit it felt awkward.

"Let's pray," said Russell. Bowing his head, he offered thanks for the food, guests and for Sara and Brenna and his Annie who worked so hard all day to give them an enjoyable evening.

Brenna blushed. She had never heard her name mentioned in a prayer before. She stood up with Sara after the prayer and together they handed out the hand-printed menus.

"What's this?" asked Karl. "I don't see any real food on here."

"You have to try to guess what food you'll be getting. That's why it's called a mystery meal," explained Sara.

Karl raised his eyebrows at Russell.

"Don't look at me. I had nothing to do with it," protested Russell. "All I know is that it smells wonderful in the kitchen."

Michele squealed. "Covered earthworms! Surely that's a joke."

"Earthworms!" Avery's face lit up. "Cool!"

"Considering your grandpa's penchant for keeping night crawlers in the refrigerator, anything is possible," teased Karl.

"Mud pie, that must be chocolate pudding or something," Nell guessed.

"Mom, you can't order dessert yet," said Sara.

"You just gave it away," chortled Bradley. "Hey everybody, the mud pie is chocolate pudding."

"Actually, it's not," Sara informed him frostily.

"But it is dessert," said Anya. "Brenna, why don't you start over there by Nick and take orders going to the right. Sara, you can start with Grandpa going the other direction. I'll go on into the kitchen and be ready to dish up the food."

"What kinds of plates will we get?" asked Michele. "Please don't tell me they're worse than the cups and silverware that we already have."

Sara looked at Brenna. Brenna looked at Sara. They burst into laughter.

"Much worse," said Sara.

"Great," muttered Michele, but she was smiling.

The girls wrote down the orders on little pads of paper and took them to Anya in the kitchen. Brenna enjoyed hearing each new wave of laughter as she brought out the food to each person in mixing bowls, saucers and even a cookie sheet. Their guests talked enthusiastically as they ate, trying to match up the food names on the menu with what was on their "plates".

"Well, I'd better get going." J.D. pushed himself away from the table and stood up as soon as his food had disappeared.

"We'd love to have you stay a little longer," encouraged Anya. "The girls fixed dessert as well, which we can start serving up right now."

""No time. Nick, come on."

Nick followed suit slowly. Brenna had not missed the fact that Nick had barely said a word during the meal. Nick often acted withdrawn, content to remain on the sidelines but tonight he had seemed awkward, almost wary. She wondered if she was being fanciful or if J.D.'s presence had anything to do with Nick's behavior. Maybe it was just the fact that J.D. made her nervous. He hadn't been fair to Nick by making him leave before dessert.

"Thanks for supper," Nick muttered, avoiding eye contact. He pulled his shoulder in tight against his neck and left the room ahead of J.D. Brenna heard the front door open and close.

"Don't know what's wrong with that boy," J.D. bluffed.

"Show him some love, J.D." Russell stood to face the other man.

"That'll only make him soft. He's too soft already."

"I'm not sure you understand children, J.D." Russell's voice became softer.

"Time he learns to be a man." J.D. shook his head and strode out.

Russell sank back into his chair. Brenna watched as his eyes met Anya's. They both looked as sorry as she felt.

"Dessert time," announced Sara. She smiled cheerfully as though nothing untoward had happened, but Brenna knew Sara's compassionate nature enough to know better.

After large helpings of mud pie, a.k.a. chocolate cake covered in rich chocolate pudding, Russell leaned back in his chair and sighed with satisfaction. "Excellent meal, girls. You did a good job."

"Yes, you did," echoed Karl. "I enjoyed myself very much."

Brenna pulled up her shoulders as words of thanks and appreciation came from around the table like a gentle barrage.

As they cleaned up from the meal, Anya put generous helpings of leftover roast beef and chocolate cake into plastic containers for Brenna to take home.

"You earned these," she said. "Thank you so much for helping put together a wonderful meal – and a very fun one at that."

Brenna watched the lights in Nick and J.D.'s trailer house as they passed it on their way home; wishing her sadness for Nick hadn't overshadowed the evening's finale. He had reached out to her in friendship with that simple note at school, yet in shyness she had ignored him. She determined to make an effort to be kind to him.

The next night, Brenna proudly set two bowls on the supper table as her father walked in the door, home from work.

"What's this?" he said in surprise.

"Brenna cooked supper," bragged Bradley. "Spaghetti and meat sauce. Brenna makes really good spaghetti. We had some last night. Only we called it earthworms."

Their father looked dazed. "Well what do you know about that," he said, shaking his head.

Brenna glowed with triumph.

Chapter 5

"I figured that today we'd haul in several loads of manure and dirt for Annie's garden space and the front yard. I hope you wore old clothes."

Nick pulled at the tail of his t-shirt. All his clothes were getting old, and small. School had let out for the summer a week ago and Nick spent at least a few hours every day with Russell. The more he was with the other man, the more Nick found himself mimicking Russell's walk and way of speech.

Nick lifted his farmer cap, the extra one Russell had given him, and scratched his hair the way Russell did.

They clambered into Russell's pickup, the exterior speckled with mud. As they drove, the pungent country air whipped years of acquired dirt and chaff around the cab. Nick relaxed a little more each time they crossed a mile-marking intersection, shedding the boundaries he erected when he was with his father.

They turned into a cattle pen and parked. Nick watched out the back window as Russell scooped dirt and manure into the truck bed with a small tractor loader.

After the back end was full, Nick felt the front of the truck tilted upwards. Russell drove home and backed up beside the newly built raised beds in the backyard.

"Now for the hard part," he said. He smiled and handed Nick a shovel. They shoveled the thick dirt out of the truck bed and down into the planters. Nick was thankful for the leather gloves Russell had loaned him even though his fingers were much too slender for them. He noted with surprise how what had appeared to be a lot of dirt in the truck barely made a pile on the ground.

They made two more trips to the pen and were ready to take the final load back to the house when Russell startled Nick by motioning for him to scoot over into the driver's seat.

"Want to try a hand at driving, Nick?"

"I don't have my driver's license yet."

Russell smiled. "I don't see any patrols out here. Do you?"

"Isn't it illegal anyway?"

"If it is, then most farmer's kids should be ticketed and fined."

Nick looked skeptical.

"The best way to learn is by doing," Russell coaxed. "I'll help you."

Nick slid behind the wheel. He could barely reach the gas pedal yet Russell's legs didn't look any longer than his.

Russell caught his look. "The seat is stuck. I'd move it closer if I could."

Nick nodded and gripped the wheel. As a younger child, he had perched in the driver's seat of Grandma Bates' ancient car when it was parked in the garage. He would make engine and siren noises and pretend to be driving a fire truck to a blazing inferno or turn on his lights and chase after the bad guys until Grandma Bates found him and insisted that he never sit in the car unless they were going somewhere. She had been afraid that he might somehow get the car started and drive through either end of the garage – never mind that she kept the keys in her gigantic purse.

"It's an automatic. Move the gear shift down until you see the orange light glowing behind the 'D' for drive," Russell instructed after he clambered into the passenger side.

Nick pulled down on the lever as though he handled a bomb. The truck rolled forward.

"Push on the gas pedal lightly, now."

Nick tried to obey but the bouncing of the truck over the mud ruts in the pen caused his foot to pound out a lurching rhythm on the pedal. Russell didn't comment.

"Where do I go?" Nick hated the breathy sound of his voice.

"Turn the truck around in a wide circle to the right and head back to the gate."

Nick looked at his hands in a sudden panic on which was his right.

"Your soprano hand – treble cleft," Russell said. "You said you play the piano, right."

Nick cranked the steering wheel around and the truck obediently circled around. He pointed the hood toward the gate.

"Give yourself a couple of feet on your side when you go through and you'll be fine. It's a wide gate."

The truck crawled through the enclosure and stopped when Nick shoved his foot down on the brake pedal. He felt relieved and wiggled his shoulders to loosen them.

Russell quickly got out to shut the gate. Nick moved the gearshift lever back up into the park position and started to get out.

"What are you doing?" Russell asked him.

"Am I done?"

"Don't you want to drive all the way home?"

Nick raised his eyebrows and tucked his shoulder into his neck. "On the road?"

Russell shrugged. "Why not? You've done a great job so far."

Nick pulled himself back into the driver's seat. Russell's praise, as usual, warmed his ears and insides but the truck still seemed a monstrous thing for him to direct. At Russell's instruction, he looked both ways and crept out onto the sandy road.

"Just keep the wheels in the worn lanes on the road, so you don't hit the soft sand on the shoulder. We'll be able to see if someone's coming and get over. Remember to check the rear view mirror every once in a while."

Nick obeyed, feeling a certain pleasure in his accomplishment. He dared to push harder on the accelerator. The speedometer needle moved up to forty miles per hour.

"Better keep it under forty," Russell said. Nick chanced a quick glance at the man. Russell sat relaxed and calm. He trusted him. He trusted his ability. Nick sat straighter and tightened his hands on the wheel importantly.

However, he was glad to turn the truck over to Russell when they reached the house and needed to back up to the garden plot.

They shoveled out the last of the dirt just as Nick's stomach rumbled with hunger. Anya poked her head out the back door.

"Lunch is ready," she called.

"Are you eating lunch with us, Nick?" Russell asked.

"I guess so," Nick said, hoping not to sound too eager. One of his favorite parts of working for the Martins was Mrs. Martin's cooking.

Nick removed his ragged tennis shoes at the door and lined them alongside Russell's cowboy boots. He followed Russell and the smell of pot roast into the kitchen.

Anya turned from the counter with a radiant smile, the same smile she always gave Russell. Nick could only dream someone would ever smile at the sight of him like that.

"Hello, Annie," Russell said, touching her shoulder affectionately before going to the sink. "Something smells awful good in here."

"It may be awful, it may be good," Anya teased.

"Guess we'll just have to eat it to find out." Russell winked at Nick who joined him at the sink.

Nick washed and dried his hands then sat down at the table while Anya bustled back and forth between the table and the stove. The doorbell rang, masking the sound of Nick's rumbling stomach.

Russell went to the door. A moment later, he and J.D. came into the kitchen.

"Let's go," J.D. ordered Nick. "Got to go pick up some parts in town." His words were slurred, his walk unsteady.

"Why don't you sit down and have a quick bite to eat first, J.D.?" Anya asked.

"Can't. I'm in a hurry. Get your shoes on, boy."

"You may not be hungry but your son needs to eat." Russell's clenched his teeth as he spoke, putting emphasis on the word son. Nick shrank against the doorframe, afraid of the anger he detected for the first time in Russell.

J.D. turned on the older man with a stronger anger. "I can take care of my own kid. I don't need your help."

Russell spoke in a softer tone, "Nick is welcome to stay here for the afternoon. I could really use his help. Surely you don't have to have him along just to pick up parts."

"He spends too much time with you already. Don't need no babysitter. Just pay me for Nick's work and we'll get going."

Nick understood then what his father wanted – money for booze.

Russell pulled his worn wallet from his back pocket. "How many hours do I owe you for, Nick?"

Nick swallowed. Was Mr. Martin going to make him go? "Eight from the last few days plus this morning."

"So I owe you for twelve hours?" Russell counted out the bills. J.D. held out his hand for the money.

"Wait a minute, J.D.," said Russell. "Nick earned it. I think I should give it to him, don't you?"

J.D. shrugged and waved his hand toward his son. "Suit yourself."

Nick took the money. He stuffed it into his front jeans pocket, knowing J.D. would confiscate it as soon as they were out the door. He wondered where J.D. would drop him off this time while he went to the bar. Nick stepped into the enclosed porch and knelt to put on his shoes. His hands shook on the laces.

J.D. followed him and held out his hand. "Give me the money, boy, and let's go."

Nick stood and pulled out the crumpled bills. J.D. snatched them from him and yanked the door open.

"If you walk out that door with that money, you're fired," Russell said.

J.D. stopped. "What?"

"You heard me. Give the money back to Nick. It's his and he earned it."

Swearing loudly, J.D. shoved the bills against Nick's chest. Nick stumbled backward. The money drifted to the floor between he and his father.

"Listen to me, J.D.," Russell said with a hard tone in his voice. "You've already been drinking. You're in no shape to be driving to town, much less fulfilling a job responsibility if it really is farm parts you're going to pick up. You don't need to take Nick with you and you know it. Go home. Sober up, then you can come back for Nick."

"You're not my boss, Karl is." J.D. jabbed his finger toward Russell.

"You show up here drunk again, nobody will be your boss."

J.D. spat at Russell and called him a foul name. Then he left, his pickup tires spewing sand.

Nick shuddered. "You shouldn't have done that."

Russell met his eyes. "Your father shouldn't have done that. Besides, I really can put you to work this afternoon. That is, if you don't mind. Come on back to the kitchen now. I know you're hungry. Your stomach's been talking for an hour now."

Nick blushed and went back to his chair at the table. But somehow the food did not smell quite as appetizing as it had only moments before.

Anya leaned against the doorframe and watched the boy position the bench the correct distance from the piano and sit down. He held his wrists arched above the keys. From the first scale he played, Anya knew.

God had given Nick an extraordinary talent. The boy already played at a much higher level than any of her piano students had ever achieved. She understood now why Nick longed to play, had to play.

Anya eased down onto the couch, watching his hands pound out an intricate scale in F sharp and move fluidly into the key of G. He transitioned into the Scott Joplin's ever-popular "The Entertainer", playing from memory. Somehow he managed to avoid the error most students made of keeping such a rigid beat that no emotion showed through.

Anya could only hope that J.D. would not show up to pick up the boy while he sat at the piano. It would only make matters worse. Quite frankly, she hoped J.D. did not come at all. If only she and Russell could keep Nick, for always.

Nick played until he clearly could remember no more and stopped. He kept his hands on the keys as though he could not bear removing them.

"There's piano music in the bench if you want to open it," Anya said.

Nick lifted the lid of the piano bench and shuffled through the stacks of music books.

"I have this one," he said, holding up the John Thompson's lesson book 5.

"Those are the series I use with my grandchildren," Anya said.

Nick looked up sharply. "You give lessons?"

"To Michele and Sara. I've also just started giving lessons to Brenna Williams, the girl that lives down the road on the corner. I believe she's in your class at school?" Without waiting for an answer, Anya went on. "I used to give lessons to my own children, although several of the boys didn't want anything to do with it."

The tips of Nick's ears turned red.

Anya instantly regretted her words. "I'm sorry, Nick. I didn't mean it that way."

Nick shrugged. "It's okay. I know I'm different than most boys."

Anya cringed. She had no wish to solidify his maidenly mannerisms. She exchanged a look with Russell where he sat in his recliner. They had discussed Nick's need for a male role model, a role that Russell felt compelled, no, called to fulfill.

"Would you give me lessons?"

Anya stalled. "I don't know if I can, Nick. We'd have to okay it through your father."

Nick sighed.

"You do have an undeniable gift, Nick. I honestly would hate to see the chance to develop it taken away from you. But ultimately it's not my decision."

Nick reluctantly turned from the piano. He covered his mouth to hide a yawn, but Anya noticed.

"If you're tired, Nick, why don't you lie down here on the couch?"

Nick complied. She lifted the afghan that lay folded across the back of the couch.

"Why don't you try and get some sleep?" she said and laid the blanket over him, tucking it around his shoulders with tender hands. She wished she could protect him from more than the chill.

Russell folded down the corner of the page he was reading in his farming magazine. "It's time for bed for this old body too."

Anya smoothed Nick's hair. "Good night, Nick."

"Good night," he whispered, his eyes wide as though he had never been tucked in before.

*   *   *

Nick rolled over to face the back of the couch. He listened to the Martins' footsteps fading down the hall. The hall light snapped off. He closed his eyes but could not relax. He wished he could have played the piano all night. His lack of practice had blatantly showed up in his playing. Though no fault of his own, the loss of skill and dexterity pained him.

After a few moments, he heard the toilet flush and footsteps coming back. He lay still and pretended to be asleep.

Russell walked to the front door and turned the deadbolt into the locked position. He came up to the couch and stood still. Nick held his breath. Then with creaking knees, the man knelt beside the couch. Nick could not keep his back from stiffening. Russell rested his hand on Nick's shoulder. Nick lay in silence.

"Father," Russell whispered. "Take care of this boy. Show me what I can do to shelter him from the tough things in his life, if I can, and if not, then to teach him the lessons You want him to learn. Help him to come to a saving knowledge of Your grace. Use his gifts for Your glory."

The man was praying for him? Nick had heard Grandma Bates pray over her rosary, chants that he never quite made out, but this prayer sounded as though Russell spoke freely to Someone whom he knew personally. The Father-God he was always talking about.

"Father, this young man has such great potential, potential to go either way. Protect him. Give me wisdom in dealing with his father."

Nick tried to keep his breathing even and slow, aware of Russell's touch.

"And Father, you know that Annie and I are beginning to love Nick. Help him to become part of our family. Let him feel that he is more than a project to us. Allow us to raise him up into a Godly man. I pray this in your Holy name."

Russell squeezed Nick's shoulder and rose. Nick stared at the back of the couch for a long while afterwards, Russell's words wrapping around his memory.

Nick slept, wrapped in the comfort of Anya's afghan, when the throaty roar of his father's truck woke him at 1 a.m. Headlights bore into the living room wall like eyes searching for him. Nick burrowed closer into the couch.

Russell walked through, hastily tucking boxers into a pair of jeans and let himself outside. He shut the door behind him.

Nick heard long periods of silence, followed by the staccato shouts of his father. Nick sat up and pulled the afghan to his chin.

Finally, the door opened and Russell came in.

"Go back to sleep, Nick," he said. "He'll pick you up in the morning."

Nick shivered. "Will you lock the door again?"

Russell complied before sitting down on the couch beside Nick. "If I ask you something, Nick, will you give me a completely honest answer?"

Nick hesitated.

"Does your father drink at home?"

Nick twisted his fingers through the afghan fringe. "Not enough to get drunk, just a beer with supper."

"Have you seen him drunk since the time Mitch told us about?"

"No."

"Has your father ever hit you or hurt you in any way?"

Nick thought of the many derogatory words J.D. slung at him on a daily basis but other than the night at the Laundromat, he could not recall his father ever touching him. "No," he answered again.

Anya entered, tying the belt on her fuzzy blue robe. "Russell, is everything all right?" she asked in alarm.

"It's fine, Annie. Go back to bed. I'll join you in a bit."

"Was J.D. here?"

"Yes. He went on home."

She sighed. "Good."

Russell searched Nick's face for several moments as Nick bit his lip, looping strands of yard from the afghan fringe over and under his fingers. Without a word, Russell tousled his hair and left.

Nick woke to the smell of coffee and sausage. He slipped into the kitchen. Anya's back was turned to him as she flipped sausages in a skillet. Russell looked out the window, a phone to his ear.

"As I explained earlier, I am a concerned neighbor just asking you to check it out." He paused. "Yes, I understand that, but the boy's safety is vital."

Nick slunk back into the hall.

"I'd appreciate that. Thank you."

Nick leaned against the wall. Shame made his face hot. Now that Russell had called to make a report, Nick would probably undergo questioning from nosy social workers. He hated having to dredge up personal things, having grown-ups fire questions at him as though he were on a witness stand, as though they would relish in any nasty tidbits he could supply. Not that all of them were as uncaring as Mrs. Anderson. Some were quite nice. He just preferred to be left alone – especially when it came to some of the nosier questions they asked him, like psychologist that interviewed him before J.D. came for him.

"Have you ever been touched in a private area by a caregiver?" she had asked.

He had reddened in humiliation. But those boys who blocked his way out of the bathroom stall at school had not been caregivers. He had answered "no" with honesty.

Anya bustled through the doorway, nearly knocking Nick over.

"Oh my goodness, Nick, I'm sorry," she said. "I was just coming to see if you were awake."

He tugged at the front of his wrinkled t-shirt.

"Are you up to having some breakfast?"

Nick shrugged, hoping that she didn't guess what he had overheard. He followed her to the table, trying to avoid Russell's cheerful greeting and smile. He bent his head over his plate as Russell offered thanks. He had grown accustomed to either Russell or Anya praying before every meal, but this time he could only remember the sound of Russell's voice praying over him beside the couch, only to betray his privacy to social services a few hours later. He stubbornly kept his eyes open.

Anya spooned scrambled eggs onto his plate. "Eat while they're warm," she encouraged.

He stabbed a sausage patty with his fork when Russell held out the plate.

"How'd you sleep last night?"

"Okay."

Russell peered at him. "You doing okay, Nick?"

Nick cut his sausage into little pieces. "I'm fine."

He could sense them glancing at each other over his head.

Russell cleared his throat. "Are you okay with going home?"

Nick put a fork of eggs into his mouth and chewed without taste. Fear of J.D. flared in a sudden electric surge through his body and he lowered his hand to the table.

"Nick?" Anya reached for his arm.

He shook her away. "I'm fine."

The early morning hours crept by. J.D. was either recovering from a hangover or too ashamed to come. Nick doubted the latter. Russell and Anya prepared for their church service. They looked nice in their dressy clothes and sat in the living room reading after they were ready. Nick went to the bathroom and finger-combed water through his mussed hair. He wondered what they would do if J.D. did not come – if they would make him attend church with them or leave him there alone. He wasn't certain which scared him more.

Finally J.D.'s horn honked outside. Russell stood and looked at his watch. He held the door open.

Anya slid her arm around Nick and walked him down the sidewalk. J.D. met them partway. Anya kissed Nick's hair just above his ear. "Call if you need anything," she said.

J.D. pointedly slung his arm over Nick's shoulders and pulled him away from Anya's side. The weight of his arm hurt Nick's neck and shoulders but he did not dare pull away.

"Come on, Nick. Time to go home." Nick felt no pleasure at hearing J.D. use his name instead of the usual "boy".

"J.D.," Russell said.

"Don't start," J.D. said. "Truth is, you know you or Karl won't fire me. For Nick's sake, you won't."

Russell clenched his fists at his sides until his knuckles turned white.

They drove away, Nick turning to watch the Martins in their driveway. The quarter of a mile from their home to his seemed far away.

J.D. smirked. "Made 'em late for church, didn't we?"

But as soon as they were inside the trailer house, J.D. stopped smirking. Anger transformed his features. "Hiding behind the neighbors? What are you, some kind of sissy boy?"

Nick cringed.

"I'm your father, don't forget. I'm the one who decides what'll be best for you and by God I'll make a man out of you yet." J.D. unzipped his tan work jacket and withdrew a bottle of vodka. He unscrewed the top and took a long swig.

"Don't you think you've had enough?" Nick dared to ask.

J.D. swung the bottle at him. Even though the bottle was too far away to make contact, Nick instinctively jumped backwards. He felt a blinding pain on the side of his face as it made contact with the sharp corner of a kitchen cupboard, the force knocking him to the floor. His eyes filled with smarting tears.

"Get up," J.D. said. "Men don't lay around and cry."

When Nick did not move, J.D. swore and kicked at him viciously, the pointed tip of his cowboy boot ramming into Nick's side.

Nick curled into a fetal position, gasping from the pain.

"Get up, I said!" J.D. drew back his foot for another blow. Nick put his arms over his head and held his knees close against his chest. He waited for the next kick.

When it did not come, Nick peeked up. J.D. stared at him, a horrified expression on his face. Their eyes met and held, Nick's wary, J.D.'s stricken.

Finally J.D. spoke. "I don't know what happened. I…" He rubbed his face with a trembling hand. "Are you all right, boy?"

Nick nodded despite the pain in his side and skull. Russell's question in the night replayed in his ears. "Has your father ever hurt you?"

"I'm sorry. I shouldn't have…" J.D. swung around and disappeared from the room, clutching the vodka. His bedroom door slammed.

Nick put his hand to his temple. No blood, just a good-sized knot. He wrapped several ice cubes in a dishrag and lay down on his bed, holding the ice to his throbbing head.

He withdrew inside himself, mentally reviewing the notes and finger positions of Beethoven's "Fur Elise" until the pain and his father disappeared.

J.D. pressed his thumbs into his temples, trying to massage away his headache. Alcohol rarely gave him hangovers. His body had become too accustomed to it. Why one now?

His son's terrified face floated into his memory. He blinked to rid himself of it. He hated the surge of raging anger that had risen in him with volcanic quickness the night before. He rarely lost his temper, but when the anger came, it was sudden and uncontrollable.

He sat up in his bed and saw the crumpled bedcovers, the empty bottle of vodka. The explosion of anger had probably brought on this headache, not the alcohol.

Again, Nick's terror haunted him. J.D. shuddered. His own temper haunted him.

If he knew where Julienne had ended up, he would load up Nick within the hour and take the boy to her.

The heat of summer toured western Kansas, its shimmering waves blending one day into another. Anya rose from her bed early each morning to work in her garden before the worst of the heat settled in for the day.

She sat back on her heels and surveyed her garden plot. Dark ribbons of standing water showed her rows of corn and green bean seeds. The earth sucked at the water in greedy thirst. She marveled at the miracle that the tiny kernels buried in mud would soon produce an entire crop.

To Anya, gardening did not only mean producing fresh vegetables. Gardening was her chance to work in the silence of her own thoughts, with only the sounds of birds to interrupt. She loved standing in the soft dirt and letting the mist from her water hose cool her off along with her plants after a hot summer's day. She loved the nearly inaudible ripping sound of weed roots letting go of the soil. She loved the random thoughts that God placed in her mind as she worked and the opportunity to respond in prayer.

Anya had learned much about the nature of God with her hands in the mud. With every seed she placed in the ground, she pictured Jesus telling his disciples that they must die to themselves and take up their crosses to follow Him, just as the kernel of wheat dies in the ground before producing a crop.

She thought about how so many people refused to believe that a loving God could not forbid anyone to come into heaven, yet the very act of weeding her garden was an example of keeping the evil separate from the holy.

But today, Anya felt burdened. She let out her breath in a long sigh, thinking how her tomato plants always seemed so dwarfed by their metal cages when she first put them in. Just as she felt dwarfed by her worry for Nick.

Russell often reminded her not to worry, to turn things over to the capable hands of God. She knew he was right. She was a worrier by nature but that didn't make it any less a sin.

"God," she spoke aloud. "God, if I had my way, I'd burst into that trailer, pack up all Nick's things and bring him home with me."

She thought about Russell's phone call to the town sheriff, a man who attended their church. Russell had made it plain that he did not want social services involved if at all possible. He knew as well as Anya that if Nick were to be taken into foster care, their input on his life would cease. Yet, if he were truly in physical danger, were they right to let him stay?

The sheriff had agreed to watch J.D., nothing more. "I can't arrest a man for drinking, only for laws he breaks after drinking," he had said. "I also can't promise you that I won't turn in the situation to S.R.S. myself if I feel there is a valid need for the boy to be out of that house."

She pushed herself up, her legs and feet full of the prickling sensation that comes from lack of circulation. She rubbed the majority of dirt off her hands and clothing and went to the side of the house to turn off the water hose. Most likely she wouldn't have as much time in her garden this summer so long as Nick came over and did most of the work. But getting him out of that dreary trailer house and having daily opportunities to show Christ to him made the time away from her garden worthwhile.

Chapter 6

Brenna slid off her bike and wiped sweat from her face. The sun angled down with intensity, even at this early hour. Weather forecasts predicted a hotter and dryer summer than last. Already, Brenna's father complained about air conditioning bills.

She leaned her bike against the side of the Martin's garage and rang the doorbell. She shifted the canvas bag with her piano books from one arm to the other.

Anya Martin answered. "Hello, Brenna," she welcomed her. "It's good to see you. How was your week?"

"F...f...fine."

"How did your practicing go?"

Brenna stepped into the cool house. "I c...c...couldn't p...p...practice m...mm...much. M...m...mother's b...been s...s...sick."

"I'm sorry to hear that. You're welcome to ride your bike down here anytime and practice, if you like," Anya offered. "Just give me a call first."

"R...really?"

"Really. Now, if you want to make yourself comfortable there at the piano and warm up with a few scales, I need to run out back and check on Nick."

"N...Nick?"

"Nick Pierce. He's helping Russell and I out with some yard work this summer."

Brenna nodded nervously. She didn't want anyone besides Anya able to hear her playing, especially not Nick. She knew from choir class that Nick played very well. He had started playing the accompaniment for all the choral classes soon after he moved. As for herself, she only had a few short lessons under her belt and struggled with 3-note songs even when she counted the beats out loud.

Anya went out the back door and Brenna fiddled with arranging her books on the piano. She tentatively pressed her thumb down on middle C. She heard the soft murmur of voices from the back door before Anya reappeared.

"I'm back. Sorry about that, Brenna." Anya bustled over to the piano and pulled up a folding chair to sit beside Brenna.

"Let's start with prayer."

Brenna folded her hands in her lap and bowed her head. At her first piano lesson, Anya had asked permission to start every lesson with prayer, the same way she started lessons with her granddaughters. Brenna had agreed, so long as Anya did the praying. She was fairly certain that God did not wish to hear from a girl who couldn't speak coherently.

Her mind wandered as Anya talked to her God. She thought about the pleasure she gained in her piano lessons. For one thing, she received one-on-one attention from Sara's grandmother. That alone meant more to her than learning to play the instrument.

Her father had acquiesced on the condition that she pay out of the allowance she received quarterly from her grandparents and ride her bike to and from lessons. Her mother had only given the stipulation that Brenna not practice while she rested, which pretty much meant all the time.

Anya raised her head. "Let's get started. Why don't you play this scale in C major for me?"

Brenna fumbled, squinting at the notes before her, wishing her fingers could replicate the exacting rhythm of eighth notes marching up the staff.

"Let me play it for you so you can hear it," Anya said. She leaned over and placed her hands on the keys. As she listened, Brenna remembered the sounds and copied them exactly, albeit slower.

"Excellent," Anya encouraged.

Brenna shrugged. "It h…helps i…i…if I c…can hear it."

Anya frowned thoughtfully. "I could teach you all kinds of songs by playing them first and letting you reproduce them, Brenna. But I want you to have the skills to read music for yourself."

Brenna flushed.

"It's a wonderful gift to be able to play by ear, Brenna. I just don't want you to be limited to that." Anya laid her hand gently on Brenna's back. "Now, let's hear that scale one more time, then we'll review the names of the notes."

The rest of the lesson flew by and Brenna forgot about Nick being in the backyard until she stuffed her music books back into her canvas bag.

"Would you like a glass of lemonade and some cookies before you ride your bike back home?" Anya asked.

"S…sure." Brenna laid her bag down on the couch and followed the older woman into the kitchen.

Anya went to the back porch and called outside. "Brenna and I are having a snack if you'd like to join us, Nick."

Nick came in, wiping his hands on his pant legs.

"Hi, Brenna," he said, his face averted, a farmer's cap pulled down low over his face.

"Why don't you two have a seat?" Anya poured lemonade from a frosty pitcher into several glasses and set them on the table. She sat with them and popped the lid off of an olive green Tupperware container. The scent of peanut butter floated upward. Brenna tentatively took a cookie with neatly crisscrossed fork marks, and laid it on her napkin. Nick took four.

Anya sipped her lemonade. "How are things going outside, Nick?"

"Fine." He spoke around his cookie and swallowed. "You've got flowers on one of your tomato plants."

"Already? I just brought them home from the nursery last week. That's wonderful."

Brenna nibbled on the edge of her cookie, content to let them visit.

"I'm almost finished with the watering," Nick said. "Did Russell say what I'm supposed to do after that?"

She shook her head. "You're such a quick worker, Nick. You're spoiling us, you know."

Nick grinned and tilted his chair back.

"Be careful," Anya warned. "These old kitchen chairs aren't as sturdy as they used to be."

Before she finished speaking, the chair slipped. Nick grabbed for the wall for balance, knocking his cap askew. Brenna's eyes widened as she saw the bump and bruise that extended from his eyebrow to his hairline.

"My goodness, Nick. What happened to you?" Anya rose from her chair.

"Nothing." He grabbed for the cap brim to pull it back into place.

"But surely... oh, Nick. Let me see it." Anya reached out to his face. He jerked away.

"It's nothing," he protested. "I left one of the kitchen cupboard doors open and banged my head on the corner."

Anya closed her eyes. "Oh, Nick, I'm sorry," she said with quiet intensity.

"Sorry for what?" He plunked down on a chair and reached for a cookie. "Wasn't your fault. I left the cupboard door open. I ran into it."

Anya turned away, pressing her body against the sink.

"I'm telling you the truth," Nick said, his anger apparent.

Brenna edged from the kitchen, looking from one to the other. "I...I need to g...g...get h...h...home."

Neither answered her. Nick deliberately took another bite of cookie. Anya's shoulders rose and fell with a heavy sigh.

Brenna backed out. She stepped out on the front porch just in time to see her bike disappear around the corner of the garage.

"H...hey," she shouted. She half tripped down the steps and sprinted around the corner. The man pushing her bike turned. Sara's Uncle Mitch.

He smiled. "We meet again, Brenna Williams. You have a flat tire. Do you want me to air up the tire, or should I steal your bike, like you thought I was going to do?"

"I...I'm s...sorry."

"Not to say I wouldn't mind having a new bicycle, but this particular one doesn't seem to fit me very well."

She tried to envision Mitch's long legs trying to pedal, his knees hitting the handlebars and smiled sheepishly.

"I...I thought you m...might l...like flowers," she teased him, pointing at the decals. Instantly she felt her neck and face warm up. Brenna never attempted more speech than the lowest common denominator required for manners. And here she was joking with a practical stranger.

"I like flowers," he said, posing to show off his biceps. "It takes a real man to like girl stuff and still be masculine."

Brenna laughed but it sounded tinny and forced after the dark undercurrents she had witnessed inside. She sobered.

Mitch tilted his head and studied her. "You should laugh more often, Brenna Williams. You have a nice laugh."

Her neck and face heated up even more until she was certain that she resembled a red tomato. She was also fairly certain that the dark shade didn't dissipate until after he had aired up the tire and she'd pedaled halfway home.

Nick straightened and brushed the hair from his eyes with his forearm. He let the hoe drop from his hands onto the soft mass of green weeds that had sprung up around Anya's new gardening beds. Russell had wanted to spray the weeds but Anya had raised an outcry.

"I won't have you killing off my baby tomato plants with chemical drift again," she declared.

"Annie, that was over ten years ago. I'll be careful. Besides, your tomatoes are in raised beds. The chemicals won't burn them."

"I don't want the stuff near them," Anya said and that was that.

Nick had gladly accepted the extra hours of work hacking out the clumps of crabgrass and kochia even though his back hurt and arms burned from the workout. Anya had helped him for an hour that morning but had gone inside to bake goodies for some church thing. When she fed him sloppy joes and baked beans for lunch, he could smell the sweet bread in the oven. He hoped Anya had made extra. Even with a big lunch, he seemed to always be hungry these days. He was getting taller. His jeans hovered higher above his shoes.

As if she had read his thoughts, Anya appeared. "It's too hot out here for you. Why don't you come inside and have a snack?" she said.

Nick should have known she would feed him again. Anya seemed to consider feeding the world her personal responsibility. He walked willingly alongside her into the house.

"I've been meaning to ask you something, Nick," said Anya as he squirted soap onto his hands at the kitchen sink. His back stiffened. Surely she wouldn't ask again about the bruise on his forehead, now that it had faded till it hardly showed. He knew he had never totally convinced her that J.D. had not hit him.

"I know the hairstyles these days are for guys to keep their hair longer but I also know that it's hot out there. A shorter haircut might be cooler. If you would like a haircut, I could give you one. I have always cut Russell's hair and I cut the boys' when they lived at home."

Nick dried his hands on his pant legs and ran his fingers through his hair. "I do need a cut," he said. His hair had grown long and shaggy, enough that he was certain it would have invited mocking jokes had school been in session.

"It would sure beat working out in the sun," she coaxed. "I can cut it right now while it's hottest outside."

Nick shrugged. "Whatever."

Anya motioned for him to sit at the table where she had laid out a napkin and a tall glass of ice water. She brought two slices of sweet bread and laid them on the napkin in front of him.

"Eat up while I go get the clippers," she said.

Nick chewed the still-warm bread and savored the homemade flavor. "What are the little black things?" he asked when she reappeared.

"Poppy seeds," she answered. "Poppy seed bread is Russell's favorite. I try to make it at least once a month for him. The almond flavoring in the glaze on top is his favorite. I have to slice the entire loaf as soon as it's cooled or Russell will slice the top off for himself."

Nick started on the second slice, stopping only long enough to let her wrap a bath towel around his shoulders.

"I'm glad you're working for us, Nick. You do such a good job with everything we ask you to do." Anya combed her fingertips through his hair. "When our sons were your age, we had a hard time getting much quality work out of them."

Nick blushed, still unsure how to react to encouragement, even after so much time around the Martins. He relaxed in the chair. Her touch made his scalp tingle.

Anya plugged in the clippers and took several conservative swipes through his hair at the base of his neck. She traded the clippers for scissors. He felt the gentle tug of the comb and heard the crunch of the blades over his hair.

"By the way, when is your birthday, Nick?"

He flushed and ducked his head. He knew she was merely making conversation, but he did not want to tell her.

"Hold still." She put her fingers on each side of his head and straightened it. "You didn't go and have a birthday without us knowing, did you?"

"Last week." He looked at his ice water thirstily but was afraid to wiggle again.

"Nick, we didn't know! What day was it?"

"May 30th."

"Oh, Nick, we'll have to do something special for you – even if it was last week. How old are you now?"

"Thirteen."

"Your first teen year," Anya said. "Well, better late than never. What can we do to help you celebrate? Is there anything in particular that you want?"

He itched his neck. "Could I have another piece of that bread?"

"That's no birthday gift, Nick."

"That means no?"

"Of course you can have more. You can take a whole loaf home if you like. I can always make more. But surely we can do something else for your birthday."

There was something, something that he would like very much. But he was afraid she would say no. He took a deep breath. "Could I play your piano? Not just tonight, but whenever I'm already over here and finished with my work. I know my dad," he swallowed on the word. Calling J.D. "dad" still didn't come naturally. "I know he doesn't want me to take lessons but I need to practice, even if I have to teach myself and I'm afraid that I'm already forgetting what I do know. I read the music in my head at night in bed sometimes, just to review the notes and timing but I need a piano. If there's anything I want, it would be that."

Anya did not respond. Nick slid his fingers under his knees as though to remove the offenders from sight.

Finally she spoke. "I don't know, Nick. I hate to keep you from doing something you obviously care so much about, especially if God has given you a talent for it. Yet, I also don't want to go against your father's wishes."

"Russell went against his wishes by making him leave me here that one day."

"That's a little different, Nick. Your safety was at risk."

"He hates me." Anger exploded in Nick's words.

She tenderly combed the hair from his forehead and touched the fading bruise above his eye. "I wish you'd tell me what really happened, Nick."

He regretted his outburst. "I told you the truth. I really did hit my head on the cupboard."

Anya was silent as she finished cutting his hair. She sighed as she removed the towel from his shoulders. "You'd better go outside and shake your shirt off. Otherwise it'll get itchy."

He obeyed and removed his shirt outdoors. He felt naked. Even the hot sun refusing to take away his goose bumps. He shook the shirt off and pulled it back over his head. The hole fit easier over his shorter hair.

Maybe when he went back inside he could convince her to let him practice on her piano.

"You'd better stop, Brenna."

Brenna looked up to see her father standing with his shoulders hunched together, like an old man whose bones and ligaments had forgotten how to straighten.

He waved at the piano keys. "Your mother is trying to sleep," he said. "Best if you not practice today."

Brenna silently pulled the wooden cover over the keyboard. When she looked up again, her father had disappeared, Bradley taking his place.

"Why do you do that?" he asked irritably. "You just roll over and play dead every time anyone asks you to do something.

Do you think that makes you a better person – always letting others take advantage of you?"

Brenna knew Bradley's anger stemmed from their parents and not her. Unfortunately, she usually ended up as Bradley's target.

"You aren't going to make them happy, you know," he went on. "Don't you know it does no good to try to please them? They're just trying to pretend to themselves that our problems don't exist. That's why they're always saying things like 'Bradley, go outside', 'Brenna, go to your room and read', 'Bradley, can't you be more quiet? Mother's trying to sleep'."

Brenna winced at the mockery in Bradley's tone. "D...Dad's just tr...trying t...t...to help."

"No, he's just trying to pretend to himself that as long as us kids are content doing whatever and staying out of trouble that our family is okay. Our perfect little family. Besides, fat lot of help he's done. Seems to me that Mother sleeps more now than ever. I think he oughta confront her, force her out of that bedroom, make her face people. I mean, truly, Brenna, when was the last time you saw Mother outside of the bedroom?"

"Th...this morning, wh...when she w...went to the bathroom."

"Besides that," Bradley said impatiently. "You are an annoying little optimist, you know that?"

Brenna rolled her eyes at him. She clicked off the piano light and started to stand.

"So that's it? You're not gonna try to play? I've heard you practice, Brenna. You know, you're getting to where you're not half bad on that thing." Bradley shuffled his feet as though giving the compliment disagreed with his nature.

"I think I...I'll go r...read."

Bradley forced air out through his nose in exasperation. "Yes, Brenna, why don't you go read? You know, you're every bit as bad as Mother when it comes to escaping life. It's just that

Mother does it by staying in bed and moping and you do it by reading for hours."

His words hit her hard.

"Are you any b…better, Bradley?" she dared to ask. "You esc…cape by g…going out with your f…friends. And when y…you're home, you h…hide b…behind acting m…mad."

Bradley scorched her with a smoldering look. "You know, the kids at school are right. You really shouldn't try to talk. You sound like the village idiot."

He stomped from the room. Even though his words stung, as usual, Brenna couldn't hold back a smirk. It felt good having bested him in a war with words, so that he had no ammunition left except a petty put-down. Still, she wondered if Bradley had a point. Was she hindering her mother's recovery from depression as equally by her silent acquiescence as her father's coddling?

Not wanting to think through the answer, Brenna walked down the stairs to her bedroom and opened her most recent library book, "Number the Stars", by Lois Lowry.

As Annemarie and her Jewish friend Ellen tried to outwit the Germans, Brenna's own difficulties sank over the horizon of Nazi occupied territory. Her troubles were quite small compared to that era and place.

She read until her neck and shoulders ached from lying on her stomach and Bradley poked his head in the door. "Dad says you need to come upstairs," he said.

Brenna glanced at her alarm clock. "Oh no! I…I f…forgot to f…fix l…lunch!"

"I don't think it's about lunch."

"B…but it's almost one."

Bradley shook his head. "Just come upstairs."

Brenna folded the corner of her page to mark it and laid her book down. Bradley looked serious, subdued, even a little panicked.

Upstairs, their father paced in circles around the living room. He acknowledged them with a nod. "Let's go outside."

Once the glass door slid closed behind them, Bradley asked, "Can you tell us what's going on now?"

Brenna perched on the edge of a lawn chair. She clasped her hands together and squeezed them between her knees.

Her father pressed his lips together until they whitened and released them. "I don't know how to say this. I just stopped your mother from doing something that would have hurt her pretty bad."

"Oh, boy," Bradley muttered.

Brenna looked at him with wide eyes. "What?"

"She was trying to take too much medication."

"On p…purpose?"

"Yes."

"W…Why?"

"She's tired of living." Their father sank down onto the wooden deck steps and rested his elbows on his knees.

"Truth is, I overheard you kids talking this morning. I hadn't realized you understood quite so much, Bradley."

"We're not babies anymore." Bradley's words spilled out spitefully.

"You were right what you said. I have been avoiding everything by working and staying away."

Brenna stared at her feet. In their own ways, each of them had contributed to the elephant in their home - the elephant called depression that refused to be ignored any longer.

"So?" asked Bradley.

"I'm going to make arrangements to get some professional help for your mother."

"H…Help?" asked Brenna.

"Your Mother is not going to get better on her own." His mouth twisted and he bent his head at an angle so that neither child could see his face. "Truth is, it's not you kid's fault, or even the loss of our first child – although that definitely exacerbated the situation."

At their surprised looks, he added, "She told me you knew about it. You mother is... well, she is just not able to handle her emotions, especially sadness, the way a stronger person might."

"So why don't you just make her get out of bed? Make her do fun stuff? Try to make her laugh? Why do you just give up and work all the time?" Surprisingly, Bradley's voice had lost its accusing tone.

Their father rubbed the heels of his calloused hands into his eyes. "I tried, Bradley. For years, I tried. I thought it was my fault. That I couldn't be the man that she needed. I wasn't rich enough. I didn't have the right ambitions in life. Later, when the two of you came along, I really thought that children might change her – that she would find the happiness in being a mother that she couldn't seem to find in being a wife. I'd hoped to spare the two of you from all this. I guess I didn't realize how old you are getting – how much you are able to figure out on your own. And now with her latest attempt..."

A long silence followed. The unspoken message lay thick on the air between them. None of them had been able to supply the woman inside with what she needed to overcome her depression, maybe no one could. Brenna bent over until her nose touched her thumbs, still clutched between her knees.

"Kids, I'm not trying to make you feel guilty by telling you this. Believe me, I've lived with enough of it." He blew out his breath. "I'm no good at this sharing thing."

"So are you taking her to a doctor or something?" asked Bradley.

"To Denver... for psychiatric assessment."

"Psychiatric? Isn't that, like, a mental hospital?"

"Yes." He spoke the word so low that Brenna could hardly hear it.

Kids at school joked about people that had to go to the "fourth floor". Brenna had always assumed those people were truly crazy, not like her mother.

"You really think that will help?"   Bradley was skeptical.

"I don't know what else to do."

"Why now?" asked Bradley. "Why are you wanting to fix things now? Why not years ago, when we needed her?"

"Because years ago, she was doing better. She took care of you both when you were younger. I'm sure you remember."

"Maybe took care of us, but she never loved us."

"She loved you." He stopped and corrected himself. "She loves you. She just doesn't know how to show it."

Brenna finally raised her head. "What a…about you, D…Dad? Do y…you love us?"

Her father would not look at her but his words swelled within her, warm and soft. "I do."

Brenna flew to him, pressing up against the arm of his work shirt, kneeling on the stair beside him. She tasted salt and wetness on her upper lip before she realized her tears.

Her father awkwardly let her hug him for the briefest of moments then he stood up, letting her fall from him like the kittens at Sara's house fell from the mama cat when the mama decided to walk away.

"I better get back in to your mom," he said, rubbing his neck. "She shouldn't be alone."

He let himself back inside. The instant the glass door slid into the casing on the wall, Bradley muttered in a radio announcer's voice, "And he disappears again, folks."

"B…Bradley?   What did he m…mean by latest attempt?"

"Suicide, Brenna. Mom tried to commit suicide again."

Chapter 7

Nick let himself into the Martin's house even though no one answered his knock. Anya had told him to make himself at home even if they weren't there.

Russell had not asked Nick to work that day but the trailer had gotten so stifling hot and nothing interesting was showing on television. He had hoped to find one of the Martins and ask for something to do, anything, even if they didn't want to count the hours for pay.

Nick snuck to the kitchen like an intruder. Anya usually had some sort of baked item or snack in the Tupperware container of the counter and his stomach growled.

He cracked the lid. The aroma of cinnamon wafted upwards to his nose. Anya had made more of the muffins she had made last week, the kind she dipped in melted butter and rolled in sugar and cinnamon. Nick eagerly took one to the table and ate it, careful not to leave crumbs. He wondered if eating the muffin were stealing.

Nick went back into the living room, grateful for the air conditioning. He trailed his hand along the cool ripples of piano keys, enjoying the sight of the afternoon sun sprinkling wavy patterns across the keyboard.

He knew he shouldn't play without their permission. He knew he really shouldn't even be in their house, even though Anya had encouraged him to come on in. She had meant when he got there early for work, not a bored afternoon. But who would know? Who would find out?

He settled on the piano bench, positioned his fingers and played and played. His fingers skipped and danced, they pounded and threatened, they flitted and twirled. He reveled in the sounds, wrapping around him like long-lost relatives separated no more.

After he had played everything he could recall from memory, he looked through Anya's songbooks on the stand and played whatever caught his eye.

When his hands felt loose and limber and his brain tired and content, he arranged Anya's music the way he had found it and stood. He was reluctant to leave the piano but even more reluctant to get caught. He looked out the front window. No sign of the Martins, no telltale clouds of dirt barreling down the road toward the house.

Bored again, Nick wandered out to the back yard. The plants in Anya's garden were plumping out with bushy green leaves. The fence he and Russell had begun building last week before Russell became too busy with spraying stood half-finished. The fence bordered the edge of the garden and the back yard and stood only three feet tall.

"Never liked a tall fence," Russell had said. "A man like me who's lived all my life in Kansas needs to see as much of the horizon as possible at all times. I feel claustrophobic if I can't."

Boards and scraps lay scattered across the back yard from cutting the posts and planks to size. Nick had helped put the posts in concrete and fasten on the crossbeams. He had watched Russell screw on the wooden planks, using a level and a long scrap of wood for a spacer. By now, Nick had used a drill enough to feel brave.

"I could work on the fence, maybe even finish it," Nick told himself. "I could surprise Russell."

Energized, Nick went to the pile of planks that still waited to be hung. He picked up the top plank and held it to the fence. It didn't look right.

Then he remembered. Russell had cut the six-foot tall planks from the lumberyard in half. He had already hung the top portion of each plank, which had two small angles cut off to form a scalloped edge. The remaining planks still needed to be cut - dog-eared, Russell had called it.

Could he do it? Nick had watched Russell cut through several planks with his miter saw. He was too afraid to use it, with its loud whine and pull-down handle.

But he had used Russell's band saw in his garage – with Russell's help, of course. It was no less noisy but at least it was stationery.

Nick carried a stack of planks into the garage and dug through the large plastic barrels where Russell kept his scraps. He found several triangles that Russell had already cut off and traced the angle that needed to be cut onto the planks with a pencil.

He was ready to cut. He turned to look at the band saw. Unlike the miter saw's thick round blade with sharp jags, this blade seemed harmless enough, just a narrow metal band with small teeth.

Russell's stern warning about using the equipment seemed like such a long time ago. He had watched Russell operate the band saw. It couldn't be that hard and he only had two small, straight cuts to make on each plank, and not that many planks either.

Nick stuck out his chin. He could do it. He would do it. He was tired of being called a pansy, a chicken, a pretty boy and much worse. He imagined Anya's pleased expression when she saw the finished fence, imagined Russell's surprise and pride.

A bit nervously, Nick flipped the "On" switch. Nothing happened. Maybe the machine wasn't working. Then he remembered that Russell kept his equipment unplugged for safety purposes.

"Better to be safe than sorry," Russell had said. "I can't afford an accident, not when I have grandchildren around. Avery's only seven years old, you know."

Nick's ears burned as if he had actually heard Russell's voice in the empty garage. He shook his head. He would be careful. He knew how to be safe. Russell had taught him. After all, he was thirteen, not seven.

Nick started the band saw and cautiously fed the wood through it. The long plank wobbled slightly, but he finished the cut, feeling sawdust speckle his face. He turned the plank around and lopped the next triangle off with a much straighter line. He inspected the cut with pleasure, his heart rate gradually slowing down.

With growing confidence, Nick fed the planks through the blade, feeling satisfied with his progress. He sped up, wanting to be sure to finish before Russell came home. He held up the next plank to the vibrating blade. The opposite end caught in the power cord and yanked sideways. Nick jerked.

The wood dropped to the floor and Nick stared in confusion at the redness that pooled on the metal plate underneath the blade. In shock, Nick realized that the saw had cut through his hand, slicing in between his thumb and index finger and not stopping until nearly three fourths of the way through his palm. His hand gaped open as though a piece of pie had been sliced from it, the thumb flopping limply.

He felt no pain, only numb horror and the agonizing thought that he may not be able to play the piano. He cupped his good hand underneath, trying to catch the blood flow, afraid to touch the wound yet afraid to leave the fingers dangling away from his palm, revealing bone and muscle under the red rivers of pulsing blood.

"Nick?" Russell's voice jerked Nick around. He tried to cover his hurt hand. Blood spattered onto the floor and down his jeans. Russell's frown transformed to shock.

"Annie!" he yelled. "Get some towels and ice. Hurry!"

Anya appeared, her face turning white at the sight of Nick. She disappeared quickly.

Russell took Nick's arm gently in his hands, without touching the hand. "Are you in a lot of pain, son?"

Nick shook his head. He felt no pain whatsoever although his knees had begun to tremble so badly he could hardly stand.

Russell folded Nick's arm up against his body to protect the injured hand. Nick felt warm liquid seeping through his shirt. Russell pulled Nick close and held him. Nick's teeth began to chatter.

"I'm sorry, I'm sorry," he repeated over and over.

"I know," Russell murmured against his hair. "I forgive you, Nick. I'm sorry you got hurt. I'm sorry I yelled at you."

Nick waited for the "I told you so" but it never came.

Anya reappeared. She wrapped Nick's hand and arm tightly in towels and ice packs while Russell turned off the band saw.

The silence hurt Nick's ears. "How strange," he thought. "My ears hurt. Nothing else."

"Let's get you to the doctor," said Russell. "Can you drive, Annie?"

Nick found himself in the backseat of their sedan, wrapped securely in Russell's arms. The telephone poles flashed by and he knew Anya was driving quite fast. Russell's arms tightened around him and he became aware that his trembling had increased.

"How are you holding up, son?" Russell asked.

"Fine." Nick leaned his head against Russell's chest and closed his eyes. He liked hearing the way the word "son" sounded in Russell's deep bass. He liked knowing the term was directed at him.

"Don't go to sleep, Nick." Russell's chest vibrated as he spoke.

Nick burrowed his face into the man's shirt. He relished the strange sensation of being held, of being loved.

"Nick." Russell gave him a warning squeeze.

"I'm awake." Nick spoke against the rough fabric.

"What were you trying to do in there?" Russell asked him. The question held no accusation.

"Trying to cut the dog ears." His voice did not sound like his own. Nick swallowed several times, trying to pop his ears.

"Dog ears?"

"For the fence planks."

"Oh, Nick." Russell laid his broad hand over Nick's head and whispered, "Take care of this boy, Father. Watch over him. Help Annie drive safely. Let the doctor be at the hospital and ready for us when we get there. Take away any pain that Nick may be feeling right now."

Nick sank deeper into the man's warmth and security.

"Hang in there, Nick. We're almost there," said Anya from the front seat.

"Bring healing to Nick's hand. Father, don't let there be lasting damage unless you plan to teach him something through it. Take care of him, Father, please take care of him."

Anya pulled onto the emergency ramp.

Nick felt himself being lifted out of the car and carried into a brightly lit area. Faces loomed above him, floating faces with fuzzy features, as Russell carefully lowered him onto a gurney.

"Don't leave me." He grabbed for Russell with his good hand.

"I won't." Russell clasped Nick's hand in both of his. "I'm right here. I won't leave you."

"I'll try to contact J.D.," said Anya. She moved out of Nick's range of vision.

"No," he pleaded. Fire wormed its way up Nick's wrist and arm. His shoulder tightened and ached. The fire flared inside him, burning, devouring. He tossed his head and moaned.

Russell's hand smoothed his forehead. "I'm here, Nick. It's okay. The doctor is going to take good care of you," he soothed.

"It hurts," Nick gasped. Unwanted tears leaked into his ears, his already plugged, roaring ears.

"They're giving you a shot for the pain, Nick. The doctor said you might feel a little sting."

Nick moaned as someone jostled him in order to slide his pants down for the shot and apologized for the movement. Russell continued to stroke him. Nick heard the rising and falling of conversation around him.

Russell bent down. "The doctor said they need to send you to a hospital in Wichita where they can do surgery on your hand, Nick."

"Are you going with me?" Nick rasped in panic.

"I'll come with you on the plane. You'll be fine, Nick. The doctor said your pain medication will make you fall asleep pretty soon. Don't worry about anything. Annie and I will take care of you."

The doctor bound Nick's hand tightly and helped him sit up enough to put his arm in a sling.

"This should hold the hand stable," he said. "It shouldn't start bleeding again, but if it does, the paramedics will take good care of him."

"Thank you," said Russell.

Nick's eyelids slid down. He forced them back open as several men transferred him to a different gurney and strapped him down.

He slept, waking once to a fuzzy sensation of discomfort and the buzz of an airplane engine. He had never flown before but didn't even care enough to wish he could look out the window.

Russell wet a tissue with water from a bottle and wiped Nick's face. Nick closed his eyes and fell back asleep.

This time he awoke in a different hospital. His head and arm ached but he could not feel his hand.

"Grandma Bates?" he croaked.

"It's me, Nick. Russell. How do you feel?"

"Not so great."

"Lie still," said Russell. "The anesthetist will be here shortly. Your surgery is scheduled in a few minutes."

"Can you go with me?"

"I'll stay with you until you fall asleep and I'll see you again when you wake up. But don't be afraid, Nick. God is with you."

God. The God that Russell called a Father. Nick instinctively knew that J.D. would never have stayed with him, spoken to him, the way that Russell had. A Father-God surely would keep His distance.

Yet Russell Martin had seven children. He was a father as well, a good father. Nick drifted into blackness to the symphony of Russell's soft promises and touch.

"I'll never leave you, nor will I forsake you. I love you, my son."

The voice echoed and swirled around him, until he was no longer certain if Russell or Russell's Father-God spoke.

Nick tossed his head fitfully on the pillow. His sleep-fogged brain couldn't tell him if he had moaned out loud or in his head. He bit his lips to hold back another cry of pain.

His hand throbbed mercilessly. Hot salty tears ran down his face and onto his ears and pillow.

He heard a rustle in the chair next to his bed and Anya's face appeared above him.

"Oh, Nick," she said, touching his hair. "It's hurting pretty bad, isn't it? Do you need more pain medication?"

He nodded. His throat felt too tight to speak. He was too exhausted to hide his fresh tears. She pushed the call button on his hospital bed and gathered him into an embrace. She rocked him as though he were still a baby. He cried into the softness of her arms until his face felt hot.

"Lord Jesus, please take away Nick's pain. Help him sleep soundly. Send an angel to stand guard over him. Let him feel Your presence and Your love." Anya rubbed his back in tiny circles as she spoke.

Part of him felt embarrassed. Did any other thirteen-year-old boy allow himself to be cuddled this way? If not, why did he seem to need it so much? Why was he so averse to pulling away?

Anya helped him lie back down and took a tissue from the nightstand and blotted at his face.

A nurse pushed aside the curtain around his bed and offered him a glass of water. She and Anya spoke in whispered tones. The water cooled his throat.

He could see from the window that it was night, most likely very late. He felt bad for Anya, knowing that she probably tried to sleep in the chair beside him. When had she come? Where was Russell?

"Thank you," he whispered to the nurse.

"You're welcome," she replied. "Call again if you need anything. I'll check in on you in another hour unless you call sooner."

She left and Anya leaned against the bed rail. She rubbed his good arm. "I'll stay right here until you fall back asleep if you like."

"Where's Mr. Martin?"

"He's sleeping on a couch in the waiting room. We're going to take turns staying up with you. Do you need him?"

Comforted, Nick shook his head no. At that moment he didn't care how old he was. Nick shifted his body so that he felt her warmth from the edge of the bed and closed his eyes.

"Of all the stupid things to do," J.D. muttered as he eyed Nick's bandaged hand and arm. Despite the words, his voice wavered.

Russell and Anya supported Nick as they led him up the driveway and onto the front porch of their home. They had made arrangements with J.D. for Nick to stay with them for several more nights so that Anya could get up and check on him but J.D. had met them anyway.

As Nick drew closer to his father, J.D. reached out one hand. His hand hovered above Nick's good shoulder as though he were afraid to touch him. That was enough encouragement for Nick.

"Dad." He reached out to hug his father.

For the briefest moment, J.D. accepted Nick's touch then he yanked away without returning it. "Men don't hug," he said.

"That's bunk, J.D., and you know it," Russell said.

Anya pushed at both men. "Move out of the way," she fussed. "And for goodness sakes, J.D., open the door for Nick. He looks about to fall over."

She situated Nick on the couch and helped him position a throw pillow under his throbbing arm.

"Give me a few minutes and I'll have some supper on. Won't you stay, J.D.?"

"Actually, Annie, you don't need to worry about supper," Russell interjected. "Nell said she'd bring food over when we get home."

"I can stay." J.D. pulled at his shirt collar and stared at Nick. Nick shifted on the couch.

"Let me go get your bags, Annie," said Russell. "Why don't you give Nell a call to let her know we're back?"

With the Martins out of the room, an awkward silence stretched between the father and son. J.D. shuffled his feet.

"You can sit down, Dad." The word "dad" came easier now that he had said it once.

J.D. lowered himself into the chair opposite the couch. "How are you feeling?"

"Much better, thank you." Nick knew he sounded formal, feminine. He winced, knowing his father would hate that.

More silence between them.

J.D. cleared his throat. "Does the ah… hand hurt you still?"

"Yeah, but the doctor gave me pills to take."

Nick heard Anya's muted voice on the telephone.

"I think someone just pulled in." J.D. went to the window as though glad for something to do and peered out. He opened the door in time for Nell, Michele and Sara. All three carried covered dishes that emitted tempting smells.

"Hello, J.D., hello Nick," Nell said, her cheerfulness a welcome diversion. "J.D., there's a basket of paper plates and plastic silverware out in the car if you wouldn't mind getting it. Sara, Michele, take the food to the kitchen. Nick, it's good to see you. Your color looks good. Are you feeling okay?"

Nick nodded, always amazed at the Martin women's ability to direct and organize, most likely from having large families.

"Dad said the doctors sewed your hand up nicely."

Nick had to think for a moment before he realized that Nell meant Russell. "Yeah, I suppose."

He remembered his reaction when the nurse had first unwound the bandages to clean his hand. Angry black railroad tracks of stitches marched over his palm and index finger. The skin and tissue had swelled and bulged in strange areas until the hand really didn't resemble a hand at all. The fear of not being able to play the piano pinched at him at regular intervals.

"You're here. I just tried to call," said Anya. She took the dish from Nell's hands and led her into the kitchen.

Sara came back in the living room and sat cross-legged on the floor next to the couch where he lay. She took a cloth bag off her shoulder and laid it between them.

"Hi, Nick. I'm sorry you got hurt."

"Yeah, well, me too."

"I brought some magazines and books for you to read if you want them. I figured you might get bored laying around." She pulled them out of the bag.

He looked at the stack with interest. "What are they?"

"This magazine is actually a Christian teen girl's magazine." Sara held it up. "But I think you'll enjoy it because there are several articles about musicians. One is about a classical pianist. The next several are from my brother. The same company publishes them, only for boys. It's for a younger age group but I read it sometimes and think it's still pretty cool."

Nick rubbed at his arm, just above the elbow. He wondered where Anya had put her purse. He knew she had put his medications in the inside pocket.

J.D. walked through and made a face at the flowery lining on the basket of plastic silverware and paper plates Nell had told him to carry from the car.

"I brought a Hardy Boys book that looks ancient but my dad said it was his all-time favorite book and that every boy should read it." She paused from her chattering. "Does it hurt?"

"Pretty much always." Nick stopped rubbing.

"Where did you get cut?"

Wincing, Nick turned his bandaged arm to point.

"Maybe you better show me on my hand," she said and held it out.

Nick traced the line on her palm. "The blade went in here and cut to here. You can kind of tell when I jerked away because then it angled up across the base of my finger like this."

Sara shuddered and pulled her hand back. "Grandpa said it took them several hours to get everything sewn back together."

"I wouldn't know. I don't remember." He smiled at her. She smiled back.

"Oh, and I brought a video too," Sara said. "It's a great video about the life of Jesus."

Nick shook his head. "What is it with you people and God?"

Sara stood and walked away from the couch to the bookshelves on the far wall.

"Hey, I didn't mean to offend you. Come back."

"You didn't offend me," she said. "I'm just looking for something."

She came back a moment later holding another thick leather bound book.

"You asked what it is about us and God," she said, laying the book on his thighs. "Read this and find out."

He read the spine. "It's a Bible."

She smiled. "That's right."

"That's a grownup book." He thought back to third grade when reading finally became easy for him. He had wanted to go to the library for books but Grandma Bates had said it was too far to walk alone. So, he had dusted off the cover of the Bible that sat on the shelf above the T.V., right next to Grandma Bates' Holy Mary candle and crucifix. The words had not made sense to him and when she caught him, Grandma Bates had told him he was offending God by touching the Book without washing his hands first. He had never touched it again.

"I read it every day and I'm not a grownup," Sara said.

"But it's thick. It's got to be a thousand pages long." Nick flipped open the book. "And it has two columns of writing on every page and the print is little."

Sara laughed. "So start with Matthew. That's the first book in the New Testament. It tells the story of Jesus, the same story in the video."

"Maybe I'll just watch the movie. Wait a minute. You said the first book? What do you mean? This big book is really a bunch of little books put together?"

"Something like that. So it really wouldn't be that bad to just read one of them, don't you think?"

Nick slid further down in the couch. "I guess not."

"Here." Sara took the Bible from him and opened it to Matthew. "Skip the first part of the first chapter. It's just a bunch of names. If you start here," she pointed, "you'll be starting right when Jesus was born."

She marked the page with a loose scrap of paper and gave him back the Bible.

Nick accepted it grudgingly. He liked Sara. She treated him kinder than most. He supposed that for her he might read one short book out of the Bible.

Chapter 8

Brenna's mother sat on her bed with her face in her hands, crying the entire time Brenna helped her father pack a suitcase. Once they got her buckled into the front seat of the car, she stopped crying and stared vacantly out the windshield, not responding to any of their attempts to converse.

They had taken her to the hospital in Denver and wheeled her into a room using a hospital wheelchair. She took no notice of her surroundings as Brenna's father spoke to a nurse and filled out paperwork. But when Bradley handed over her suitcase to the nurse, she cried out, realizing that they intended to leave her there.

Brenna still wanted to plug her ears against her mother's pitiful cries and clutching hands. The nurse had told them to leave quickly, not to prolong the separation, that their mother would be fine in time, but part of Brenna's heart muscle had torn off and stayed with her mother in that sterile, white room with the keypad lock on the door.

They had stayed in the city for several days. Just in case, Brenna's father had said. They visited her each day but she would not look at them or speak. The hospital personnel gave them a list of what they couldn't bring into the facility and Brenna noticed that they had taken away her mother's shoes – because of the shoelaces, a nurse explained when Brenna had asked. She wasn't sure she wanted to know why her mother wasn't allowed shoelaces but the resigned look on her father's face told her that he wasn't surprised.

To fill the rest of the time, Brenna, Bradley and their father drove up into the mountains and tried out several hiking trails. Water blisters formed on Brenna's heels so her father bought band-aids for her at a convenience store. Bradley helped unwrap them so she could pad the sore areas from her shoes.

Brenna felt a togetherness between she, her father and Bradley begin to unwind, as a tight flower bud that loosens its first petals ever so slightly. She wondered briefly if her mother's absence was actually helping them become a family. But then she would see her father's Adam's apple bob as he swallowed and looked in the direction of the hospital. For possibly the first time, Brenna realized that her father loved her mother.

She wanted so badly for her mother to improve, for the psychiatrist to convince her mother to live life and enjoy it, for her father and Bradley to be happy and always treat her with the attention and kindness she had received from them the last several days.

On their third evening in Denver, their father called Karl Martin who was handling their farm chores during their absence. When he hung up, he turned to his children.

"Your grandparents found out," he said, his voice heavy. "They've been trying to get ahold of us. I guess they're waiting at the house. Best we go on home in the morning."

Brenna understood his obvious reluctance. Her mother's parents disapproved of her father and no doubt were horrified that he would hand over their pampered daughter to a psychiatric hospital.

Grandmother demanded perfection from everything and everyone around her and if the perfection itself could not be attained, then heaven forbid that you ever let it show outwardly.

"Besides," Brenna's father went on. "I guess school starts next week. I totally lost track of time. I'm sorry."

"Don't be," Bradley said. He dumped more corn nuts into the palm of his hand from the sack he had bought at the vending machine down the hall. "Suits me just fine to stay in this motel forever with nothing to do but go hike the mountains and watch T.V."

Their father smiled a half smile. "We'd run out of money sooner than later doing that, Bradley."

Bradley rolled over on his back, his feet dangling off the edge of the bed. "So let's at least stay here until our grandparents get tired of waiting for us to come home and leave."

"Not going to happen, Bradley. You know that." Their father shook his head. "Unfortunately."

"Dad!" Bradley shook his finger.

"I guess I shouldn't have said that, at least not out loud."

Brenna smiled at their exchange. Her father and Bradley seemed to have formed a bond on this trip. At least Bradley no longer oozed sarcasm and anger.

Despite the reason for the trip, she, like her brother, wanted to stay forever.

Nick slurped on his Dairy Queen milkshake as Russell turned onto the interstate.

"What did you think of your first physical therapy session?" Russell asked him.

"It was okay, I guess."

"I noticed that the therapist was careful to have you stop any exercises that really hurt."

"Yeah. She said that she would be nice the first time but that she would make me push harder later."

"And you have the list of exercises that she gave you to do each day?"

Nick nodded and patted his pocket. "I just wish we didn't have to drive all the way to Wichita every week."

"It will be every other week soon. Then not at all."

"But I feel bad having you drive me."

Russell glanced at him. "Your accident happened on my property, Nick. Not only that, I was the one who taught you how to run that band saw. I take some of the responsibility for what happened. Besides, I enjoy spending time with you."

"You do?"

"Yes, I do." Russell reached across the console to squeeze Nick's shoulder. Nick giggled.

"I think you're ticklish!"

"No, I'm not," Nick protested, but he scooted away from Russell. Not for the first time, he wished Mr. Martin were his father, not J.D..

Russell laughed and pulled his own milkshake from the cup holder for a sip. "Actually I'm glad for these trips in more ways than one, Nick."

"So you can go shopping at all those big stores like Home Depot and Lowe's?"

"Partly. Although you really should have cut your hand a year ago when we were right in the middle of building the house. That would have been more handy."

"Sorry, I'll remember that next time," quipped Nick. Russell laughed.

"Actually, I've been wanting to get to know you better, Nick. It seems that even though you've worked for us for what, just under three months now, I still haven't gotten the chance to really talk with you. Pretty soon school will start and I won't see you as often."

Nick felt himself closing up. "You tell me how to do stuff."

"No. That's me talking to you. Tell me about yourself, Nick."

Nick looked out the window. "What do you want to know?"

"Well for starters, tell me about living with your grandma."

Nick bit his lip. "Grandma Bates was pretty old, even when I was a baby. I don't think she liked having to raise me that much."

"But she clearly taught you a great deal. You have excellent manners, you show respect and you know how to clean up after yourself."

"Yeah, I suppose so. She liked things clean. Maybe that's why she didn't really like kids. As long as I didn't make messes, I could pretty much entertain myself and she didn't care what I did."

"She fed you and clothed you, didn't she?" asked Russell.

"She didn't have a lot of money, but, yeah, she always made sure I had enough to eat. She made me take these horrible vitamins." Nick paused to suck melting ice cream through his straw. "She mended my clothes too and knit me a scarf and mittens one year for Christmas."

"She loved you," Russell said. "She probably just didn't know how to show it."

Nick studied his cup. "I guess she probably did," he said, surprised.

They drove in silence. Nick chewed on the end of his straw after he finished his shake.

"So how did you come to live with your Grandma Bates?"

"My mom left me there."

"Did she ever come visit you?"

"No. I don't remember her at all. I overheard Grandma Bates saying once that she figured my mom would never come back. I don't know where she is. Maybe she's dead." He heard the bitterness in his voice.

"Your mom missed out on a great blessing by not staying and getting to know you, Nick."

"Maybe," Nick spoke around his straw. "Not many people have liked me. You're the first one. Well, you and Mrs. Martin and maybe Sara."

"What makes you think people don't like you?"

"Because I'm different. I don't really know how. Everyone seems to see it but me. I always get teased and made fun of in school. That's why I like summer."

"I'm sorry to hear that, Nick." Russell flipped on the blinker and checked over his shoulder before easing into the passing lane. Nick read the advertisements to a furniture company painted on the semi trailer as they drove past.

"So, what do the other students say?" asked Russell.

Nick folded his straw and shoved it into his cup. "That I'm a pretty boy, I talk funny, I walk funny. Sometimes they call me names."

"Is the teasing constant or has it been just a few times?" Russell's forehead crinkled with concern.

"In some ways it's not so bad as Wichita. When those guys ganged up on you, they could be pretty cruel. But it's harder to blend in the background at a smaller school." Nick paused. "Once, in Wichita, some guys backed me into a bathroom stall and..."

He stopped and stared out the window, feeling his face burn red. Why had he chosen to tell Russell about that?

"Did they hurt you?" Russell prodded.

"No." Nick shoved at the floor mat with his foot.

"What exactly did they do?"

Nick pressed his lips together, feeling shaky inside. His heart rate sped up. How could he describe to Russell how the bullies had yanked his pants down and mocked his private areas? How could he explain how they had pinned his arms behind his back and stroked him until his body responded? Nick couldn't add that the experience had felt simultaneously humiliating and enjoyable. The realization had caused an enormous load of guilt since that day.

"Did they touch you anywhere they shouldn't have?"

Nick instinctively pulled his shoulder around toward the window to turn his back toward Russell. He kept his legs tightly together. He nodded once, not sure if Russell had even seen it while watching the road.

"Did you tell anyone about it?" Russell asked. He sounded upset.

"No, just you."

"I'm glad you told me. What those boys did to you was wrong, Nick. If anything like that ever happens to you again, whether it's touching or even the teasing and name calling, you tell me. That's not tattling. That type of thing shouldn't go on. You are a unique and special creation of God, Nick."

Nick exhaled. "You say God created me, right?"

"That's absolutely right, Nick."

"Did He create everybody?"

"Yes, He did."

Nick shook his head in frustration. This Father-God created everyone, even the Tate Masons of the world. What kind of good Father would make people like that? Then God only paid attention to his favorites, people like the Martins, never kids like Nick. Not that Nick could blame Him. Anyone would like the Martins. But if God thought he was unique and special, like Russell said, then surely God would take away the different feeling inside him. Surely God would have protected him from the meanness of life.

He remembered the many times he had prayed alongside Grandma Bates as she fingered her rosary, prayed his own words instead of the memorized passages she quoted, prayed for his mother to come back for him and for her to be loving and kind and treat him the same way he saw mothers treating their children at the park. God had never listened, or at least it had not appeared so.

Nick leaned his head back against the headrest and closed his eyes, hoping Russell would stop asking questions and hoping that time would somehow stop so he wouldn't have to go back to school next week.

"Such a shame. Such a pitiful shame," clucked Brenna's grandmother. "This room looks as though it hasn't been cleaned for ages. You really should have hired a housekeeper. It isn't all that expensive, you know." Her tone implied that her daughter never would have suffered a nervous breakdown if her husband had seen to her needs suitably.

Brenna's father opened his mouth then clamped it shut.

"Why, I don't believe that this bedding has been aired for some time. Surely you don't expect us to sleep in a musty bed?"

"L...Let me g...get y...you some c...c...clean sheets," Brenna said.

"Are you still stammering about, child? Haven't they taught you how to speak properly by now?"

Brenna hung her head and retreated to the hall closet for the clean bedding.

"Old biddy," Bradley muttered.

"What did you say, young man?"

Bradley plopped down the large suitcase he had carried in from their grandparent's shiny car and didn't answer. The surly glare had reappeared on his face since they had gotten home.

"Please, be careful with our things." She turned to her husband. "I tell you, Wilfred, young people these days have no respect. No respect, I say."

"Go on outside and get the last two suitcases, Bradley," Brenna's father ordered softly. He stood with his shoulders hunched and his hands in his pockets. Brenna knew his posture hid the way his hands shook when he got nervous. She supposed she had inherited her inability to handle interpersonal situations from him.

"And where can I expect to unpack our belongings if the drawers in here are already full? You would think that after we built you this spacious of a home that you would have room for guests."

"I'll empty the two largest drawers for you," said Brenna's father.

"Two? That's hardly enough."

"It will be fine, Mildred," soothed Brenna's grandfather, speaking for the first time. "This closet is mostly empty and most of our clothing is on hangers anyway."

"Well, I suppose." She stalked around the room as though searching for more to criticize. "Goodness knows this should be better than that flea bag of a motel we were forced to stay in while waiting for you to come home and unlock the doors. Really, we should have our own key made."

Brenna tiptoed into the room and laid the clean sheets on the dresser. She pulled at the bedspread.

"Well," said her grandmother. She ignored Brenna. "I'll just go on down to the kitchen and make certain that Bitsy is adjusting. Are you coming Wilfred?"

The grandparents had brought along their poodle, Bitsy. The poor dog had lived a long life of nearly fifteen years and had only deafness and partial blindness to show for it.

Brenna's grandfather shook his head. "I'll unpack some of our things. You go on ahead."

Mildred Roth left the room, still clucking. Brenna felt a surge of hurt. Her grandmother treated them as though they were all her slaves to unpack and clean for her, yet lavished affection and care upon her poodle.

Brenna yanked off the bedcovers and put on the clean sheets with jerking motions. Bradley stepped up to help her, yanking equally as hard. He was angry. He scared her when he became angry. No one ever knew when his anger would erupt. She tried to smile at him.

He avoided her eyes.

"I am sorry about Mildred," their grandfather spoke again in that cultured distinct voice of his. "She doesn't handle change very well, I'm afraid. With all the upset in our schedule, the long trip, the worry about your mother... I'm certain that you understand."

"I understand." Her father spoke. He still used an uncommonly soft voice.

"How is Deborah, really? You know that you can shoot straight with me."

Brenna's father shoved his hands deeper into his pockets. "I honestly don't know."

"You don't know?" The question contained a lance. For all his politeness, sometimes Grandfather could be as nasty as his wife.

"I call every day but at this point I'm not allowed to speak with her. The doctors tell me she's doing fine but they are fairly vague."

"Well, I'll see what I can find out tomorrow." Brenna's grandfather patted her father on the shoulder. His statement implied that her father hadn't tried hard enough. "Things will get better now that we're here. You'll see."

Brenna hated the way her father hunched his shoulders and bowed his head without standing up for himself or their family.

She missed the first three days of eighth grade due to all the family upheaval. Now, Brenna slid into an open seat in her homeroom with a feeling of intense relief to be out of the house and away from her grandparents, even if it meant facing Tate Mason.

The last five days had consisted of fetching for and obeying her grandmother's constant demands while running as peacemaker between her father and Bradley who were once again at odds. This time, however, Brenna sided with Bradley in thinking that her father should put his foot down and ask her grandparents to either change or leave.

Her grandmother had thrown a fit when Brenna and Bradley prepared to start school.

"How can they even consider going off to school to be with their friends and have fun while their poor mother..." She had let her voice trail off with a sniffle and dab to her eyes.

"There, there, Mildred," their grandfather had soothed in his cultured, routine way that bespoke years of dealing with her manipulation. He didn't even turn toward her or stop polishing his Rolex watch.

In the end, her father had set his foot down. The children would attend school no matter what, he said. He didn't need truancy added to his list of troubles. Her grandparents had complied, yet Brenna knew her father had only found the gumption because he wouldn't be in the house. He was leaving for Denver after being told that he could spend a few hours with his wife. Brenna couldn't blame him. She was every bit as non-confrontational as he.

Grandmother had walked around the house several hours after that making statements about how sacrificial she was being to stay behind and care for the children, even though they all knew it to be a front.

Brenna pulled out a pencil. The lead formed a sharp point but the pencil's eraser had been flattened to the silver binding. Fumbling in her backpack, she located her large pink eraser. She had written her name across it in black permanent marker at the beginning of last year. The "a" had nearly disappeared, leaving the word "Brenn". The teachers allowed them to write in ink now that they were in junior high, but Brenna never felt confident enough.

Feeling a soft hand between her shoulder blades, Brenna looked up. Sara stood beside her.

"I'm glad you're back, Brenna," she whispered. Brenna knew she meant it. She started to say thank you but clamped her mouth shut before the first "th" sound could multiply and smiled instead.

"Well, well, if it isn't B...B...Brenna b...b...back from a v...v...vacation!" Tate's mocking voice broke over the classroom noise.

Brenna flushed and looked at her hands.

"Of course," Tate looked around them, making sure he had captured others' attention before he continued. "I guess it isn't much of a vacation when you take your mom to be locked away. Heard she got put into an asylum. Isn't that where crazy people go? I'll bet she went crazy trying to teach you how to talk without stuttering!"

Brenna's heart rate surged. Blood pumped violently through her body. She shot out of her chair and shoved Tate with years of pent-up anger providing strength to her arms. Tate flew backwards against a desk and fell to the floor, his books and papers scattering.

"What's going on here?" The teacher marched up the aisle. Students parted like the Red Sea for her approach.

Tate stumbled to his feet, the hatred in his eyes strong enough to turn Brenna's boldness to raw fear. "She pushed me," he spat.

"I saw that much. My question is why?" The teacher looked at Brenna. Brenna stood in silence, unable to defend herself without speaking.

"It wasn't Brenna's fault," Sara said. She stepped up beside Brenna. "Tate egged her on. He made fun of her all year last year. Now he's starting in on it again,"

The teacher looked at Tate. "Is that true?"

"If you want the truth, ask Brenna. She won't be able to tell you anything." Tate shot a look of triumph at Brenna.

"See, you're doing it right now. You're making fun of her," Sara said hotly.

Tate gave Sara a dirty look.

The teacher looked back and forth between them. "I should give all three of you time after school for this fighting. Consider this a warning. If I hear about anything going on again, anything at all, there will be consequences. Now get along or stay away from each other, understand?"

"Yes, ma'am," Sara said meekly.

"Yes, ma'am." Tate echoed, his sarcasm evident.

The teacher ignored him and turned to Brenna. "And you?"

"Y...Y...Yes," she whispered.

"Fine, then. Now, I want all you students to take your seats. We need to start class." The teacher walked back to the front of the room.

Tate pushed away from the desk. "Don't think you can hurt me and get away with it, rich girl," he hissed.

"Don't think you can hurt Brenna and get away with it," Sara spat back.

"You can't always protect her, Sara." Tate smirked.

"No, but she'll have help," said a new voice behind them. They turned in surprise to see Nick Pierce standing with his arms crossed.

"Oooh, like Pretty Boy can do anything," Tate taunted.

"Stop it, Tate. We're all tired of your meanness," said another student.

"I second that," said another.

Tate stood in the center. His eyes flitted from face to face. When he realized no one sided with him, he shoved between two students and stomped to his desk.

Sara knelt to pick up Tate's dropped items and took them to him. He jerked them out of her hands without giving Sara a chance to speak and slammed them onto his desk.

Nick grinned at Brenna. "I don't think he'll dare bother you again."

Brenna sighed. "F...for a wh...while anyw...way."

Chapter 9

Nick smoothed his hair behind his ears as he stepped into the church foyer. In front of him, Anya greeted a woman with a hug. Russell held the glass door open behind him for a mother and her two small children.

The foyer teemed with people. Nick pulled his shoulder up towards his ear in a protective gesture and crossed his arms to hide the scars on his hand.

J.D. had gone out of town for the weekend with Karl Martin. The two of them had driven up to Wyoming for a horse sale and Nick was staying at the Martin's. Coupled with the time he had stayed there after returning home from the hospital, Nick was beginning to feel as though the Martin's house was home, more so than the trailer house.

"This is Nick Pierce, our neighbor," Anya introduced him to the woman at the door. Nick unbent his right arm to shake the woman's hand then re-crossed his arms.

Russell belted out a friendly laugh at something one of her children had said.

"Let me show you where you'll go for Sunday School." Anya tucked her hand into Nick's elbow. He let her lead him down a hallway and into a small room with folding chairs set up in a circle.

"Nick!" Sara waved at him. She sat between two girls he recognized from school. "I'm so glad to see you."

She got up and patted an empty chair. "Here. I'll move so you can sit by me."

"Thank you, Sara," Anya said when Nick remained in the doorway. She squeezed Nick's arm. "I'll see you in a little while."

"But…" Nick watched her leave. He sat down by Sara.

"Hi, Nick," one of the girls said. She and the other girl giggled.

"Hi." He tried to smile. They giggled again.

Several boys bounded in, along with an older man whom Nick assumed was the teacher.

"It looks like we have a visitor," the teacher said. He held his hand out to Nick. "I'm Darrell. And you are…?"

"Nick Pierce." He took the proffered hand, already tired of handshakes.

"Nice to meet you, Nick. Are you from around here?"

"Nick is my grandparent's neighbor and he goes to our school," Sara explained.

"Well, it's nice to have you today," Darrell said.

Several of the boys sniggered. Nick knew them from school as well. While not as openly mocking as Tate Mason, they clearly viewed him as an oddity as well and Nick knew of nothing that he shared in common with any of them.

Darrell seated himself in the circle opposite Nick. "Open your Bibles to Daniel chapter three for our lesson."

Pages rustled as the students bent their heads and obeyed.

"We'll go around the circle and let each of you take a turn reading a verse."

Nick bit his lip and looked at his empty lap. Sara held out a corner of her Bible toward him. He took it gingerly with his good hand. He had made no effort to read the Bible she had loaned him when he first came home from the hospital, despite his intentions. Anya had told him to keep it when he moved back home so he had taken it to the trailer but for some unknown reason, he detested the idea of reading the Book. Maybe it was the stereotype of religion being for weaklings. He could not afford any more affirmation of his own weakness in his father's eyes. Then again, perhaps the video about Jesus, which he had watched on Russell and Anya's VCR had disturbed him more than he had thought.

"King Nebuchadnezzar made an image…" Darrell began and Nick listened as the story unfolded. This king had declared that all his subjects bow to a huge statue of himself whenever certain music was played.

What a ego trip, Nick thought. When his turn came to read, he fumbled over the strange musical instruments listed and couldn't help but wonder what each sounded like and how it was played.

The king in the story didn't seem to deserve the worship he demanded and Nick silently applauded the three Hebrews who refused to bow down to the king's statue of gold.

But as the soldiers bound the three men and threw them into the fiery furnace, so hot that even the soldiers burned to death, Nick stopped his mental applause. Now their refusal seemed just plain stupid. So much for stories with a happy ending, he thought. If this was the kind of lesson Christians studied, no wonder so many of them walked around so puckered up.

The next verse jolted him as Sara read that the king leaped to his feet in amazement saying, "Look! I see four men walking around in the fire, unbound and unharmed, and the fourth looks like a son of the gods."

He read the verse again to himself and wondered what it meant. Had the three Hebrews not died after all? Who was the fourth guy? Was it truly a god? Were gods real?

With a blush, he realized the others waited for his turn. He quickly read verse twenty-six. "Nebuchadnezzar then approached the opening of the blazing furnace and shouted, 'Shadrach, Meshach and Abednego, servants of the Most High God, come out! Come here!'"

The three Hebrews were completely unhurt. Their God had saved them from the fire. Nick sat back in satisfaction. It had been a good story. Every bit as far-fetched as Hansel and Gretel, but good.

Nick listened without joining in as Darrell led the students in a discussion of what the story meant and how to apply it to their lives at home and at school. With the exception of Sara, the girls giggled after every answer they gave while the boys jabbed at each other or stared at the floor. Nick almost felt sorry for Darrell.

Sara answered many of the questions, somehow managing to not come across as the teacher's pet. Nick liked her statement, "We shouldn't be ashamed to stand up for what we believe in." It sounded like a slogan that should be printed at the bottom of a poster, maybe with a picture of a flag or a bald eagle.

Sara walked with him to the sanctuary doors afterward where they waited for Russell and Anya.

"Is it always like that?" Nick asked her.

"What do you mean?"

"You being the only one who really seems to care."

Sara fingered the worn edge of her Bible. "Not everyone who goes to church loves Jesus," she said sadly. "I just wish…"

"Wish what?" he prodded.

She shook her head. "Never mind. Oh look! Here comes Grandma and Grandpa."

"What did you think?" asked Russell as they walked up.

"It was a good story," Nick answered honestly. Sara smiled at him.

"Not just a story," said Russell. "It really happened. But, we'd better go on in. It looks like it's filling up in there."

They stepped into the sanctuary. Sara left to join her family.

Anya stopped to visit with a woman in a blue dress. Nick stood beside her stiffly until Russell clapped him on the shoulder and turned him around to introduce him to a smiling couple.

People milled all around him, talking and hugging as though they had not seen each other in years. Nick smoothed his jeans at his hips, aware that most of the men wore dress pants and button-down shirts.

He used to own a pair of dress pants. Grandma Bates had bought them several sizes too large for him at the Goodwill store. She had hemmed them up only to let them down a few inches every year as he grew. He had worn them to Mass on Christmas Eve every year until Grandma Bates had stated she was too old to get out on cold nights. By then, the pants no longer fit anyway.

"Hello, Nick."

Nick turned to see Russell's son, Mitch, approaching him. "Hi." He ducked his head. He saw Mitch around the farm when he helped Russell, but never failed to flush with embarrassment thinking about the night Mitch came to the Laundromat and found J.D. drunk. He avoided Mitch as best as he could in order not to remember.

"Dad tells me you're a hard worker."

Nick glanced at Russell, still in conversation with the couple.

"Anytime you want to learn how to work on engines, come on over to the shop. I can teach you if you like." Mitch patted him on the shoulder and moved farther down the aisle.

Nick edged closer to Russell, relieved when he motioned for them to sit down. Anya came and joined them so that Nick sat between them.

"Good morning everyone," said a friendly voice over the sound system.

"Good morning," the congregation responded.

Nick looked at the platform to see a man wearing a tie and holding a microphone.

"We're glad to see you all here today. Please find your seats and stand as we begin by singing praises to our Lord and King," the man said.

To the accompaniment of a piano, the man began to sing. Russell and Anya stood and joined in singing. Nick stood as well, watching as groups of chatting worshipers scattered and filed into pews and began singing.

Grandma Bates had sniffed at what she called the "irreverent Protestants". The Catholic Church's sonorous pipe organs, robed clergy and worshippers who crossed themselves did appear more reverent, Nick thought.

But Nick had to admit that he enjoyed the music. The church roof nearly lifted from the voices that filled the sanctuary with joyful songs. He found his body swaying slightly to the rhythm.

As one, the leader and pianist changed keys. Nick couldn't hold back a tiny smile of satisfaction at their professionalism. To his left, Anya's voice rang out sweet and clear. To his right, Russell growled out an off-key form of bass. Nick couldn't resist. Following the words on the overhead projector, he sang along.

He didn't understand much of the sermon. The pastor used words like "justification" and "sanctification" and said that no human was without sin. He felt an uncomfortable tightening in his abdomen. If everyone had sin, then so did he. Maybe the part of him that made him so different from other boys his age was his sin.

But surely the Martins were without sin. They had never hurt him. He glanced at them. Seeing their rapt attention to the pastor, he felt confident of their perfection.

"Wait right here, Nick. I have a surprise for you," said Russell.

Nick leaned back in his chair, his stomach comfortably full of Anya's Sunday dinner. "What is it?"

"If I told you, it wouldn't be a surprise, now, would it?"

Anya stacked the dinner plates together and laid the used silverware on top. "Are you finished with your glass, Nick?"

"Yes, thank you." He stood to help her clear the table.

"Do you know what the surprise is?" he asked her.

She laughed. "Enjoy the suspense, Nick. I'm not going to tell you. All I will say is that with time, I think you will like it."

Nick heard Russell coming down the hall. He carried something that bumped against the walls. Unable to wait, Nick peered around the corner.

"No fair. You're peeking," Russell complained good-naturedly. He carried a guitar case.

"Is that what I think it is?" Nick asked. He was not certain that he liked the idea.

"It sure is. Come on into the living room." Russell followed him to the couch and laid the case onto the floor. "My pop played this guitar while my granddaddy played the fiddle. They used to sit together on the front porch of the house - you know the one Sara lives in now - to play. The rest of us would gather round and sing whenever we weren't kept too busy swatting mosquitoes. People don't sing many of those old songs anymore but we sure enjoyed them."

Russell smiled and stroked the hard leather-bound case. "Now you probably figured out already if you heard me singing this morning that I'm not the most musical sort so I never learned to play. But after Pop died, I inherited the guitar. My first wife Elin picked it up a few times but with all the kids, she just didn't have time. Said it wasn't a ladylike instrument anyway."

"I didn't know that you'd been married before."

"It was a long time ago." Russell sighed. "Elin died of cancer. I met Annie later. She was teaching music at the grade school. I never thought I'd love again, but there she was."

The clanging dishes stopped and Anya poked her head into the room. "I heard my name," she said.

"Just telling Nick how much you bowled me over when I met you." Russell waggled his eyebrows at her. She blew him a kiss and disappeared.

Russell leaned over and unsnapped each fastener on the guitar case. Nick scooted to the edge of his seat as Russell opened the lid and Nick saw a flash of golden gleaming wood.

Russell extracted the guitar and laid it on his lap. He stroked the top. "The finish is cracked and I don't think the guitar is worth much but I figure it still plays enough for a learning instrument."

"A learning instrument?" Nick held his breath.

"Annie and I figured that a boy with as much musical talent as you needed to use it. That's why I'm giving it to you."

"But I don't know how to play the guitar. What I really want is a piano." Nick looked at Russell worriedly. "I don't mean to offend you or anything."

"I know. But your dad, for whatever his reasons, is against you playing the piano. He is your father, so you must honor his decision while you are under his authority, even if you don't like it. Annie and I talked with J.D. about giving you this guitar and he has agreed to let you have it."

"You talked to my dad?"

"We wouldn't go behind his back, Nick."

Nick rubbed at his injured hand and tried to think of an excuse. Mrs. Plum at the music store in Wichita had carried a strong aversion to guitar, much like an English aristocrat who might choose fine teas over coffee. The only joke he had heard her deign to tell had been, "If you want an electric guitarist to stop playing, hand him sheet music".

"My hand still hurts quite a bit to move it too much. Maybe I shouldn't play," he said.

Russell smiled. "That's another thing. Annie and I talked to your physical therapist and she said that limited playing would actually be very good for you to do. Learning to place your fingers on the right strings will re-teach your brain and fingers to work together quickly. Guitar playing can also be a great finger stretching exercise. Personally, I think it's a perfect solution since you're almost done with therapy."

Nick reached out to slide the tips of his fingers over the strings. A disharmonic sound vibrated through the guitar's body. He winced.

"It needs tuned. Annie bought some guitar books for you. I'm supposing they'll tell you how."

Nick folded his hands in his lap, refusing to look at Anya's piano. This gift only confirmed his fear that they would not let him play for them again, that if he wanted to bad enough, he would have to sneak in when they were gone. After the catastrophe of the last time, he wasn't sure he had the nerve.

"Nick, I need you to make me some promises before I hand over this guitar. First, promise me that you will not hide the musical gift that God has given to you. Whether it's playing the guitar, the piano someday later in life, or who knows, even a cello in a famous orchestra someday, promise me that you will not let your talent go to waste."

"I can promise that," Nick said. That was easy. He knew that music would always be a priority for him.

"Can you promise to at least give the guitar a fair chance?"

"I suppose so." If anyone but Mr. Martin had given him the opportunity there was no way he would have agreed, he thought.

"The next part won't be as easy," Russell warned. "I want you to promise that you'll try to find out everything you can about the Person who gave you the gift of music. And I want you to promise that you will at least consider following after Him."

Nick frowned. "What do you mean?"

"God, Nick. I'm talking about God. He gave you the ability to not only hear and reproduce music but to feel it and live it as well. Give God a chance in your life, Nick. Don't shut Him out. Just because your father here on earth has not always been the best at fathering doesn't mean that God the Father will treat you the same way."

Nick looked away.

"At least try, Nick. That's all we ask of you, both with God and with the guitar."

Nick closed his eyes. "All right. I'll try." But he had no intention of keeping the last promise.

*   *   *

Brenna sat next to Sara on the piano bench.

Sara pointed to the music in front of them. "Let's try it first with me on the bottom notes and you on the top. Then we can trade places. Grandma said we can experiment with both and then decide who plays what for our duet at the recital."

At her most recent piano lesson, Anya Martin had told Brenna about the piano recital that several other piano teachers along with herself put on each year. She had asked Brenna if she would be willing to practice a piece for it.

"I like for my students to get accustomed to playing in front of others," Anya had explained. "Not only is it good practice for adulthood when you may be called upon to give a speech or presentation or play the piano for church but it also teaches us not to hide our abilities and horde them for ourselves. We want to share what we can do and give God the glory for it."

Brenna's natural reaction was to flat out refuse. She had absolutely no desire to get up in front of a crowd and let them hear her play. Anya's rationale made no sense in her world. Chances were highly unlikely that anyone would ever voluntarily ask her to speak in front of a group with her speech impediment and she couldn't play at church if she didn't attend.

But when Anya explained that most of the other teacher's students would be beginners and that she would be willing to help Brenna and Sara work up a duet, Brenna agreed in a rush of wanting to please. But she was having jitters.

Sara started to pound out the lower part of the song, playing the first few bars several times until she had the rhythm correct.

"Now join me," she said. "We'll sight read."

Brenna tried to read the music and keep up with Sara. The end result turned out so discordant that both girls doubled over laughing. Their next attempt sounded no better.

"Let me try the l...lower part," said Brenna. "I...it's easier." For some odd reason, she found it easier to remember the note placements on the bass clef. She also figured it would be better if Sara carried the melody. Not only did Sara have more experience and ability, but Sara had poise in front of people. Brenna had no guarantee that she wouldn't just freeze up when the time came to play at the recital.

Sara switched places with her and flexed her fingers. "Here goes nothing," she announced with a grin.

Together they stumbled through the first page. Brenna found it much easier to stay with Sara's lead rather than play the melody herself.

"Not too bad," said Sara. "I'm starting to hear it now."

"Well I'm not," proclaimed Michele. She stood up from the couch with her magazine. "I'm going outside until you're finished."

Sara made a silly face at Michele's back and Brenna giggled. They turned back to the keyboard.

"Let's try starting on the count of three, since there are three beats to a measure," Sara suggested. "And one and two and three..." She began to play as she said three.

Brenna jerked with surprise, thinking that Sara would start on the "and" after three.

"You have to play, Brenna." Sara shook her finger.

"Okay, s...start over."

"And one and two and three." Again they began on different beats.

"When am I s...supposed to start?"

"On three."

"It sounds better to s...start on the down beat of f...four, doesn't it?"

Sara rubbed her lower lip. "Okay, let's try it."

Again she counted and this time they began together. They limped through the song.

"Aaaah! I can't take it anymore!" Sara's little brother Avery emerged from his bedroom and streaked outside.

"Are we really that bad?" Sara asked.

Brenna burst into laughter. "Worse!"

"We haven't even made it to page two," Sara moaned, flopping from the piano bench to the couch.

"At least there's only three p...pages," Brenna consoled and the girls burst into laughter again.

Sara covered her face with her hands. "We need so much practice."

Brenna carefully closed the music score and laid it inside the piano bench compartment. "We c...could just say we can't do it."

Sara shook her head. "We can't quit after we said we would. You have a copy to practice with at home, right?"

Brenna nodded. "If my g...grandmother lets me practice."

Sara got up from the piano bench and flopped on the couch. "Do you enjoy having your grandparents staying with you?"

Brenna joined Sara on the couch. She copied Sara's relaxed position, leaning against the arm and propping her feet up on the cushion. Her mother or grandmother would be horrified if she put her feet on the couch at home but Sara's mother didn't seem to mind.

"Grandmother is picky." She chose her words carefully. "She doesn't l...like my dad because he's not from a rich family. She doesn't really like B...Bradley or me either, but I'm not sure that she really likes anyone."

"Maybe she's never learned to like herself," said Sara.

Brenna fiddled with the edge of her shirt. "I'd r...rather not talk about it."

Sara adjusted the throw pillow behind her back. "Okay," she acquiesced.

"I've been w...wondering something," said Brenna. "How old are your parents?"

"They're both thirty two. Why?"

Brenna calculated the math. "If you're t...twelve, then they were only n...nineteen when you were born."

"That's right. They got married the summer after they both graduated from high school. Lots of people said they were too young, but Grandpa and Grandma say that they were both more mature at eighteen than most twenty-five year olds."

Brenna rubbed her forehead. "But M...Michele?"

"Michele's adopted," Sara explained. "She is actually my mom's niece but my aunt and uncle on that side were killed. Mom and Dad adopted Michele when she was six. I was only three years old so I don't remember Michele ever not being my sister."

"Your f...family is really n...nice." Brenna felt envious. She would have never guessed that Michele was not Karl and Nell's biological daughter. They treated her as lovingly as Sara and Avery. Brenna's grandmother complained about having to disrupt her life to come and live in the barren wasteland of western Kansas in order to properly care for her grandchildren, as if she expected sainthood to be bestowed upon her for the sacrifice.

"You know, Brenna," Sara said, "I'm really sorry that we weren't friends a long time ago. We've gone to school together since Kindergarten but I never realized how much we're kindred spirits, you know, like Anne of Green Gables says about Diana. I'm glad that we ride the same bus and live close to each other now, aren't you?"

"Yes, me too." Brenna agreed, surprising herself by not stuttering. She smiled at Sara and savored the word "friends".

Nick sat cross-legged on the floor. He opened the guitar book to page one and laid it flat on the floor in front of him. He picked up the guitar and ran through the strings, following the page's instructions on how to tune the instrument, an easy task with the electronic tuner Anya had bought with the books.

Satisfied with the sound, he turned the page and attempted to place his fingers on the guitar as the diagram showed for a C major chord.

He strummed down the strings with his right thumb. Half the strings reverberated too loud while the other half emitted a strangled buzzing sound. He pressed harder. The second strum sounded better although the thickest string at the top of the guitar sounded totally wrong. Nick checked the diagram again. It showed a tiny "X" above the string. What did the "X" mean?

He skimmed through the introduction pages. The "X" stood for a closed string, which meant not to play it.

He painstakingly placed his fingers on the correct frets and strings once again and strummed. Yes, now he had a C chord, not the most harmonic, perhaps, but a C chord nonetheless.

Nick rubbed the fingertips of his left hand with his thumb. The strings pressed into the tender flesh, leaving imprints. Frustrated, Nick envisioned a C chord on the piano keyboard, where his fingers could instantly find the correct keys.

Not only that, but the prospect of only learning chords, which seemed to be the main theme of this book, frustrated him. What about melody and rhythm and multi-faceted complexity? This strumming up and down reminded him of the country music that blared from his father's truck.

The trailer door screeched open. J.D. came into the living room, stomping mud from his cowboy boots on the newly vacuumed floor. "What's this?"

"I'm practicing guitar," Nick said. He swallowed.

"Guitar?" J.D. shook his head. He resembled the confused cattle Nick had watched him prod into the corral. "Oh, that's right. Russell told me about that."

J.D. sank into his recliner and yanked off his boots. He propped his stocking feet up. "Do we still have any leftover pizza?"

"Three pieces."

"Get them for me, will you? And a beer while you're at it."

Nick laid the guitar aside and stood to his feet. He laid the cold slices on a paper towel and took them to his father who had already turned on the television with the remote.

J.D. took a large bite and popped the tab on his can of cold beer. "I'm going to watch some T.V. Play that thing somewhere else."

Nick gathered up the guitar and books and tried to ignore his own hunger. He chided himself for not eating before J.D. got home. Yet even then, he might have incurred his father's wrath if the pizza had been gone.

"Oh, and Russell said to tell you he'd pick you up at eight in the morning for your last trip to Wichita." J.D. waved the pizza slice in Nick's direction.

Nick nodded and went to his room. He closed the door and sank on his bed. He rubbed at the soreness in his still healing hand.

Nick and Russell crossed the steaming hot parking lot after Nick's final check-up with the physical therapist in Wichita.

"Why didn't you tell me that you've been paying for all this?" Nick asked. He had caught Russell filling out paperwork and writing a check. He didn't know why it hadn't occurred to him - it didn't seem right that the Martins should have to pay a debt that he had incurred by his own foolishness.

Russell dug in his pocket for the car keys without answering. He unlocked the passenger door.

"You have paid for it, haven't you?"

"Yes."

"Did your insurance cover any of it?"

"Some of it. It's not something you need to worry about, Nick."

"But why? Why would you do that?"

Russell held the door open. "I already explained to you that I feel responsible for what happened. Besides, J.D. doesn't carry health insurance and we can afford it."

"But it was my fault. I disobeyed you."

"You apologized already and I forgave you, Nick. Let Annie and I take care of it."

"How much was it?"

Russell sighed. "It's a gift, Nick. You don't turn away gifts. Get in the car. It's hot out here."

Nick slid into the car, feeling the hot vinyl of the seat through his jeans. As soon as Russell got in the driver's side, Nick said, "I'll pay you back."

Russell inserted the key into the ignition with a little smile. "How?"

Nick paused. "I don't know. I could work without wages until I pay it off."

"No, Nick. This is a debt that you cannot pay. Please don't take away my blessing of paying it for you."

Nick stuck out his jaw.

Russell met his eyes. "Truly, Nick. Just keep your promise to give God a chance in your life. That's all the payment I ask."

"But I can't accept… it's too much…"

"It's a lot less than the debt Jesus paid for each of us." Russell started the car and adjusted the air conditioning. The blowing air cooled the sweat on Nick's neck and forehead. "The money isn't important anyway."

Nick rubbed at his hand. Ever since his accident, he had begun massaging it, at first to ease pain, now more as a nervous habit. "I'll still pay you back somehow," he said obstinately.

Russell waved his hands. "You and Annie are both stubborn as mules," he exclaimed. He slapped his hands down on the steering wheel and Nick jumped.

"Enough of that," said Russell. "Now, since this is our last official visit to Wichita, would you like to drive by your old house?"

Nick shifted in the seat. "Why?"

"Sometimes looking at where you've been brings closure, perspective on where you are now. It's up to you, but I'd be interested in seeing where you moved from."

"You would?" Nick couldn't imagine why Russell would care. He remembered Mrs. Anderson using that word, "closure", and not with fondness.

"When are you going to start believing what I tell you?" Russell teased.

Nick blushed. "I'm sorry."

"So what do you think?"

Nick paused. "That'd be okay I guess."

He gave Russell directions the best he could remember by landmarks and after several false turns, they were driving down the familiar street, past his old elementary school, even though his former classmates now attended at the junior high building. Nick felt a bit superior as he drove around town on a Friday, with permission to miss school for the day.

Businesses had sprung up around the small residential area as Nick was growing up. Many people had moved from the area, leaving houses abandoned. Renters came and went, many treating the property like miners who scrape the beauty from the land and leave a scar behind. Those who stayed were old, too old to care for the property any longer, like Grandma Bates had been. The houses showed their years in decay and dilapidation. Weeds and shrubs overtook many of the yards.

"Slow down. It's the second house to the left."

He peered out at the house standing desolate, a real-estate sign hanging crookedly in the front yard.

Russell parked across the street.

"Would you like to get out and walk around?"

"Not really."

"Any friends or neighbors you'd like to visit?"

Nick shook his head.

Russell turned to face him. "Were you happy here, Nick?"

Nick looked at the sagging front porch. He could remember hours sitting on the top step, watching ants on the sidewalk below, hoping his mother might decide to come back for him after all and pull up to the curb in a nice car and whisk him away to a happy ever after.

"I don't know," he said.

They sat in silence. Nick listened to the quiet pinging of the engine as it cooled. Heat began to seep into the car's interior without the steady cool air of the air conditioning to ward it off. He thought of Grandma Bates pulling his old red wagon to the grocery store to save money on gas. He thought of her endless complaints about how much he ate, how much toilet paper he used. He thought of the hours she had set him down at the kitchen table to practice the hated alphabet sounds and blends when he had difficulty learning to read. Maybe he hadn't been happy in that house, but he had been secure. He never knew what to expect with life at his father's house.

If he were honest with himself, Nick didn't even understand what exactly happiness was other than what he saw in Russell and Anya's faces - contentment, security, serenity, hope - as though flawless music flowed through their lives, rather than the dissonant cacophony of sounds that plagued Nick.

"There is one place I'd like to visit," he said.

Russell reached for the ignition.

Nick unbuckled his seat belt and opened the door instead. "We might as well walk. It's just around the corner."

A sonorous bell rang as Russell followed Nick into a music store. Russell looked around. Racks of music scores and lesson books stood in the front part of the store. Rows of grand pianos and uprights stood at attention toward the back, away from the hot sunlight flooding in the front windows. He should have known that the only tie Nick might still feel would involve music, namely piano.

"Nicholas Pierce, is that you?" A tall silver-haired woman approached the door. Russell had to smile at her obviously practiced English accent, like some of the announcers on national public radio.

The woman lifted the glasses that hung on a silver chain around her neck. "Why, it is you!"

"Hello, Ms. Plum," said Nick shyly.

"Look at you." She patted his arm. "You've filled out. And you've gotten such a tan." The last statement held a disapproving tone.

Nick brushed his hair behind his ear self-consciously. "Ms. Plum, I'd like you to meet Mr., uh... I mean Russell, Martin."

"Pleased to meet you," Russell said and held his hand out to her.

"Likewise." Ms. Plum nodded her head elegantly and turned back to Nick. Russell dropped his hand. "We've all wondered where you've been. It seemed as though you fairly disappeared. How is your grandmother?"

Nick rubbed his hand in the nervous gesture Russell had noticed before. Russell hesitated then answered for Nick. "She passed away some months ago."

"I'm so sorry to hear that. Where are you living now, Nicholas?"

"With my dad in western Kansas." Nick picked up a music theory workbook off the shelf and flipped the pages, clearly wishing to change the subject.

Ms. Plum looked at Russell sharply. "Are you Nicholas' father?"

"Nick's father works on our farm," Russell explained quickly. "I'm just Nick's taxi driver for the day."

"Oh?" She cocked her head like a little bird.

"We came to Wichita for…" Russell stopped. He wasn't sure if Nick wanted him to share anything personal or not. Nick seemed to like this Ms. Plum, though Russell couldn't see why. "For the day," he finished.

Nick repositioned the workbook on the display.

"Nicholas! Whatever have you done to your hand?" This time, Russell heard genuine concern in her voice.

"I cut my hand in a band saw and had to have surgery." Nick seemed to consider hiding the hand, but held it out for Ms. Plum to inspect.

"Oh my goodness! What a terrible thing," she exclaimed. She examined his scar without leaning closer. "How did something so terrible occur?" She glared at Russell as though he had pushed Nick into the blade.

"It was an accident," Russell said blandly, aware of Nick's embarrassment over disobeying.

"Is everything healing normally?" She focused back on Nick. "Do you still have all your movement?"

"Yes, although parts of this finger are still a little numb. The doctor said that the feeling would probably come back but that it may take several more months."

"And you are still able to play the piano, I hope?"

"I'm still able."

Russell noted how Nick evaded her question. "Actually, Nick is learning to play the guitar now as well," he offered, noticing Nick's wince too late.

"The guitar!" She spoke the word as though referring to a barbaric cultural practice. Russell's mouth twitched with amusement. "Why ever do you want to give up the piano?"

Nick shrugged.

"But you are so gifted!" She turned on Russell. "Did he tell you that he came over to my store almost every day and taught himself how to play the piano? He listened in on lessons that I gave in the back room and read the books on this shelf. Within a year he could play some of the simpler Beethoven pieces. Such talent as this I have never before seen. He is a maestro, Mr. Martin. You must not allow him to give up on this ability."

Russell understood her passion. He believed firmly in the Biblical mandate to use talents and spiritual gifts from God to further His kingdom. Still, he believed in the command for children to honor and obey their parents. He had asked himself internal questions about what point children should disobey parents if the requests a parent made contradicted the Biblical command and made no progress on knowing what to do in Nick's case. It wasn't as though J.D. asked something immoral or unethical of Nick.

"I don't like it either, Ms. Plum," he said. "But Nick's father forbids it and we must, for a time at least, abide by his wishes."

"What kind of father is this who will not allow his child to blossom in the garden of that child's gifts?"

"The kind of father who does not care for flowers."

Ms. Plum's thin lips tightened. "Then this is a shame," she said. "I am very sorry, Nicholas."

Nick looked up from a music score he studied with feigned concentration. Russell laid his hand on Nick's shoulder.

Nick jumped and Russell inwardly scolded himself for forgetting that Nick did not react to everyday touches in the same way his grandchildren did.

"Would you like to play something for us right now, Nick?" he asked.

"Yes, please do," said Ms. Plum. "I would so enjoy hearing you play again." She steepled her fingers together with rapture.

Nick hesitated. "I haven't played for a long time and my fingers still aren't very strong on my right hand."

"Just do your best," Russell encouraged. "And enjoy yourself. We have time before we need to leave."

Nick took a deep breath and turned toward the pianos.

"I have a Steinway parlor grand in the corner." Ms. Plum pointed with the eyeglasses that hung on her thin chest. "We just set it out yesterday. The sound is exquisite. You must try it out."

"You really mean I can?" Nick's eyes sought Russell's.

"You mean you may," Ms. Plum corrected. "And of course you may. You know you're welcome to play any piano in my shop."

Russell nodded. Nick's usually guarded expression slipped off and his face came to life so rapidly that Russell felt a lump in his throat.

He had wanted so badly to get to know the boy, to mentor him, partly because he sensed that without a male role model's intervention, Nick would most likely experience gender confusion very soon if he hadn't already, but mostly because Russell felt an urgency to introduce Nick to Jesus.

How do I connect a soul with the Father of love when that soul has rarely, if ever, experienced the sensation of being loved, he wondered?

Listening to Nick play with tentative notes giving way to joyful abandon told Russell the truth. Nick's ability to interpret and define music through his fingers proclaimed his ability to feel and understand emotion, even if he were not yet aware of it.

Russell prayed for the chance to explain.

Chapter 10

"And now Sara Martin and Brenna Williams will perform a duet for you," Anya Martin announced to the small crowd, causing Brenna's already tight stomach to clench.

Anya nodded at the girls encouragingly as they stood and made their way to the piano. As practiced, Brenna turned to face the audience while Sara announced their piece and the composer. So many faces smiled at her. Instead of friendliness, their bared teeth seemed primed to laugh at her mistakes. Brenna's knees trembled.

Sara turned to sit down. Brenna joined her stiffly. She rubbed her palms on her dress, aware that her grandmother would no doubt scold her for it later.

"Bodily secretions do not wash out of certain fabrics, you know," she would say with a sniff, and probably feel victimized for even having to mention such a vile thing as sweat.

Her father, grandparents and Bradley had all come to the recital, Bradley only under duress and with much struggling. Grandmother approved of Brenna's piano playing, citing that for centuries cultured and "accomplished" young ladies were distinguished by their ability to paint with watercolors, dance and play the pianoforte.

But she couldn't think about anyone else now. Sara's fingers were poised on the keyboard, ready to play. Brenna lifted her own shaking hands.

Sara counted soft enough so only the two of them could hear her. Somehow, Brenna's fingers complied and she played, her bass notes a robot to Sara's flighty soprano. The rest of the auditorium blacked out around her, leaving only the piano keyboard and Sara in her vision. Before she could blink, they were finished, the audience clapped and Brenna stumbled back to her seat. She panted as though she had run a race and realized

that she had held her breath through most of the song. She tried
to still her breathing so no one would hear.

Sara patted her arm. "We did it!" she whispered with a
wide smile. "You did a good job."

Brenna smiled back as best she could. She felt shakier
now that she was finished, if that were possible.

Nick slouched in a back seat of the sanctuary. He
smoothed the recital program over his thigh. Since the program
only listed fifteen piano soloists and two duets, the families and
friends barely filled the first five rows in the center section. No
one saw Nick in the back.

He had come with Russell and Anya. J.D. had given
permission for him to spend the evening with them, but Nick had
not divulged that they would be spending it at a piano recital.

Michele Martin, Sara's sister, stood at the grand piano
and announced her piece. As the eldest student, she was the last
to perform. Nick had suffered through the first choppy
performances by young elementary students.

Brenna and Sara's duet had been a great improvement
yet he still heard the mechanical rhythm in their playing as
though they tried to stay together rather than enjoy the notes.

Michele sat down to play. Nick listened with
discernment. She knew her piece well and played with
confidence. The program said that she had taken six years of
piano lessons from Anya. Nick had never taken a single piano
lesson in his life and he knew that he could have played her
piece with more musical interpretation and smoothness.

He did not begrudge Michele her ability, but knowing
that his far superior ability lay pushed aside by his father's
stubbornness caused a bitter gall in Nick's stomach. He
slouched lower in his seat and crumpled the program in his fist.

Nick thought of the guitar leaning against the closet door
in his tiny bedroom. The instrument had proven itself more
complex than the piano keyboard. Rather than pressing a key

and consistently receiving the same note, he had to memorize positions on the fret board to press down before a string could give him the same note. He found the lack of octaves frustrating when he tried to pick out melodies of favorite piano pieces and could not stretch his left-hand fingers far enough to produce the harmonies he heard in his memory. Worse of all, he could not seem to evoke emotion in the strings. He supposed that would come; piano playing hadn't always come easy either. But there were days when he hated the sight and sound of the clunky wooden instrument, hated the dark gray grooves the strings made in the tips of his fingers.

Why couldn't his father accept that he could play the piano? Why did he forbid it?

Nick clenched the program harder. He knew the answer. Because his father was close-minded. Because his father wanted Nick to develop his masculinity. Because his father no doubt believed the same thing about him that bullies like Tate Mason called him at school.

Nick knew other boys his age were changing as testosterone and puberty raged through their systems. Nick watched facial and leg hair sprout and thicken. He heard voices crack and deepen. Yet his own legs remained slender and smooth, almost shapely. His own chest and even armpits were still devoid of hair. His voice had become husky, but by no means deep.

Why did this masculinity thing matter so much anyway? If being a man meant sitting around on his derriere drinking beer every night to a flashing television screen, he wanted no part of it. If it meant hard work and faithfulness to a wife, like Russell Martin, then being a real man was out of reach to him – no woman in her right mind would ever marry him if she knew about the thoughts and images in his brain.

Nick watched as the audience began to file out a front side door after an announcement of refreshments in the church's fellowship hall. The last people left and the door closed behind them.

Nick sat in the semi-darkened sanctuary, staring at the cross that hung on the front wall. Shadows made the cross seem ominous, as a thing of death rather than beauty, unlike the glorious brilliance that shone onto the cross when he had came with the Martins to a Sunday morning service and the sun had shone into the eastern facing windows. He stood and made his way down the carpeted aisle toward the front, his footsteps muffled.

The sheen of the grand piano pulled him forward. He stroked his fingers over the keys and relished the silky feel of the ebony, the slickness of the ivory.

The shadow of the cross fell across the stage. It pointed toward him. He thought of his grandmother's Catholic church with its dark wood pews and ornate stained glass. Jesus still hung in agony on that cross. Nick recalled the story from the video Sara had lent him.

The Sunday he had visited church with the Martins, they had sung a song about the cross, a wondrously haunting song. Nick lowered his head to remember. Perhaps the song was in the hymnal here as well.

"Man of Sorrows, what a name…"

Nick found the page number and propped the thick book on the piano's music stand. He glanced around him several times to make sure no one was coming back into the sanctuary and sat.

He played slowly, careful to follow the notes. The tune became fresh in his mind again when he heard it. He paused to look again at the shadow of the empty cross, wondering what sort of man would allow others to kill him, would take punishment for someone else.

Nick played the song again and this time focused on the words to each verse. He felt the intensity of the lyrics washing over him, intensity that found its way into his fingers.

"Bearing shame and scoffing rude,
In my place condemned He stood;
Sealed my pardon with His blood;
Hallelujah! What a Savior!"

Nick recalled the many times he had stood before scoffers. He understood the man on the cross's shame.

"Guilty vile and helpless we;
Spotless Lamb of God was He;
Full atonement, can it be?
Hallelujah! What a Savior!"

What did the song mean by calling Jesus a "Lamb of God"? Nick remembered the camera on Sara's movie zooming in on Jesus holding a tiny lamb as children in dusty robes danced around him. Jesus had been smiling in that scene.

"Lifted up was He to die,
It is finished was His cry;
Now in heaven exalted high;
Hallelujah! What a Savior!"

Chills broke out over Nick's spine, as though the condemned man had shouted out his victory in the empty sanctuary and drowned out the noise of the piano. Exhilaration exploded over him and Nick pounded his hands down in the glorious ecstasy of the final verse.

"When He comes our glorious King
All His ransomed home to bring,
Then anew this song we'll sing;
Hallelujah! What a Savior!"

A Savior. One who saves. From what? Nick bowed his head over the keyboard, drained. The final chord still vibrated in the air.

Nick tilted his head to look at the cross. In his mind's eye, he pictured the statue pinned to the crucifix he had seen as a child, the man's head still slumped over toward the left, his face bearing the same frozen expression of pain. Had Nick only imagined the joy? He rubbed his face. The cross hung in silence.

*   *   *

Brenna hugged the wall with her back and willed herself to sink into the shadows. Nick would soon stand from the piano and turn. She had no wish for him to notice her.

She had never heard such playing before, not even from Mrs. Martin. Nick's song had made her want to weep and shout for joy at the same time.

She jumped as Nick snapped the hymnal shut. He stalked over to the pew and dropped the book back into the holder with a thud.

She did not understand his mood. Surely someone who could play the piano with such brilliance, someone who had just finished playing a masterpiece would feel contentment, satisfaction.

She shrunk back as the door opened and spilled light into the darkened sanctuary. Nick turned and scowled.

"I wondered if I might find you in here." Russell Martin entered. "Were you playing?"

"You won't tell him, will you?"

Russell shook his head. "No." Brenna couldn't miss the sadness in his voice.

Nick rubbed his hand, the one he had injured. His voice cracked as he said, "I wish you were my dad."

Russell closed his eyes. When he opened them, he reached for Nick. "So do I, Nick."

Nick buried his face against the older man's shirt.

"I love you like a son, Nick," Russell choked out. "I know that's not enough right now but it's all I can give. I wish…"

"I love you, too." Nick's words were muffled.

Brenna dared not move, embarrassed to have intruded on such a scene and fearful that they would see her kept her motionless. Another emotion surfaced, surprising her. Jealousy.

*   *   *

The faint sound of the telephone filtered over the sound of the vacuum. Anya turned off the vacuum and hurried to pick up the phone before the answering machine came on.

"Mom, it's Karl."

The phone receiver in Anya's hand suddenly felt weighted with stones. Something was not right. Something in Karl's voice.

"Mom, are you there?"

"Yes, Karl, I'm here."

She heard Karl swallow.

"Karl, what's wrong?"

She heard voices in the background, panicked sounds.

"Karl, where are you?" she asked sharply.

"I'm at the farm shop." Another swallow. "Mom, there's been an accident. Dad's hurt. You'd better come."

The hallway swirled around her and she braced her hand against the wall, knocking a family photo askew.

"How bad?"

No answer.

"Karl?" she pleaded.

"Just hurry, Mom. You need to get here before the ambulance. Pray." The phone line clicked as Karl hung up.

Anya numbly dropped the receiver into its cradle.

"Pray, pray," she told herself. "Oh, Russell. How bad is it, God? Please, dear Lord, let him be fine."

But she knew that Karl would never have called for an ambulance unless it was indeed very serious. Russell himself would not allow it if he was in any shape to argue. She remembered the time he had broken his pelvis when a horse threw him. He had limped to his truck and drove himself to the hospital.

She gathered together her purse and car keys, as normal a task as preparing for a trip to the grocery or the beauty parlor, yet her insides trembled.

Dust billowed behind her car as she made the drive to the farm shop. Two miles had never seemed so far.

When she pulled up, she saw Nell holding the children back in their yard and the men kneeling in the drive next to a pickup and tractor.

Anya parked and pried her hands off the steering wheel, surprised at their soreness from gripping so tightly. She stumbled toward the huddle on the ground. Karl and Mitch knelt at Russell's side. Mitch held his hands over his face as though he could not bear to look. His shoulders convulsed. J.D. leaned against the tractor as though he had no strength to stand on his own.

Karl saw her and jumped up.

"The tractor," he said. His face looked gray and haggard, much older than his thirties. "J.D. didn't look behind him before he started to back up. We were all yelling but he couldn't hear. Dad was right behind it."

Anya pressed her hand against her stomach. Karl laid his hands over both of hers to squeeze them but she felt his trembling.

"It went right over him. We were afraid to move him. That's why we called the ambulance."

It. Anya's brain took a moment to realize Karl meant the tractor. The tractor had run over her Russell. J.D. had run over her Russell.

Anya sank down on the dirt beside Russell, her legs quivering. Karl sat down with her.

He lay motionless, his eyes open. His stomach protruded oddly as though someone had inserted an air pump and expanded it. She laid her hand over his, not sure if her hand or his felt colder.

"Russell? It's me, darling. I'm here." She bent close to his face. His skin held an unnatural blue cast. She sternly told herself not to cry. Her flesh hurt with almost physical pain as she looked at him. Her husband. The man whom God Himself had proclaimed to be one with her.

Russell blinked and looked at her. He mouthed her name, his special nickname for her. "Annie." Dirt and sand caked his lips.

"Yes, I'm here." She leaned closer.

"Wh…wh…?"

"You've been hurt but an ambulance is on the way." She was unable to keep the tremble out of her voice.

Spittle trickled from his mouth. She wiped it away with her bare fingers, leaving a muddy streak. If only she could take this dirt and saliva and put it on his body for healing, as Jesus did with the blind man's eyes.

Russell struggled for breath and tried to speak. One side of his face sagged similar to a stroke victim.

"Shh, darling. Don't try to talk," she murmured. She caressed his forehead, his hair, traced his jaw, memorized every crinkle around his eyes, every stubbly whisker, every pore. "You're going to be fi…"

"Annie," he whispered. "It's time."

She couldn't swallow against the expanding pressure in her chest and throat. "No."

He tried to lift his hand in hers. She held it to her face. His fingers curved around her cheek.

"So soft," he said.

She began to weep. Her tears ran through his fingers and onto her own.

"Russell," she implored. "Don't go."

His body stiffened. His gaze suspended on each face, and stopped on Anya.

"We love you, Dad," Karl said in a low voice. Mitch murmured assent.

J.D. turned and staggered away.

Russell nodded without breaking eye contact with his wife. Anya watched his face change subtly, the intense lines of pain melting into a contented smile.

They looked at each other, simply looked, memorizing, silently saying everything.

His lids lowered, hiding his eyes from her, separating her from him.

"Jesus," he exhaled.

She held her own breath and willed him to inhale. He did not.

Her knees weakened even as her hand tightened around his limp one, still pressed to her face. No one spoke. The silence seemed reverent, holy.

In a trance, Anya bent to kiss him, the last kiss she would place on her husband's warm lips. Her own mouth trembled as she prolonged the contact.

"Mom." Karl held her shoulders.

She sat up. The small movement away from her husband caused a tearing, wrenching inside her, as though she were deserting him. She turned her face into Karl's chest and allowed numbness to overtake her.

Chapter 11

Funny how a funeral and a wedding seemed so similar. Anya found herself in the middle of a flurry of phone calls and preparations to ask friends and family to speak, perform music and act as pallbearers. Several of the same friends had acted as groomsmen and musicians nineteen years before in she and Russell's wedding.

Then there was the meal to plan, just as she had once planned a reception complete with cake, punch and those little hand-pressed mints that no one ever truly liked. The church ladies had taken over that job.

Nell fussed over cleaning and pressing Anya's nicest dress, along with Russell's suit and best shirt and Anya could not resist thinking about the yellowing bridal gown in the back of her closet and the tie Russell had squawked about having to wear. He had looked uncomfortable and formal in their wedding photos.

A steady influx of cards arrived in the mail, complete with memorial funds and handwritten notes. She recalled the excitement she and Russell had shared as they opened each wedding card and tallied up the cash gifts. She had no excitement now.

At the viewing the previous evening, Anya had wandered through the mortuary's chapel. While she greeted those who had come to pay their respects, her eyes continually returned back to the open casket where she could see Russell's face so peaceful, so still.

She remembered the day of their wedding, and the days after, how her eyes naturally searched him out in a room crowded with people simply because she enjoyed watching him.

And although it seemed deranged to think it, she had to admit that she enjoyed the evening in a sentimental way. This was the last opportunity she had to be in the same room with Russell, to glance across the room for him, to keep her identity as his wife one last night. After tonight, she would be his widow.

Before the funeral service, she found herself sequestered in a Sunday school room, away from sight, with the rest of the immediate family. She was surprised to feel nervous as the funeral director led her solemnly out of the room where she waited at the back of the church, the long aisle stretched out before her.

Unlike her trip down the aisle as a bride, she and Karl led the procession of family members. At first, she was conscious of the friends and loved ones who watched her. Then her focus switched to the shining wooden casket in front of the podium, surrounded by fragrant arrangements of cut flowers and plants.

She blinked, as though the casket momentarily became Russell, wiping his broad hands down the lapels of his suit coat, a proud smile wide enough to split his face. They had said their vows to each other in the same place where his body now lay.

"Till death do us part..."

Anya took her seat and her family filled in around her. She wanted to concentrate on every word, wanted to remember all the memorials and tributes to Russell, but her mind wandered, an apparition flitting over a wispy landscape, only grazing its feet on the firmament.

She studied the flowers and wondered how the tradition of giving them as memorials ever started. The blossoms vibrated with color, life and perfume, a symbol of life in direct juxtaposition with this place of death.

But, she realized, the stems had been cut from the mother plant. Their vibrancy would dull, so quickly, so irreversibly. Maybe the flowers showed death more than life. In truth, despite their beauty, they were already dead.

No, she thought. That thought was too depressing. Maybe a better perspective might be that the limited time of the flower arrangements only increased their beauty, just as life becomes more precious with the realization of how little time a life really was.

Time. She had assumed that she and her husband still had so much time. Russell was only 67 years old, she a mere 54.

Then the pastor was handing the microphone to people in the audience who wanted to share memories about the man who had affected so many lives. After a number stood to share, Karl patted her shoulder to say it was her turn.

She had agreed to speak at Russell's service. To keep silent about what he was to her would almost seem cruel. She stood on shaky legs and leaned forward until her knees touched the pew seat for support. A microphone appeared in her hand. She gripped the microphone in one hand and Karl's hand in the other and let her gaze travel over the filled pews. People also filled rows of folding chairs added to the back. Some stood against the far wall and beyond in the foyer. Karl had told her that more people sat downstairs with a video screen of the service in front of them. She swallowed. Her husband had been a loved man, a respected man, and many people had come as a result.

Many of the guests she would love to visit with, catch up with, many she had not seen for years, but she would much rather have Russell alive and beside her than all the caring visitors in the world.

The children were all there as well. Her family had teased her about being a mother hen who liked to have all her chicks in one nest, since Anya loved it when all the children could be home. But she would be content to have the children scattered to the four corners of the earth on this day if only Russell could be back.

She loved the children deeply, her stepchildren as much as her own. But Russell was her one flesh, the part of her that no longer existed as though half her body had withered and disappeared and left the phantom pains of amputation.

Now the children sat in the pews around her, instinctively in the order of their ages.

Karl and Nell sat in the front with their three children, Michele, Sara and Avery. Nick Pierce sat next to Sara, his jaw clenched tight. Anya felt guilty. She had not thought of Nick since the accident.

Cassie sat at the end of Karl and Nell's row. She wore a tailored suit, her hair neat as ever. She and her husband worked as partners in a law office and only those closest to Cassie ever got to know her as a woman with a sense of humor as well as the deep, hidden pain of infertility. Her husband had been unable to come.

Peter, who had been seven when she married Russell, and his wife Lin Zhu had driven through the night from their home in California. Lin Zhu held their son on her lap. All three looked tired.

Next sat Kathleen. A recent nursing graduate, Kathleen had taken a job at a mission outreach in Bolivia and was slated to leave the states in several months. She had been going through a rigorous training and briefing session in Texas. Anya thanked the Lord that Kathleen had not already left the country. She needed the girl's unwavering faith.

Mitch sat with his arm around Kathleen. The mother in Anya knew that Mitch held onto his sister more for his own comfort than Kathleen's.

Her only biological children, the twins, sat together as usual. Their light hair and features matched so perfectly that, to Seth and Jayne's amusement, strangers often commented that they must be identical twins.

"Exactly identical," Seth would quip. "One of us just dresses up as the opposite sex. Bet you can't guess which one!"

Only, today, the twins' faces were somber and ashen.

"Pastor asked me to speak a few words," she began, backing away from the microphone when the first "p" sound exploded over the sound system. She looked at her family. They nodded back encouragingly.

"He thought you might enjoy hearing Russell and my story."

Russell. Such a precious word that she had spoken with joy, called for him with, whispered into his ear in their bed. Such rending to say it now.

Her family smiled. They knew the story well.

"Russell, of course, was married before me. He and his first wife, Elin, had five children, now my stepchildren. Elin became very sick with a sudden cancer and passed away several months after Mitch was born." She cleared her throat. The trembling eased in her knees.

"Not long afterward, I moved here to begin teaching music and band at the elementary and high schools. I had one particular student, and I won't mention any names but his initials were P.M.," Anya looked pointedly at Peter.

Chuckles rippled through the audience. Peter ducked his head with a sheepish smile.

"Peter asked if he could stay after music class one day. Since it was his recess, I agreed. Before I knew what was happening, he pulled out pictures of his family and told me how his mother had gone to heaven and how his daddy needed a new wife and would I please go home with him after school and marry his dad and be his new mother.

As it was, I did not meet Peter's father until several months later when I was asked to serve as a spelling bee judge for the county spelling bee. You know small town school systems. Everyone helps out everywhere, whether it's your specialty area or not.

Cassie got first place at that spelling bee after a very close showdown with another student. I went up to congratulate

her, and Peter nabbed the chance to finally introduce me to his
father.

To my surprise, Russell invited me to celebrate Cassie's
victory with the family that evening over ice cream and as they
say, the rest is history.

We were married six months later, just before Mitch's
second birthday. To some, that may seem rushed, but I knew
that Russell was the man I was meant to marry and I never once
regretted it.

I suppose that's been what holds me together these past
few days. I was created to marry Russell. He was so good for
me. His faith, his love for Jesus, his steadfast dedication to me
and the children have all made me a better person. Even though
Russell and I only had nineteen years of marriage, with children
in the house eighteen of those years, I have no regrets and I
would marry him again, even if I knew the eventual outcome."

Anya's voice faded to a whisper. "It has been worth
every moment of it."

The casket blurred from her tears when she turned to
look at it - the casket that held the shell of her husband.

"It has been worth every moment," she repeated. Anya
looked across the faces before her. She saw neighbors and
friends, some with the assurance of heaven in their eyes, others
with the empty pained look of not understanding death. Her
heart pounded with an insistency that she recognized as the Holy
Spirit's urging. She knew she had more to say.

"But if I had not made the decision years ago to love
Jesus more than Russell, I would feel that I had just lost the most
important thing I could ever lose. As it is, I lost the second most
important thing, and that's hard enough. But I know Russell is
not gone forever and I know that even though the rest of my life
will seem long without him, it won't be long before I go to join
him and my Jesus. If there is anything more that Russell would
want for you to do, it would be to please, please consider your
own future. Russell very well may have died at such a surprising

time so that you would have to think about death and what comes after. Do not resist God. He loves you. He wants to forgive you for every wrong. He wants to adopt you as His own."

Faces in the audience had changed. Some nodded in agreement, some looked down, several looked confused or mutinous. But the pounding in her chest had eased and she knew she had done her part.

"Thank you, Lord," she breathed inwardly as she took her seat. Only God's strength could have given her the courage and clearness of mind to testify the truth at her own husband's funeral.

Nick folded his arms across his chest, as though he could force his emotions to remain inside his body. He turned to look at the continual line of cars that snaked their way down the sandy road and into the cemetery. Townspeople and family members crowded in and around the dark green tent until he could no longer see the gleaming wooden casket, positioned above a yawning hole.

Wind insistently buffeted the group, clawing at men's ties and streaking women's hair across their faces. The scalloped flap that hung along the top edge of the tent whipped up and down with a slapping noise that grated on Nick's already raw nerves.

The pastor began to speak, shouting in competition with the wind. Nick stared at his shoes. He had sat through the funeral service, tuning out the words of hope and clenching his jaw during the open mike session as many friends and family members stood to testify of the impact Russell had made on their lives. He had refused the comfort of Sara's hand touching his and defiantly kept his eyes open and his head high during the closing prayer.

Anya's own words had made an anger inside of him so fierce that he was afraid of it. If the Martin's Father-God loved him so much as to want to adopt him, then why had this God taken Russell from him. Had God been jealous of the love Nick had for Russell? If so, then Nick wanted nothing to do with Him. He hadn't played fair.

The night before, J.D. had driven him to the mortuary for the viewing. Neither of them had wanted to go. Nick had balked at walking up to the open casket. If there was ever anything he did not want to see, it was the corpse of the first man who had loved him. He had stubbornly stared at the ceiling, the floor, the trailing flower arrangement that draped across the foot of the casket. He had studied the polished wood of the casket but had not looked upon Russell's body.

J.D. had been equally uncomfortable. They had not stayed long.

Today, the mourners would go back to the church for lunch after the graveside service, and then he and his father would go home. Strange how he longed for the day to be over and wished he was alone in his bedroom, yet he also wanted to prolong the day, put off the inevitable future, ignore that the days of hopping into Russell's truck were over.

J.D. shifted his weight from one foot to the other, stiff in his black jeans and button-down shirt. His greased hair did not move in the wind. He ran his tongue over his lips, as though thirsty for a beer, something to forget the day with.

But Nick didn't think his father would end up at the bar tonight. J.D. had seemed subdued since the whole accident. He hadn't gone to work and Nick had found his alcohol in the burn barrel behind the trailer.

Nick eased away from his father's side and back to Sara. She was weeping into her hand. Without thinking, Nick drew her close and she huddled against him.

He looked at the sky and told the Martins' Father-God what he thought of Him.

Anya woke to the sunlight and rolled over automatically for Russell's warmth.

"You'll never believe the horrible nightmare I've been having," she wanted to tell him. She wanted him to hold her, convince her that everything would be all right.

Nothing. The left side of the bed sheet felt cool. The present roared into her senses, heavy and oppressing. She moved her head onto his pillow and wept, as she had wept every morning since his death.

After the physical tears stopped, she knew she would spend the rest of her waking hours that day in a state of mental tears that would break forth into real ones at a simple mention of Russell, a smell, the sight of something in the house, a memory.

Anya had heard the cliché many times that the bereaved would expect to look up and see their loved one walk in the door simply out of habit. Now she found herself watching for Russell to pull in the driveway at certain times of the day, listening for him in the bathroom after she crawled into bed, fixing extra toast in the morning, similar to trying to push up a pair of glasses that aren't on your nose or glancing at your wrist throughout the day even though you forgot to put on your watch.

When she came home from the hospital after Russell's death four days ago, she had wandered around the house in restless disbelief, looking for something to do to keep herself busy so she would not have to think, frustrated with Nell, who dogged her steps and kept asking her if she was okay.

She had started to finish her vacuuming job, the job she had been doing when Karl had called, then she thought of the mud clods on the floor that Russell had tracked in. She could not bear to erase them from the floor. She put the vacuum away instead.

She went into the bedroom to gather laundry but ended up bringing Russell's dirty undershirt to her face and inhaling the scent of sweat. She rubbed her hands over the inside of the cloth, thinking of his skin touching it.

The kitchen had only dirty dishes to wash. That was a safe enough chore. Anya had started a sink of hot water and dropped a handful of silverware into it. She reached for the cup on the windowsill in front of her and stopped. Russell kept his drinking glass there so that he could reuse it. The sunlight shone through the glass and showed every fingerprint and even a lip print on the rim.

She had dried her hands and picked up the glass along the bottom edge. She placed her fingertips over his fingerprints, brought the cup to her mouth and let her lips touch the spot his lips had touched.

Then Anya had crumbled to the floor and cradled the cup to her chest while Nell held her.

Yet even with the awfulness of knowing he was gone, the magnitude of Russell's death had not even begun to sink in yet during those first few days. Now after she had left him buried and alone, the finality hit full force and her entire body hurt for it.

"Mom?"

Anya raised her head from her pillow and swiped at her eyes and nose.

"Mom?"

"I'm in the bedroom," she answered. She knew she looked a fright but couldn't drum up the energy to move.

Nell appeared. "Did you get any sleep?" she asked. Her face looked worn as well. She had slept in the guest bedroom each night since Russell's death so that Anya would not have to be alone.

"Some."

"Michele called and said that she needs some help with Avery this morning so I need to go home for a little while. Will you be all right or should I wait and take you with me?"

Anya tried to smile. "I'll be fine. You need to be taking care of your own family, not me."

Nell bit her lip.

"Go, don't feel guilty." Anya waved her hand.

Nell disappeared. Anya rummaged under the covers until she found Russell's undershirt. She wrapped it in her arms, close to her heart, and willed the refuge of sleep to overtake her a little longer.

Brenna swallowed as she watched her father brush her mother's hair.

"Did you need something, Brenna?" he asked.

"N...No." She didn't move.

He continued to move the brush through his wife's hair in even strokes. "You'd better get some breakfast. The school bus will be here before too long."

"I alr...ready ate."

"Good. Don't forget to say goodbye to your grandparents. They'll be on their way home by the time you get home from school." Her father reached for a barrette. He smiled at Brenna, the same tired and accepting smile he had born since her mother came home.

Her mother never looked up from the pale hands that lay motionless in her lap but at least she was up. The doctors had told them it might take several weeks before the medications made a significant improvement. Brenna figured improvement had already been made if they had allowed her mother to come home but the changes were small.

Brenna went to the kitchen and found Bradley eating his second bowl of cornflakes. She sat across from him and moved the cereal box from between them.

"Hey," he protested.

"Q...Quit hiding, Bradley."

His spoon halted halfway to his mouth and milk dripped into the bowl. "Was I hiding?"

"Yes."

He set the spoon down. "Sorry."

"Will she ever g...get better?"

Bradley's breath came out in a hard sigh. "I don't know."

"But we'll be okay, won't we?"

He gave a crooked smile. "Yeah. We will."

"Brenna? Bradley?" Their grandfather came in, tying his silk robe over his pajamas. He smoothed his gray hair. "I'm glad I didn't miss you. Have a wonderful day at school."

"Okay," Bradley said around his cereal. The older man winced.

Brenna stood and wrapped her arms around her grandfather. "G...Goodbye, Grandfather."

He patted her back twice and moved away. "Goodbye, Brenna. You take care now."

"Where's Grandmother?" asked Bradley.

"She's getting ready. She won't come out without her hair done, you know. But she did request that I relay her goodbyes."

"T...tell her bye." Brenna gave him another squeeze as the school bus honked outside.

Chapter 12

Nick leaped out of bed and grabbed the phone before it could ring twice. The last thing he needed was J.D. getting angry about being woken before nine a.m. on a Sunday morning.

"Hello... Nick?" It was Anya Martin in her new voice, the voice full of pain and hesitancy, so unlike the Anya of before.

"Yes."

"I was wondering if maybe..." Nick heard a sniff and rustle as though she wiped at her nose or eyes. "Could you go to church with me this morning? The last two Sundays, Karl and Nell took me but I told them I would be fine going alone today. But when it came right down to it, I realized that I don't want to go alone."

She paused and Nick wondered why she had chosen him.

"You don't have to if you'd rather not. I would understand."

Nick heard the loneliness in her voice. He understood loneliness even if he was four decades younger.

"I'll go," he said.

"Oh, thank you so much, Nick. I'll tell you what. Since you're doing me this favor, can I fix you lunch?"

Nick smiled. That sounded like the old Anya. "I never turn down food, Mrs. Martin."

"Let's plan on it, then. I'll come by in twenty-five minutes."

Nick hung up. Church. He had told God at the graveside service that he would not cater to Him. A God that allowed death was no God at all, Russell's death, Jesus' death, Grandma Bates' death, even the death of Mrs. Martin's joy.

He was going for her sake, he told himself, her sake and Russell's. She needed him and he would not turn his back on her. He would not treat her the way her God had.

Anya clung to Nick's arm as she stood up from the pew, her knees stiff from sitting.

Her body had aged over the past weeks, as though Russell's passing on to heaven had dragged ten or twelve years out of her.

Nick kept his elbow pointing toward her for her to hold, his head leaning inward. She recognized the mannerism for what it was. Protectiveness. As though he were somehow able to sense all the well-meaning condolences and questions that would assault her in seconds and wanted to spare her.

He was only thirteen. Yet Anya knew that Nick hurt much more than he let anyone else see and needed her even if he didn't think so.

Several ladies headed up the aisle toward her, no doubt prepared to hug and encourage her. Nick moved his foot and shifted his position. She wanted to tell him that she didn't mind the ladies, that their motives were sincere, that sometimes by allowing herself to be comforted she helped give comfort to others.

"Anya?" The voice came from behind them.

She and Nick turned as one.

Pastor Dean slipped into the empty pew behind them. "I'm glad to see you here today."

"I had some help," she responded with a nod toward Nick.

"I'm glad." Pastor Dean gave one firm jerk of his chin in a nod of approval. He spoke in his pastoral voice. "Welcome to our fellowship, Nick."

But his tone gentled when he turned back to her. "Is there anything I, or the church, can do for you, Anya? Anything at all?"

She hesitated. She had never been one to ask for help and even now with the constant influx of volunteers that offered to bring food, wash and return dishes to their rightful owners, clean her house, keep her company, whatever they could to help, she found herself unable to focus on what needed done.

Oh, she had plenty to do. The insurance company still hounded her for information on the accident, the bank needed her to come in and update paperwork, Russell's woodworking magazine subscription should be cancelled, thank you notes still waited to be written for the memorial funds given to the Gideons for Bibles. But how could anyone truly help her with those?

"There is one thing," she said.

"Name it and I'll do my best."

"I'd like to start giving piano lessons on a more regular basis but since I live out in the country, it would be nice if I could use the church's piano."

She knew that Russell had made certain that he had finances in order at all times and she would have enough to get by, but maybe the extra lessons would force her to overcome this lackadaisical numbness that kept her from wanting to accomplish anything.

"Of course,' Pastor Dean agreed. "The piano in the fellowship hall or this one in the sanctuary would both be available most times. Just let us know when."

"I'll try to slot my times so that I could give the lessons all on the same day, hopefully all in a row."

Pastor Dean twisted to look at the piano on the podium. "Naturally," he said. "Would you like for us to help you advertise, put a notice in the church bulletin?"

"I don't think that would be necessary," Anya said. "I'll let it spread word of mouth. I know from the other piano teachers that there are always new recruits. They have each had to turn several students down recently because their time is full."

Pastor Dean crinkled his brow. "How many students do you currently teach, Anya?"

"Only three. I teach my granddaughters and Brenna Williams. I really haven't taught formal lessons for years other than to family members with the exception of the Williams' girl but I suppose I'll try to get as many students as I can."

Pastor Dean pointed his thumb at Nick. "I assumed you taught this young man. I hear he has an exceptional gift."

Nick ducked his head and Anya felt his tension.

The pastor cleared his throat. "Anya, I need to ask, but tell me if this is none of my business, all right?"

She nodded, Nick's nervousness transferring to her.

"Is there, that is, do you have financial concerns? Is this why you are considering more lessons?"

"Oh, no," Anya said quickly. "Russell left things well taken care of. He was always conscientious about things like that. I'd like to give more lessons so that I can stay busy. I seem to rattle around that new house all by myself all day long."

"Might I suggest another venue? One that you could do as well as piano lessons?"

"Certainly."

"I noticed an ad in the local paper from the nursing home that they are looking for volunteers to come in and play games with or read to the residents once or twice a week. I go over there myself and enjoy morning coffee with several gentlemen. I find that I am most always given more wisdom and enjoyment than what I can offer. If you're interested, I can get you more information."

Anya took Nick's elbow with her hand again. "I'll consider it," she promised.

Nick dried off his hands as best as he could with his already damp towel.

"Where do these pans go?" he asked Anya. She stood at the sink, watching the water drain and swishing the bubbles around in a lazy circle.

Anya had fed him re-warmed casserole for lunch, with potato chips and store-bought cookies, all leftovers from the many food donations she had received. He missed her cooking.

The house felt cold and dim. She had not opened many of the blinds. He could see dust collecting in the corners of the kitchen floor. The Anya of before would have clucked at the sight and fetched a broom.

He hated seeing her so despondent, almost listless about life. He had been glad to hear her speak of her future plans with the pastor.

She looked up belatedly. "Oh, those pans? Just leave them on the counter. I can put them away later."

"It's no trouble," he said.

Not answering, Anya rinsed out her dishrag and laid it over the sink divider. She lowered herself onto her chair at the table like an old woman.

Nick hung the towel over the back of his chair and joined her at the table. He rubbed at a spot on the tabletop that he'd missed when he had wiped it off.

After church, Karl and Nell had invited them over to eat at their house and even Mitch had offered to take them out for pizza, but Anya had declined. Today, she seemed to cut herself off from her family and even though Nick sat there with her, she seemed far away.

"You have quite a bit of mail here," he commented, motioning toward the stack of envelopes on the edge of the table, against the wall.

"Yes." She cupped her hands together on the tabletop.

"Is it all cards?" The mail at home consisted of junk mail and bills addressed to his father. Just once, he would like to get a personalized card or letter, but who would ever write him?

Anya sighed. "Pretty much. I've been slitting the envelopes open to check for money or memorials so I can write thank you notes but haven't had the heart to read them all."

She tightened her fingers and her knuckles whitened. "People have so many things to say, so many stories to tell about how Russell affected them. I'm learning things about him that I never knew. But I can only read a few every day. It's too painful."

Nick estimated the stack to be nearly a foot deep. He could not remember a single card after Grandma Bates had died.

"Sometimes, the grief gets so intense, I just need to step back from it. It seems wrong to not want to grieve. I loved Russell so much and I feel unfaithful when I want to feel nothing, but I'm half afraid I'll lose my sanity if I don't distance myself."

He realized with a sudden jolt why she wanted space from her family. Her grief for Russell was strong, apparent on the lines in her face, the slow movements of her body as though she were in physical pain. Her children's faces bore that same grief. It was almost too much hurting to fit into one place.

But Nick grieved and raged and wept too. His pillow could testify to that.

Anya unbound her fingers and swiped at her eyes. "I'm sorry, Nick. Here you are, a young boy with your whole life ahead of you. You don't want to sit here and listen to an old woman ramble on about pain."

"I know about pain, too," Nick said.

Her eyes met his. "Oh, Nick. You loved him too. I'm sorry."

"He was the first man I remember ever showing me that he loved me." Nick swallowed.

Anya nodded. "He did love you. You know, he would share with me how he enjoyed all the talks you had on your trips down to Wichita. He felt honored to be able to be part of your life, Nick."

"So why did he have to die?"

Anya lowered her head. "I don't know," she whispered. "I may never know."

She clenched and unclenched her hands. "I run myself in circles asking 'Why, God, why?' and I always run right back into the same conclusion. God has no obligation to tell me why. I am only responsible for my reaction. How will I respond? What will I do now? What attitude will I take? Will I choose to be angry and bitter or will I trust God to continue working in me?"

"It's not fair!"

"No, Nick. It's not fair. But I'm still responsible for my reaction." She flattened her hands on the tabletop. "I should probably take you home, now. Your father is probably wondering where you are."

Regret filled Nick. He had burdened her with his own questions when she needed someone to help carry hers. He leaned back in his chair. Dampness from the kitchen towel he had draped there to dry seeped through the back of his shirt. "I'm sorry, Mrs. Martin. I should be able to help you more."

"That's not your responsibility, Nick." She pushed in her chair. "It was enough to have someone to sit with during church and someone to fix a meal for. I really needed that today and am so thankful that you were here."

Nick followed her outside to the car parked on the gravel in front of the garage.

"You don't have to take me," he said. "I can walk."

"Oh, I don't mind. I need to be needed."

Nick looked around at the overgrown lawn. "I need to be needed too. Why don't you let me mow your lawn?"

"Today? It's Sunday, Nick, a day of rest."

He shrugged. "Then tomorrow, after school."

"I hate to impose…"

"Russell showed me how to take care of your lawn and I want to keep it up."

Anya pushed at a clump of foxtail with her foot.

"It is kind of weedy. Would you mind spraying it as well?"

"Not at all. There are still chemicals mixed up in the hand sprayer."

"I can pay you same as Russell paid you." Anya squinted at him in the sun.

"You don't have to do that," he protested, feeling sorry for her even though he knew her words earlier that morning held truth. Russell was the sort of man who would have kept things in order financially in case of emergency. She probably needed the money less than he did.

"It's only fair, Nick. Besides, one more mowing will most likely be all the yard needs before winter sets in."

Nick smiled without humor. "I thought you said that life wasn't fair."

She gazed pensively at the wheat stubble across the road. "Yes, I guess I did."

Part 2

Chapter 13

Five Years Later

"The man took the stairs to his apartment two at a time," Anya read aloud. "His fingers fumbled with his keys. He had to get that packet in safekeeping before anyone found out he had it in his possession. He stumbled to his desk where he had left it but the packet was gone."

Anya picked up her library issued bookmark and closed the paperback novel.

"You can't stop there, dearie. We have to find out what happens next."

Anya smiled at the elderly woman sitting in the wheelchair to her right. "I have to stop, Elma. It's twelve o'clock and time for all of you to go to the dining room for your lunch."

"Oh, but you can't just leave us hanging. Give us a hint. Where did the packet go? Who has it?" The words came from the far end of the table. Fred Finley leaned forward, his age spotted hands gripping the table's edge.

"I can't do that. It would give away too much of the mystery. Besides," Anya said, "I have to make sure you all come back to hear me read next week."

"Next week. With our short term memories you should be reading to us every 10 minutes," Elma quipped. Cackles erupted around the table.

Gordon Smith's bald head jerked up from his chest. "Wha...?"

"It's all right." Elma patted the thin blanket over his leg. "You just slept through the most exciting part, that's all."

Anya watched them interact as they shuffled to their feet or carefully wheeled their chairs away from the table. Spending

time with these men and women, people she remembered
working in the community in not too many years gone by, helped
focus her mind on something other than her own loneliness.
Most of them, like she, had lost a mate. She saw the wisdom and
pain in their faces, right next to the patience and tiredness and
felt blessed to know them.

But she had not wanted to come in today. Today marked
the fifth wedding anniversary she had spent without Russell.

During those five years, Anya's acceptance of
widowhood had grown into contentment. She enjoyed her
family, her piano students, and her volunteer efforts at the
nursing home. But today, thoughts of Russell lay heavily on her
mind. She missed him, wanted to tell him how his children and
grandchildren were, wanted to share how proud she was of them
all. After so many years, she did not expect anyone else to
remember their anniversary, but it would be nice if someone
noticed and gave validity to her melancholy.

Only the night before, Nell and Karl had teased her
about a widower from church, a very nice man. She knew she
could remarry – that Russell would have wanted her to do so if it
made her happy. But the truth was, she felt no interest. She had
spent many years satisfied with being a single woman before
meeting Russell. She supposed he would be the only love of her
life.

Anya tucked the book into the bag she had stowed under
her folding chair and looped it over her shoulder. Fred wobbled
slightly and grabbed for the wall.

"Can I give you a hand, Fred?" She touched him, felt
his pointy shoulder blade.

"I never turn down offers from pretty ladies." Fred
leaned against her strength. Together they made their way to the
cafeteria. She helped Fred sit at his table and turned to go. Fred
gripped her hand. She looked at him in surprise.

"I lost my girl close to fifteen years ago," Fred said
softly. "I still reach for her every morning. End up with my

hand on the bars of my bed instead. I used to lay and cry for her. Now I lay and remember the good times we had. I look forward to waking up now. It's almost like knowing that I'll get to spend some time with her first thing every morning."

Anya bit her lip, tried to extricate her hand. The elderly often spilled over their sad stories to her, looked upon her as a friend and counselor of sorts. Most days she enjoyed sharing a burden or two but today, she couldn't muster the strength.

The old man's cloudy eyes pinned hers. "You can still cry, you know, even years afterward. Just when you think you're done grieving, it comes back. I know. But when you feel like you can remember again without the memory punching a great big deep hole into you, then you make a priority of spending time in your memories."

Fred squeezed her hand and let go. Anya gave him a wobbly smile.

"Thank you, Fred," she whispered. How had he known what she needed to hear?

Fred smiled back toothlessly as he picked up his napkin with shaky hands and tucked the corner into his front shirt collar. "Now I'd invite you to stay and share some dinner with me, but green jell-o and pureed turkey casserole probably isn't your standard fare."

Anya laughed. "I'd love to, Fred. But there's something I need to do." She thought of the cemetery and the potted mum in the front seat of her car.

"Mother, d...do you want to go on to the intersection?" Brenna spoke without turning her head, letting the Kansas wind carry the words to the woman beside her.

Brenna's mother clung to her arm as though the wind planned on ripping them apart. "I think I'm ready to turn back."

They stood at the half-mile point on the dirt road, marked only by the turn-in for tractors to go into the field to the north.   Another 200 yards and they would pass Nick Pierce's trailer house.

Brenna thought nervously of the piano duet she and Nick had been asked to perform at their high school graduation ceremony. She had protested that Sara would do the song much more justice, but since Sara was salutatorian and already giving a speech, her arguments failed to move the planning committee.

She and Nick had practiced after school nearly every day that week at Anya Martin's – Brenna on the keyboard her grandparents had bought her and Nick on Anya's piano. Anya seemed to relish the company and fed them baked sweets and lemonade just like old times.

Brenna practiced much more than usual in order to keep up with Nick even though keeping up with talent like his was pointless. The song seemed effortless to him while she struggled to play with any semblance of fluidity. She plugged a set of headphones into the keyboard so the sounds would not bother her mother.

Secretly, she was glad for the excuse to spend so much time with Nick and hoped now for a glimpse of him at his house. Maybe he was out in the yard or something.

But her mother tugged at her arm. "It's windy, Brenna. Let's go home."

"It's always windy in Kansas, Mother," Brenna wanted to say, but she didn't. Instead, she dutifully changed directions. Like Sara's horses, her mother balked the entire walk away from the house then picked up the pace as soon as they started for home.

But despite their turning around so soon, days like today were a triumph. When they had started, they had only walked to the end of the driveway and back. Even that short distance from the house had worn her mother out and made her resist the idea of another walk for several days.

"Prolonged depression can make the decision to do anything active difficult," the psychiatrist had explained. "It takes your mother much more energy than you realize just to do simple things you take for granted."

Brenna understood, or at least tried to. She gradually lengthened the walks. The exercise seemed to encourage her mother to move around the house more freely, and helped her stay in the kitchen or living room with the rest of the family rather than secluding herself away.

Brenna sighed internally. The progress seemed so victorious one day and so minute the next. She preferred to think about Nick.

She loved watching him play the piano, the way he tilted his head forward to read the music in front of him. She loved mixing her notes with his, watching his long fingers stretch and dance, wishing she knew how it felt to have those fingers hold hers.

She and Nick had always held an uncommon friendship with each other. Well, maybe not always. She remembered the awkwardness of the first years when he had moved to Western Kansas. But throughout high school, they had ridden the bus together, the only older students to use the bus system. Bradley had gotten a car from their grandparents just before leaving for college but there had been no mention of such a gift for Brenna.

On those bus rides, Brenna would sit in the straight-back green vinyl seat and steal looks at Nick. Unlike many other boys in the senior class, Nick hadn't matured much physically. Other than his height, he still looked fourteen. But his features were pleasant, his manners even pleasanter and when he played the piano, everyone stopped to listen.

She knew that the cross-country and track coaches had asked Nick to participate – on account of his physique - but he refused.

Nick had shrugged when Brenna asked if he regretted missing out. "I don't like sports. Never have," he said. "Besides, how would I get home from practice?"

However, he had not given up music or band class despite his father's blustering protests. Nick often made a point of sitting beside Brenna on the way to music contests. They would talk music the entire way, or at least Nick would talk and Brenna would listen. She was always surprised that he would openly seek her friendship in front of their classmates, not just on the bus ride home with all the little kids.

Sara sometimes teased her. "I bet you two get married someday," she would say.

And Brenna would secretly hope so even while she teased Sara right back about some boy or another. But Sara had set her sights high and no boys seemed even remotely close to her expectations. Brenna figured her friend would either marry a sold-out, all-for-Jesus missionary or remain single.

"Brenna." Her mother tugged on her arm.

Brenna halted and looked up.

"There's a strange car in the driveway."

"That's Sara. Her family got a new car last week. She said she'd stop by to show me her salutatorian speech. She w…wants me to proofread it."

"Oh," said her mother but she didn't move.

Brenna saw the uncertainty forming in her mother's eyes. "We'll go in the back door. You don't have to talk to her."

Graduation Day. After driving through the high school parking lot in a futile attempt to find a parking space, Anya settled for a spot several blocks away.

She hated parallel parking – living in a small town made the number of parallels she had made in the past ten years easy to count.

She stuffed her car keys in her purse and walked toward the gymnasium. A crowd had gathered at the doors, slowly siphoning inside. She joined the throng, nodding politely at those around her, nodding hellos to those she recognized.

Moments like these, Anya missed having Russell at her side. He had had the ability to strike up a conversation with the most unlikely people and she had always felt bolstered to be more outgoing with Russell beside her. She squeezed in through the doors and made her way to the bleachers, climbing up several stairs, her eyes searching for any familiar face with an extra seat.

Folding chairs took up the entire gym floor with a podium at the south end. People had already nearly filled the chairs and the bleachers. How could she find anyone?

"Grandma, up here!" She looked up to see Avery and Michele waving at her from nearly the top row – Avery with his crackling voice changes and Michele with the grown-up confidence that comes from earning a college degree. Those trite sayings about time flying by somehow didn't seem so trite anymore. Anya felt old when she stopped to think about her grandchildren's newfound maturity. Goodness. She felt old just thinking about climbing all those stairs with no railing to hold onto.

"Oh, for goodness sake, Annie," she scolded silently. She often used Russell's pet name when she talked to herself, a habit she had formed from living alone.

Then Avery was bounding down to her. "Grandma, Mom and Dad saved you a spot closer to the front. I'll take you to them."

She realized she had been blocking the stairway and quickly followed Avery back onto the gym floor and to Karl and Nell. Nell picked up her tailored jacket from the bleacher where she had saved a seat.

Anya settled herself next to them, wondering if she should take off her sweater. The heat index in the gym was already rising with the afternoon heat. Nell looked much cooler in a loose fitting silk shirt. Nell also wore a corsage, a gift from Sara, Nell explained with a proud smile.

Karl looked uncomfortable in his white button-down shirt and tie. He pulled at the collar and swiped at the sweat on the back of his neck. Anya couldn't help but notice the physical resemblance Karl bore to his father, especially the older he got. His neck and jaw were thickening while his hairline receded and grayed. She sometimes got lumps in her throat looking at his features.

"Should I be sitting here?" she asked Nell. "I don't want to be in the parents' section."

"You're fine, Mom," Nell reassured her. "You're not the only grandparent sitting here."

The first notes of the ever familiar "Pomp and Circumstance" prodded spectators to stand and the first robed graduates appeared, parading up the center aisle in alphabetically ordered pairs.

Anya watched the pianists instead. Nick and Brenna played the song flawlessly. Nick had made Brenna practice to the point of overdoing; he was so obsessed with perfection, but Anya had thoroughly enjoyed the late afternoon practices in her living room.

So many years had passed without her having much contact with Nick, it seemed. One of my life's regrets, she sighed. The day of his graduation had come too soon and too soon he would move off to parts unknown. Had she failed the boy by ignoring him in her own grief? Had she failed Russell? Had she failed God?

Then Sara emerged in her cap and gown, a happy bounce in her march, the classmate next to her reaching to slow her down. The girls were the last students to come in - the long stretch between Sara's "M" in Martin and the other girl's "Z" name testified of the small class size, even with the "P" in Pierce and "W" in Williams both at the pianos.

The song ended and Nick and Brenna stood at their pianos to bow. The audience clapped with enthusiasm and Anya thought of the comments locals made about the Pierce boy making it big someday – something they would brag about since he came from their little hometown. And wasn't it funny that such talent had come from J.D. Dobbs?

As for Brenna, Anya had seen a growth in maturity and confidence through her years of piano lessons and caring for her mother after school. Anya knew that Brenna would most likely go nowhere as long as she was needed at home.

Why is it, Anya mused, that folks looked at Nick's obvious talents and admired him yet they completely overlooked Brenna's selflessness?

As the two crossed in front of her to sit down with their classmates, Brenna peeked up at Nick. Something about her expression caused Anya to catch her breath with comprehension. The girl was infatuated with Nick. Anya should have figured it out before now.

"Oh, Brenna, Brenna", she told the girl in her mind, "Don't you see that he does not return your affection?" But she couldn't fret now. Sara stood at the lectern to give a student-led prayer as an opening.

Nick remained close to the wall in Sara's living room, balancing a cup of punch on his plate of hors d'oeuvres. He speared a little Smokey with a toothpick and nibbled off the end.

He supposed he hadn't had to come to Sara and Brenna's joint graduation party but he had no ties with any other classmates and couldn't even imagine his father agreeing to host such a party in his honor. And even if he had, who would they have invited?

Besides, coming here had to be better than staying home in the empty trailer. When Nick dropped off his diploma and sheet music, J.D. had not been in sight. Nick didn't even know for sure whether or not J.D. had attended the graduation. If he hadn't, it was because of his anger over Nick's piano duet. J.D. seemed to ignore all the well-wishers in the community and held fast to his idea that male pianists were nothing but sissies. It hurt, but Nick had learned long ago to stuff his feelings down.

Sara and Brenna stood beside a card table overflowing with gifts brought by the guests. Sara chattered with anyone and everyone, spreading her contagious laughter. Brenna simply smiled.

Brenna's father and brother were in the house somewhere – probably in the kitchen since Nell kept coaxing everyone to go help themselves to the mountain of food on the table. Her mother had not come to the graduation ceremony or to the party, not surprising considering that Nick only saw the woman when Brenna took her for walks.

As for himself, Nick preferred not to go into the kitchen where Anya had taken up residence plying food on everyone who entered, which was why he had taken nearly five minutes to consume his last little sausage. He knew he shouldn't avoid Anya. Last night, she had given him the title to Russell's S-10 pickup and promised to pay the insurance and taxes for the first year as a graduation gift.

"It's not exactly new and certainly has seen its fair share of miles, but it's still in good condition and I had it serviced last week for you," she told him. "I approved it with your father so as soon as you sign the title and have it notarized, it's yours."

He knew she wanted to establish a new bond between them but the gift made him want to evade her. It raised up the old guilt of abandoning her, as though watching over her should have been his responsibility after Russell's death, and the old anger that she seemed to survive and enjoy life so freely and perhaps hadn't even needed him after all. He couldn't understand her inner joy – unless it had something to do with that whole God thing.

And, he couldn't help but resent what the truck represented. Many memories of Russell came back to him as he drove his new possession – Russell helping him learn to drive, the two of them loading supplies in the back, Russell's work-worn hands on the radio knob, tuning to hear a sermon on the Christian station.

Nick had spent the first several years after Russell's death in a reeling sort of shock. If he were to admit it, Grandma Bates' death, his move from Wichita and the strained relationship with his father had much to do with his emotions as well, but he preferred to blame his resentments on God for taking the man who had promised so much to him. He had never heard much about what happened other than some accident with a tractor. He hadn't wanted to know more. If God was God, then God would have stopped it.

Nick learned stoicism as a coping mechanism. The only bump that made Nick occasionally want to break out from under his self-inflicted shield of un-emotionalism was that he knew the depth of his music suffered. Classmates and teachers raved over his ability to play the piano. But Nick knew the true extent of his capability. He knew that he always held back from letting the music's tone and emotion guide him. He played mechanically, technically perfect, afraid of where the music might take him if he gave it control.

Anya knew. She had come to the state music contest with Sara's mom. He had felt awkward, knowing that she had made a special effort to find out the program in order not to miss his performance even though she had primarily come to hear Sara sing.

After his piano solo, in which Nick earned top ratings and a round of spontaneous applause from his panel of three judges, Anya cornered him in the hall.

"You played very well, Nick," she had said, a tender sadness pulling at her mouth. "Nearly perfect in every way except for the soul. Oh, Nick, if only you would..."

She had stopped and he had hidden how deeply her words hurt him by making a joke about how a white boy couldn't play soul. He already played much better than any other musician his age. Wasn't that enough?

"Nick, I have something for you."

Nick juggled his plate and cup into one hand self-consciously as Sara's mother handed him a large beige-colored envelope.

"You don't have to give me anything."

"I know. That's why we did. Besides, Sara made the card." Nell put her arm around him and gave him a motherly squeeze.

His back felt rigid. Was he supposed to hug her back? Both hands were full. Apparently not, since Nell dropped her arm.

"Before I forget to tell you, Nick, I very much enjoyed hearing you and Brenna's duet at the program. You both did a fine job."

"Thank you."

"Oh, and make sure you find Mom before you leave. I know she didn't want to miss you."

He sipped the last of his punch so that he wouldn't have to answer, the frothy carbonated fizz collecting on his upper lip. He licked it off. Brenna shyly accepted a gift and hug from Michele, then her eyes met his briefly, as though she were keeping tabs on where he was. She smiled timidly and he nodded back.

He thought of the times he and Brenna had upheld each other, how he appreciated her friendship, yet lately it seemed she had fallen into the same mode of the rest of their classmates. She watched him as though he were some kind of hero, musical magician. Ironically, he hated her idolization even as he craved it. Her life had seemed to stabilize – he knew about the summer hiking trips she took with her father and brother and the slow progress she made with her mother – but he missed the needy Brenna. It seemed that the more her family leaned on her, the less she leaned on Nick. And Nick did not like that.

He also found himself unreasonably jealous of her close friendship with Sara, and of the time she spent with Sara's family when she went with them to church and youth group.

If Russell had not died, he might have been the adoptee into this family. Instead, it sometimes seemed that Brenna had taken his place.

"Read this brochure," Sara said, tossing it onto the bed next to where Brenna lay flopped on her stomach. "Tell me what you think."

"Serve the Lord in India," the front page read above the photo of a young girl wearing a sari and holding a Bible.

"India!" Brenna wrinkled her face. "Surely you don't want to go to India."

"I don't know where I want to go," Sara answered seriously. "All I know is that I've wanted to be a missionary for I don't know how long. Every time Aunt Kathleen comes home and tells stories about how hard and rewarding life overseas can be, I'm captivated. I really think God wants me to go somewhere."

Brenna didn't like the thought of her friend moving so far away even though she had grown accustomed to Sara's ever-growing pile of mission pamphlets and dream lists.

"Why can't you s...stay in the States?"

"I could. But I love foreign customs, cultures, learning words in other languages."

Brenna thought of the many people who stopped at the gas station beside the interstate exit. "You can see all that right here, or at least close to here in Denver or Kansas City."

Sara blew out her breath. "That doesn't sound quite as exciting, you know? I want to go somewhere where I can be immersed in the culture."

Brenna opened the flyer. "This organization wants teachers, nurses and doctors and mechanics. And they want you to commit for 3 years minimum."

"Three years," Sara echoed. "That's a long time. Besides, I'm not qualified to do any of those things, except maybe teach."

"It says y...you have to be a certified teacher with experience." Brenna handed Sara the pamphlet. Sara reluctantly threw it into the growing stack of rejections.

"I so wanted to wear a sari," she said.

Brenna giggled. "You hate wearing skirts. A s...sari would be much worse, I would think."

Sara scrunched up her face. "What about you, Brenna? What do you think you will do?"

Brenna shook her head. "I know I w...won't be going to India or Russia or anywhere like that."

"Seriously, Brenna. What do you want out of life?"

Brenna rolled over and sat up, crossing her legs underneath her. She shrugged her shoulders. "To be happy, I g...guess. Isn't that what everyone wants?"

"Partly." Sara thumbed through her stack of short-term mission applications. "But don't you want more than that? Happiness doesn't always last."

Brenna looked at her feet, letting her hair sway around her face so she could not see her friend. "I guess I w...want to b...be loved."

"Are you looking in the right place for love?"

Brenna raised her head. "Where is that?" Her heart thumped as she thought of Nick, wondering if maybe he had shared anything with Sara.

"I've told you many times, Brenna. Only Jesus can give you the perfect love you want and need."

Brenna bit her lip. Yes, Sara had shared over and over how her heart had changed because of Jesus. She had invited Brenna to church and youth group activities and prayed with her, but Brenna had never felt any different. The kids at youth group were also her classmates at school and Brenna often felt invisible at their activities with their clichés so cemented in place. The adults at church intimidated her with their over-interest and well wishes, as though they each wanted to claim her as a personal convert.

Yet she knew Sara loved Jesus. No one could stay around Sara for long and not know that something about her was drastically different and very real. But Brenna didn't know how to get to that point, even though she wanted to please Sara and be able to say she felt the same.

For a while, Brenna had thought that attending church with Sara and reading the Bible would make it happen, whatever "it" was. But after a while, she stopped. The services and scriptures only confused her. She knew her lack of interest in spiritual things hurt Sara, but didn't know what to do about it.

"You never answered my question, Brenna, about what you want to do with your life. I know you were offered scholarships from several colleges. Do you think you'll go to college?"

"No. I'm staying home."

Sara frowned. "To take care of your mom?"

Brenna studied her fingernails. "Someone needs to."

"Brenna, you can't put your life on hold for your mom. She may never get any better."

Sara's words stung, but Brenna knew that Sara was the only person who could tell her such a thing without her taking offense. She met Sara's eyes, wanting her friend to understand.

"You want to travel the world, Sara. You want to serve other people in far away places. You've told me that it's like a b...burning inside you, s...something you just know you are supposed to do, you have to do. I f...feel that way about taking care of my mom."

Sara smoothed a glossy brochure over her knee without speaking.

"One d...doesn't have to go far away to help others."

Sara bit her lip and spoke after a long moment. "I'm sorry, Brenna. I shouldn't downplay what you're doing. It's noble of you – and admirable, and sacrificial. It makes me feel like I'm only doing what I'm doing for the adventure and excitement of it."

"Oh, Sara, anyone who knows you, knows that you're d...doing this because you love Jesus."

A troubled look appeared on Sara's face. "I hope that's true. But here I am, supposed to be a Christian example at all times and my non-Christian friend outshines me."

Brenna laughed. "Hardly." The thought of herself, little hide-in-a-hole Brenna outshining such a vividly joyful person as Sara seemed ludicrous. She changed the subject. "Here. Hand m...me that application over there, the one about needing orphanage workers in Eastern Europe. That might be just what you're looking for."

Chapter 14

Mitch wished for the hundredth time that he'd taken time to fix the radio. Spraying could be monotonous enough with entertainment. Without, it was sheer boredom. When his older brother Karl had asked him to help with spraying, he had groaned but with only a few vehicles to repair in his shop, simple repairs at that, how could he say no?

The spray coupe bounced and wobbled over the uneven ground. Mitch leaned forward to eye the sky. Clouds had gathered to the north, forming stark white thunderheads that ballooned in size and height. Now the clouds had begun to darken ominously. He wished again that he had a radio, wondering what Doppler radar showed.

Mitch glanced around the field. "Only another hour and I can finish," he told himself. Surely, the storm would stay north. He made several more loops around the field, continually glancing at the sky. He wished he had a cell phone to call Karl. Was this a spray that needed water to soak in or would rain simply wash away his efforts? He wished he had paid more attention to farming details.

The wind abruptly picked up in speed, buffeting the sprayer and sending the fertilizer spattering to the side, missing where he wanted it to go. There was no sense continuing. A storm was imminent. He felt irritated at himself, knowing he should have stopped earlier.

Mitch turned off the spray nozzles and drove over to the edge of the field where his motorcycle waited for him.

The air whipping his tee shirt felt surprisingly cool after a series of rising temperatures that promised a hot summer ahead. He reached up with his left hand to lower the bill of his cap and twisted the throttle with his right as he swung out onto the sandy road.

Dark clouds screened the sunshine, creating a pseudo-dusk so Mitch switched on his headlight. Clouds swirled and churned closer overhead. When the rain hit, it felt as though a bucket of cold water had been dumped over his head. Water fell from the sky as though from spigots rather than individual drops. Within a short moment, visibility became dangerously poor.

Puddles appeared in the packed tracks on the road and splashed up on Mitch's work boots. He swerved slightly to drive on the shoulder but the sand was too deep. Peering out from under his cap, he tried to see ahead as he raced down the road. Rain dripped steadily off his cap brim, further hampering his efforts to see. He was less than four miles from the farm shop - his stepmother's house less than two, yet continuing on was crazy. Maybe he should stop at J.D. and Nick's. Even though he couldn't see their tree row through the driving rain, he knew it must be close. He wouldn't be stranded long. Hard rains like this usually came and went quickly.

"God, keep me safe," he prayed silently.

The shadowed shape of a car loomed up behind him. He felt it more than saw it. Mitch yanked the handlebars sharply. The bike slipped on the sandy shoulder and spilled him into a cold puddle at the bottom of the ditch.

He scrambled to stand, suddenly aware that the slickness underneath him was not just mud. What looked like stacks of papers lay in the tall grasses flattened southward by the water and mud. He scraped the mud off of a paper, revealing the title of a girlie magazine and the nude photo of a woman standing in a seductive pose. Someone had dumped his trash in the ditch, that someone most likely J.D. considering that he lived the closest to here. Thinking of his nephew Avery possibly being exposed to this stash filled Mitch with anger.

"Are y…you all right?" An anxious voice hollered to him over the wind.

Mitch squinted under the rivulets of water running off his cap. A woman, girl really, half hidden by slashing lines of rain, stood beside the car, holding onto the open door. He didn't answer her, just grunted as he tried to lift the bike up; afraid she may come to him and think the magazine belonged to him. Mitch swiped at the mud and grass to cover the offensive picture. He set the bike upright. He'd have to check it over for damages once the rain stopped.

"A...Are you h...hurt?"

The stutter made him look at her – the rain glistening on her perfect face, the wet molding her shirt to her upper body, the splashes of rain across her pant legs, very shapely legs. He forced himself to look back at her face.

"Brenna? Brenna Williams?"

She nodded, nervously pushing sodden hair out of her eyes. "I...I'm so s...sorry. I d...didn't mean to, that is, I didn't s...see you..."

"It's okay," he told her. "It's hard to see out here in this rain, especially just a dirt bike."

"A...Are you okay, then?"

"I'm fine. Didn't hurt a bit," he lied, although his tailbone felt a little bruised and his pride very much so.

"Can I t...take you h...home?"

He looked at his muddy jeans. "I can't get in your car like this."

She shook her head. "You c...can't stay out in this. The radio s...said possible funnel clouds."

"I've lived in Kansas all my life and never seen a tornado. We only get a bad rap because of Dorothy."

"Just get in. I'll take you wh...where you need to go."

He looked at her with surprise. For such a timid thing, she could boss him around. He wouldn't have expected it. "Let me get my bike on higher ground first," he said.

She got back in the car as he swung his leg over the seat and stepped down on the kick-start. The motor would not turn over. He smelled the fumes that told him the bike had flooded when it tipped over. It was a good thing that Brenna had offered him a ride or he'd be hoofing it. He pushed the motorcycle up out of the ditch and leaned it against a telephone pole then ran back through the muddy ditch to join Brenna.

As soon as he shut the car door, he felt the intimacy of the interior, steamy from their wet clothing and closeness. He shifted awkwardly in his seat.

Her hands shook as she pulled the car into drive. Apparently she felt the tension as well.

"I h…hate driving in the m…mud," she confessed.

So much for her feeling the same way. He had to look straight ahead so as not to let his eyes linger on the shape of her body that would not have shown so apparently had she not been wet.

"Get a grip, Mitch," he told himself. Twenty-five years old and single, Mitch practiced reigning in the physical desires of his body and imagination as a way of life. Maybe her figure was quite attractive. Maybe he hadn't been alone with a female in the confines of a car for a long time. Maybe the image of the woman on the front of the magazine had affected him. But Mitch couldn't dare let a few minutes with this teenager destroy years of careful discipline.

"You're doing fine," he told her. "This car does a nice job in the mud. Is it a front wheel drive?"

She looked baffled, then flushed red. "I d…don't know. It's my p…parents' car."

He winced inwardly. He hadn't meant to embarrass her. How many teenage girls knew the difference, anyway? He shouldn't have asked.

He listened to the windshield wipers flopping across the glass before braving more conversation. "You've really grown up since the last time I talked to you. Remember the time we had brown cows at Karl and Nell's?"

She tightened her fingers on the wheel as the tires hit a mud puddle and brown water splashed over his window and part of the windshield. "I remember."

"You look a lot like your mom." Maybe he shouldn't have said that. Even if Mrs. Williams was a pretty woman, everyone knew of her struggle with depression. What if Brenna took offense at the likeness?

But Brenna smiled slightly. "Where should I t...take you?"

Mitch felt awkward. "I was heading to the farm shop – you know, the buildings right behind Sara's house, but that's several more miles and I hate to make you drive any farther than you need to. Really, you can just drop me off at my mom's house."

She seemed to stiffen but nodded. "All r...right."

The noise of raindrops on the car roof eased and Brenna turned the wipers to a slower setting. Mitch had been right about the rain not lasting long. The sun began to win out over the clouds, casting an eerie orangish-green glow over everything.

Mitch seized another opportunity to get her to talk. "You were in the same class as Nick and my niece Sara, weren't you?" Maybe calling Sara his niece out loud would help him remember Brenna's age.

Brenna nodded and pulled into Anya's driveway and turned off the ignition. She looked at him shyly. He wondered why she had turned the car off.

"Thanks for the ride, Brenna Williams," he said, holding his hand out to her. "And thanks for not running me over and leaving me in the rain."

She took his hand after a hesitation. Her skin felt cold. "Y...You're w...welcome."

He enjoyed the sight of her wet hair and large brown eyes for a second longer before releasing her hand and jumping out of the car.

At Anya's door, he turned back to wave and nearly hit her with his hand. She had followed him up the walk.

"Aaah! You scared me!"

She backed up several steps. "I'm s…sorry."

He felt instant regret. "No, I'm sorry. I didn't realize you were behind me."

She joined him under the shelter of the porch roof and he noticed her bag of piano books.

"I take it this is where you were already coming."

She nodded.

Then Anya was opening the door and ushering them in, clucking over the story of their near collision and wet condition and heating water for hot tea even though it was the beginning of June.

Brenna seemed nervous and Mitch saw his mother watching him closely, so at the earliest opportunity he excused himself to the basement where he found a dry shirt and pants in his little brother Seth's old closet and turned up the television set to drown out the sounds of Brenna's piano lesson.

J.D. worked late again. At least, that was his excuse. Nick knew his father would stagger in around midnight, drunk as a cat on catnip.

Nick didn't mind. He much preferred to be at home alone. He emptied the bills from his pockets, payment for mowing lawns for Mr. Cobb's Lawn Care. Thirty dollars. Not much, but at least something. He added the bills to the empty bleach bottle he kept under the bathroom sink. The money was safe there. J.D. had never made any effort to clean the toilet in the six years Nick had lived with him. Chances were good that he would never be compelled to pull out the bleach.

"It's only seasonal work," Mr. Cobb had warned. "I can't keep you on past August."

But Nick was glad for any job, and for the S-10 pickup to take him there.

Nick went to the kitchen. His mouth felt dry. He wanted something cold to drink but the only thing in the refrigerator was beer and Nick knew better than to touch J.D.'s stash. He settled for a glass of water.

There wasn't much to eat either. He would need to use his own earnings for groceries. Again. Which meant he probably should take today's money right back out of the bleach bottle. At this rate, he would never be able to afford going off to school, scholarships or no scholarships. If only he were as good at academics or sports as he was at music. Then maybe he could have gotten a full ride scholarship.

Nick's stomach growled hungrily and he opened the cupboard resignedly. To his shock, the nearly bare shelves had been stocked with layers of canned goods – all kinds of vegetables, soups and fruit stacked neatly with their labels toward the front.

He opened the next cupboard. Cereal boxes, crackers and snack foods filled the space.

The refrigerator had been visited as well. J.D.'s beer cases had been pushed aside to make room for milk, fresh fruit, vegetables, cheeses, bread, butter and eggs.

Anya Martin. It had to be her. Just last week she had told him he was too skinny. Part of him wanted to go to her and thank her. Part of him wanted to box up the food and return it. She couldn't keep giving him so much.

His stomach won out so he made himself a deluxe sandwich with two kinds of deli meat and lettuce and cheese from the newly stocked refrigerator. As he washed down the last bite with cold milk, Nick noticed one more change – a beige envelope propped against the toaster.

He slit the envelope open with his index finger. Inside, he found a church bulletin announcing a special guest the following Sunday – a Christian singer and songwriter that he'd never heard of. Probably some amateur. With the references to the guest's piano accomplishments, Anya had clearly banked on Nick finding the envelope before J.D.

Was Anya bribing him with all this food to get him to church? He shook his head at his cynicism. More likely, Anya had brought the invitation, seen the empty cupboards and subsequently visited the grocery store. Wasn't that Anya's personal mission – to feed anyone she could? At least, it had been when he'd first moved to Western Kansas.

He grabbed a handful of cream filled cookies and carried them to the living room. Nick ate while he flipped channels. Commercials flashed by in succession, intermingled with the canned laughter of sitcoms. Nothing on TV interested him. But the ever-welcoming stash of magazines in father's bedroom did, one series of photos in particular. Photos of two men together.

Nick hated himself for becoming such a slave to his body, but the desire was strong. He snuck down the hall, his adrenaline pumping as he listened for the sound of his father's truck in the drive, his signal to rush into his bedroom and pretend to be asleep as the images reviewed themselves and seared into his mind.

Brenna carefully affixed postage stamps to the right-hand corners of the envelopes before dropping them in the out-of-town mail slot. Her father routinely signed blank checks in order for her to pay bills each month. He hated paperwork of any kind and was more than glad to leave it up to Brenna.

"Hello, Brenna Williams."

She knew the voice before she looked up.

"H…Hello, M…Mitch." She could feel her face heating up with the dreaded blush. Being with him in the car the other day had shaken her. She remembered the child-sized crush she had nursed for him in junior high and was surprised to feel attraction still. She had cared for Nick so long, she just assumed that feelings like this would always be for Nick now.

"Busy doing errands?" The scent of motor oil and grease from his clothing dominated the small lobby of the post office.

She nodded as she gathered up her purse and leftover stamps. "S…Something like that."

He held the door open for her. "I was next door in the auto parts store and saw your car parked in front of the post office. Thought I'd stop by and see if you had a little time for a bite of lunch."

She looked at him, startled.

"Maybe go to the café here on Main Street for a sandwich and cup of coffee."

"I d…don't drink c…coffee," she said lamely, hating her stuttering.

"A soda, then. After all, I owe you for giving me a ride the other day."

"I n…nearly ran you over," she protested. "That makes us even."

Mitch followed her out the door, his disappointment evident.

"I couldn't anyway," she hurried to explain. "I…I have cold groceries in the c…car and I need to get them h…home before everything melts into soup."

"Oh." His face cleared. "Maybe some other time?"

"Maybe."

He opened the car door for her. Goodness, she thought to herself, two doors in less than five minutes. She ought to start feeling like royalty.

"How about Saturday?"

Brenna's mind went blank. "Saturday?"

"Would you like to go out to dinner on Saturday?"

Brenna froze. Was he asking her out? How old was he anyway? She remembered him seeming like a man already when she was just a kid visiting Sara's house.

He seemed to read her mind. "I know I'm a bit older than you. But I'd like to get to know you better, Brenna Williams."

"How old are you?" she dared to ask.

"I'm twenty-five. And I'm guessing you're seventeen, eighteen?"

She nodded.

"Seems like a lot to you, huh?"

"N...Not for friends," she said. "I think of your m...mom as my friend and she's in her sixties."

"Good point." Mitch crossed his arms over the top of the car door. "Would you like to be friends?"

"I would," she said, before her shyness had time to assert itself.

"So what about Saturday?"

"I d...don't know." She couldn't keep her eyes off his muscular arms, streaked with grease.

"Okay. How about Sunday instead? We could meet after church. Where do you attend?"

She looked down. "N...Nowhere, actually."

"I just assumed..." He stopped. "I'm sorry. How about if I pick you up and take you to church? We can sit with my mom if you like."

Brenna heard the subtle change in his voice. She knew from going to youth group with Sara that most Christians stayed in a tight circle, knew that non-Christians were considered part of the "world" and were a project to proselytize, certainly not date. She tossed her purse into the car.

"No thanks. I...I'd better go. It was nice talking to you, Mitch."

He lifted his arms from the door and backed up a step. "Yeah. Take care, Brenna Williams."

"Brenna, wake up. The phone is for you."

Brenna rolled over and groggily took the cordless receiver from her father. "Hello?"

"Hey Brenna? This is Nick."

Brenna held the phone to her ear and sat up in bed. "Good morning, Nick," she said, trying to sound awake.

Her father backed out.

"Listen, Brenna? There's this pianist that's supposed to be playing at Anya's church this morning and um... well, I thought I'd go but I didn't want to go alone. I was wondering if you'd like to go with me."

Brenna groaned inwardly. What did that say about her when the closest thing she could get to a date was an invitation to church – two invitations to the same service no less?

"Brenna? Are you there?"

"Yes, I'm here."

"I woke you, didn't I?"

She rubbed her face with her hand and did not answer. Nick laughed. Brenna pressed the phone closer to her ear, feeling pleasure in her stomach at the sound.

"So will you go?"

How could she tell him no? "Of c...course."

"Good." He sounded pleased. "I'll pick you up in 20 minutes."

"Twenty minutes?" Brenna threw back the covers and stood in panic. "What time is it?"

"It's a quarter after eight."

She checked the alarm clock beside her bed. "Why so early? Church starts around ten, doesn't it?"

He paused. "I want to be gone before my dad wakes up. I figured we could go to the park or something to kill time."

The park alone with Nick – she was glad she had said yes. "I'll be ready," she said.

Despite her promise, Brenna had not finished her makeup when she heard the doorbell. She hurriedly dashed eye shadow on her eyelids and went to meet Nick.

He stood in the foyer talking with her father, his posture rigid. She had noticed that Nick often showed discomfort when talking with other boys or men. He seemed at ease with her and Sara.

"It probably has to do with his dad," she thought to herself as she approached them. "J.D. scares me too."

Her father frowned when he saw her. "You're all dressed up."

"We're going to church, Dad."

He looked at his watch. "Church must be starting earlier these days than it did when I was little."

Her eyes widened. She had not known her father to ever have entered a church, save for his own wedding.

But her father shrugged. "Whatever. Get going. Have fun or whatever it is you do when you're at church. I guess I'll cover things this morning."

Guilt gnawed at her insides. She had totally forgotten about her mother. "D…Do you want me to stay?"

Nick backed up to where Brenna's father could not see him and shook his head at her, motioning impatiently to the door.

"Go on ahead. You need your time too." Her father sounded weary. She knew he had worked late the night before cutting alfalfa.

"If you're sure." She hesitantly followed Nick, turning to blow her father a kiss. He frowned with embarrassment as he always did when she showed him affection.

At the small city park, Nick and Brenna walked along the creek under the tall gnarly cottonwood trees. The wind tousled the crisp cottonwood leaves, making sounds of waterfalls and whitewater rapids despite the dry creek bottom that only filled up after an infrequent torrential rainfall – like the one the other day when she had nearly mowed down Mitch. But she couldn't think of Mitch now.

Other than warning her not to step in a patch of poison ivy, Nick did not speak. Brenna, used to his moods, kept silent as well. She found herself daydreaming that Nick was trying to build up courage to tell her how much he loved her and that he would take her hand in his as they walked side by side.

She quickly uncrossed her arms, letting her hands swing free, just in case. Nick bent over to pick up a piece of cotton that had burst from the cottonwood seed before floating to the ground. He fondled it and let the wind pick it out of his fingers. Brenna wondered if she should try to say something witty, something to draw him out and take notice of her.

"So h...have you decided what you will do this fall?" she asked.

"No."

"You'll probably go off and become some famous musician."

Nick tossed her an irritated look. "I'm not a god, Brenna."

"You'll be flying from stage to stage someday and forget all about me." She stopped. "Will you? Forget about me?"

"Maybe."

"Maybe?" Her face flamed in embarrassment when she realized how plaintive she sounded.

"I meant maybe about the stage part, not about forgetting you. You're the only friend I have."

"Am I more than a friend?"

Nick jerked away from her. "Brenna, don't." He sounded strangled. "I can't..."

She was exposed. He had seen how she felt – and rejected her. Brenna folded her arms protectively around herself and walked away from him, away from the trees. He did not follow.

She went to the playground equipment, new plastic equipment that the city had just installed last summer. Sitting down on a swing, she kept her feet on the gravel and swung back and forth slightly, letting the wind dry her tears so Nick would not see her wipe her face, would not see her shame.

The church bells on Main Street rang out and she wondered how much time she had before they had to leave for the service.

"Hi." Nick sounded subdued as he came up from behind and sat in the swing next to her.

"Hi." At least her voice sounded normal.

"Brenna, about…"

"What time is it?" she interrupted.

He didn't answer. She could feel his eyes on the side of her face. To her horror, he rummaged in his pocket and handed her a rumpled tissue.

"Your makeup," he explained.

Brenna scrubbed under her eyes, ashamed by the amount of mascara smearing the tissue.

"Brenna, I have something I want to tell you. Something that I've wanted to tell you for a long time now but never knew how to bring up."

Nick scuffed his feet in the gravel. "This isn't easy. I had no idea that you felt about me the way you do. If I'd realized sooner I would have told you sooner."

Brenna steeled herself. Whatever he was going to say couldn't be good.

"The truth is, Brenna, I could never like you back – at least not like that. I've never been attracted to girls. I don't know what's wrong with me, or if there is anything wrong with me. Maybe it's the way I was born because I've always felt different. It's like I can't relate to other guys, yet I find them, well, attractive."

The air sucked out of Brenna's stomach, and if she was surprised, it was surprise at herself for not being surprised at his statement. She had known the truth deep inside, even though she had persisted in her silly romantic dreams. Her times with Nick had given her a chance to pretend, but now her foolishness stood out in the open. She risked a glance. Nick stared straight ahead.

"I've tried to overcome these feelings," Nick went on. "I wanted to like girls. I even tried to imagine myself dating someone like Sara or you but I just couldn't."

Nick let go of the swing chains and rubbed the jagged scar on his hand nervously. "I guess what I'm trying to say is, I think I'm gay."

The word hung between them; it couldn't be retracted. Brenna finally looked at Nick. "You can't be," she whispered.

"Why not?" His brows came together in quick anger.

She had no answer.

He blew out his breath forcefully. "Look, I don't expect you to understand. I don't understand it either. It's just, me, you know? I guess if you don't like the truth about me then the truth is maybe you never liked me at all because I've been this way the whole time you knew me."

"Nick." She started to protest but closed her mouth. He was right. He had withheld this part of himself from her, from everyone, but that did not negate the fact that it was a part of him. And he was right that she could not reject this part of him without rejecting all of him.

They sat in silence.

Nick looked at his watch. "We'd better go now."

She stood and walked with him to the Chevy S-10. What little dignity she had left kept her back straight.

They arrived at the church on time according to the clock on the dashboard. Brenna always felt awkward going in to church when she came with Sara, as though she did not belong. She felt even more so now with Nick. She made certain that she walked far enough away from him so that no one would mistake them for a couple. Maybe she could find Sara and sit with her. She needed distance from Nick in order to process what he had told her.

"Nick, Brenna, how lovely to see you both here." Anya came up between them, putting a hand on each of their shoulders.

"You shouldn't be surprised," Nick said caustically.

Anya looked hurt. "I invited you because I thought you would enjoy the special music today."

"And the groceries? What was that about?"

Anya's hands dropped. "To be honest, Nick, the cashier at the grocery store mentioned that you always buy the groceries. I figured I'd help you out with college savings."

Brenna looked from one to the other. She had no idea what they were talking about but she did know Nick was taking out his anger on Anya. "M...Maybe we should s...sit d...down," she suggested.

She found herself leading the way into the sanctuary and picking a pew toward the back, leaving a space for Sara. Sara would surely rescue her. Nick sat stiffly on her other side, with Anya to his left.

Brenna searched the sanctuary but she did not see any of Sara's family. Maybe they had gone on a trip or something. She couldn't imagine them ever missing a Sunday - and of all Sundays for them to miss!

The music began and the congregation stood. At the leader's request, Brenna picked up a hymnal and turned to the correct page. Anya already shared her hymnal with the woman on the opposite side of her and Nick stood empty handed. Brenna swallowed nervously, unsure of whether or not to offer sharing. Nick seemed to sense her dilemma and turned his body slightly away from her, sending a clear signal of no.

Brenna brought the hymnal close to her face as though she couldn't see the words clearly. She mouthed the words; unable to sing for fear Nick might hear her.

After the third verse, she glanced sideways to see Mitch start down the aisle and do a double take when he saw her. He smiled and to her dismay, headed back to slip in beside her.

"Hey, Brenna Williams," he whispered, his breath hot on her ear. "You decided to come after all. I'm glad."

"Oh no," she thought frantically. "He thinks I came because of his invitation."

Mitch boldly took a corner of the hymnal from her and began to sing without reserve. Nick craned his neck to peer around her at the newcomer.

When the guest musician stood to speak, Brenna found it hard to pay attention, squashed in between Nick and Mitch. Mitch sprawled out his legs comfortably while Nick crossed one knee over the other, careful not to instigate any body contact.

Mitch raised his eyebrows at her when Nick wasn't looking and made a tiny flopping motion with his hand that indicated he had noticed the feminine manner in which Nick sat. Brenna pressed her lips together and stared at her lap in silent anger – anger at Mitch for making subtle fun of Nick, and anger at herself for ignoring what she had instinctively known and ignored.

Nick was different. He always had been. Nick never felt comfortable with the guys at school. He had picked the obvious for friendship – a female. Not only that, but a reject female, someone who would take in his friendship like a starved puppy. She felt ashamed.

Her head jerked up when the speaker's words suddenly sounded like megaphones in her ears.

"I wanted love so desperately. I tried to earn my parents' love by being perfect. I thought if I ever failed at anything, they would stop loving me. I went from boyfriend to boyfriend for love. When that didn't work, I thought that maybe having a baby would. I'd have a sweet precious little somebody who would always love me. Instead, I had a child who was diagnosed with autism, a child who could not even handle my touches of affection."

"I finally came to the point where I sank into the arms of Jesus and asked him to love me. And to my amazement, He did."

The woman went to the church piano but Brenna did not pay attention to the music. A semi-conscious side of her knew that the woman played with great skill since Nick leaned forward to listen but the woman's testimony kept repeating in Brenna's mind.

"I wanted love desperately... I sank into the arms of Jesus and asked Him to love me. And He did."

Brenna found herself fighting tears, clenching her hands in her lap. She wanted the same thing – love. She had even told Sara so. But what if her sudden desire for spiritual things was only an attempt to assuage the hurt Nick had dealt her? What if looking for love from Jesus would just be one more attempt in a line of attempts that had started with her mother? Sara had told her she could find love in Jesus, but Brenna wanted a tangible love instead. This woman said the tangible loves would fail her. She needed something supernatural. She needed Jesus.

It made sense.

"Jesus," she whispered in her mind, "can you love me?"

She cowered at her boldness. If her mother couldn't love her, if Nick didn't, why would God want her? Didn't God choose people who were like Sara – joyful, exuberant, and stable? Brenna was just a candidate for severe depression.

Wetness perched on the lower rims of her eyes. She closed them to hold the moisture in. She didn't need Nick to see her cry a second time today. She had to choose now. Would she believe everything Sara had taught her about Jesus, or would she continue muddling around after love?

"I'm trusting you, God," she thought. "I'm trusting what Sara has told me – that You can love me."

She kept her eyes closed. She listened and heard nothing. But Sara said it was that way sometimes. If God always spoke, you wouldn't need faith.

"Can you forgive me for not coming to You sooner?" She trembled. She had done many things she shouldn't have, thought many thoughts she shouldn't have. "Can you forgive me for everything?"

Instantly, Brenna felt different, as though she were wrapped in a cozy blanket and standing on a precipice in icy wind at the same time.

Brenna opened her eyes and saw the sanctuary with a surprised feeling – as though the room had somehow changed while her eyes were closed. Nick and Mitch still sat on either side of her and the guest still played the piano.

Then she realized that Pastor Dean stood at the podium. "I'd like to give an altar call this morning to those of you who may want to confess a new faith in Jesus by your action of raising your hand so that we can pray with you and disciple you in a new way of life."

Fear snaked through her body. She couldn't dare, wouldn't dare draw attention to herself, especially with Nick beside her. The coldness of the wind at the precipice hurt her lungs. The warmth of the blanket faded. Could she jump?

She chanced a look around. The congregation sat quietly with bowed heads and closed eyes, even Nick. Almost before she became aware of making a decision to do so, her hand slipped into the air. Mitch apparently felt the movement for he opened his eyes.

She lowered her hand slowly.

Mitch wrapped his arm around Brenna's shoulders and pulled her against him in a half hug. "Praise the Lord," he murmured.

People began to stir about, indicating the end of the service. Nick started at the sight of Mitch's arm around Brenna and frowned.

"Do you want to talk to someone about your decision?" Mitch asked.

She hesitated. She didn't want to make a big deal out of it but she also remembered Sara saying the importance of not hiding faith.

"Would you be willing to tell Mom?"

Brenna peeked at Anya, who watched them with wary curiosity and concern. She nodded.

Mitch led her out into the aisle and motioned for Anya to join them. "Mom, Brenna has something she'd like to tell you," he encouraged.

Brenna bit her lip. "I r...raised my hand," she whispered.

"You mean..."

"Yes. I want Jesus to be my Savior." She knew it sounded cliché but there were no other words for it.

Anya opened her arms to the girl. "Oh, Brenna. I have prayed for you for so long. You couldn't tell me anything else that I'd want to hear more."

To her surprise and consternation, Brenna began to cry as soon as her face fell against Anya's shoulder.

"I'm not even s...sad. I don't know why I'm crying," she sobbed. "I just feel so..."

"I know, child. I know. That's the Holy Presence of God you're feeling right now. You just enjoy it."

Pastor Dean approached and prayed over her and a circle of churchgoers gathered around her, all eager to welcome her as the news of her conversion spread around the room. Brenna felt embarrassed by the attention, and overwhelmed with a sense of belonging in this place.

Then Nick stood beside her. "I'm leaving," he said, his face set and hard. For the first time, Brenna recognized J.D.'s features in Nick's face.

"Oh, Nick, I wish you could..."

"No." The word came out vehemently. He lowered his voice. "Look, I have to go. Just find another ride home, okay?" Nick stepped backward, bumping into the pastor.

"Excuse me." Pastor Dean quickly moved out of the way.

Brenna watched him go. Mitch stepped forward as though to follow Nick but Anya shook her head.

"Do you have to be home anytime soon, Brenna?" Anya asked.

"I p...probably shouldn't be too late."

"Can you come over for lunch? I would like to visit with you more in depth about the decision you just made. We can stop by your house first to check with your parents."

Mitch backed up. "I guess I'll get going," he said.

Brenna watched him go.

"All right," she told Anya.

Anya and Brenna pushed aside their plates after finishing the omelets they had prepared together "with all the fixings". Anya felt embarrassed to serve eggs to her guest for Sunday dinner but she just didn't keep that much food in the house anymore with only herself to feed.

Her mother radar had warned her of Mitch's desire to come over for dinner along with Brenna, but Anya knew it wasn't wise. Mitch was by nature a fixer, and Brenna needed to learn to trust God, not people.

Brenna fiddled with her spoon, laying it sideways then flipping it over. "So the next step would be baptism?"

"Yes."

"I still don't understand why. It seems like a strange tradition."

"My parents explained it to me long ago as being like taking a new sponge out of the package and getting it wet. The water changes the appearance of the sponge forever from thin and hard to soft and useful. You come out of the baptismal waters as a transformed creation, ready for God's use and cleansed from sin."

Brenna tapped the spoon lightly, thinking. "It sounds embarrassing – in f...front of all those people."

"Being a Christian is something you can't hide, Brenna," Anya told her. "If you're nervous, think of it like a wedding. Do the bride and groom ever seem to pay attention to the audience?"

"No, they only watch each other."

"Precisely," said Anya. "And your baptism will feel much the same way – just you and God. But don't forget all the other things I told you as well, Brenna. You need to read your Bible, pray and spend time with other believers."

Brenna rested her arms on the table. "Those are all the things that I tried when Sara wanted me to and they did nothing for me."

"They don't save you. But a Christian trying to live without them is like a man choosing to never eat. You will find, Brenna, that those things will feed your soul and keep you close to God. Sometimes it's hard when we can't see God. Sometimes it's hard when we don't understand why some things happen the way they do." Anya thought of her husband's grave. "You will need to have an intimacy with God that no circumstance or tragedy here on earth can break."

"Like you?"

"No, like Jesus."

"But I don't know as much about Him as I do about you."

"That's why you need to read your Bible, Brenna, dear."

Chapter 15

Nick unhitched the company trailer from his S-10 just as his boss Mr. Cobb came out of the office. It had taken many times of practice for Nick to get accustomed to pulling the trailer, especially backing up. He still didn't like driving the riding lawn mower up and down the ramp into the trailer. He always felt nervous about tipping. He was glad to have the trailer backed into position before Mr. Cobb was there to watch him.

"Nick, come over here a minute, will you?" Mr. Cobb stood in the doorway. Another man was with him.

Nick obeyed, wishing he could pocket the straight earnings currently in his pocket for mowing. If only he owned a mower, even a push mower, he could earn more by running his own lawn service. But he handed over the money without comment, knowing Mr. Cobb paid him fairly.

"Nick, I'd like you to meet Les Howland, a landscaper from the Wichita area. He brought up a load of sod earlier this afternoon for the Downing place."

"Hello, Nick." Les took off his leather work glove and held out his hand.

Nick appraised the man. Something about him seemed familiar.

"Nick, I'd like you to go help him lay sod this evening."

Nick had already put in a full day of mowing but Mr. Cobb knew he would always work overtime for the extra pay.

"Are you ready to go now, or do you need a break first?" Les Howland said.

"Now is fine." Nick knew that the longer they waited to start, the longer it would be before he got home for any supper.

"Do you need to notify your parents that you'll be late?"

"No." As long as Nick kept out of his father's way, J.D. never commented on Nick's schedule. J.D. probably didn't even know Nick had a job. If he had, he most likely would have asked for money.

"All right then, let's go." Les slapped one glove against the other and started for his vehicle.

The gesture told Nick why Les seemed familiar. The man looked like a younger Russell Martin. Nick studied Les as he climbed into the passenger side. Les's build and coloring were similar to Russell's but even more than that, the way he walked, held his head and the way his eyes crinkled at the corners.

Les turned on the ignition. "Better buckle up," he advised.

Nick scurried to obey, impressed by the man's concern for his safety. Russell had always shown solicitude like that. As had Anya. Nick scolded himself. Why did he even want to think of the Martin family? Now that they had established Brenna as one of them, he was probably forgotten. They had their little convert. Now they could sit back and pat their backs.

After finishing a good portion of the Downing's new lawn, Nick's arms ached from laying heavy rolls of sod. He stood and stretched his back, squinting in the harsh glare of the sun's setting angle.

"Tired?" Les asked.

"I'm okay."

"Well, I'm tired. I've got some food packed in a cooler in the truck if you'd like to join me," Les offered.

Again, the man reminded him of Russell. Nick knew the man probably hadn't counted on company when he had packed his meal, but Les handed him one of the sandwiches and let him choose between the granola bar and apple.

Les bowed his head and prayed a brief silent prayer before biting into his sandwich.

Nick could not resist asking. "Are you a Christian, Mr. Howland?"

"Call me Les," the man answered. "And yes, I am. How about you, Nick?"

"I believe in God," Nick hedged.

"There's a difference between just believing in God and being a Christian."

Nick tore open the granola bar wrapper. He knew what Les said to be true when he compared Anya and Sara's lives to his own – and now Brenna's. He felt jealous of all the attention Brenna had received at church. If those loving church members had known what he had told her at the park only hours before, they would have chased him out of the building.

He half wished he had pretended for Brenna's sake to care about her. If he had, he supposed they would have done more together, maybe go on a few dates. Maybe keeping her out late several nights would get his dad off his back about still being a virgin. And Brenna would have looked to him for whatever she needed, not Anya or church or Jesus. Mitch somehow fit into the puzzle as well, but Nick had no idea how.

And if he had pretended, she would not have responded to him with such revulsion. He couldn't help but notice the way she had walked so far apart from him as though she were afraid to contaminate herself by touching him. Would everyone feel the same way as her, even though he had never acted on his desires? Would Anya? He knew what Anya's church preached. He knew what the fundamentalists said about people like him when they ranted and raved on T.V. talk shows.

"What's on your mind, Nick?"

Nick shrugged. "Just thinking about this girl I know. She just became a Christian - like you, I guess."

"A girlfriend?"

"No."

"Someone you like, then?"

"No. I never liked any girls – at least not like that."

Les wiped the apple on his shirtsleeve before taking a large bite. He chewed and swallowed. "What do you mean by 'any girls'?"

Nick became still. "Nothing," he said carefully. He changed the subject. "So what is being a Christian all about then?"

Les smiled. "It's about liberty, Nick. Freedom. Christ loves us and accepts us no matter who or what we are."

The guest speaker at Anya's church had also talked about Jesus' love. Brenna had babbled to Anya about knowing now that Jesus loved her.

"Becoming a Christian means entering into God's family," Les went on. "God adopts us and loves us like a perfect Father."

"There's no such thing as a perfect father," Nick muttered.

"My dad wasn't that great either – or any of my stepfathers. But God truly is perfect."

The open manner Les talked about God made Nick feel as though he were thirteen and working with Russell again. But he wasn't sure he wanted to hear about Russell's Father-God after He had ruthlessly wrecked his life.

"Thanks for the food," Nick said, tucking his granola wrapper into his pocket.

"Thanks for showing interest in my faith, Nick." Les reached over and squeezed Nick's knee familiarly. "God loves you, too, you know."

Nick's knee tingled. "Yeah, I've been told that before."

"Believe it," Les said seriously.

The sky waited until after nine o'clock to darken. Just when he and Les could no longer see enough by streetlight, they finished installing the last patch of sod and waited for the homeowner to turn on the sprinkler system.

Les drove to Nick's S-10 and parked so his lights shone the driver's door. "Guess I'm used to the city," he said. "But light always means safety."

Nick reached for the door handle.

"Wait," Les said, digging in his pocket and pulling out his wallet. "I need to pay you."

Les held out several bills. "You worked hard and steady tonight, Nick. I'll be honest with you. It's usually pretty hard to get good help as young as you. I was very impressed. I know you're supposed to give this to Mr. Cobb, but I want you to keep the top bill for yourself. Consider it a tip."

Nick took the money, too awkward to count it in front of Les. He savored Les's kind words.

"You know, Nick. I'd be willing to hire as good a helper as you if you'd move down to Wichita."

"Wichita?"

Les nodded. "That's where I live. My employees and I landscape in the spring and summer and contract out for laying tile in the winter. I'd have work for you year-round if you're interested."

Nick stared through the windshield and thought of the cash saved up in his bleach bottle at home. "I've been wanting to go to college somewhere," he said.

"You could attend Wichita State," Les said. "In fact, Wichita State isn't far from my duplex. What are you interested in studying?"

"Music." He felt the familiar blush of shame at admitting his love and the anger that quickly followed. Why did people have to pigeonhole jobs into masculine and feminine slots?

Les simply nodded. "I don't know anything about the music department there, but I can check for you if you like."

"No, don't," Nick said. He opened the door and several moths appeared, attracted to the dome light. "I don't have money saved up yet."

"We could work something out," Les said. "I've given out grants for education before under the name of my company. Maybe part of your work hours could go for education funds."

"You would do that?"

Les smiled. "I like you, Nick. I'd hate to see your potential wasted in a small town like this one."

Something deep inside Nick shot off a warning. How could Les know his potential? Les had not heard him play the piano. But maybe Les saw something worthwhile in him besides his musical abilities. Russell had. Nick told himself that Les was like Russell. Les would treat him right.

A June bug found the door opening and buzzed through, landing in Nick's lap. "I'd better go," he said. He brushed the bug to the floor with his glove.

"Think about my offer, will you Nick?"

"I will," Nick promised.

"Here." Les took a pen and small notepad from the storage space in the middle armrest. "I need your full name, address, phone number, and e-mail so I can be in touch with you."

Nick quickly wrote down the information. When he got into his S-10, he saw the denomination of the top bill that Les had given him to keep. A fifty.

Brenna instinctively turned down the volume on the kitchen radio when she heard her mother stirring in the bedroom.

A few moments later, her mother appeared, bleary-eyed and rumpled in her bathrobe even though the clock read one-thirty in the afternoon.

"Hello, Mother," Brenna greeted her, trying to be cheerful.

Her mother walked over to the table and sat down.

Brenna opened her mother's pill bottles and dumped the daily amount into her palm.

"Turn off the radio, will you Brenna? My head is throbbing."

Brenna turned to see her mother rubbing at her temples with her fingertips. She swallowed the irritation that rose inside her. Anya had introduced her to the local Christian radio station and Brenna had begun soaking in all the teaching and praise music. She had also followed Anya's advice and began reading her Bible daily. Brenna had always enjoyed losing herself in a book and this Book made her feel as though she could never read enough.

Brenna obediently flipped off the power button. Sadness wove into the kitchen through the silence.

Brenna set the pills on the table along with a glass of water.

"Here's your medication. Do you want some lunch, Mother?"

Her mother curled her fingers tentatively around the coffee mug. "No, thank you."

"You need to eat."

The woman's lips quivered and she lowered her head, letting her hair hide her face. "I can't."

"Why don't I heat up some leftovers for you just in case." Brenna put a slice of ham and a spoonful of peas on a plate and slid it into the microwave.

But her mother pushed the glass of water away, and lowered her face to the table.

"It's one of those days again," Brenna sighed inwardly. "I don't know if I can take this, Lord."

She wanted to escape to her bedroom and find a good book – either that or sit and feel sorry for herself. Goodness knows she had enough reason between her mother's persistent depression and Nick's recent revelation, which still hurt her when she considered the implications. But she wouldn't be any different than her mother if she chose to do that.

She took the food from the microwave and placed it on the table with a spoon and fork.

Thinking about Nick made her guilty. She had ignored him since that Sunday, afraid of what he would want to talk about, if he wanted to talk at all after she had let him see her heart. Surely he hadn't meant what he had said about thinking he was gay. Surely this was only a phase he was going through and he would get over it.

The phone rang and Brenna hurried to answer before her mother could complain about the noise.

Sara spoke on the other end of the line. "Brenna, I have great news. My application was accepted!"

The news meant that Sara would be leaving soon for Thailand, a country Brenna had hardly taken notice of until Sara pointed it out to her on a map.

"That's wonderful," she managed to say.

Sara went on to tell her about the mission organization and the work she would be doing.

"Mostly we'll be working with street children and relief aid for the poor. The missionary family that lives there permanently gives medical care from a clinic attached to their house. They also hold church services. I'm so excited I could burst, Brenna!"

"When do you leave?"

"In two months, which really isn't that long when you consider I need to raise support during that time. Oh, and I need to get a passport and buy supplies. They sent me a whole list of things I will need. But I won't be going to Thailand yet. I'll be spending close to six months in Canada for training first. I may even get to come home for Christmas."

Brenna enjoyed hearing the excitement in Sara's voice even if Thailand was on the other side of the world. "If I can help you get ready, count me in."

"Oh, I will," promised Sara. "You know, Brenna, one of the things I most dreaded about leaving Kansas was leaving the mission field of you. I am so indescribably glad that you are a Christian now."

Brenna thought of the past several weeks and the changes inside of her. "I am too, Sara," she said with feeling.

Nick pitched his old suitcase, the one that had come from Grandma Bates, into the back of his pickup alongside several boxes of belongings.

He was going to Wichita, with barely more than he'd had when he left the city as a child.

"So you're really going through with this, huh?" J.D. leaned against the rickety railing on the front steps.

Nick didn't bother answering.

J.D. spat into the bushes. "You sure I can't talk you into staying?"

Nick looked at his father long and hard. Now that he was leaving, J.D. seemed to have suddenly formed a regretful attitude, as though he would miss his son.

"He will miss me," thought Nick. "He'll miss the groceries, the cooking, the laundry…"

"Gonna seem awful lonely now," said J.D. He rubbed his chin.

"Maybe you should get a wife," Nick told him. He couldn't hide the acidity in his tone.

J.D. shifted his weight from one foot to the other. The railing swayed behind him. "You call me when you get there, you hear? So I know you made it okay?"

Nick swung into the driver's seat and started the vehicle. He glanced out at his father, still standing there. In a moment of softness, Nick rolled down his window. "I'll call."

J.D. touched his cowboy hat with one finger.

Nick answered with a half-hearted wave of his own. Now he only had one thing left to do before leaving.

The beat up guitar propped in the passenger seat had to go home. He may have learned how to play it decently enough but the tones and velvet feel of the piano keys spoke to him in languages that knew nothing of Russell Martin. Nick drove toward Anya's house.

"I can't take this back," Anya fussed, just as he'd known she would.

"I'll never play it," Nick said. "Find someone who can make it sing."

"Keep it a bit longer. You never know. You might enjoy playing it. You don't have to return it today."

Nick gestured to the truck in the driveway. "Yes, I do. I'm moving. Leaving today. Got all my stuff packed up."

Her face flashed surprise. "Leaving? College?"

"Back to Wichita. A landscaper I met at work offered me a job. I plan on trying to save up enough money to start college after Christmas."

"This landscaper – do you know anything about him?"

"Oh, you'd like him. He's a Christian. Actually, he reminds me of Mr. Martin." Nick fell silent, looking around uncomfortably. In the years since Russell's death and that one Sunday when he went to church with her, Nick had not allowed Anya to get too close or to talk to him about Russell.

He looked at the planter that he and Russell had built along the front of the house, overflowing with perennials and shrubbery now.

"Russell loved you like a son, you know." Anya spoke quietly. "Did you know that he checked into the possibility of adopting you?"

Nick gaped at her.

"He even approached J.D. about it."

"What did my dad say?"

Anya shook her head. "I don't know. I never found out. Russell died that day."

Nick exhaled in frustration. "You see? That only proves that God didn't take care of me."

"Oh, Nick."

"He didn't! Otherwise He would've let Mr. Martin live. Why didn't you tell me sooner?"

Anya sighed. "Some things are better left unknown. That way we don't beat ourselves with the 'what could have been's. But remember this, Nick. Even if you don't understand why things have happened the way they have, God does care."

"He has a rotten way of showing it." Nick turned away from her. Then something occurred to him. "So why didn't you go ahead and adopt me anyway?"

Anya touched his chin tenderly and turned his face toward her. "You needed a father, Nick. I couldn't give that to you."

"A father like that one?" Nick jerked his chin from her touch, pointing it toward the trailer.

Anya's hand fell. "I'm sorry, Nick. I've regretted not doing something for years now, I truly have. I was so blinded by my own grief. I was wrong and now you're all grown up and going off on your own. I guess I've run out of chances."

Her repentance surprised him. He had expected excuses. His anger dissipated.

"You'll write or call me, won't you?" Panic flared her eyes.

"I will," he promised, his second promise of the day. When he had made plans with Les Howland to move to Wichita, he had assumed he would sever all ties.

Then she was hugging him tightly.

"Goodbye, Mrs. Martin," he whispered even though he made no move to pull away.

"God's blessings to you, Nick," she murmured. "May you find peace in His love."

He left, with the guitar back in the passenger seat at her insistence. As he drove away, the cloud of dust behind his truck hid her from view but he knew she still stood on the front porch watching.

He passed the trailer. J.D. was no longer in sight. Then at the turn onto the main road, he saw Brenna at her mailbox. She lifted her hand in a partial wave. Nick missed her friendship. But maybe it was best that things had turned out the way they had.

Right now, he had a chance to escape his father and that was enough.

Nick tightened his fingers on the steering wheel as traffic doubled and tripled. When he had lived in Wichita, he had not even noticed the traffic. Of course, the only driving he had done back then had been in his imagination behind the steering wheel of Grandma Bates' parked car. Accustomed to only one stoplight, the city's bombardment of road signs, billboards, and interstate exits butterflying in all directions instilled nervousness into him.

Nick glanced frequently at the paper draped over his knee to follow the instructions to Les Howland's duplex. The directions were concise and Nick pulled up in front of the building without any trouble although his hands were sweating. He stuffed the paper in the glove box and swiped his hands on his jeans.

A park spread over the block across the street, creating a peaceful atmosphere. Nick liked it much better than the concrete he had seen from the freeway. Instead of a traditional duplex with spaces on both sides, floors separated the homes. Les had told Nick to come to the second floor so Nick walked up the wooden staircase.

Les stepped out before he reached the top. "Nick! You made it, I see. It's so good to have you here finally."

To Nick's surprise, Les reached out and pulled him into a full body hug. Nick instinctively backed away but Les tightened his hold.

"Don't back up," he warned. "You'll fall down the stairs."

Nick laughed nervously as Les let go and motioned the way in.

"Let me show you around, then we can go down and carry in your things."

"We can leave some of them in the truck," Nick said. "Until I find my own place, I mean."

Les made a little face of dissent. "Oh, you don't want to leave your things out there. It could take several days or even weeks to find an apartment. I have plenty of space."

"Weeks?" Nick echoed.

Les nodded. "To tell the truth, Nick, I kind of hoped that you might stay here with me – for the first few months at least. I get lonely living all by myself and you need to save up money for school. I think it might help both of us out."

"I couldn't do that," Nick protested.

"I like you, Nick. I'd like you to at least consider it."

Nick rubbed his hand, the hand he had injured so long ago, between the thumb and forefinger. "I guess I could think about it," he said finally.

Les brightened. "Good. Now for the grand tour."

Les showed Nick around the home, a living space much larger and much nicer than J.D.'s trailer.

Two bedrooms sat at the back with a large bathroom tucked between. Les demonstrated how to pull out the futon in the spare bedroom that Nick would use as a bed. A king-sized bed with a soft comforter and throw pillows dominated Les's bedroom. The room had been decorated in blacks and browns.

"I hired a decorator for this room," Les said sheepishly. "A bedroom is the most important room of a home."

Nick didn't agree or understand but he nodded anyway.

A third and smaller bedroom served as office space for the landscaping and tiling businesses, Les explained. He rented a separate building for storage of his equipment on the outskirts of town but he liked to have the paperwork at home so he could work whenever.

Nick smiled at his phrase "the outskirts of town" as if Wichita were the same size as the town he had just left, even though in comparison to other U.S. cities, Wichita was small.

They carried in Nick's things and Les commented on how little he had brought. "You pack light," he teased.

Nick flushed. He had brought all he owned.

"Feel free to take over wherever," Les said. He showed Nick several empty drawers in the bathroom that his previous roommate had used as well as an empty space in his own closet for Nick's clothing.

"The spare bedroom closet is full of junk," he explained.

Nick felt uncomfortable about having to go into another man's bedroom for his clothes but reasoned that if the other roommate had done the same, it would be fine.

"Why did your roommate move out?" Nick asked, curious.

Les waved his hand vaguely. "We weren't getting along. Besides, I have a new roommate, you, at least for a while. Have you eaten yet?"

"No."

"Let me treat you to a Chinese place that's great. You do like Chinese food, don't you?"

"Never had it."

"Are you feeling brave?"

Nick had already used up his bravery in breaking away from J.D. and Anya and driving to his new home. "Sure," he lied.

Chapter 16

Wild sunflowers and gaillardia spotted the ditches along the lonely expanse of highway through Eastern Colorado.

"Radar patrolled," Mitch laughed as they passed a speed limit sign. "I wonder if police even bother to patrol out here."

"I think we've only passed two cars since we turned on highway 94 and that was over 20 minutes ago," said Sara. "But that's still no excuse to speed, Uncle Mitch."

"I'm not," he protested. "At least not too much. We have plenty of time to get to the airport."

"Let every person obey the higher authorities," Sara quoted. "That's in the Bible somewhere."

Mitch made a fist and gently punched her shoulder. "Don't try to make me feel guilty, little niece of mine. I'm doing you a big favor here."

Mitch had offered to drive Sara to the airport in Colorado Springs where she would then fly to Canada for her basic training since her parents couldn't. Sara had asked Brenna to come along.

The family had hosted a large going-away party for Sara with many church people and special prayer.

"I'm glad you are going, Brenna," Nell had confided to Brenna at the party. "She appreciates your friendship so much."

Sara wrinkled her nose at Mitch then turned to smile at Brenna who sat in the back seat. "When I was younger, our family came on a trip to Colorado Springs. When we stopped at a gas station in one of those little towns back there, Michele and I went into the restroom but it was so dirty that we couldn't make ourselves use it. We ended up on this long stretch of nothing with nowhere to stop and nothing to even hide behind."

"Was that the time you went to the top of Pike's Peak?" asked Mitch.

"Yes. Anyway, Dad told us that we had to hold it and that we should have used the bathroom at the gas station and yada, yada, but he finally stopped at a spot where a huge culvert ran under the road, almost big enough to stand up in. Michele and I didn't care anymore. We were too desperate."

"You didn't!" Brenna burst out laughing.

"We did! And while we were under there, a car came along and stopped and the man inside asked Dad if he needed any help so Dad had to explain why we were stopped along the side of the road. I think it was the only car we saw the whole time. Well, at least the only car that Mom, Dad and Avery saw. Michele and I hid out under the culvert until it was safe to come out."

"Your family always took great trips," Mitch said. "Nell must've had to drag Karl off the farm at first. Mom and Dad hardly ever took us anywhere. What about you, Brenna?"

Brenna realized he watched her in the rear view mirror. "W…We didn't travel when I was little, but now we like to go hiking."

"Where is your favorite place?"

"Anywhere, so long as it's in the mountains."

"Do you like the mountains better than Kansas?"

Brenna watched the endless barbed wire fence slide past her window in order to avoid his eyes in the mirror. "The m…mountains are beautiful but I'd miss the openness of Kansas."

"I know what you mean," answered Mitch. "I've always felt closed in when I can't see all of the sky. Are there mountains in Thailand, Sara?"

"Not very high ones. And not where I'll be."

Brenna felt content to sit quietly in the back as Sara bubbled on about her training in Canada and what she expected in Thailand, with Mitch asking questions and making comments.

The faint shadows of mountains in front of them grew larger and larger and they began to see small towns and housing developments.

"Lots of folks moving out this way," Mitch commented. "Seems like they want to move out to the country but then they live tight together."

Mitch found the airport without difficulty.

"Don't walk me inside or anything. I don't want you to have to pay for parking," said Sara. "Just drop me off at the front entrance."

"Your mother would quit bringing me her lattice-top cherry pies if I did that," said Mitch. "We'll take you in. What's a few dollars, anyway?"

They found a parking space and walked into the terminal. After a brief wait in line, Sara surrendered her large suitcase to the attendant and rejoined Mitch and Brenna, tickets clutched in hand. She drew in her breath deeply as though steadying herself.

"The lady at the desk said you can't walk me to the gate. Only people with a boarding pass can go through security now. You know how tight it's been since 9-11."

"Are you nervous?" asked Brenna.

Sara breathed again. "Very. I've never flown alone before but someone from the training center will meet me in Toledo. The worst part will be finding my connecting flight in Chicago."

"You'll do fine. Just ask a flight attendant for directions." Mitch drew her close in a one-armed hug and began to pray. "Lord, give my niece an ease of heart and mind on her trip. Take away any anxiety that she may have and help her to remember that she is following Your will and Your plan for her life. Let the next six months teach her more about Your character and help her to grow and mature in Your Word. Prepare her for Thailand. In Jesus' precious and holy name, Amen."

Sara reached out and took Brenna's hand during the prayer to include her. She lifted her head and laughed, a little shakily. "I'm sure this solo flight will be nothing in comparison to the new things I'll try in the next couple of years but thank you ever so much for praying, Uncle Mitch."

"I'll pray for you too, Sara," said Brenna. She pulled her friend close as soon as Mitch let her go. "Every day. And I'll miss you."

"I'll miss you too, Brenna," Sara whispered. She pulled back. "Although it's so much easier going, knowing that you will be praying for me."

The girls hugged again then Sara was off, walking toward the metal detectors and her new adventures. She turned for one last wave before Mitch and Brenna stood alone together. Brenna quivered inside at the thought of driving four hours home without Sara to buffer the conversation. Why hadn't she thought ahead to this when she had said yes to Sara's invitation?

Without speaking, they went back to the car. Brenna hesitantly took the front passenger seat.

"Are you in a rush to get back home?"

"N...No, not really." Brenna had told her father that she didn't know what time she would be home. She had assumed they would wait the several hours before Sara's takeoff. Her father would be late getting in anyway with corn harvest and her mother would probably sleep without Brenna to coax her out of bed.

"Would you like to drive up into the mountains?"

"It's quite a ways, isn't it?"

Mitch shrugged. "Or we could drive up Pike's Peak."

"That's expensive," she warned, thinking of the hair-raising stories Sara had told about the narrow sandy roads switchbacking up the steep mountainside. She always felt better on foot than in a vehicle when it came to heights.

"I've heard that Garden of the Gods is pretty. What do you think?"

She hated to be a naysayer three times in a row. "That sounds n…nice."

"Great! Now where did I leave my atlas?" He leaned over the console, rummaging in the back seat. "Karl and Nell sure keep a lot of stuff in their car."

"I put it in the pocket on the back of the seat," Brenna said timidly. He was so close she could see the blond streaks in his brown hair.

"Not the back of my seat," she added. "Yours."

"Oh." He found the atlas and opened it to Colorado. "I don't suppose I'll be lucky enough to have a map of the Springs in here. Never mind. There is one."

Mitch studied the map for a moment. "It looks like it will take twenty or thirty minutes to get there from here. Is that okay?"

"It sounds like fun." She tried to infuse enthusiasm into her voice.

They left the airport and drove through the city until they reached the entrance to the rock attraction. Brenna forgot to be nervous as they walked along the red paved sidewalks and gawked at the huge stones jutting into the sky with sheer cliff-like sides.

"It's amazing," she murmured.

"Lot of people," Mitch said. "Let's take this path."

She followed him around a group of Japanese tourists.

"I'm sorry," Mitch apologized suddenly. "I should have let you go first."

Something in her look must have told him she felt perfectly content to let him lead for he laughed and fell in step beside her.

They walked on, Mitch admiring the color of the rocks, the brilliant blue of the sky, and the wildflowers beside the path.

Seven years. That's how much older he was than her. Surely he couldn't be showing interest in her. Perhaps Mitch looked at her as another niece.

Besides, why was she even thinking this way? Hadn't she learned not to hope for romance through her childish experience with Nick? Not that it mattered now, with Nick gone off to Wichita. And hadn't she made a decision to allow God to fill all the needs in her life? But now Mitch was looking at her questioningly. "I...I'm sorry. D...Did you ask me something?"

"I asked you which way you wanted to go." Mitch indicated a fork in the pathway.

She looked up at the rock faces and pointed toward the path that led around to the other side.

"Good choice." He smiled and shortened his steps to matched hers.

She figured she should say something. He probably thought she was as socially inept as her mother. Maybe even as crazy. No, no. She shook her head. That was her insecurity speaking. God looked at her so much differently.

"So you like cherry pie?" she ventured.

"With a lattice top." Mitch licked his lips.

"I suppose a lattice top tastes better?" She wondered what reservoir of courage she had pulled the ability to tease from.

"Much better - even better than streusel."

"Why is that?"

"Because presentation counts. The more appealing the food looks, the more appealing it is to eat."

"I never thought of it that way."

Mitch stopped walking. "Brenna," he cleared his throat. "I'm not sure if you realize this or not, but I find you very attractive too. Not just the lattice top part of you, which is very nice, by the way, but your character and maturity, your actions in the way you care for your mother and show loyalty to Sara. And the way you've taken a step of faith to follow God. I know you probably think of me as nothing more than Sara's uncle, but if you'd be willing, I'd like to spend more time with you, get to know you better."

"We have four hours in the car on the way home," she hedged, trying to hide her embarrassment and pleasure and yes, panic. "Is that enough time?"

He laughed, red sweeping up his neck and over his face. "It's a start."

They came to the end of the circle and backtracked to the car, tentatively asking each other questions about family members, jobs and commonalities.

Mitch found a McDonald's on their way out of the city and they got their food to go and ate in the car, still talking. Somehow food made things more relaxed.

When Mitch opened the cardboard pouch containing his rectangular cherry pie, he made a face and Brenna couldn't resist. "It's all in the presentation, right?"

After Les's cajoling, Nick agreed to attend church with him on his first Sunday in Wichita. When Nick walked into the building with Les, he recognized the song that the congregation sang. He couldn't remember if he'd heard it in Anya's church or on her radio.

Les immediately joined in singing, clapping and bobbing his knees. Nick raised his eyebrows. He couldn't imagine Russell acting so demonstrative. Nick had to admit that Les reminded him less and less of Russell as he spent more time with him. They were two separate people after all.

Les nudged Nick with his elbow, encouraging him to clap along. Nick clapped on the second and fourth beats half-heartedly while looking around.

The majority of the people were adults, young adults. He didn't see many children, but maybe they were still at Sunday School or children's church. He also didn't see many worshippers that looked over fifty. Anya's church had a spattering of all ages.

Then to Nick's surprise, the two women in front of him reached toward each other, clasped hands and smiled a secret kind of smile, their facial expressions reminding him of the way Karl and Nell looked at each other. His skin prickled. Surely they weren't...

But they were. The women leaned toward each other and shared a brief kiss. He looked around and saw more same-sex couples in worship together. These people dared to approach God just as they were?

The more Nick had become convinced of his own same-sex desires, the more fear kept him from buying into Anya's belief in a God who acted as a loving and forgiving Father. He believed in a "God", yes – a God of either judgment, neglect, or malice. He had heard of gay churches and wondered if it were even possible. Wasn't God supposed to strike down homosexuals with lightning or something like that?

When guys at school had taunted Nick with cruel names, Nick had felt ashamed of his desires and fantasies. Was he as depraved as they all thought he was? Nick had seen plenty of gays caricatured on TV sitcoms. He had heard plenty of discriminatory comments, some snide, others outright hateful.

But here he sat amongst men that acted and looked like men, women that acted feminine and pretty, stylish people in suits and classy dresses, yet clearly coupled up with those of the same sex.

Nick rubbed the scar on his hand thoughtfully. Apparently, a gay didn't have to be someone crass. A gay didn't have to be someone involved in the lowest of depravity. A gay could have dignity.

Nick sat straighter. Maybe he could have a place in society after all, without trying to change. Maybe he was fine just the way he was. Maybe God loved him anyway.

He slid a glance at Les, who sat with his eyes on the pastor, an open Bible on his lap. Les, who reminded him of Russell Martin. Les, who accepted him with ease and friendliness. Les, with a clear, open face. How did Les feel about it? Could Nick ever be brave enough to share his own struggles with Les?

After the song, the leader set his guitar in a stand behind him. Adjusting his tie, he walked to the podium. Apparently, he served as pastor as well.

The service entertained Nick as well as confused him. The majority of the pastor's talk consisted of announcements regarding numerous outreach efforts the church sponsored with an occasional question or joke tossed in. The atmosphere seemed more like a casual business meeting with parishioners answering the questions or joking back. Even though the relaxed attitude surprised him, Nick liked it. He also liked the evidence of good deeds that the church was involved in with their community services.

Then the pastor gave a call to the altar for communion. Les questioned Nick with his eyes but Nick shook his head. He knew enough from his visits to Anya's church to know that taking communion was a sacred act and not to be engaged in by nonbelievers. He watched as couples lined the front of the church and took the bread and cup together.

Doubt filtered through Nick. What if these people were wrong? Wouldn't God punish them for their actions? But no, they exhibited peace and joy as they filed back to their seats, quiet and reverent now.

A woman took the podium, opened a book and read a prayer as the last of the bread and wine was served. One phrase stuck out in Nick's mind, asking God to help those who felt rejected by the rest of the Christian community. Nick knew she meant gays.

He swallowed. Several of the "Christians" from Sara's youth group had been the rudest to him in high school, letting

him know in no uncertain terms that God could never love a fag
– their word, not his.

Their accusations had hurt deeply. He had never acted
on his inner desires, had never yet done anything to be labeled
with the derogatory word.

But according to this group, God loved him. God would
not punish him for being who he was.

When Les put his arm around Nick's shoulder in a
friendly manner after the benediction and asked Nick what he
thought, Nick smiled and said he had liked it.

Anya answered her phone on the third ring. She had
debated on not answering at all, so involved was she in the novel
she was pre-reading in preparation for her weekly reading
session at the nursing home. Fred Findley had shared with her
how he liked spy novels best so Anya tried to find the most
suspenseful ones she could. But when she heard Nick's voice on
the line, she closed her book without even saving her spot.

"Nick! It's so wonderful to hear your voice. How are
you?"

"I'm fine," he answered. He sounded fine, upbeat.

"How are things going in Wichita? You've been there,
what, close to two months now?"

"Only one and a half. I like it here, Mrs. Martin. I'm
glad I came. I'm sorry I didn't call you sooner."

"I've worried about you." She bit her lip, wishing she
hadn't sounded quite so grandmotherly.

"You shouldn't. Everything is really great here."

She didn't want generalizations but found herself asking
another generic question. "How is your job?"

"Now that it's September, there isn't much landscaping
to do so Les, that's my boss, takes on contracting jobs for tile
work. We're working on a new housing development and laying
tile in all the bathrooms and laundry rooms.

"Do you enjoy it?"

"I enjoyed the summer work much better, but laying tile isn't bad if you wear knee pads. Les says it gets harder on his back every year so he usually runs the wet saw and does all the measuring while Zack and I do most of the floor work. Zack is another employee. Sometimes I run errands to pick up supplies or new tile shipments. The tiles come in crates that are really heavy. Les says it's a fitness program and job all rolled into one."

"How many employees does Les have working for him?"

"During the busiest part of the summer there were four of us but now the two high school guys have gone back to school."

"And college? Have you started yet?"

"No. I'm going to start second semester when I have more money saved up. Besides, Les says that after I've been an employee for six months, they can give me financial aid."

"As in a loan or a grant?"

"A grant. And living with Les helps me save more too."

Was it her imagination, or did Nick mention Les in nearly every sentence? She hoped this man was a good influence, as she had prayed for the past weeks. "So you aren't going to look for your own place?"

"I don't think so. Les's duplex is a lot nicer than anyplace I've ever lived before and he only asks that I help with cleaning and groceries. He's great to live with, Mrs. Martin. We get along really well. He gives me advice and help with stuff, which is more than my dad ever did."

The thought of Nick staying with Les should have made her more comfortable about him being alone in the city but for some reason, she felt a check in her spirit. "What kinds of things does he help you with?" she asked casually.

"Oh, how to do accounting papers for his business, pay bills, get around town, do my jobs."

That sounded benign.

"Oh, and you'll like this. I go to church with him."

She brightened. "What church is that?"

Nick laughed. "You know, that's crazy, but I don't even know the name of it. I'm not sure what denomination it is, but I really like the people there. They are always doing service projects in the community, like helping out with Special Olympics, Big Brothers and Sisters, tutoring, and last week we made sack lunches and took them out to the homeless people downtown around the Century II building."

"It sounds like they stay busy."

"Yeah. The pastor says that whenever we help out others, we are actually doing those nice things for God and God will love us."

"God loves us without our good works, Nick. We don't have to prove our love to Him or try to maneuver Him into loving us."

She heard the immediate defensiveness in his voice. "Well, maybe that wasn't exactly what he said. I can't remember."

Anya didn't want to ruin this precious conversation. She had prayed fervently that Nick would contact her, hoped that she had not lost him. "You said you took sack lunches to the homeless. Tell me about that."

"It was really sad, Mrs. Martin. Wichita is a small city but it has crime and inner city conditions like anywhere else. I was really surprised at the number of people we found. We went out in the evening as people were finding places to sleep for the night. Some were in sleeping bags in trees near the river and some were sleeping on the stairs of the Century II building and around the fountains. Most of them acted really thankful for the food we gave them, but others acted angry even though they took it."

"It probably takes a lot of humility to accept help from others."

"Yeah. And I think some of them thought we were just trying to assuage our consciences before we went back to our nice homes."

The phrases didn't sound like Nick, like "assuage our consciences" – more as if he were quoting someone, possibly Les or Les's pastor.

"It's not true, though," Nick went on. "The pastor and Les and several other guys from church volunteer at the rescue mission every week. Well, Les doesn't go every week like the others, but he does go when he can. He's a great guy. I think you'd like him."

"I would like the opportunity to meet him sometime," she said. "Tell me, Nick, do you think of Les as a father?"

"No. Maybe. I don't know what a real father is supposed to be like. I guess he's more like a friend." Nick paused for a long moment. "How is my dad?"

"I think he misses you."

Nick snorted. "Is he still working for Karl?"

"Yes." She paused. "He's drinking quite a lot, though." She didn't tell him that whenever Karl confronted J.D. and threatened the loss of his job, J.D. straightened up, but only for a while.

When Nick said nothing, Anya changed the subject. "Sara left for Canada several weeks ago. She's going to be in mission training for six months before she leaves for Thailand."

"Thailand? Why there?"

Anya explained and they talked a while longer about safe topics such as Anya's grandchildren and the weather. Nick gave Anya his address so she could write to him. "Send cookies," he said, in reference to her statement that she had sent Sara's favorite oatmeal and chocolate cookies to her in the mail. She laughed and promised to do so.

"This is silly," she told the Lord after she hung up. "I should be overjoyed that he contacted me but instead here I am worrying about him even more. He didn't say anything that should cause me to fret, but I am. Please show me how to pray for Nick."

   Nick stood tentatively in front of the electronic keyboard, his right foot reaching toward the pedal, wrists arching, fingers spreading instinctively into a C chord formation. The angle felt different than sitting at a piano, his balance awkward with his weight on one foot. He pressed several keys until he felt comfortable with the pressure needed and response of the notes.

   He closed his eyes and listened. The music was there, gently throbbing with his heartbeat, swaying in the moving air of his breath, solid as the cold keys beneath his fingertips. He waited a hint of a second before his left hand pounded out a strong, deep question. His right hand lilted over the high notes in response. The two hands continued their conversation, dancing closer and closer until they met in the middle.

   He played a series of chords, filled in with intricate melodies. Then the music became minor, plaintively calling. His body leaned closer to the keyboard with each stroke, his head bending back. He began to pile the notes, one on top of the other purposefully, faster and faster, until they spun out from under his fingers, swaying and twirling with a life of their own. When it seemed they could no longer possibly keep up, his hands crashed down on the last chord, powerful and sure. The notes hung, suspended, before dissipating in the breathless hush. Not as pure as a grand piano, but it would do.

   Applause burst forth from the small group standing around him, enthusiastic and sincere. Nick couldn't hold back his smile of pleasure at their approval. He had not felt so accepted in a long time – maybe not ever.

   "I told you he was good, didn't I?" Les bragged. Les sometimes went with Nick to music stores and listened while

Nick played the pianos although Nick never got to play enough to satisfy.

"Nick, you have a true gift on that instrument," Les's pastor told him. He clapped a hand on Nick's shoulder. "We desperately need a keyboardist on our worship team. Would you be interested?"

Nick's eyes hesitantly sought out the other guitarists and drummer. They all nodded enthusiastically.

"I...I don't know," he stammered, disgusted that he sounded like Brenna. He stood up straighter. "I'm not sure you really want me on your team."

Over their dissent, he forged on. "I may attend church with Les but I'm not what you'd call a Christian. I haven't been saved or anything like that."

Pastor Jeff squeezed his shoulder. "We all were at a place in our lives like you at one time or another, Nick. Truth is, we're all going to the same place eventually. You're just at a different spot on the path. We'd still like to have you play if you're willing."

Nick felt relieved that they hadn't pushed for him to drop to his knees then and there and confess whatever sins one had to confess in order to receive salvation, or however the lingo went. Although, he had to admit, confession of sin had not exactly been a topic on the front burner at this church.

"It would get you more involved if you were on the team," said Les. "Let you see more what we're about. In fact, I could let you off early on the nights when the worship team has practice."

Pastor Jeff nodded in approval and Les unsuccessfully tried to hide his satisfaction at being noticed as generous. Nick stifled his irritation. He supposed it was normal for people to try to please their pastors. If there was one thing he was learning here at this church, it was not to judge.

He knew he could easily play with the team, even without much practice. The chords and keys to the music on Sunday mornings were usually systematic and simple.

"All right," he agreed. "I can try it for a little while."

On the drive home, Les questioned Nick. "Are you excited about being on the worship team?"

Nick watched the endless headlights sweeping by them in the opposite lane. "I guess so. I've never played with anyone else before. Unless you count Brenna."

"Brenna?"

"A girl from my class in high school. She and I played a piano duet for graduation. You know, the song while everyone walks in?"

"Pomp and Circumstance?"

"Yeah."

Les cleared his throat. "This Brenna, was she a girlfriend?"

Nick felt uncomfortable, as though anything he said could be misconstrued. "I already told you I never had a girlfriend," he said defensively, thinking of how Brenna's soft brown eyes filled with hurt when he had told her his secrets.

"M…hmmm." Les did not speak the rest of the way home. Nick found himself wishing he could tell Les how he really felt about girls – and men. He knew by now that Les would never judge him. But years of silence kept him from speaking.

To his surprise and pleasure, Nick found that he very much enjoyed playing with the worship team. He thoroughly enjoyed his practice times playing alone in the sanctuary. He taught himself new songs and did drills from his classical training from Ms. Plum during those stolen lessons at the music store so many years ago.

Nick had tried to find her without success when he first moved back to Wichita but a pet store had moved in where the music store had been. He only knew her last name, which wasn't much help in the phone book.

Nick anticipated Thursday nights when the team practiced. The other men in the group accepted him and gave him praise and attention. He had never felt so comfortable with other men before.

Pastor Jeff still led the group on his guitar but he allowed Nick to do most of the introductions and finales as well as the offertory and altar calls. He was the only member of the group to sing, but then, his voice fulfilled the job quite well. Where Nick had a gift on the keyboard, Pastor Jeff had a gift with his tenor.

Tim and Cal, clearly a couple, played electric guitar and bass, although Cal usually hit a number of incorrect notes and had to keep asking for his monitor to be turned up because he couldn't hear himself. Nick suspected that the sound guy turned his bass down. Tim worked patiently with him to teach him the music and by Sunday morning, it usually worked out fine. Nick had to wonder if Cal only played because of Tim. The two always came in swinging their guitar cases and laughing together. Nick envied their closeness.

Marc played drums. He worked evenings as a waiter and couldn't always come to practice on weeknights. When he did, he seemed distracted and in a hurry, though he always had a smile for Nick. Nick appreciated Marc's clean rhythm much more than the Ms. Plum's hated metronome. Marc's partner, Andy, came to the warm-up practice with him early on Sunday mornings and sat on the front pew tapping his fingers to Marc's drumming.

Nick sometimes felt awkward during the actual service when Pastor Jeff would throw back his head and utter loud and long prayers during the middle of a song or people would flock to the altars but he would continue to play at Cal and Tim's nodding. People often found him after service and thanked him for his "inspired playing" and he and Les would laugh afterwards.

One night Cal and Tim invited Nick to the men's Bible study and support group that they co-led. When Nick felt too nervous to go alone, Les promised to go along.

The first time he and Les attended, Nick was shocked at the openness of several men who shared about painful circumstances they dealt with, but the true shock was not in sordid details; what the men said about their struggles and emotions resounded in Nick. Here were others who understood pain.

One of the men shared how distant his relationship with his father had become since he had come out as a gay. The father's actions reminded Nick of his own father and Nick sympathized with the man who shared.

Nick shuddered at how J.D. would react if he knew what Nick's new friends stood for – if he knew about what Nick was becoming more and more convinced of within himself. J.D. had wounded Nick internally with words much more than he had ever hurt Nick physically. But at least Nick had never been close to his father, like the man sharing. That man's father had turned on him and denounced him, betrayed him after years of camaraderie.

Nick listened carefully as the man testified how the members of the church had accepted him and loved him when no one else did, which eventually made him realize that even though his earthly father had turned his back, God the Father had not.

For the first time since Russell's death and his subsequent anger at God's betrayal, Nick felt a stirring in his spirit. Perhaps God had not turned His back after all. Nick rubbed the scar on his hand thoughtfully.

The group gathered around the men who spoke, laid hands on them and prayed over them.

"Jesus will never condemn," Les explained after they went home and Nick asked what made the men so trusting. "If we stand in the seat of judgment and criticize our brother, then we are trying to take God's place. That's why men feel so comfortable about sharing. They know we won't judge them or hate them based on what they share."

"I remember hearing a song about that," Nick said. "A girl from school, Sara, sang it at a music contest." Brenna had accompanied her on piano, but Nick did not mention that.

"There is no condemnation to those who are in Christ," Nick quoted the words. "But that wording makes it sound like you have to be in Christ in order to escape the condemnation."

Les smiled as he pulled a root beer from the refrigerator. "And aren't we all in God's family? You want one?"

"Sure." Nick flinched as Les tossed the can at him, but he caught it.

Les went to the living room and sat on the couch. He popped the tab on his can and drank deeply. Nick watched Les's Adam's apple bob up and down. Les lowered the can and smiled at Nick, an intimate smile that made Nick wonder how much Les eschewed and even indulged in the lifestyles of his friends.

"Do you have a Bible, Les?" he asked, tugging on his shirt with embarrassment.

"Yes. On my bed stand."

"Where does it talk about condemnation?"

"I can't tell you off the top of my head but I have a concordance. Just be forewarned. Condemnation was for the Old Testament. Jesus changed all that."

Les came back a moment later with a Bible and a large hardbound volume. "This is an extra Bible. You can use it for as long as you like," he offered.

The last time Nick had held a Bible had been after he had cut his hand and Sara came to visit him.

While Les flipped through channels on the large screen, Nick acquainted himself with the table of contents in the Bible and the format of the concordance.

He found a several verses using the word "condemnation" and labored to find the books of Jeremiah and Romans in order to look up the first few on the list.

What he read did not make much sense to him, especially the verses in Jeremiah about God pouring out condemnation on some people who wanted to move to Egypt. That didn't sound like the pleasant God he heard about from Les and Pastor Jeff.

Romans talked about one man causing the condemnation of all – Nick assumed Adam – and another man's goodness eliminating the condemnation. Jesus?

He found the verse he sought at Romans 8:1. "Therefore, there is now no condemnation for those who are in Christ Jesus." The Bible stated it just like Sara's song.

Nick peeked at Les, who sat absorbed in a "how-to" landscaping show. He still didn't really understand but hated to ask Les any more questions. He had seen the irritation Les sometimes showed toward Zack on the job and Nick didn't want Les to think he wasn't smart.

The next day, Les announced that he would be in Texas for a week to check out an opportunity to put in tile for a housing development in Houston.

"If it works out, I'll go back down to Houston for a few months," he said. "I should be able to get a crew down there hired for the job."

"Do you want me to go too?" Nick asked.

"No. You stay here and finish up on our current job. Besides, I trust you to watch Zack and make sure he shows up to work."

Nick didn't exactly feel comfortable with the prospect of babysitting Zack, who complained more about the hours than summer high school help even though he was twice their age.

"Don't worry, Nick. I don't have the job yet. I'm just flying down for a week to check it out and give them a proposal."

Zack, as Nick had predicted, liked the idea of more freedom with the boss out of town. Nick shuddered to think about trying to keep Zack engaged on the job for a week. If it would be hard for this week, then it would be doubly hard for several months if Les got the job.

As it turned out, he didn't have to worry. Not long after Les left for Houston, the water main at the building site broke and work halted due to flooding in several houses. They had no water or electricity to run their wet saw and the building contractor would have to replace some of the sub-flooring before they could tile. To Zack's delight, the site manager told them not to come back the rest of the week while they sorted out the mess.

Nick sequestered himself in the duplex for most of the week and read voraciously about the life of Jesus from the Bible Les had loaned him.

He would have liked to have lived in Israel during those years, he decided, Romans or not. Jesus seemed so purposeful everywhere He went, with everyone He addressed, so forceful one moment, gentle the next, like he always knew what to do.

Nick already knew the basics of the story – how Jesus had been falsely accused and executed and how he rose from the dead – but Nick could not have predicted his emotional reaction as he read the details for himself.

It seemed that many of the things Nick had experienced, Jesus had gone through tenfold. Jesus endured mockery that made anything Nick had faced seem easy. Jesus had a close friend die too.

At first, Nick became angrier and angrier with the Father-God who allowed the Son-God to go through such misery. He had been right about God being a God of revenge and cruelty. But as he read about why Jesus had to die and what Jesus had accomplished through death, Nick began to understand. God had let Jesus take the penalty for everyone else.

By the time Nick reached the end of the book of John and read Jesus' words as he asked Peter to follow Him, Nick made up his mind. He slid down beside the futon bed buried his face in the mattress.

"God," he whispered. "I don't know why You let Russell die. I don't know why You didn't let me have a mom or dad who loved me. But I do know things could be a lot worse if I had to pay up for everything I've done wrong. I don't understand why you let your Son take the brunt for everything, but I believe He did it for me. I don't know how or why, but I do believe it. I've sinned, God. I've been cold toward people who wanted to be nice to me. I've held hatred in my heart for those who have ridiculed me. I've been angry with you."

He stopped and pressed his hand into his abdomen, which cramped painfully.

"I want You to be my Father." His voice broke on the last word. A Father. Could he somehow make God love him enough to adopt him as His own? Would God treat him with the kindness and patience of a father like Russell or would He turn on Nick like J.D.? Would He ignore Nick like Grandma Bates?

It was a risk, he knew. But he had taken it and it felt good. He felt tears exploding from his chest and did nothing to stop them. His cries sounded loud in the quiet apartment, devoid of Les's friendly chatter or the television.

He cried for the years of loneliness with Grandma Bates and had a strange sense that God whispered, "I will never leave you, nor forsake you."

He cried for the neglect and verbal abuse from J.D. and God comforted him with, "My Son was despised and rejected by men but by His wounds you are healed."

He cried for Russell, the years of love and advice he would never have. "I am a Father to the fatherless," God breathed.

He cried for the sins he had committed. "I will cleanse you from all unrighteousness. Come out from among the world and be separate."

"Teach me how to be a good son," he whispered. "Teach me how to follow you like Russell did."

As the wetness flowed down his face and dripped from his chin, he felt reborn.

That Sunday, he drove to church alone, the old S-10 standing out in the parking lot full of foreign-made cars and sparkling wax jobs.

As the worship team quickly ran through the songs before the service, Nick found himself understanding the lyrics with a freshness and excitement that he could not contain. He blurted out what he had done the night before. Tim and Cal gathered around him with hugs and congratulations and Pastor Jeff laid his hand on Nick's shoulder and prayed a prayer of thanks.

For the first time in his life, Nick felt as though he completely belonged somewhere.

Chapter 17

Nick greeted Les with a smile and wave when he saw him standing by the baggage claim.

"You're late," Les said.

"I'm sorry," Nick apologized. "Traffic was bad. Do you have your luggage?"

Les silently held up his bags.

"Are you ready to go?"

Les started walking. Nick tried to tamp down his irritation at the other man for not showing at least a little appreciation or enthusiasm. He wanted nothing to spoil the joyous high he had ridden on for the last two days.

"So did you get the job?"

"No." Les walked out the terminal door and into the brisk October air.

Nick half jogged to catch up. "I parked over there." He pointed.

Les frowned and changed direction.

"Can I take one of your bags?"

Les stopped. "Aren't you the chipper one today?" He held out the heavier of the two bags.

"I have reason to be." Nick took the bag, unable to keep from smiling the same goofy grin that crept onto his face every time he thought of what God had done for him. "I became a Christian."

"You what?"

"I became a Christian. I asked God to forgive my sins and..." Nick's words faltered to a stop. "Aren't you happy for me?"

Les ran his hand over his chin. "Yeah, I'm happy." He smiled, forcibly. "That's really great news, Nick. So how did this happen?"

"I've been reading that Bible you loaned me since I had so much free time…"

"Free time?"

"Oh, you haven't heard yet about the water situation. I left a message on your cell phone but I guess you didn't get it."

Nick explained as they walked out to the pickup. He tried not to let Les's mood affect him but he could feel his enthusiasm slipping away.

Anya leaned her head back against the headrest of Russell's old armchair. The fabric had nearly worn through in several places and Nell had offered to sew a slipcover for it, but Anya declined.

After Russell's death, Anya took to sitting in the chair with her legs curled under her, wishing that the bulky arms were Russell's. The chair had become as much of a habit for her to sit in as it had once been Russell's and even after five years, she still felt close to her husband in that chair.

Today, Anya held a letter from Nick on her lap. He had never written her before and the letter thrilled her. She had assumed that his one phone call had only been obligatory and steeled herself to not hear from him again. The contents of the letter thrilled her even more. Nick wrote excitedly about his turn to God and Christianity.

Anya's fingers caressed the pages as she thanked the Lord for moving in Nick's heart. But something niggled at her and she picked up the pages to re-read the paragraph where Nick told of his realizing that God had not abandoned him, the part that talked about the church Bible study and support group Nick attended.

"It's a great group and I get so much more out of it now that I know the Lord. Many of the men have gone through tough times and they still believe that God is faithful. I'm only beginning to understand how faithful."

Anya shook her head in confusion. Nick had said nothing contradictory, nothing to fuss over. Why did she feel unease? And why had she sensed such a strong need to pray for him lately?

"Why, Lord?" she asked. The heavens remained silent.

Les smiled at Nick from across the candlelit table. They sat at a corner table, Les sipping from his wine glass, Nick from his Coke.

The waiter came to their table and took their order by memory. After he left, Nick felt the dark walls close in uncomfortably.

"Relax, Nick. You act like you've never been in a fancy restaurant before," Les teased.

Nick pulled at the tie Les had loaned him. "I haven't."

"Then enjoy it."

Les seemed back to his amiable self after several weeks of black moods. Nick chalked Les's irritability to the loss of the Houston job. But as soon as he had landed a large contract with tiling a new restaurant, Les had cheered considerably. The new job had given Les the idea of going out to celebrate.

"We'll be making enough money soon to eat here every week," Les said. "Then you'll feel comfortable."

"Don't count your chickens before they're hatched," Nick quoted.

Les laughed. "Where did that come from?"

"My grandma used to say it."

"You've never mentioned your grandma before."

Nick shrugged and toyed with his silverware, wrapped tidily in a cloth napkin.

"Seriously, Nick. We've been living together for, what, a little over six months now and I still don't know much more about you other than that you grew up in Western Kansas with your dad."

"Actually, I grew up here in Wichita with my grandma. I moved out to live with my dad just before I turned thirteen."

"You're kidding."

Nick pulled out his spoon and watched the light dance upside-down on the silver.

"Were you happy here? I mean, did you like living with your grandma? I bet she was one of those granny types, always giving you milk and cookies."

"Not really." Nick laid the spoon down next to his overturned wine glass. "You haven't told me that much about your family either."

"Point taken." Les fell silent for a moment. "And I think I'm ready to share some of that with you. But I am interested in your life, Nick, and we did start with you."

The candlelight flickered between them while the background violin music swayed through Nick's head. For a moment, he feared Les's intent in bringing him here but Les sat across from him, his face curious and compassionate, the same Les he saw every day. Nick pressed his lips together nervously.

The waiter efficiently slid their plates onto the table and disappeared. Les lowered his nose to his plate and sniffed appreciatively.

"Shrimp scampi," he breathed. "My favorite."

As Nick sank his fork into his safer order of lasagna, he found himself confiding in Les. He told of Grandma Bates' austere and silent house. He told of his father's sneers and alcoholism. He even told a little about Russell Martin and how he had wished he belonged to the Martin family. He talked until their plates were taken and large slices of airy cheesecake with raspberry sauce appeared in their place.

Les simply sat, listened and nodded, and occasionally inserted a comment or question. When Nick finally stopped, spent and vulnerable, Les reached across the table and patted Nick's hand.

"I'm so sorry you've always felt alone, Nick. But know this. You're not alone any longer."

"I know," Nick said. "Ever since I made things right with God, I've felt different. Hopeful. Like I have a chance at doing something meaningful with my life."

"I wasn't just talking about God," Les said. He squeezed Nick's hand. "You have friends at church now and you have me."

The soft sound of a throat clearing made them both look up. Nick pulled his hand away with a red face.

Les slid some bills into the black leather folder the waiter held lay on the table.

"Keep the change," he said grandly.

They pushed back from the table and left.

When they got home, Les opened the door for Nick. Nick automatically reached for the light switch, but Les stopped him.

"Don't," he said. "It's been a perfect evening. Bright light would only spoil it, don't you think?"

The soft darkness of the house did seem preferable, especially after he had told Les so much about himself. Nick dropped his hand.

"I enjoyed listening to you this evening, Nick. I felt like I got to know you better in the last two hours than in the last six months put together."

Nick rubbed his forefinger and thumb over the scar on his hand. "Thanks for listening," he said.

Les lightly tapped Nick's hands. "I've noticed you do this when you get nervous. Are you nervous right now?"

"No." But Nick did feel nervous. He had odd little bounces in his midsection, as though gnomes jumped on a miniature trampoline. He started walking down the hall toward his bedroom but stopped.

"I almost forgot." He pulled off his necktie and handed it to Les. "Thanks for the loan."

"No problem." Les allowed his hand to linger on Nick's as he accepted it back.

Nick headed back down the hall.

"Say, Nick, are you still seventeen?"

"Yes."

"When do you turn eighteen?"

"April."

"April." Les sighed. "That's three months away."

"Why does that matter?"

"Oh, no reason. Good night, Nick." Les passed him in the hallway and disappeared into the darkness of his bedroom.

Sara burst out of the bathroom, her hair dripping wet from a shower. She squealed when she saw Brenna. "I thought I heard your voice!"

Brenna hugged her friend. "Welcome home, Sara."

"And you're here too, Uncle Mitch."

Mitch made a face. "You can drop the 'uncle' bit. Makes me feel old."

Sara wrinkled her face. "Since when have you started feeling old?"

"I don't think you're old," Brenna protested for the hundredth time. She would continue protesting until he stopped bemoaning how much he was robbing the cradle by dating her. The familiar fear that Mitch would decide their ages were too much of an issue to overcome rose within her.

"Look at this." Mitch lowered his head toward Brenna and rubbed his hands through his hair. "See that? Gray."

"Where?"

"Right there, and there."

"That's not enough to count."

"So you do see it."

Brenna made a face and ruffled his hair. "On you, it looks good."

Comprehension dawned on Sara's face as she looked from her uncle to her friend and back again. "No way. Is this what I'm thinking? Are you guys…"

Brenna reddened and Mitch raised his head and laughed. "Yes, way," he said.

Sara squealed again, jumping up and down. "This is too classic! I never would have guessed."

"You just did," Brenna pointed out.

"So how long has this been going on? I mean, you really are dating, right?"

"Yes," said Brenna.

"A couple of months," said Mitch at the same time. He and Brenna looked at each other and laughed.

"You'll have to tell me the story," ordered Sara. "Let me get a towel for my hair first."

"Um, you may want to put on your shirt right-side out too," Brenna said.

"I was in a hurry," Sara protested. "I wanted to see if it was you. I tried to call your house as soon as I got home but there was no answer."

"I was with Mitch when your mom called Mitch's cell phone," explained Brenna. "We came over right away."

"I didn't interrupt anything, did I?" Sara waggled her eyebrows.

"No, you didn't," Mitch said, firmly pointing his niece toward the bathroom. "Go fix yourself up or whatever it is girls do. We'll wait in the kitchen with Nell."

"No 'we' stuff," Sara said. She grabbed Brenna's arm and pulled her into the bathroom behind her. "You can wait in the kitchen, Uncle Mitch."

As soon as the bathroom door closed, Sara put her hands on Brenna's shoulders. "You really are dating my Uncle Mitch?" she asked again.

"Yes, I really am." Brenna couldn't contain her huge smile.

"But, he's so much older than us."

"Only seven years." Brenna had grown accustomed to inquisitive looks from town and church people when they saw she and Mitch together.

Sara looked at her friend carefully. "Are you sure this is what you want? Uncle Mitch hasn't dated anyone for as long as I remember, maybe never. I might not be telling you anything you don't already know, but I'm fairly certain he's going into this with more than just dating for fun."

"I already know that," said Brenna. "Mitch talked to my dad about his intentions before he ever took me out – unless you don't count the Garden of the Gods."

"Garden of the Gods?"

"That's kind of where it all started," Brenna said. "At least for me. I guess Mitch was interested the day I almost ran him over with my parent's car."

"What! You never told me about that."

"Last summer, not long after we graduated. It was raining hard and I nearly hit his motorcycle. I didn't see him until the last second."

"And you never told me?"

"I didn't think too much about it." Brenna held her palms upward in surrender.

"Okay, start from the beginning." Sara put her hands on her hips. "I only have a few days to catch up on all the news before I leave for Thailand and believe me, I want to hear it all."

Brenna was only too happy to acquiesce.

Nick slid lower in his theater seat as the movie characters blundered their way through comedic bloopers and stupidity. The previews on television had depicted a hilariously tangled mess and true enough, it was. What the previews had not foretold was that a large amount of humor was derived from sexual jokes and making fun of the stereotyped gay guy.

Les glanced over at Nick. "Enjoying yourself?"

Nick shrugged and tried to smile. "Wish they'd let up on the gay jokes."

"I know. It bothers me too. Why don't we show them?"

Nick felt Les's hand close over his, their fingers intertwining. Nick stiffened but did not remove his hand.

During the past months, Les had shown Nick more and more attention, teaching Nick how to fill out his own tax forms, paying to service Nick's truck and throwing a surprise eighteenth birthday party for him at the church. Les had also become more and more affectionate. Nick cowered from him and craved for more all at the same time. He wasn't ignorant of Les's objective and even though he had told Brenna what he thought he was even before he moved to Wichita and made friends within that circle, Nick wasn't certain he wanted to take the dive into the lifestyle. Then again, he wasn't certain he could continue to hold off what seemed so inevitable and attractive.

The guys at church had noticed Les's pursuit of Nick and teased them, but Les always seemed to check Nick's reaction before he allowed the ribbing to progress.

Nick supposed that his friendships with Tim and Cal and others from church had much to do with the reason why he sat here with his hand enfolded in Les's, watching a movie he didn't want to see, with his heart beating faster than ever before.

Nick had indulged in fantasies about other men before; now he had an older, experienced and nice looking man showing interest in him – someone who could love him, provide for him, and help him overcome his past. Surely this was what God wanted for him.

Les gave Nick a sidelong, slow smile of promise. Nick swallowed his fears and laid his free hand over their linked hands.

Chapter 18

From then on, a shift occurred in Nick's relationship with Les. No longer did he feel that they were testing the waters with one another. They seemed committed, almost married. Despite the stares and sometimes glares from onlookers, they held hands in public and enjoyed each other's company. Their friends at church gave their blessing and Nick felt as though he had finally found his place. He was special to someone – not just an unwanted addition to a household.

Spring arrived with a flurry of new customers until summer pushed her out of the way and demanded endless lawn care.

One evening, Nick and Les sat on the front steps of the duplex to watch the stars come out.

"We have been treated unfairly from the very beginning, you know," Les said.

"Who's 'we'?"

"Us. Homosexuals. All of us have experienced hate and persecution simply for being who we are. It's no different than being treated cruelly because of skin color or religious beliefs. Sometimes I think it all started back in the days of Adam and Eve."

Nick frowned. "How? Adam and Eve were a man and woman. If God created an opposite sex for Adam, then does God want all of us to be heterosexual?"

"Of course not. That's my point. God naturally set up the first couple to be heterosexual because he wanted them to procreate, to have children. They were supposed to fill the earth. But now everyone assumes that just because Adam and Eve were, we all should be too. It's the same argument as 'would you jump off a cliff just because everyone else is doing it'. I'm telling you, Nick, it doesn't make sense. My granddad was an oilman, but my father was a banker and now I work in landscaping and construction. No one thinks it's a sin that each generation has chosen different careers, so why should our sexual preferences be expected to remain the same?"

Nick shrank back a little from Les' intensity. "I guess I never thought about it that way."

"Yeah. Apparently, neither has a large percentage of the population. The gay rights movement may be making headway to protect our rights but there's still a long ways to go within the church community."

Nick thought of Anya Martin and her church. He couldn't imagine ever convincing her or her friends that God accepted all lifestyles equally. But maybe if he could convince her even the slightest bit, he would feel his own unrest ease up.

He swallowed. Maybe he would try. Despite all Les's approval, Nick still felt the need for Anya's – and, if he were to admit it, his father's approval. Maybe Nick would put her to the test. See if she loved him as much as she said she did.

Anya thumbed through her mail and stopped when she saw an envelope with Nick's name and address in the upper corner. He hadn't written or called in such a long time. The summer had come and gone without a word. She tore into the envelope.

Maybe this letter would give her insight as to why she had felt an increasing burden to pray for Nick. She scanned the opening paragraphs until she came to the reason he'd written.

"Les and I have gotten very close throughout the time I have lived here and share many things in common, including a love for each other. Be happy for me, Anya. I'm happier than I ever have been in my life.

We attend a church that accepts us and I feel that I am finally allowed to be the person I always was on the inside.

No doubt you are surprised, shocked maybe. I know your church doesn't agree with our ideology. But I know you care about people, which is why I trust you to know."

Anya flung the paper away from herself, an instinctual movement, as though the paper contained poison. She watched it float to the driveway and rest on the gravel.

The emerging spring sun scrambled back behind the cloud cover as though afraid and Anya half feared a bolt of lightning to sear the page into nothingness.

How could Nick turn to such a life? How could he be so deceived as to believe that God was pleased with him? And what exactly was he hoping to accomplish by telling her?

A gust of Kansas's leftover winter wind snatched the page and tossed it across the drive and into the field between her house and J.D.'s. She could not let J.D. see this letter. She did not know if Nick had communicated with his father since he had left but if J.D. was to find out, it needed to come straight from Nick.

Anya fetched the letter, holding it with her thumb and forefinger, much the way she held empty beer bottles when she picked up litter along the road.

She went inside and tossed the offensive words into the trash can only to dig them out again.

Nick had been right about one thing. She did care about people, even when those people messed up. Nick had trusted her with his revelation and she could not turn her back on an opportunity to stand in as a witness of the truth.

"Lord, Jesus," she moaned. Her mind could barely comprehend the magnitude of what Nick had told her, yet she ached all over. Sweet, susceptible Nick. How could she have let him go with this strange man? Why had she done nothing to find out more about the situation? She had felt checks in her spirit for some time now regarding Nick. Had the Holy Spirit prompted her to do something that she had not done? Was it her fault?

After Sunday service the next day, Anya tried to make excuses to Nell rather than go to their home for Sunday dinner – as was her habit.

"Oh, you have to come, Mom," Nell encouraged. "I invited Mitch and Brenna and have chicken and rice in the oven – your favorite. Of course, if you don't feel well..."

"I feel fine, just tired," Anya said. The last thing she needed was Nell going into "super mom" mode and fussing over a supposed illness. "I didn't sleep very well last night."

"You don't have to stay long. As soon as we've finished eating, you should go home and take a nap."

Despite her wishes, Anya allowed Avery to drive her since he was excited about getting his first driver's license. His chatter soothed her churning emotions and she was able to smile her way through the meal.

Mitch's careful consideration toward Brenna gave her reason to smile. Despite their age difference, Anya hoped that their relationship would work out. She enjoyed watching Brenna glow under Mitch's admiration.

But watching Brenna made her think of Nick. Both Nick and Brenna came into the Martin family around the same time. Both had been neglected and starved for love. Brenna's current happiness with Mitch only reminded her of Nick's false security under Les. Anya picked at her food and concentrated on laughing at all the correct places.

After the meal she offered to wash the dishes so she wouldn't have to go in the living room with the others. That way, she could excuse herself as soon as the dishes were done.

Nell cleared the table and dried dishes, pausing at the archway between the two rooms to engage in conversation.

Anya rubbed a scratch pad in circles over a particularly crusty pan. Her nose prickled and she swiped at it with her

wrist. This pain felt so debilitating. Why did it hurt so much –
as though she had experienced a sudden death? Maybe that was
it. She had. Perhaps not a physical death, but the death of
certain hopes and dreams for Nick.

"Lord," she thought. "It was almost easier when Russell
died. At least I could make sense out of that. I knew you were
orchestrating everything. With this, it feels as though the enemy
is winning and I can do nothing."

"Mom?"

Anya stopped rubbing. Small wonder she hadn't
scrubbed a hole in the pan.

"Mom, you're crying! Are you okay?" Nell peered at
her, concern puckering her face.

She could not pretend, not with the tears Nell had seen.
"No, not really." She gave Nell a wobbly smile.

"What is it?"

Anya knew that Nick had shared in confidence so she
only shook her head silently.

"Can I pray with you about it?"

From anyone else, the question might have sounded like
an invitation to share juicy news under the holy auspices of
prayer. But Nell was not a gossip and Anya knew that she would
pray fervently even without details.

"I'd like that very much," Anya whispered. Before she
could dry her hands, Nell wrapped her arms around Anya and
prayed a simple prayer that God would intervene in a mighty
way and that Anya would be comforted.

"Is everything all right?" Brenna joined them hesitantly.
Seeing her freshness and purity gave Anya a fresh batch of tears.
She turned back to the sink.

"Is it Sara?" Brenna's voice held panic.

"No," Nell answered quickly. "For all we know, Sara is
fine."

"It's Nick, isn't it?"

Anya turned slowly. Brenna held her hands over her stomach in a vulnerable gesture.

"Is he all right?"

"Brenna..." Anya tried to read the girl's face. Did Brenna still harbor feelings for Nick? Anya cleared her throat. "No, he's not all right. He thinks he's all right, but he's not."

"Then he told you." Brenna spoke flatly.

Anya stared at Brenna, not even breaking eye contact when Nell pressed a dishtowel in her hands.

"You're dripping all over the floor," Nell apologized.

"You already knew?"

The girl looked away, flustered. "At least if you're r...referring to what I think you are."

"I thought Nick was doing well. You told us about his decision to follow Christ," Nell interjected.

Anya wrung the towel over her fingers. "I know. But it seems he's allowed himself to be drawn into false theology."

"You don't think he's saved?" asked Brenna.

"I don't know."

"What kind of theology?" Nell asked gently.

Anya hesitated. "Well, it's very liberal."

"He told me he thought he might be g...gay." Brenna strangled on the word. "That's what you're talking about, isn't it?"

"Oh, Mom," Nell breathed.

"That man who offered him a job – the one he's staying with – I guess he..." Anya flapped her hands helplessly. "I feel so guilty. I should have done so much more for that boy."

"It's not your fault, Mom. You can't bear the burden of his choices," Nell said.

"But I am partially responsible. God placed a burden on both Russell and I regarding Nick when he first moved here. I feel like I've failed God, failed Nick."

Nell took the dishtowel back and hung it over the stove handle. "I guess this confirms what Brenna and I were talking about earlier. We were discussing how we both felt called to be more involved in intercessory prayer ever since Pastor Dean preached a series about it. Maybe this is the situation God is asking us to lift up."

"I've been w…wanting to be involved in a Bible study, too," Brenna said shyly. "But with Mother, it's hard to get away."

"Perhaps just the three of us should meet every week," suggested Nell.

"We could meet at my house," said Anya. "That way Brenna is not far from home."

"Or, m…meet at my house. Mother usually takes long naps in the early afternoon if that time works for both of you. And even if she's awake, she might actually join us."

Anya knew that Brenna prayed for her parents' salvation. "That sounds wonderful," she said.

When Anya turned back to the sink, hope rose within her. God performed miracles through the faithful prayers of His loved ones. Surely God would perform a miracle in Nick's life. That is, if Nick allowed it.

Nick reread the postcard from Anya with trepidation. She was coming here? He had written so boldly of his life and choices, wanting to justify himself in black and white but the instant the letter had fell from his hand into the narrow slot at the post office, he had regretted it. Now he supposed she would come with hellfire and damnation to win him back. Or worse yet, with tears and disappointment. He couldn't face her tears.

Anya parked beside Russell's old S-10. The duplex in front of her must be where Nick lived with that man, Les. No matter how hard she tried, she felt revulsion. She got out and tucked her purse strap over her shoulder as she locked the car.

She never locked her car at home but one had to be cautious in the city.

Nick had told her to meet him in the park across the street from the duplex. She didn't know if he wanted her to meet Les or not. She wasn't sure she wanted to meet Les.

Anya scanned the grassy area until she saw a young man sitting on a park bench, his back to her.

Taking a deep breath, Anya crossed the street but before she could approach him, the man stood and sauntered away. A glimpse of his face revealed that he was not Nick.

Anya frowned in confusion. Where was Nick? The S-10 meant he had to be near. Should she go to the duplex? Nick had not told her which duplex number, just to meet her in the park. She turned in a little circle, feeling silly.

A young mother passed her on the sidewalk, pushing a baby stroller and coaxing a dawdling toddler along. Anya smiled at them and said hello but the mother quickly looked away.

Anya sighed and made her way to the vacated bench. She sat and folded her hands over her purse. Distant sirens and traffic noise competed with the birds, but the park was a pleasant place to wait.

"Lord, help this meeting to go well," she prayed as she watched the young mother hoist the toddler into a kiddie swing. He chuckled as his mother pushed him. Had anyone ever taken the time to push Nick in a swing when he was that young?

Anya tightened her fingers over her purse in anxiety. Her stomach had felt fluttery ever since she had gotten in the car to drive here. Maybe God was trying to tell her this was not the time for her to be here. Then again, maybe she was supposed to be here and the enemy knew it and tried to make her awkward and cowardly.

"Mrs. Martin?"

She jumped.

Nick appeared from behind the bench. "I'm sorry I scared you," he apologized. "I figured you'd hear me walk up."

She quickly stood. "It's all right. I was just lost in my thoughts, I guess."

"Well, anyway, hi." Nick held out his arms for a hug.

That surprised her. Nick had never been demonstrative. Was his relationship with Les changing that? After the briefest of hesitations, she stepped forward.

"Hi yourself." She could feel the difference in his body as she hugged him back. He was filling out, becoming a man. She stepped back. "You're growing up."

He blushed. "I figured we could go out for lunch, if that's all right."

"That would be fine."

"There's a sandwich shop not too far from here. We can take my truck."

"That sounds lovely."

They began to walk toward the S-10.

"How is everyone back home?"

"Well, Sara emails her parents quite regularly. She is homesick but adjusting. She says the climate and constant noise of the city are the hardest to get used to but she loves the people. She tells very sad stories about street children begging for food and shanty towns within the city but she's also shared incredible stories of miracles. Her last email said that she felt as though she was gaining much more than she could give."

Nick smiled. "That sounds like Sara." He held open the truck door for Anya.

"Can she come home for a visit?" Nick asked as they pulled away from the curb.

"Not for a long time."

"I bet you miss her."

"I miss all my grandchildren when they move away. But it's easier than when my own children grew up."

"You have some kids in California, don't you?"

"Peter and Lin Zhu. Cassie and her husband live in Oregon, the twins are in Kansas City, Kathleen is in Bolivia, and of course, you know about Karl and Mitch."

"Sara talked about Kathleen a lot."

"She looks up to her aunt a great deal." After a pause, Anya said, "You remember Mitch, of course."

Nick nodded.

"He and Brenna Williams are seeing each other."

Nick stepped on the brakes a little too sharply for the red light in front of them.

"Isn't he a little old for her?"

"That's what I thought at first. Seven years doesn't seem like much if you are thirty and thirty-seven I suppose, but at eighteen and twenty-five it is quite a maturity gap. But Mitch and Brenna seem well suited. He is gentle and considerate with her and she adores him."

Nick winced. "She used to like me, did you know that?"

"I was aware of it."

Nick pulled around the corner when the light changed to green and parked. "Did she tell you?"

"No. I figured it out by watching. I also knew that you didn't return the feelings."

"Yeah. Well, I guess you know why, now."

There it was, hanging between them. The awful truth. Anya had come with the intent of confronting Nick in love. Now was the opening she had waited for, yet she felt a strong inner check.

"Lord," she argued. "Is this from you or the enemy? How can I keep silent? Am I condoning his actions if I do not speak out against them?"

Nick pulled the keys. "Are you hungry?"

She wasn't but she picked up her purse from the seat between them and followed him inside.

After ordering their food and engaging in a brief tussle over who should pay the check, with Anya as the winner, they enjoyed their deli sandwiches in relative silence.

On the way back, Nick took a short detour to show her a neighborhood where he had done landscaping. He pointed out retaining walls, bushes and perennials, and different types of fescue grasses. His knowledge impressed Anya and she told him so.

"I already knew some of this before I came here," he said. "But Les taught me a lot. But with laying tile, I didn't know a thing. Les could have laid me off until next summer but instead he trained me."

"Oh, Nick," she wanted to say. "Les has been training you in other ways as well. Dangerous ways." But again she kept silent.

"Which is a good thing," Nick said with a self-deprecating laugh. "I'd probably end up working as a Wal-Mart greeter without this job."

"There's nothing wrong with being a Wal-Mart greeter. But you would have many more options open to you. What about college? What about becoming a world-famous pianist?"

Nick acquiesced with a smile and shrug. They pulled in front of the duplex.

"Thank you for eating lunch with me, Nick. It was wonderful seeing you." Anya reached for the door handle.

"Wait." Nick touched her shoulder. "Would you like to go inside, meet Les?"

"Are you sure?"

"Yeah. I'd like for you to."

"I assumed you didn't when you said to meet at the park." She wondered if she sounded too bold.

"To tell the truth, I wasn't sure," Nick confessed. "I figured you came down here to lambaste me and that it would be better if I saw you by myself. But you haven't, at least not yet

anyway. I have to admit, Mrs. Martin, I was all nervous and
prepared to do battle."

Anya silently thanked the Lord for stilling her tongue
earlier.

"I know you don't agree with me," Nick went on. "And
I understand that. So, thanks for just being here."

She felt choked with sudden tears. "I love you, Nick.
You know that, don't you?"

He laughed. "You tell me practically every time you see
me." Then he sobered. "You are a mom to me, Mrs. Martin. If
there is one thing I've learned in the last nine months, it is how
to show appreciation and affection so I'll tell you now before I
lose my nerve. I love you too."

Anya cringed inwardly at his statement of learning to
show affection. But even with his choices, his ever-so-wrong
choices, she could not refuse his declaration. "Thank you for
telling me, Nick," she whispered.

Anya gathered her emotions as they climbed the stairs to
the upper level of the house. Now that he offered, she didn't
want to go inside. She didn't want to see the house where Nick
and his lover did only God knew what, didn't want to see the
man who held such influence over her Nick.

She had come, as Nick had guessed, to do battle and as
she entered the home, a spiritual heaviness came over her. This
was the battlefield. Her first impression of Les solidified the
feeling.

"So you're the lady who sent us cookies?" Les asked as
he shook her hand.

"Yes, that's me."

"How grandmotherly of you."

Anya flushed at the derogatory tone in his voice.

Nick looked back and forth between them nervously.
"Why don't we sit down?"

Anya perched on the edge of the couch and eyed Les's
impressive entertainment center. Nick sat in an armchair while

Les made a show of sitting on the arm and resting his hand on Nick's shoulder. Nick shrugged almost imperceptively and Les removed his hand.

"So, what brings you to our fair city?" Les asked.

"I came to see Nick." She shifted uncomfortably. Nick had told her that Les reminded him of Russell. She could make out a faint resemblance physically but the direct stare and antagonism coming from his face took away any nostalgia.

"Nick? No other reason?"

"Nick and his father were my neighbors for many years. Nick worked for my husband the first summer he was in Western Kansas."

"I know. He told me about you. Said you had thought about adopting him or something like that but never did."

Les had gone straight to her guilt. She sat straighter, refusing to let him make her feel inferior. "Nick is a special young man."

"I agree," Les said. Ignoring Nick's tiny sound of dissent, Les took Nick's hand in his. Anya kept her face as impassive as she could.

"Mrs. Martin plays the piano," Nick said hurriedly.

"Really? Did you teach Nick how to play?"

She shook her head. "Nick could already play when I met him. The first time I heard him on the piano, I was dumbfounded by his gift."

"He plays on the worship team at our church," Les said. "You should have come on a Sunday so you could hear him."

He was deliberately taunting her, she knew. She did not want to attend his church and he knew it.

"I would like to hear you play again sometime, Nick. I'm sure you've gotten even better, if that's possible."

Nick took a breath as if getting ready to speak but Les spoke first. "Nick's playing has improved since he got saved. We used to tease him about playing at church before but now I guess you could say his music is truly sanctified."

She couldn't hide the reaction on her face to the term "sanctified" in relation to this strange business of Nick and Les together in this house, going to church together at that church. Les saw it and jumped.

"So why don't you tell us why you really came?"

"Les," Nick protested.

"Come on, Nick. We all know it. She's worried about you and wanted to check up on you, to try to talk you into turning away from evil." He spoke the last word with derision.

Anya sat speechless. What could she say? Les was correct.

Les turned back to Anya. "You're just a homophobic," he accused.

Now that she could answer. Anya folded her hands over her purse. "I'm not phobic of you or Nick - of spiders, maybe."

Nick blinked.

"You know what I meant," Les said.

She felt her face redden as she answered him with the bluntness he seemed to want. "You meant that I disagree with your morals. And yes, I do. What do you say we agree to disagree?"

After a brief and bare silence, Les stood up. "I've got paperwork to do," he said and left.

"Did I make him angry?" Anya asked.

Nick truly looked confused. "I've never seen him like that before."

"I'm sorry, Nick. Maybe I should go."

Nick didn't argue. He stood and walked her to the car.

"How's my dad?" His eyes told her how hard it had been to ask.

She met his eyes. "Karl had to let him go. Your father found a job in town but didn't hold on to it. I don't know what he's doing now. His vehicle isn't at the trailer often."

Nick nodded slowly. "Does he ever talk about me, ask about me?"

"Nick, I rarely see him, much less talk to him. That doesn't mean he never thinks about you."

They stood in silence. Anya had the distinct impression that Les watched from an upstairs window.

"Nick, are you still thinking about college?"

"Not for a while. I'd need to get started on applications right now if I wanted to start in January but I don't think I will just yet."

She sighed. He always seemed to put it off one more semester. "Don't neglect your musical gift, Nick."

"I'm not," he said. "I play at church, remember?"

She took the plunge. "Are you still considering your own place?"

His face hardened. "Don't, Anya."

She nodded. "Well, this is goodbye then."

"Thanks for coming."

When he hugged her she didn't want to let go. "I'll pray for you, Nick."

"And I'll pray for you," he rejoined quickly. His words sent a needle through her heart.

Somehow she got into her car and dug her keys out of her purse. She drove away, waving at Nick's blurry figure on the stairs, blurry from her tears.

"Sara says to tell you both hello and that she misses you very much," Nell said as she joined Brenna and Anya at the dining room table in Brenna's home. "That's why I'm late. She was on the phone."

"What time is it in Thailand right now?" Anya accepted a mug of hot tea from Brenna.

"It's 2:00 in the morning."

"Which day?" asked Brenna.

"I had to ask Sara. The International Date Line always confuses me. It's 2:00 tomorrow morning."

Brenna shook her head with a little laugh. "It always amazes me that Sara is a half a day ahead of us."

"Did she get up in the middle of the night to call you?" said Anya.

"Yes. Next month, Karl and I get to set our alarm. We have an agreement that we will talk once a month and take turns getting up in the night.

"How is she doing?"

"She's fine. She sounded tired but she talked quite a bit about a little girl named Esha that the mission staff just took in. Sounds like she stole Sara's heart."

Brenna set two more mugs on the table. "That wouldn't take much."

Nell smiled. "No. Sara falls for children, needy or not. But Mom, I want to hear about your trip to Wichita. How did things go yesterday?"

Anya traced the top of her mug with her finger. Funny how old her hands looked these days. She told Nell and Brenna about her time with Nick and meeting Les.

"After seeing Nick and Les together," Anya went on, "I realized that Nick has placed Les in the role of a father, perhaps without either of them realizing it. Les is so much older and experienced. He has taught Nick a great deal about working on the job and Nick clearly follows his lead. Yet Nick still asked about J.D., as though he still longed for things to be right with his own father. Maybe somewhere deep inside, he's trying to find a father's love when he seeks another man's approval."

"That makes sense," Brenna said. "I always wanted people to like me. I thought if they did, then my parents' lack of involvement wouldn't make me feel so empty." She spoke softly, as she always did when she talked honestly about her family, even though her mother usually slept through their Bible studies.

"It's hard when families don't provide what God designed them to give," said Anya. "Children grow up not understanding God's nature and sometimes try to find fulfillment in destructive behaviors."

"Let's pray," said Nell, always ready to enter the throne room when Anya tended to continue bemoaning situations.

"Yes, let's," added Brenna.

Anya held out her hands to the younger women and they bowed their heads in unison.

"Father, God, we approach you in humbleness and love for you." Nell spoke with fervent sincerity. "We ask that You reach down to Nick this afternoon. We know that You have already touched him and made him curious about You. We know that You have begun a work in him that You have promised to complete, if Nick is willing to allow You to do Your plan. Give him a dissatisfaction with where he is. Let Your Spirit convict him of truth. Cause Nick to experience a change in his life that will affect a great number of people for the cause of Christ. Let Your name be glorified through Nick and the inerrant truth of Your Word be undeniable to him. We ask this in Your Son, Jesus' holy, holy name. Amen."

"Amen and amen," Anya added mentally.

Chapter 19

Anya recognized Nick's handwriting on the envelope and sent up a prayer of thanksgiving. Her visit to Wichita had not scared him off, then. It did surprise her that he wrote instead of calling. She had encouraged him when she was there that he could call her collect. Maybe he had inherited some of J.D.'s stubborn independence.

"Dear Anya, thank you for coming to visit me. I enjoyed our lunch together and apologize for Les. I think he felt threatened by you somehow. He says he's embarrassed about it now."

"I'll bet," Anya thought and immediately chastised herself for her attitude.

"Les and I have had some long talks since you were here about the verses that seemed to condemn homosexuality, at least at first glance.

I don't know why I want to tell you what I've learned about those verses, because you may choose not to believe what I write, but I guess I want to legitimize things to myself on paper more than anything else.

Les says that when Leviticus and Romans talk about men involved in homosexual acts, it was a bad thing because they were temple prostitutes to false gods. That is what made God hate it.

Les also explained God's destruction of Sodom by reading Ezekiel 16:49-50 to me. It says that the real sins of Sodom were that the people were arrogant, overfed and unconcerned about helping the poor and needy. Ezekiel says nothing about Sodom being destroyed for the "sin" of homosexuality.

Knowing all this fits what I am learning about God's character, about how He is a good Father. I have had a hard time learning to love and obey a heavenly Father, for you are well aware that my earthly father did not deserve it. But as I read the Bible and listen in church, I see how loving God is and I want to call Him my Father. He deserves the title. My own father certainly doesn't.

Anya folded Nick's letter. Les clearly had Nick's ear when it came to Biblical interpretation. But not entirely. He may have said that he needed to flesh out his thoughts on paper, but he had sent the letter. To her, that was an open door to rebut Les's teachings with the truth of God's Word. The Holy Spirit had restrained her when she was there, but now she was compelled to answer.

Anya went to her Bible. She needed the guidance of the Holy Spirit more than ever before as she studied the passages Nick had mentioned and penned a reply.

"Dear Nick, first of all, thank you for your honest letter. I am pleased to hear that you are spending time reading the Word of God. That is the best thing you can possibly do.

Regarding the scriptures you quoted in your last letter, lend me your ear (or eyes) for a moment.

I agree with you that it is entirely probable that the people were committing acts of homosexuality in conjunction with idolatry but think about the other sins listed – witchcraft and child sacrifice and more. Does that make child sacrifice all right as long as it is not done for idolatrous reasons? Either something is okay or it isn't.

As for the verses in Ezekiel, you are right that Ezekiel never says Sodom was destroyed because of homosexual sins. However, Jude 7 does. Jude writes, "In a similar way, Sodom and Gomorrah and the surrounding towns gave themselves up to sexual immorality and perversion. They serve as an example of those who suffer the punishment of eternal fire." (NIV)

Perhaps this is what Ezekiel referred to when he said, "they… did detestable things before me [God]" Ezekiel 16:50. Be very careful to make sure you get the whole story.

When people, well intentioned or not, pick apart the Holy Word of God or only choose bits and pieces, they cause God's truths to falter and waver in the eyes of man. Make no mistake though, Nick. God's truths themselves never change – only man's perceptions of them.

I care about you, Nick, and I am only mailing this letter after I have spent much time in prayer over it. Please understand that despite the fact that I used the letter as a debate, I would sincerely love to hear from you as often as you wish to write or call. And don't feel like you can't share more of your viewpoints with me. I would like to hear them. Perhaps we can challenge each other to greater growth and maturity.

With much love and prayer,

Mrs. Martin

"Don't believe what that woman tells you, Nick. How does she know any better than you or I? Is she a Bible scholar?" Les slammed his bottled water down on the kitchen countertop. Droplets of water sprayed on his shirt but he didn't seem to notice.

Nick smiled wryly. "She's the closest to a scholar of anyone I know."

Les shoved the square pizza box into the round trashcan with vengeance. "I get so sick of right wing conservatives smashing their theology down my throat when what we all need to remember is that God created and loves us equally."

Nick watched silently. He hated when Les worked himself up like this. He shouldn't have said anything about Anya's letter.

Not that Les's blue funk stemmed entirely from Anya – several of their largest landscaping clients had switched to a new company that promised lower rates. And lower quality, Les complained. Now Les was irritable about anything that had to do with money, including Nick's paycheck. No mention had been made for some time about Nick's going to college, much less the grant money Les had formerly promised. But to keep the peace, Nick never brought it up.

Maybe he needed to make sure he picked up the mail each day in case Anya wrote again. Nick felt sad that the two most important people in the world to him did not like each other.

"Brenna!" Mitch bounded down the apartment steps toward her. "How was your day?"

"Good," she said, turning to drink in his features. More and more she felt compelled to be close to him and hated their time apart, even though they saw each other nearly every day now.

"How did lunch go?" Mitch knew about his mother's and Brenna's conspiracy to ease Mrs. Williams into social situations.

"She didn't eat much and we stayed l...less than 20 minutes but she didn't go straight to bed when we got home so I consider it a major accomplishment."

"Good. I'm proud of you." Mitch beamed at her and she longed for him to touch her, hug her, to give her some physical token of approval. She knew Mitch cared for her deeply. She could see it written on his face, yet he never touched her, if she didn't count the hug he had given her when she had become a Christian. They had dated nearly a year now and he still hadn't even held her hand.

"Speaking of walks, do you want to take one before we go out to dinner?" Mitch asked.

Her stomach told her she needed to eat but she would gladly wait if he wanted. "That sounds nice."

Mitch shoved his hands into his jacket pockets and a strange look crossed his face.

"What is it?" she asked.

"I think I forgot something," he said, groping around in the pockets then checking his jeans' pockets as well. "Would you mind waiting while I go back upstairs?"

"Did you lose something?"

He wouldn't meet her eyes. "I hope not."

"I'll wait," she said. Mitch had never invited her up to his apartment. She knew he guarded their reputation carefully.

"Thanks, you're a jewel," he said and disappeared.

Brenna listened to his feet pounding up the stairs and before she had time to wonder, she heard them pounding back down. He reappeared, out of breath and red-faced.

"That was fast."

"I guess it was in my pocket the whole time," he said sheepishly.

Brenna's curiosity begged her to pry but she had never seen Mitch so flustered. He started to walk across the street without looking and Brenna pulled him back when she saw a car coming. Her hand on his sleeve seemed to startle him more than the reason she had touched him.

They walked to the park as they often did. Mitch made a point for them to spend time together in public places – the park, the library and restaurants, even the Laundromat once although he hid his underwear from her sight. Mitch led the way to a picnic table and sat down across from her. He dug in his pocket and pulled out a white paper, folded over until it was small and taped shut.

He took a deep breath and laid it between them.

"This is for you if you want it," he said.

Brenna frowned at the paper in confusion. "W…What is it?"

He pushed it closer to her. The paper caught in the crack between the boards of the tabletop and Brenna cautiously pulled it out. She broke the tape with her fingernail and stopped. Mitch watched her with an intensity that made her hands shake. She started unfolding the paper.

"Careful," Mitch warned.

One more fold and something fell out and lay on the splintered wood, something small and round and glittery.
Brenna sucked in her breath. It couldn't be – could it? She blinked, stared, blinked again. The diamond on the ring winked back at her.

"Do you want to put it on?"

She looked at him, seeing his nervousness and wanting to ease it but years of inbred low confidence washed over her. What if the ring was just a gift? What if he didn't mean engagement by it? Wasn't he supposed to ask those four special words, "Will you marry me" and say he loved her?

"Brenna?" His voice shook.

"W…What…" She couldn't continue without stuttering badly and chose silence.

"Don't you like it, Brenna?"

She found her voice. "D…Do you l…love m…me, Mitch?"

"Of course, I love you, Brenna Williams. I wouldn't be asking you to marry me if I didn't."

"Are you asking me to m…marry you?"

Immediately, Mitch came around to her side of the table and knelt beside her on one knee. "Is this better?"

She couldn't hold back her tears of relief. To hide them, Brenna pulled his head toward her and buried her face in his hair.

He looked up and the small movement was enough to bring their mouths together. His kiss sent waves of adrenaline through her and a desire that surprised her with its intensity. Mitch groaned and pulled away.

"I didn't intend to kiss you quite yet," he said. She could feel his arms trembling where they rested at her waist. "But I'll take that as a yes."

She could only nod. Mitch moved to sit next to her on the narrow bench and picked up the ring. "Give me your hand."

She held her breath as Mitch carefully slid the diamond ring onto her finger. She reached for him but he took her hands and held her at arm's length.

"I can't," he said.

That same feeling of inadequacy came rushing over her. Mitch must have seen some of the uncertainty for he squeezed her hands. "Oh Brenna, my sweet innocent," he said. "Here. There's one more thing we need to do."

Mitch flattened the paper that he had folded around the ring and took out a pen. He printed three words across the top, "Contract of Conduct".

"First of all, if we're engaged now – we are aren't we?" He waited for her nod before continuing. "We need to have a standard to stick to regarding physical touch. I know you've wondered why I never touch you. Truth is, when I'm with you, it is very difficult not to think about things that should be reserved for marriage. Not touching you helps me."

"Many times, I was afraid that you were just g…going out with me for friendship," Brenna confessed hesitantly.

"I know. I should have been more open with you before now. I wasn't fair to you. By protecting myself, I left you open to self-doubt and I'm sorry for that. I guess now I need to stop thinking like a bachelor and start thinking like a man committed to a woman. Because, Brenna, I am every bit as committed to you right now as I will be after we say our wedding vows. I waited to ask you until I was absolutely certain that you are the woman God intended for me."

"Does that mean we c…can kiss again?" She looked at his lips, anticipating, blushing at her boldness.

"That's what I'm talking about, Brenna. You make me hungry for so much more than I think you realize."

She looked away, chastened. "C…Can we hold hands?"

"I think so." He reached over to take her hand in his, writing down the words, "No kissing. Handholding allowed." on his sheet of paper.

"After we come up with a standard, let's have someone sign it with us to keep us accountable," he said.

"Karl and Nell?" she asked. Her head felt light. Had he just proposed? Was it real? She looked at the ring on her finger for reassurance.

And this whole business of a contract was new and odd. It certainly wasn't included in any of the romance novels she had ever read. Brenna thought of the hardships her own parents had faced as a result of marrying out of necessity and the barbed comments her grandmother still handed out. Mitch's approach gave her a sudden rush of thankfulness.

"That's who I thought of." He was smiling at her approvingly.

"Thank you for doing this," she said, squeezing Mitch's hand, her fiancé's hand. She would relish using the word.

Mitch squirmed as though he were nine years old again and trying to hide something from his stepmother.

"Are you certain about this, Mitch?" Anya asked him.

"More certain about Brenna than I've ever been about anything in my life, short of knowing I need a Savior," Mitch said fervently, almost too fervently as though he were on the defensive.

"She's very young."

"You never complained before."

"I know. I've enjoyed watching the two of you and I thought – still think – it's a good thing. I know you love Brenna deeply, Mitch. And I know she loves you, adores you even."

Mitch reddened at her words.

"And that's precisely what concerns me," said Anya. "I see her adoring you almost too much."

"Too much? We're getting married, Mom. I would hope she adores me."

"Lately it seems that her adoration is almost turning into a type of worship, Mitch."

Mitch flinched.

"I'm afraid that she will place all her hopes and dreams in you," Anya persisted.

"Isn't that what she's supposed to do? I'll be her husband, her protector. It will be my job, my God-given responsibility to take care of her, to make sure she is happy."

"To a point, Mitch. You can only provide those things for her to a point. Don't promise what no human can deliver."

Mitch threw up his hands and stood up from Anya's table.

"Only God can truly satisfy her, Mitch. You know that."

"It's not like she's some adolescent with rose-colored glasses on. She's more mature than others think. Look at the selfless way she serves her mother."

"I didn't say I don't like her, Mitch. I do. And I know she's good for you. I just want you to be aware that she's still a baby in Christ and naïve enough to see a fairy tale ending. I don't want her to put her faith in man instead of God."

"What are you saying, Mom? What do you want? Do you think we shouldn't get married?" Mitch couldn't hide his hurt.

Her reticence baffled him. No one else had shown any negativity to his engagement announcement. Karl and Nell had given their blessings and best wishes and complimented Mitch and Brenna's wisdom in writing out and practicing barriers to protect their pre-marriage purity. Brenna's father shook his hand and told Mitch that as long as Brenna was happy about it, so was he.

"I'm not saying you shouldn't get married," Anya said. "I think you should. However, I do think you should wait. You, personally, may be ready right now and goodness knows, I'd imagine your physical desires are telling you to speed up the process, but Brenna might need more time to grow up."

He felt his ears go hot as he thought of the strong urgings his body had been giving him and at the thought of his stepmother knowing what he felt like.

"I'm twenty-six, Mom. I think I'm old enough to make this type of decision now."

"But Brenna just turned nineteen."

Mitch walked to the back door and looked out the window at Anya's garden plot. The plants had dried and withered after the first frost and lay flat on the ground, not unlike his balloon of giddiness. "We haven't talked about a wedding date yet," he said, a little gruffly. "I'll do some praying about it."

"Pray with Brenna, Mitch." She walked up behind him and patted his back. "You'll make a good decision together, I'm sure."

"Les, I've been wondering about something," Nick paused his even strokes with a damp sponge over the grout work on the newly laid tile floor. He and Les were working in the renovated entryway of a church large enough to boast 1,000 members. The stained glass windows along the front depicted Jesus with lepers, Jesus holding children on his lap, Jesus preaching on a mountainside, Jesus on the cross and Jesus ascending back to heaven.

Nick rinsed his sponge in a bucket of water. The windows made him nervous. He knew this church's stance on homosexuality. The denomination had made bold statements against his kind last summer when gay activists organized a parade in Washington D.C.

That, coupled with Anya's gentle rebuttals to everything Les told him made Nick almost afraid to look at the artist's depiction of Jesus' face.   He worried every time Les affectionately snuck in a caress.

Les teased him about his prudishness, saying that it would do the pastor good to see them, but Nick was more concerned about Jesus' eyes watching them from the stained glass. Maybe he had less faith than Les, but he could never seem to feel completely at ease with his choices.

"What have you been wondering?" asked Les.

"You know the Bible says that 'all scripture is God breathed'," Nick said, "but if there are mistakes in it, or misinterpretations by the interpreters, how do I know what parts to take literally and what to not?"

Les sat up on his heels and stretched his neck muscles. Nick hoped Les would not see through his question to the doubts Anya had placed in his mind.

"I struggled with that for a while too. I agree that everything in the Bible is true and you can trust what it says. The catch is, you can trust what it says in the original language. The problem is that many years and cultural changes have passed, so it has become impossible for men, even trained scholars of Greek and Hebrew, to translate exactly what the original writers meant. I guess my conclusion after lots of thought was this - I don't totally trust what the Bible has been translated to say, but I do trust the original text to be perfect and infallible. Does that make sense?"

Nick nodded even though Les had not really answered anything. How could he know what to and what not to trust if he couldn't trust the translations, since that was all he could read? Did he have to learn Greek and Hebrew? If the scholars couldn't be accurate, how could he hope to be?

Anya's philosophy was simpler – believe it all or not at all. But to go back to a literal belief in the Bible would mean that he was wrong, very wrong. And what would that mean for his future? If only Les could give him a more satisfactory answer. Nick felt even more troubled.

He worked up the courage to ask about Les again as they cleaned up their tools at an outside hydrant before going home.

Les sighed as he squeezed water from a sponge. "Nick, Nick. When are you going to quit beating yourself up over this? Let it go. Relax. You know you have experienced the Holy Spirit. Do you question that experience? You said you felt clean and changed after praying the prayer of faith. Did you imagine that feeling?"

Nick shook his head no to each of Les's questions.

"God loves you, Nick. Believe that when nothing else makes sense to you."

"I feel okay until I read the Bible."

"Then stop reading it. Follow the Holy Spirit. Listen to what He tells your heart. The Bible isn't the only way God speaks, you know. Do you believe that God is big enough to speak to His people today, the same way He spoke to Abraham and other patriarchs in the Bible?"

Nick flushed. Les had a way of making him feel as though his doubts were childish and immature. Maybe they were.

"Hey." Les rubbed his fingers over Nick's cheek affectionately. "Questions are good. I'm glad you asked me and I promise I won't stop loving you no matter what you ask."

Nick pushed down the handle on the spigot to turn off the water and resisted the urge to glance around and make sure no one had seen Les touch him.

"You're still worried about those verses that seem to be against us, aren't you?"

Nick didn't answer.

"Jesus never said anything about homosexuality, ever. Think on that for a while."

Nick did. And he wrote Anya about it too. She wrote back promptly.

As soon as Nick heard Les turn on the water to take a shower, he retrieved Anya's latest letter from where he had hidden it when it came in the mail earlier that day. He grabbed one of Les's gardening magazines and sat on the couch, using the magazine as a cover in case Les finished faster than usual.

"Dear Nick," she wrote. "You are correct that the Bible does not record Jesus saying anything for or against homosexuality. However, I'm sure you understand the triune nature of God. All three parts of God are one – God the Father, God the Son (Jesus), and God the Holy Spirit. None of the parts of God can act in a manner inconsistent with the others. God (all three Persons) wrote the entire Bible, inspiring men with what to write down. God (including Jesus) did, in fact, have much to say about homosexuality, adultery and fornication when you refer to other books in the Bible besides the Gospels. You see, Nick, God is unchanging. All the books of the Bible are equally true and important and their truths merge together. If God the Father said it in the Old Testament, you can be sure that God the Son is in full agreement.

But your argument remains that Jesus said nothing about the issue while on earth. Think for a moment. If you were to write a memoir about Russell and try to capture on paper everything he ever did or said, could you? John wrote in the Gospel of John, chapter 21 and verse 25 that if all the things that Jesus did were written down, the whole world could not hold all the books.

Jesus may not have been recorded as talking about homosexuality but He did talk about heterosexuality. Read Mark 10:6-9. "But at the beginning of creation God 'made them male and female. For this reason a man will leave his father and mother and be united to his wife, and the two will become one flesh. So they are no longer two, but one'. Therefore what God has joined together, let man not separate." (NIV)

Now consider if Les were to tell his clients that he had decided to stop pulling weeds from his sod – because weeds have just as much right to be there. The customers would laugh at him and go to a different company for their lawns.

Nick stopped reading and frowned. That much was true for gardening, but if the weeds represented homosexuals, then surely Anya did not suggest they be pulled out and thrown away. Les had warned him of people's hatred and intolerance. With difficulty, he continued reading.

"Weeds (or sin), when left in a person's life, will grow and re-seed until they have multiplied so much that the desirable plants (good works or blessings) become choked and unhealthy, maybe even die completely."

Nick shifted uncomfortably. He wished he could talk to Les about it, but he was afraid of pushing Les' patience.

As if hearing his name in Nick's thoughts, the bathroom door banged open and Les came out rubbing his wet hair with a towel.

Nick turned the magazine page over the letter and pretended to read.

"The shower feels great, Nick. You should have joined me but I made sure there would still be hot water left for you."

Nick could feel warmth from the shower's hot water emanating from Les's skin. He hated his attraction and wanted it at the same time.

"Thanks, but I think I'll finish this first." Nick held up the magazine carefully so that the letter would not fall out.

Les shrugged and left. Nick looked at the pages before him. The article ironically outlined weed control.

"I'm so glad you're here." Brenna greeted Anya and Nell at the door. "I want to show you something."

They followed her to the kitchen bar, their usual spot for Bible study. Brenna had spread bridal magazines and computer printouts on the table.

"See this? Isn't it beautiful?" she enthused, holding out a page with a picture of a woman modeling an upswept hairstyle and lacy bridal veil.

"Quite," Anya told her. "So is the price in the bottom corner."

"Oh, that." Brenna waved her hand. "I'm obviously not getting it from there. I'm just trying to get ideas."

"Have you done any shopping yet?" asked Nell.

Brenna glanced quickly over her shoulder. Anya looked beyond the girl to see the shadowed shape of Mrs. Williams, huddled in the darkened living room. Anya wished she could understand Brenna's mother. No matter how hard she tried to reach her, to communicate past the despondent look in her eyes, Anya felt powerless. Brenna had not been able to convince her to come back to Anya's for another meal, even though Anya and Brenna both agreed that the sooner Mrs. Williams could come again, the better.

Anya stepped into the arch between the dining area and living room. "Hello, Mrs. Williams," Anya said softly.

The woman lifted her hand in a limp wave but turned her face away. Anya slipped back to Brenna and Nell.

"I've mostly window shopped on the Internet," Brenna was saying soft enough for Mrs. Williams to not hear. "I figured I might need to do most of the shopping through the mail so I don't have to leave Mother alone too long."

"Oh, but that takes away half the fun," protested Nell, adopting the same low tone. "Mom and I can take you sometime. Surely she would be fine for a day or two."

Anya knew of the suicide attempts that had sent Mrs. Williams into psychiatric care in Denver more than once. To her knowledge, Brenna had not shared with anyone but her and Mitch about her fears of giving her mother any opportunities.

Anya also knew that such fear and loyalty could cause conflict during the first formulative days and years of marriage, especially if Mitch began to feel that he was less important to Brenna.

Mitch had gone ahead with wedding plans for the coming Christmas, despite her warnings. Anya knew that her role now was to support but she couldn't keep back the questions that she knew the two of them needed to consider. "What will you do after the wedding?" she asked.

"Mother was assigned a new case manager who recently moved to the area," Brenna said. "She's supposed to be really good. We're also working with some new drug combinations. For now, I plan on coming over every day to make sure she's doing all right and taking her meds but I want to be home with Mitch in the evenings. My grandparents have offered to hire someone to come in kind of as a housekeeper and company for Mother, just to watch out for her. Grandmother is insistent that I shouldn't have to now."

"That will be expensive," Nell said.

"My grandparents are willing to pay for it. They are quite wealthy," Brenna said matter-of-factly. "It's a little hard for my father to accept their financial help but it's either that or grandmother threatening to come live here again."

All three women winced. Anya had met Brenna's grandmother and had been treated with all the scorn the woman felt necessary to bestow on a mere Kansas peasant. Nell had likewise heard tales from Sara.

"Let's remember that your grandmother needs the Lord too," Nell quickly reminded. "Another prayer need."

"Yes," Brenna said fervently. "Let's sit down and start, shall we?"

Anya rubbed her fingers over the worn cover of her Bible, tracing the spidery lines of the leather. She sighed heavily. "If we're sharing prayer concerns, I got another letter."

Brenna and Nell didn't have to ask where the letter came from.

"I just can't seem to get through to him," Anya told them. "Every time I get a new letter, it's full of 'Les says this' and 'Les says that'. He never responds to my answers. I don't know if he is even paying attention. He just brings up a whole new argument, as though Les is coaching him. Sometimes I wonder if he's trying to convince himself by writing it all down and other times I wonder if he thinks he can change my mindset or maybe he's deliberately trying to hurt me. I don't know anymore. I'm so frustrated."

Nell reached over and curled her hand over Anya's fretting hand movements. "Mom, the important thing is that he continues to write. As long as you stay in contact with him, you have opportunity to proclaim the truth. I think it's a good thing that he's willing to discuss the issue. I'm surprised he hasn't avoided it altogether. It doesn't sound as though he's trying to hurt or proselytize you. It sounds as though something deep inside him wants to check what Les says to see if it is really true. He may not realize it himself but it sounds as though he doesn't fully trust Les. And he obviously does trust you."

"He shouldn't." Anya spoke indignantly. She stopped sheepishly. "I mean, shouldn't trust Les. Aside from the obvious 'older man taking advantage of younger man' trick, Nick has never trusted men. Well, I take that back. He was learning to trust Russell, but that was so long ago and Nick never had time to learn what it was to be a man himself before Russell died."

Anya took off her glasses and rubbed her nose. "I just kick myself over and over for not having stepped in and done something during those years after Russell died. If only I could do something now."

"I know," Nell murmured. "Karl and I have regretted that as well. We had our perfect little family but Nick could have come and lived with us. Karl says he should have taken over the father role that Dad started."

Brenna cleared her throat. "Forgive me, but should either of you worry about the past? Can you change anything? Our job right now is to give Nick the truth. You know, sow the seed. Isn't the rest up to Nick and the Holy Spirit? He's reading his Bible. He's asking questions. The word of the Lord never returns void."

Anya lowered her head. The young teaching the elder.

"That sounds good in theory," said Nell, "but is Mom right that we should do more?"

Brenna smiled the sad little smile she always got when she spoke of her mother. "I learned early on that I could do nothing to help my mother get well. That was something she had to decide. It stings that she has chosen sickness rather than her family or God's love but m...maybe Nick told the truth when he said he really did have a conversion experience. If so, can we trust the Holy Spirit to convict him? I'm not saying that you quit writing to him, Anya," Brenna added quickly, "or that we quit p...praying but the burden of change is not ours."

That evening after Anya went home, she thought long and hard about what Brenna had said. Truly, the girl was right and Anya felt proud of her progress and maturity – proud to know Brenna would soon become her daughter-in-law. Maybe she had been wrong about Brenna's not being ready for marriage. She hoped so.

Anya pulled her Bible across the table and opened it to the bookmark that kept place for her daily readings. She used to read from God's word early in the morning. That time had worked best for her after marrying Russell with all his children to care for once they woke up. She would kiss Russell while he slept and sneak from their bed to sit at the table with a cup of hot tea and God. Russell had once told her that when she came back to bed to snuggle, her face shone, not unlike Moses whose face had shown with radiance after being on Mount Sinai with the Lord.

But now in the long evenings of widowhood, she sought refuge in the words of her Lover, the morning hours not quite enough to fulfill her.

She was reading from the book of Jeremiah, the prophet who foretold not only the eventual destruction of the Israelites but also the tender way in which God would restore His people.

Anya opened to the thirty-first chapter. Her mind wandered as she read, worrying about Nick, and she found herself backing up to read verse 16 again in order to focus. "This is what the Lord says: 'Restrain your voice from weeping and your eyes from tears, for your work will be rewarded,' declares the Lord. 'They will return from the land of the enemy.'" (NIV)

If only she could capture the verse and force God to uphold the promise as a promise regarding Nick. How she would love to rest in the surety that Nick would return to her from the enemy. How she longed to know that her communication with Nick was bearing fruit.

The ringing of her phone surprised her. Who would call late in the evening? She felt a dread seize her as she picked up the receiver – a dread that came every time the phone rang at a strange hour. It was Karl. The news he delivered wasn't good - and it had to be passed on to Nick.

Nick saw the name on caller ID and briefly considered letting the answering machine take the call. Then he thought about what Les would say if Les knew that she had called. Better for him to answer now than have Les see her name.

"Hello, Mrs. Martin."

"Hello!" Anya's voice sounded surprised on the other end. "You must have caller ID."

"Yeah."

"I can't quite get used to everyone knowing who I am before I even speak. Of course, back in my day everyone had party lines and your neighbors could listen in on your conversations. I much prefer today's technology."

Nick laughed in spite of himself.

"How are you, Nick?"

"I'm fine. And you?" The commonplace phrase came out of him from long practice.

"All right, I suppose."

Her voice told him otherwise. He braced himself but she continued with small talk.

"Are you planning on coming to Mitch and Brenna's wedding at Christmas?"

Nick thought of the invitation he had dropped in the side pocket of his pickup door. "I hadn't decided."

"I'll have some family staying here at the house but I'll save you a room if you want."

Nick rolled Les's computer chair across the room to pull out the pages he had been printing when she had called. "If I did end up coming, I guess I'd probably stay with my dad."

Anya sighed. "Actually that's the reason that I'm calling. When was the last time you talked with J.D., Nick?"

"When I left to move down here."

"That's been close to a year and a half."

"I know." He couldn't help sounding impatient even though he regretted his snappishness. "Did you call to jump on me about that?"

"No." She drew out the word.

"What is it? What's he done?"

"Your father's in a bit of trouble, Nick. He was arrested as a suspect in a hit and run accident. He claims he didn't do it but the police think he was too drunk to remember or even realize."

Nick's mouth became dry. "Was anyone hurt?"

"Yes." She seemed to struggle before continuing. "Max Greeley's granddaughter was killed."

"Max Greeley?"

"You may not have known him. He ran the town Laundromat for many years."

"I remember him. We used the Laundromat until I was in high school."

"His family was visiting from out of state – from somewhere north, I think. The granddaughter was out jogging."

"And he didn't see her? Whoever hit her?" Nick clung to the hope that his father told the truth.

"His truck has a dent in the front fender that wasn't there before. They found blood. Apparently he sideswiped her and never even knew it."

Nick lowered his face onto the desk in front of him, ignoring the bleep of the computer when his forehead touched a key that the machine didn't like.

"The evidence is fairly clear. They're keeping J.D. in the county jail until his trial or until someone posts bail."

"When is the trial?"

"I'm not sure."

"Do you think they'll convict him?"

"I don't know for sure, Nick. But it's looking very likely, especially with the other accidental death on his record."

"The other one?"

"Russell's," she said, as though he should know.

The office chair seemed to swivel and spin him around the room. "What are you talking about?"

"You... didn't know?"

"Know? How would I know? No one ever told me anything about that day." He was snapping at her again and this time didn't care.

"J.D. was driving the tractor the day Russell... got hit. He had been drinking. That's why he didn't work for nearly two months afterwards and started going to A.A."

Nick had been lost in his own fog of grief during that time, not even noticing his father's troubles. If he thought about it hard enough, Nick could recall J.D.'s sleeping in late and not going to work. He could also recall the absence of alcohol for a short time. But J.D. had never said anything about the accident to him, not a word.

"I'm sorry you had to find out this way, Nick. I just assumed that you knew. I assumed that was why you seemed so angry and distant with everyone, especially your father."

Nick thought of how he had blamed God, how he had nearly refused to accept God as a Father because of his bitterness over Russell's death. And here his earthly father had been responsible the entire time, never once admitting to it, never once apologizing.

The old anger rose up within him – anger that he thought he had put aside forever.

"Nick, why don't you come home?"

"Home?" he spat. "He never made it much of a home for me."

"Nick..."

"Why should I be there for him? He never was for me. I've made a new life for myself here. I'm happy here. I have absolutely no desire to go back. Don't try to make me feel guilty."

"Are you happy, Nick?" She put the emphasis on the word "are".

"Yes!" Even to him, his voice sounded rebellious and forceful. "And don't give me any of your 'living in sin' spiel."

"I didn't say anything about that." Her defensiveness was like waving the proverbial red flag in front of a bull.

"You didn't have to."

"Nick, we were talking about your father, not you."

He didn't want to accept her peace card. He wanted to lash out at something, somebody. "Tell the truth, Mrs. Martin. You don't think I can be all right in God's eyes. You don't approve of me, do you? Truth is, I've always been gay and you never would have approved, not even if you'd done the Christian thing and adopted me. You only write and call because you're trying to fix me."

His words hurt her. He knew by her silence. The explosions inside his head disappeared with a wave of remorse.

"I'm sorry," she finally said. "I didn't realize you felt my disapproval so strongly."

He rubbed his nose. "It's just that… I want so much for you to understand."

"Nick, this is one area where we'll have to agree to disagree."

He wasn't ready to let go. ""But God loves me. And I am saved. I know this without a doubt. I had a salvation experience in a large part because of the prayers and love I felt at a gay church and from Les. So how can gay be wrong?"

"Nick, I read a story once about the man who wrote the song 'Amazing Grace'. You know the song, don't you?"

"Don't change the subject."

"I'm not. I'm trying to make a point here. How much do you know about the author of the lyrics?"

"Nothing." Nick fiddled with the mouse, drawing invisible circles on the computer monitor.

"The author was John Newton. He was the captain of a slave ship. He became a Christian but he continued to work in the slave trade for a number of years. His salvation experience did not make his actions any more tolerable to the Africans who found themselves torn from their homeland and families. Just because we are saved does not mean we can do anything we want."

"Did he ever stop?"

"Yes."

"What if he hadn't?"

"I believe that since he wanted to follow the Lord and read the Bible diligently in order to know what the Lord required, then there was no possible way for him to continue in his sin for the rest of his lifetime. The Bible convicts of sin and lays out God's standards. Because of the Bible, John Newton knew he had to stop slave trafficking, not only his own slave ship, but others' as well. He later helped pass a law in England that stopped the practice of slave trade."

The phone felt clammy. Nick wiped it off on his jeans and switched to the other ear.

"Nick, I didn't call you to argue about this."

"I know."

"I felt that you deserved to know what was going on with your father. It's your choice what you do from here. Just know that you have a place to stay if you ever need it."

Nick gave her the obligatory thank you and hung up. Not that he had any intention of going – what would he do, go visit J.D. in jail? He couldn't imagine having anything to say to his father, wasn't too sure he even had anything to say to Anya anymore either.

He went back to the computer but instead of finishing his work, he looked up John Newton on the Internet.

Chapter 20

Les slid onto the bar stool and slapped the seat next to him. "What'll you have, Nick?"

Nick sat, trying to look more adult than he felt. He could feel the music vibrate through the stool and through his body and the swirling lights made him dizzy.

"I'll have a Coke," he said.

Les laughed. "A Coke?"

"I'm only eighteen," Nick reminded him in a low voice.

"So. They let you in here. They can give you whatever you want."

Nick looked at the glitzy rows of hanging wine glasses above him and thought of how Les had winked at the bouncer who took their I.D.'s at the door. The bouncer had given Nick's driver's license back without comment and stepped aside.

"I'll have a Coke," he said stubbornly. He wasn't about to become like his father.

Les smirked a little as though Nick had asked for something funny but he ordered one for Nick when the bartender came. Les turned and leaned back against the bar with his elbows. "Tim and Cal are having a great time."

Nick turned as well. Their friends had joined the many same-sex couples out on the dance floor and laughed as they moved with the music.

"Too bad you don't dance," Les said.

Nick hated when Les treated him condescendingly. But he was glad that Les didn't try to make him dance. He was uncomfortable enough sitting at the bar.

Their drinks appeared in front of them and Nick tentatively stirred his before taking a sip. Les gulped whatever he had and slapped his glass down.

"You'll be okay here?" Les asked.

"Um, fine."

"Be back in a little bit." Les left him and found a dance partner. Nick watched them in irritation and hurt.

"What's a kid like you doing in here?"

Nick turned. A man wearing sunglasses had sat down in Les's empty seat, a frothing mug of beer in his hands.

Nick wasn't sure how to answer or even if he should.

"I'd better warn you, kid. Les Howland isn't the best commitment material."

"You know Les?"

"Know Les? I lived with him for over 5 years until Les decided he likes 'em younger. Looking at you, I'd say he's making a new record."

"I'm 22,' Nick lied.

"Yeah, and I'm a millionaire."

The man's sunglasses bothered Nick. If a man's eyes really were the window to his soul, what would this man's eyes tell him?

"Did you want to talk to Les? Should I go get him for you?"

The stranger ignored his question. "So how does Les hit on guys these days? Is he still doing the nice guy routine of offering the spare bedroom and a job? Don't tell me. He offered you scholarship money too."

The man knew too much to be bluffing.

"Trouble with Les is he always tries to put religion into everything. Me, I just admit I'm a sinner and enjoy it." The man laughed into his beer and took a long draught. "How about you? You into religion?"

"I'm a Christian, yes," Nick said.

"Christian." The man laughed again. "You guys seem to think that having a nice label will earn you more rights. Good luck. Listen, kid, when Les turns out to be a jerk, and I guarantee he will, look me up. I don't mind leftovers."

"Come on, Nick." Les approached them and stood between Nick and the stranger, putting his back to the stranger with what seemed to Nick to be a deliberate snub. "They're clearing the dance floor for the contest Tim and Cal told us about. Let's go watch."

Nick stood up.

"Les, Les, you wouldn't walk off without saying hello, would you?" The man slid over onto Nick's empty stool so that he was no longer behind Les.

"Gary, what a surprise," Les said coolly. "I would have thought things were much too busy in Houston for you to come back for a visit."

"Houston?" Nick's voice squeaked. He thought of Les's trip down to Houston and the testy weeks that followed. Had Les's business proposal been something else altogether?

Les shot Nick an irritated look. "It's not what you think, Nick."

"Yes it is," said Gary.

"Don't believe him," Les said tightly. He stalked off.

Nick followed Les, only too glad to escape but he couldn't help glancing back. Gary, the sunglasses man, watched him with a half smile, the fingers of one hand tracing around the rim of Nick's barely touched Coke. He lazily brought his fingers to his lips and Nick shuddered.

What had Les seen in that guy – if Gary had told the truth? And had Gary told the truth about Les's hook and bait for him and other young men - and Houston as well? Nick felt shaken off the sturdy security he had found in Les.

Les pushed until they reached the front of a crowd that had formed on the far end of the dance floor where the lights were dim and the music was loud and demanding.

Tim and Cal grinned at them and motioned to a line-up of models, no, Nick realized, men in drag. The men began to prance down a makeshift runway through the center of the crowd to the beat of the music.

"There he is," Cal pointed. "We told you it would be a surprise. Doesn't he look great?"

Nick looked at the figure, curvy and full-chested despite the hairy legs that stuck out underneath the red dress.

"Don't you recognize him?" Les was laughing.

It was Marc, drummer Marc. The Marc who prayed in such a soft voice that no one really heard him now strode boldly down the runway, flaunting and jouncing and making Nick's face flush in shame.

What little security Nick had left disappeared as he watched his church friends hooting and catcalling. He watched only a moment longer and left, shoving back through the mass of flesh and underlying evil until he was free on the sidewalk outside.

He breathed in and out deeply, wondering what he should do. A group of men standing along the outside wall of the club stared at him in a way that made him feel nervous. He stuffed his hands in his pockets and began to walk.

"Hey, Nick."

He recognized the voice. The sunglasses man. Gary.

"That's what Les called you, right?" Gary caught up with him. "That is your name?"

Nick kept walking.

"What are you doing out here all alone?"

Gary's tone reminded Nick just how alone he really was. He stopped, not wanting to stay at the club but not wanting to get any farther away either. The people that made him so nervous just moments before meant safety. This Gary guy wouldn't try anything in front of others.

"I left something out in the car," he said. "But now I can't remember where we parked."

"What's Les driving these days? Maybe I can help you find it."

"No thanks. I'll just go back inside. I don't need it that bad." Nick stepped away.

"Suit yourself." Gary leered and Nick knew he didn't believe him. "Remember what I said, Nick. I'll take you in when Les is tired of you. Just tell him to give you my number."

Nick rubbed his face as he walked back inside. He felt like a prisoner.

The first two weeks of confinement had been nothing but shivering, sweating and screaming for booze but finally J.D. felt he could bear it. The thirst for alcohol still burned in him and made his hands tremble like an old man's, but at least he felt sane.

When the bars had clanged shut behind him the morning after the night he couldn't remember, J.D. had felt certain that no one would remember him past the few token hours worth of a trial that would send him to another hole in a different part of the state. He knew he deserved it.

But Karl Martin surprised him by coming to visit once a week. They talked about crops, weather, horses, even news from Nick if the boy had written or called Anya that week. J.D. learned more about his son during his imprisonment than all the months before. Every Tuesday J.D. would become convinced in his gut that Karl would never show - but still Karl came.

J.D.'s court date was set for a month from now. The court-appointed lawyer had only come in to see him once and J.D. held out no hopes for a release. God had caught up with him and would mete out punishment for all his crimes and sins. The Bible in his cell said so.

"Don't forget to pick up the check from the church secretary before you leave," Les told Nick when he sent him to put on the last coat of grout sealer.

Nick admired the tile in the church entryway after finishing, liking the way the stained glass windows spilled colors onto the ceramic. He loaded up the last of the tools before he remembered Les's instructions. He went back inside, using a side door so that he would not have to walk on the wet grout lines.

The secretary's chair sat empty. Nick wondered if he should write a note or just leave.

"May I help you?" The pastor entered the office, carrying a stack of thick books. His glasses were slipping off his nose and when he reached for them, the top two books began to slide. Nick quickly took the books from the stack and set them on the secretary's desk before they could fall.

"Thank you," said the pastor. He set the other books down as well. "What can I do for you?"

Nick hated asking for money. He would have preferred to bill the church through the mail.

"Oh, of course," said the pastor before Nick could answer. "You're here for payment for the tile job. The floor looks fantastic, by the way."

"Thank you."

"Connie said she had the check ready for you. I wonder where she put it?" He began nudging around papers on the secretary's desk. "You know, we were extremely blessed to have the funds for this project. God provided the last amounts we needed through a special offering last Sunday."

"That's great," Nick said, trying to sound enthusiastic.

"Here it is." The pastor handed Nick the slip of paper. "I believe it's made out for the full amount."

"I don't know what it should be," Nick said. He folded the check and slid it into his pocket. "I'm sure Les will let you know if anything needs to be different."

The pastor leaned back against the desk and folded his arms across his chest, only to unfold them in order to push up his glasses again. "May I ask as to the nature of your relationship with Les?"

Nick stiffened. "That's none of your business."

The man smiled genially. "Your soul is my business. That's part of being a pastor."

"I have my own pastor."

His eyebrows rose. "I see."

Nick started to leave and stopped. "Why do you hate us?"

"I don't hate you."

"Your little booklet on homosexuality in the foyer calls us sinners."

The pastor removed his glasses and pulled a soft cloth from his suit pocket. "You read that?"

"Yes. Les got a good laugh out of it." Nick wasn't sure why he said that. Maybe to get a reaction, maybe to see if this man really believed what he had written.

The pastor wiped the cloth in slow circles over the lenses. He put the glasses back on his face. "If you have time, we could go in my office and talk."

Nick swallowed. "All right." He followed the man into the office and sat down on one of the upholstered chairs that sat in front of a massive walnut desk. To his surprise, the pastor did not sit at the desk but sat beside him.

"Just so I have it straight, you and Les are practicing homosexuals?"

"Yes."

"And how long have you been together?"

"Six months." Nick had lived with Les for longer than that, but he supposed he should answer how long they had been a couple.

"How did you meet Les?"

Nick told him briefly.

"How old is Les?"

Nick was ashamed to admit that he didn't know, but that Les was probably in his late thirties.

"Do you feel that the age discrepancy between you and Les causes friction?"

"No."

"Do you think the age difference is strange?"

Nick frowned, tired of the questions. "What are you getting at?"

"In my experiences of counseling young men or women with similar desires, or shall we say situations as you, a striking age difference between partners usually indicates that the older is taking on a parent role and the younger is drawn to the older person for that reason. Maybe the younger person has never had a loving family home. Perhaps you are looking for something that you never had, but are looking in the wrong place. Do you have a healthy relationship with your father?"

Nick resented being pigeonholed. The pastor had not even asked his name and already seemed to think he had him figured out. No doubt, the pastor believed he could lay hands on Nick and Nick would be miraculously healed.

"My dad and I get along great," Nick lied. "He and my mom see Les and I as no different than my sister and her husband."

The pastor squinted at Nick through his glasses in a way that told Nick he didn't believe him. "Were you raised in a Christian home?"

"Of course. I'm a Christian, just like you."

"Well, not exactly."

Nick stood up. "I suppose you mean that you're going to heaven because you're straight and I'm going to hell."

"If you read my pamphlet, then you are aware of what God has to say." The pastor pushed up the persistent glasses again. Nick didn't know why he even bothered since they immediately fell back down to the end of his nose. "The Scriptures are quite clear about men seeking after the affections of other men."

Nick sneered. "The Bible has plenty to say about the sin of judging as well." He walked out, proud of the fact that he had closed the door softly.

As he got in the company truck, he heard a knock on his window. Nick rolled it down grudgingly.

"I apologize if I offended you. I wasn't trying to judge. I try to leave that up to God and the conviction of the Holy Spirit."

"Is that all you came out to say?" Disgusted, Nick put his finger on the automatic button to roll the window back up. Next, the man would rant to him about how God's judgment was forthcoming – maybe even quote some of the slogans Nick had seen on protester's signs on T.V.

"No. I wanted to tell you that should you ever change your mind about your choice of lifestyle – should God's Word ever convince you of what I said in the pamphlet you read, please contact us. You are welcome here anytime – even if you aren't convinced."

"I doubt that."

The pastor put his hand on the truck door. "I know several men who have made commitments to walk away from homosexuality. I can put you in contact with them if you want."

Nick frowned at the hand on the door that kept him from driving off. "No thanks."

The pastor removed his hand and stepped back. "Maybe someday, then."

Nick resisted the urge to squeal his tires on the way out of the parking lot. But he couldn't help thinking about the part of the conversation about the conviction of the Holy Spirit. Was guilt something caused by the anti-homosexual culture, as Les claimed, or was guilt from the Holy Spirit? Could anyone approach God in prayer without a sense of unworthiness – and was that unworthiness a result of harboring sin or just being human? Nick had no answer.

"I am so glad to meet you, Brenna."

"And I, you," said Brenna, blinking at the strength of Sylvia Strainer's grip.

Brenna had spoken with the new case manager on the phone several times before today. The Sylvia in person matched the Sylvia of the phone. Her graying kinky hair was cut short and her stocky frame was covered in an oversized button-down shirt and khaki pants. Everything about her spoke of sturdiness and capability but her eyes, buttery brown, spoke of caring. Brenna liked her immensely.

"You have a lovely home."

"Thank you. May I show you around?"

"I'd really like to meet your mother," said Sylvia. "After all, that's the reason I'm here."

Brenna led her down the hall and knocked on the bedroom door. "Mother? Sylvia Strainer is here."

When there was no answer, Brenna opened the door a crack. Her mother sat in the chair in the corner. She held an afghan over her chest like a shield.

"Can we come in?"

Mrs. Williams' eyes got very large but she didn't reply. Brenna led Sylvia into the bedroom.

"Mother, this is Sylvia." No other explanations were necessary. Brenna had already explained to her mother about the woman coming.

"Hello, Deborah." Sylvia didn't bother to change her robust tone. Brenna felt startled at the cheerful noisiness of it when everyone else tended to whisper around her mother. And strangers rarely dared use her mother's first name.

"Hello." Her mother spoke warily but at least she spoke. The two women eyed each other.

"Brenna tells me that you grew up in Louisiana. Western Kansas is quite a change from there, isn't it?"

Brenna's mother nodded.

"My family comes from Louisiana – way back – but I've never been there. My grandma taught me how to cook some Cajun dishes, though. Do you like Cajun food?"

Another nod.

"Well, we'll just have to do some cooking together one of these days. Of course, I'm assuming that everyone loves to cook as much as I do. Maybe I should ask what you like to do."

"I used to enjoy knitting." Mrs. Williams lowered the afghan slightly.

"Did you make that lovely afghan?"

"Yes."

Brenna couldn't hide her surprise. She didn't remember her mother ever knitting.

"You will have to teach me how," declared Sylvia. "I admit I tried to crochet once and was a dismal failure but if you are patient, maybe I can actually make something. What do you say – you cook with me and I knit with you. Does that sound fair?"

"I suppose." Mrs. Williams shook her head as though dazed.

"Well, don't let us stay in your hair too long," said Sylvia. "Brenna, weren't you going to show me the rest of the house?"

"Of course."

Sylvia led the way out. Brenna marveled. The woman seemed to know exactly how to handle her mother, finding the delicate balance between challenging her and leaving her alone.

Even though Brenna could hardly wait for her wedding and honeymoon, her mother's care had eaten on her. Now that she had seen Sylvia with her mother, she knew the case manager would not breeze in and breeze out. If anything, Sylvia might be better for her mother than Brenna could be. Brenna let some of her worry slide away.

"Would you like to see my wedding dress, Sylvia?"

Sylvia turned, her bulk nearly brushing the walls on both sides. She clasped her strong hands in front of her. "Would I? I would love to!"

*   *   *

Even though a majority of the state was under a winter-weather advisory, the skies glittered with frosty sunshine above the sidewalk as Brenna and Nell walked from the car to the church. The wind wrestled with the plastic-wrapped wedding dress they carried. Avery held the door open for them as they blew into the warmth of the church.

"Brenna?" Anya hurried over as soon as she saw them enter. "Do you know where the guest book is? We've looked all over for it in the fellowship hall. Your hair and makeup look beautiful, by the way."

"It should be on the back pew with the programs."

"Oh, good. We already have people arriving so I need to get it set out."

"People are here already?" Brenna wiped her hands nervously on her jeans. She felt silly in old clothes and a wedding veil.

"You can't do that once you have your dress on." Nell slapped Brenna's hand lightly.

"Is Mitch here?"

"Yes, but you know you can't see him yet," said Anya.

"Says who?" Mitch poked his head around the corner.

Nell stepped in front of Brenna to hide her, then realized she held the dress in full view and tried to hide it behind her as well.

"Can't I see my bride?"

"You'll have to wait," said Anya, pushing Brenna toward the classroom.

Brenna looked back at Mitch helplessly and blew him a kiss. He pretended to catch and savor it.

It was raining cold sleet in Wichita. The weatherman on the radio advised listeners to get home and stay home before the sleet froze to ice. Nick pulled up to the duplex and made a dash inside.

"It sure is cold out there," Nick said. Even with the front door closed, he could still feel icy air sneaking in around the doorframe. "Maybe we'll have snow for Christmas."

Les did not answer. It was then that Nick saw Marc sitting opposite Les. Marc held a box of tissues, his nose redder than Nick's even though Nick had just come in from the cold. Nick still felt a small electrical shock whenever he remembered that this mild, small man had boldly flaunted himself on stage dressed as a woman.

"Sorry. I didn't mean to interrupt anything."

"Sit down, Nick. You might as well know what's going on too." Marc gestured to the couch.

Nick sat, wishing he didn't have to.

"Andy left Marc," said Les.

Nick looked from Les to Marc. Marc's fingers rested on the box and Nick realized that he had never seen Marc's hands still. He was always beating out a rhythm on something.

"I'm sorry," he said. It sounded lame. He really was sorry, but hadn't Marc brought some of it on himself? Could you act that brazen in front of other men and call yourself chaste with your lover?

Marc shrugged as though it didn't matter. "Just the way it goes, I guess. I've never been able to have anything lasting. Maybe something's wrong with me."

"Nothing's wrong with you." Les's vehemence startled Nick.

"Admit it, Les. Few of us ever have more than a decade with someone. Doesn't that say anything?"

Les sighed. "Commitment is what's important, however long we have."

"Commitment?" Marc laughed bitterly. "Is it commitment when you don't stay together for life? If we could have legally married, Andy and I would have. I know we would have because we talked about it so many times. Now I feel like I'm going through a divorce."

"Are you sure it's over?" asked Nick.

"Yes." Marc tossed the tissue box onto the coffee table. "He moved out all his stuff already."

"It happens," said Les. "It's hell when it does, but it does."

"Why should it?" asked Nick. "Why can't we be just as committed as heterosexual couples. If we're always saying we're better, then why don't we show them up?"

Les and Marc exchanged a look. "Oh, if we could all be so idealistic," said Les. "Nick, do you still have anything in the spare bedroom?"

"A few things, yes."

"Can you go move them into our bedroom? Marc is going to stay with us for a while. Without Andy's part of the rent, he can't afford his apartment anymore."

Nick stood. He had a feeling that he was being dismissed.

Brenna felt a thrill run through her body as she watched in the mirror as Anya fastened the back of her wedding dress.

"You look stunning, Brenna." Anya rested her cheek lightly against Brenna's. "I am so honored to have you in the family."

"Thank you." Brenna felt tears welling up in her eyes.

"None of that," said Nell. "You don't want to ruin your make-up."

"Brenna?" Sylvia Strainer opened the classroom door a crack. "I have your mother with me."

Sylvia eased her mother into the room. Brenna rushed to her, aware of the billowing and rustling of her skirts and veil, and held out her arms. Her mother accepted the embrace with a fierce one of her own.

"My baby," she whispered against Brenna's neck. "Getting married."

"I can't tell you how much this means to me that you are here," choked Brenna.

Nick tossed an armload of jeans onto the floor of Les's closet next to Russell's guitar and a stack of sheet music. There really was nowhere else to store his things from the spare bedroom. All the drawer and shelf spaces were taken and Les despised having things on the floor around the bed. He stubbed his toes on too many things in the dark getting up to go to the bathroom in the night, he said.

Nick didn't know how he felt about Marc coming to live with them. How long would Marc stay? Would Marc's presence change things between he and Les? The sunglasses man from the bar – Gary –said Les would get tired of him eventually. He said that Les had a habit of giving out the spare bedroom to his next interest. Was there any truth to that?

Nick rubbed his temples. No. This was a totally different situation. Marc needed help. Nick knew he should feel proud of Les for doing the right thing.

"You made Marc feel bad back there, you know." Les stood at the walk-in closet door, his arms folded across his chest.

"I did?"

"Your little comment about if we just stayed committed did. Marc was as committed as anyone ever could be – homo or hetero. You made him feel like it was his fault we look bad to the fundamentals."

Nick adjusted the guitar so that it leaned against the wall and would not fall out into the walking space. He could see Les's point but didn't feel like apologizing.

"You know," Les said. "Sometimes I wonder whose side you're on. One day you're enjoying all the freedoms I can offer you; the next, you're acting all uptight like you feel you have to prove that we're okay. You aren't still talking with that right-winger old lady who visited you, are you?"

Nick glared. "You always blame everything on her."

"Well, apparently she holds a considerable amount of sway in your opinions."

"Her views don't have anything to do with what's been bothering me."

"Oh, really." Les smirked and leaned against the doorframe.

Nick felt trapped with no other way out of the closet except past Les.

"So, what's been bothering you then?"

"If you really want to know, the night at the gay bar."

"What about it?"

"That Gary guy. Did you live with him?"

Les lost his smirk. "Yes."

"For five years?"

"Yes."

"Was he the real reason you went to Houston?"

Les's face contorted with anger. "What did he try to tell you?"

"What should I know?"

"You and I weren't together yet when I went down there. Don't try to lay claim on my past."

"What about your future? Do I have any claim to that?"

"We're not talking about the future."

Brenna floated toward Mitch. He took her hand, his eyes gleaming with promises. The familiar words of the wedding ceremony flitted past. Brenna couldn't have concentrated on them even if she had tried. Only one thought ran through her head. "I'm getting married today. I'm getting married to this man beside me."

Mitch squeezed her hand and smiled at her.

"In richer in poorer, in sickness and in health," Brenna echoed the pastor, her eyes locked on Mitch's. "To love and to cherish until death do us part."

Her voice cracked on the last word, but from the way Mitch beamed at her, it didn't matter.

He repeated his vows to her and before she could grasp the moment and hold on long enough to make a memory, the pastor was announcing them husband and wife and Mitch pulled her into his embrace.

Nick looked at Les with a new awareness. Les would talk about how important and wonderful commitment was, then avoid any promises for the future.

In sudden resolution, Nick shoved aside several pairs of Les's neatly ironed pants and pulled out Grandma Bates' old hardback suitcase.

"What are you doing?" Les sounded sharp - angry and anxious at the same time.

Nick clicked open the latches and laid the suitcase on the floor. He randomly tossed in items of clothing. Grandma Bates would have had a conniption if she could see the haphazard packing, no folding, no stacks, but he didn't care.

"Look, I didn't mean anything. Don't get so upset over nothing."

Nick picked up the case, still open, and holding it like a battering ram, headed toward Les. Les stepped out of the way.

His face whitened. Nick tossed the case on the bed and began taking things that he would need from the dresser drawers.

"I have to go home."

"I thought you said you'd never go back there."

"My dad needs me."

"Your dad?" Les laughed. "You talked with him?"

Nick crammed in an extra pair of shoes.

"Is this a new development or are you just making it up?"

"I was leaving anyway," Nick lied. "I was going to tell you when I got home but with Marc here…"

Les leaned back against the wall. "So how do I know you're not going off to some Houston of your own somewhere?"

Nick gave him a scathing look.

"It was a joke, Nick."

"It wasn't funny."

Les straightened. "All right, it wasn't funny."

Nick tried to close the suitcase. He had to take out the extra shoes before it would latch. He sucked in his breath from the growing fear that cutting himself off from Les would leave him with nothing. "It's not like I'm leaving for good or anything."

"Just a visit, huh?"

"Long enough to take care of a few things." Like thinking through what he had done with his life.

"Before you go, I'll need your set of keys to the duplex."

Nick's heart dropped. This was it? This thing with Les was over so quickly? All because in a fit of hurt, Nick had grabbed a suitcase?

"Marc needs a set."

"What, is he my replacement?"

"Nobody said anything about me wanting to replace you, Nick."

True or not, that wasn't the reassurance of love that Nick had hoped for.

Chapter 21

Anya met Nick on the front porch. He felt like the proverbial prodigal son as she hugged him.

"My goodness, let me look at you. You're changing so much. You look older."

He blushed. "That's good, I hope?"

"You look wonderful, Nick. I can't tell you how glad I am that you are here. I was thrilled when you called me to say you were on your way."

"I thought I'd give you fair warning."

"Warning? Oh, no, not at all. It was the best of news. But I didn't have time to ask you - can you stay here with me? I have the house cleaned up from wedding company. And, how long will you be here?"

He thought about saying forever but Les still held a huge part of him back in Wichita. "Only a few days. I thought I'd stay in the trailer but it looks like someone is living there – at least there were toys in the front yard."

"Your dad is renting it out to a family from town. They had a small fire in their kitchen and needed a place to live until the repairs were done. They have two children and their house isn't safe yet."

"How can my dad rent it out?"

"Karl actually thought of it and asked your dad if he would consider it."

"Has Karl seen him, then?"

"He goes to see him every week. I'm sure you heard about the sentencing."

"Remind me," Nick said, not willing to admit that he didn't know. He hadn't even heard that his father had gone to trial yet. Maybe Anya had tried to call him to tell him. Maybe

Les had intercepted the message and not passed it on. No, he couldn't place blames on Les that he had no proof of.

"The original sentencing was for two years in the state penitentiary but it got changed to a year in the county jail. He'll be on probation for another two years after his release. I think he has a certain number of community service hours as well as losing his driver's license for a while."

"Why did they reduce his sentence?"

"The judge decided it would be cheaper on the state to leave him where he was. It was a lenient sentence," said Anya. "The Greeley family isn't happy about it. They might appeal."

Nick wondered if she agreed with the Greeley's, considering her husband's death by J.D.'s carelessness.

"Do you think I can see him?"

Anya eyed him closely. "Do you want to see him?"

"That's why I came."

"Why now?"

The two-noted call of a quail echoed her question – low, high, low high. "Why now? Why now?" Nick spotted the bird hopping along the grass clumps at the edge of the road.

"Are things going all right in Wichita, Nick?"

"Not really."

Anya waited a few moments but Nick didn't feel like sharing.

"Well, if you need to talk, I'll listen."

"No thanks." He looked at her. Wrinkles had appeared around her eyes that hadn't been there when he had left over a year ago and her hair had dulled from blond to a dirty white. He should have come to see Anya sooner. He owed Russell that much.

Pleasure lit J.D.'s face as he stood from behind the table and held out his hands toward Nick.

"You came," he said.

Nick looked at the guard who nodded. Feeling no way out, Nick stepped close to his father and accepted his hug. He closed his eyes and remembered when he had longed for a hug or even a loving touch. "Men don't hug," J.D. had told him after his accident with the band saw.

J.D. stepped back and patted Nick's shoulders with shaking hands. "You look good, son. You look real good."

Words stuck in Nick's throat. He couldn't say the same about his father. J.D. looked skinnier than ever and more haunted. But he had called Nick "son", not "boy".

Nick backed up several steps. "I'm sorry I couldn't come sooner," he said. It was the truth.

J.D. waved to the folding chair on the opposite side of the table as he sat down. "So how are you doing?"

"Fine. I've been living in Wichita."

"Yeah, I know. How's work going?"

"All right."

"Are you enjoying it?"

"Yes." Nick tapped his hands on the table nervously at the silence between them. He knew he should answer his father's questions in more than a few words but he couldn't think of what to say. "How are you, Dad?"

J.D.'s mouth twisted. "Can't complain. They have better food here than at home. Don't have to work, just watch T.V. all the time."

"You never were much for cooking, were you?" Nick held his breath. He had never teased his father before.

J.D. laughed. "Why bother when I had you around? You always did the cooking and cleaning."

"Is that what I was to you – a maid and a cook?"

"Course not. You were Julienne's kid – and mine. I had to take you in. You had nowhere else to go. A real man doesn't turn his back on his responsibilities."

The words hurt. Nick remembered time after time when J.D. had used the phrase, "a real man" to cut him down.

"I guess I'll never be a man to you, will I?" He couldn't keep the bitterness out.

J.D. rubbed the back of his neck where, after years in the sun, lines crisscrossed like the top of a molasses cookie. "I never understood you, Nick. You were always so girlish. Guess I was afraid you'd turn out to be a fag."

Nick closed his eyes.

"Sorry – I was just scared. I didn't know how to raise a kid. I figured if my boy turned into one of those, I'd done the worst possible job."

"Well, congratulations, then," Nick said through gritted teeth. "You're a failure of a father because you're looking at 'one of those'."

"What are you saying, boy?" There it was again – that disparaging "boy".

"What do you think I'm saying?" Nick challenged his father with his eyes.

"You saying you're a fairy?"

The guard put his hand on the gun at his hip.

"Yes, that's what I'm saying."

J.D. swore and stood up. "You make me sick. You're no son of mine."

Nick leaned back on his chair and folded his arms across his chest. He would not let the man cow him. "I don't need you to be my father anyway. I'm God's son."

J.D. laughed. "You think God wants a pervert any more than I do?"

"I hardly think you're in any position to judge me." He paused with calculation. "Drunken murderer."

J.D. came after him, enraged. The guard jumped to life, restraining J.D. and forcing him to the door. J.D. spat as he passed Nick. The spittle landed on the floor but Nick felt the hate from the action bind around him. Another guard appeared to escort him out.

"Are you all right?" asked the second guard.

"I'm fine," Nick said. He put his hands in his pockets to hide their shaking.

"How did it go?"

Nick stepped out of the S-10, wondering if the truck instinctively knew it was home on the gravel in front of the Martin's garage.

"About like I expected."

"How is he?"

Nick blew out his breath in the frosty January air. "He hasn't changed."

Anya rubbed her hands over her arms. "I'll bet he was glad to see you. He's always telling Karl how much he misses you."

Nick schooled his face. "You look cold, Mrs. Martin. Where's your coat?"

"I wanted to hurry and meet you."

"Let's get inside," he said. The gray sky threatened snow but then weather was unpredictable out here. It could promise one thing and deliver another – just like his father's initial hug and greeting.

"I have company." Anya started walking with him back to the house.

"Who's here?" Nick had noticed the car parked alongside the garage when he pulled in. He had just assumed Anya had a different car.

"Mitch and Brenna. They just got home from their honeymoon and brought pictures by."

"Oh." Nick stopped walking. "Do you want me to go somewhere for a while? Give you time with your family?"

"Don't be silly, Nick. You are family. I just thought I'd give you a little heads-up, that's all."

"It's not like I'm heartbroken or anything," he said, feeling defensive. "I wasn't the one with a crush on her." He followed Anya, stopping to grasp a pillar on the front porch and clear his head. His joints ached and his stomach hurt – physical symptoms of the stress he was under, he supposed.

Mitch and Brenna sat mashed together at one end of the couch.

"Hello, Nick," Mitch said.

"Hello, Mitch. Hello, Brenna."

Brenna smiled and waved. She looked beautiful in a way he'd never noticed before. It wasn't a change in her outward appearance, he decided. She seemed confident and comfortable with herself. Nick felt ganglier than ever. If love had perfected Brenna, then why had love brought him low?

Nick thought of the verse, "Greater love has no one than this, that he lay down his life for his friends." He knew from the night at the Laundromat years ago that Mitch would do a great deal to help anyone – friend or not. Mitch probably wouldn't hesitate to lay down his life for Brenna. Would Les do the same for him?

"How've you been, Nick?" asked Mitch.

"Fine." Nick had always felt a little cowed by Mitch's muscled physique but judging by the way Brenna stroked his arm affectionately, she wasn't.

"Mom says you have a landscaping job?"

"We lay tile this time of year," said Nick. "Not much growing right now."

Mitch laughed. "I admire anyone who can get things to grow. Mom wouldn't let me water her houseplants."

"That's why we have a fake tree," said Brenna.

"A tree?" Nick noticed that she did not stutter.

"It's only four feet tall. We have it standing in a corner of our living room."

It seemed strange to hear Brenna talk about their living room. He didn't feel old enough to be married, hadn't thought any of their classmates old enough to be married. But was he any different? He had been living with Les in a marriage-type relationship all this time. He referred to the duplex as "our house". Nick winced as he thought of Marc sleeping in the spare bedroom. At least, he hoped Marc was still sleeping in the spare bedroom.

"Do you enjoy it in Wichita?" Mitch asked.

"Mostly. Mrs. Martin said you had pictures from your honeymoon?"

"Oh, yes," said Brenna. She picked up several large envelopes from the coffee table and held them out. Nick took them and sat on the floor.

"Nick, you don't have to sit on the floor." Anya stood up from her recliner. "Here. You can have my seat."

"No, I'm fine. Really." He pulled out a stack of pictures. "Where did you go for your honeymoon?"

"Colorado." Brenna looked at Mitch while she answered.

Mitch laughed. "You would have thought we'd pick somewhere warm after a winter wedding but we went skiing. It was Brenna's first time to ski and she did really well, didn't you, darling?"

The two smiled at each other with delight and Nick wondered if they were talking to him or to each other. He raised his eyebrows at Anya. She shook her head as if to say, "young foolish love", but her eyes were soft as she looked at the couple.

Nick flipped through the stacks of photos as Mitch and Brenna interjected occasional comments about their trip. When he finished, he handed them back.

"So, Nick. When are you going to get yourself a girl?" teased Mitch.

"Mitch!" Brenna hissed the word out of the side of her mouth. Her face reddened and she avoided Nick's face.

"What?" Mitch held up his hands. "You are the best thing that ever happened to me. I just want the same thing for Nick."

"Jesus is the best thing that ever happened to me," said Nick tightly.

Mitch lowered his hands. "Well, when you put it that way, Jesus is the best thing for me as well. But Brenna is definitely in second. A girl might be just what you need, Nick."

"I don't think so." Hadn't Brenna told Mitch about him? By the strained look that passed between Brenna and Anya, they had. Mitch apparently had taken it upon himself to assume what so many fundamentalist Christians believed – that if he could just find the right woman, the desires for other men would fade away.

"Brenna and I can introduce you to some girls, if you like, maybe go out on a double date."

"Would anyone like some hot tea?" interrupted Anya, standing up. "I have zucchini bread thawed out too, if anyone is hungry."

Nick almost laughed. Some things never changed. Anya still answered every complication with food.

"That sounds nice," he said, taking the lifeline she offered.

"No thanks" said Brenna. She stood as well. "We need to be going."

"We do?" asked Mitch.

"Yes, we do," she said.

"Thank you so much for coming by," said Anya. "And for bringing your pictures. I'm glad your honeymoon went so well."

Brenna hugged her mother-in-law. "Thank you for all you did to help out at the wedding. I never had time to thank you properly."

"It was just too bad Sara couldn't make it back. She loved the pictures you emailed her."

Mitch hugged his mother as well while Nick stayed on the floor, well out of hugging range. The hug from his father had been enough for one day.

"It was g…good to see you again, Nick," said Brenna. Nick noticed her slight hesitation. She had been embarrassed for him and he appreciated it.

"You too, Brenna. I wish you the best."

"Thank you."

"How long are you in town, Nick?" asked Mitch.

"I'm not sure."

"Well, maybe we'll see you around." Mitch put his hand on Brenna's back and guided her out of the door.

Anya closed the door behind them. "I'm so sorry, Nick," she said. "I know that was awkward for you. Mitch means well, he really does."

Nick unfolded his legs and stood, stomping his foot a little to get the blood flowing. "Is your offer of zucchini bread and hot tea still on or was that just a diversionary tactic?"

She laughed and led the way to the kitchen. Nick sat at her table and let her serve him, just like old times. He wasn't hungry. The pain in his abdomen had increased, almost to the point where he wondered if he had a touch of flu. But surely he could try to eat something to appease her maternal side. He put a hand to his face. It still felt hot. Maybe he really was feverish.

"Mitch and Brenna seem happy together," he said.

"Yes, they are. Deliriously."

Nick snorted. "You think it's too good to be true?"

"No. But I do know that a good marriage takes work. At this stage, I'm not sure they realize that."

"Relationships take work," he said and thought of his father.

Anya sat down across from him. "Nick, I've wanted to talk to you about that."

He frowned. "There's no relationship to talk about."

Relief flooded her face. "You aren't seeing him anymore?"

"I just saw him today," Nick said in confusion.

"Les is here?"

"Oh! I thought we were talking about my dad. No, Les isn't here."

Anya blew on the liquid in her mug before taking a tentative sip. "So, you are still seeing Les?"

"Yes." Why bother telling her about the conflict between him and Les or the fears he had regarding Les's commitment? She would only think that now she had a chance to bring him around to her point of view.

"Why?"

Why? How could he answer that? How could he explain to her that when Les focused on him, he felt special in a way no one had ever made him feel? How could he describe the feeling of community and belonging he had in Les's church? She might understand – she had experienced closeness with Russell and community in her own church.

"Nick, I've been thinking a great deal about what you said when I called to tell you about your father."

"What about it?" Nick asked warily. He broke off a bite-sized piece of bread and fingered it without eating.

"You said that you couldn't change who you are or what you are. Do you mind if I read a verse to you from I Corinthians?" She reached for her Bible.

"Let's not war with verses," he said.

"Just hear me out, please?" The pleading on her face undid him so he nodded.

"'Do not be deceived: Neither the sexually immoral nor idolaters nor adulterers nor male prostitutes nor homosexual offenders nor thieves nor the greedy nor drunkards nor slanderers nor swindlers will inherit the kingdom of God.'"

Nick glared at her. "I don't need your judgment, Mrs. Martin." His head began to pound. He put a hand to his face.

"The next part is the most important. It says, 'And that is what some of you were. But you were washed, you were sanctified, you were justified in the name of the Lord Jesus Christ by the Spirit of our God.' You see, Nick, some of the people Paul is talking to used to be just like you and they changed."

"I'm not sinning."

Anya laid her hands flat on her Bible. "But you are, Nick," she said. If her voice had not broken and the tears had not come to her eyes, Nick would have gotten up and left immediately. He sat in silence and shame.

Anya swiped at her eyes. "If I didn't love you so much, Nick, I wouldn't say that."

His defensive mechanisms kicked in. "You fundamentalist churches always have the right formula for the only way you think Christians can be. You say people like me need to change, but how can I change what is me? I've always been this way and I don't know how to be any different. When I prayed, God accepted me – just as I was. I know he did."

"How did you feel after you prayed?" She spoke softly.

"Clean, pure, ecstatic, like someone finally cared and listened."

"When was the last time you felt that way?"

Nick shut his mouth. He couldn't remember any time since that first prayer. If anything, when he prayed now, he felt… dirty.

"Oh, Nick. Sin is pleasurable for a season. The truth is, Nick, none of us enjoy turning away from sin. It's hard. Even Paul fought sin constantly. Don't use the excuse that it's too hard to give up so God must approve or he wouldn't have made it so hard. Talk to anyone who has tried to overcome smoking or alcoholism or even pornography."

Nick winced. Somehow it didn't seem right for Anya to even know pornography existed, much less that it made up so much of his life, the bookmarks on Les's computer bearing testimony. "But God created me to be this way," he argued. "I was born this way."

"Were you?"

"As long as I can remember."

"That doesn't mean you were born with it. I have a scar on my arm that I can't remember getting but I wasn't born with it."

"You can't prove I wasn't."

Anya sighed. "True enough. But think about it this way, Nick. People are sometimes born with serious deformities, such as cleft palate or blindness. God allowed those people to be created that way, but that doesn't mean that the deformity is desirable. If medical intervention is possible, the parents do everything they can to fix it."

"You're saying it's a disease or something?"

"Sin is a disease, Nick."

He didn't respond.

"I took the liberty of going on-line, as they say, with some help from Nell – you know, Sara's mother. I found several addresses and phone numbers of places that offer counseling for those who wish to become straight. I wrote them down for you if you'll take it." She took an envelope out from underneath the front cover. "I also listed several websites that give testimonials of men and women who are living straight. Some of them say that they are completely healed of homosexual desires."

Nick opened his mouth to argue.

Anya held up a finger. "Others still struggle with the temptations but have chosen to walk away regardless. I think you should at least look into it. Then you can say that you are making an informed choice even if you decide to stay where you are." She slid the envelope across the table.

Nick swallowed a bite of zucchini bread without tasting the flavor and took a prolonged drink of tea. He made a point of ignoring the envelope. The heat from the liquid made him break out in a light sweat.

"Please, Nick?"

"I can't," he said, strangled.

"Why not?"

"I just can't." He pushed back his chair.

"Are you confident before God that you are right?"

He tried to laugh. "I guess I'll take my chances."

She frowned. "It doesn't work that way, Nick."

He sobered. "I know."

"Have you felt any questions, uncertainty?"

"Doesn't everyone?"

"I suppose so. But if you come to the conclusion that your lifestyle isn't right, and you continue to live that way, you will be sinning willfully. And you can't claim ignorance if you haven't studied it out for yourself."

Nick stood, leaving the rest of his bread on the table. He couldn't remember a time when he had ever turned down her food before. "I'm going to bed."

She waved the envelope at him. "You forgot this."

He swiped it out of her hand with a muttered curse and stomped to the spare bedroom. When he slammed the door, he realized that he had sounded just like his father.

Nick got up before the sun so that he would not have to face Anya. He wrote a curt note of thanks for a place to stay – no "call me's" or "I'll write's".

His headache felt worse this morning, accompanied by nausea. In hopelessness, he drove back to Wichita, wondering how he could think of continuing on with Les, wondering if he would ever be welcome back at Anya's, wondering what he was supposed to do when what he really wanted was to run away from everywhere.

Chapter 22

"Hi, Hon." Mitch came in and draped his coat over a chair.

Brenna kept her feet tucked under her and her eyes trained on the book in her hands instead of coming to him for the usual kiss. Mitch sighed. Was she still mad about his comments to Nick the day before? She seemed to accept his apology, but maybe not.

"Brenna? Everything okay?" He slipped out of his coat and draped it over a chair.

"Oh, hi," she said with a distracted smile.

"You reading?" He reached for the book but she yanked it back.

"Don't bother me. I'm in a good part."

"Aren't I more important than your book?" He hoped he sounded like he was teasing. His blood pressure was rising.

"Of course," she said and turned up her face for a brief kiss.

"So what's for dinner?"

She made a face. "Let me finish this. Then I can fix something."

"What are we having? I can get started on it. I'm starving."

Brenna tried to focus on the pages. "I haven't decided yet."

"Do we have any meat thawed?"

"No. Can we decide in a bit Mitch?"

He stood over her for a moment longer but she was concentrating on her story. Frustrated, Mitch went to the kitchen to make himself a sandwich. He banged the cupboard doors

more than necessary, hoping she would get the gist that he
wasn't pleased. She didn't seem to notice.

He took his sandwich to the couch and sat next to her to
try again. "Hey beautiful," he said.

"Hey." She didn't turn from her book.

"Are you finished with the good part yet?"

"Shh." She waved her hand at him.

He ate his sandwich to the soft swish of her page
turning. She jumped when he put his hand on her thigh. At least
she hadn't been pretending to be involved. That was a good
sign. She wasn't ignoring him out of spite over the whole Nick
thing. He squeezed her leg.

"Mitch," she chided.

"I want to touch you. Is that a problem?"

"Yes... no."

"Which one?" He made a grab for the book and pulled it
out of her hands.

"You lost my place!"

He narrowed his eyes. "You aren't trying to escape
something, are you?"

She sighed. "It wasn't a good day for Mother today. I
was trying to unwind."

He shook the book at her lightly. "We talked about this
– about how you lose yourself on purpose. It's not healthy,
Brenna. I don't want you choosing your mother's moods over
me."

Her eyes flashed. "I am not like my mother."

"Prove it."

"All I did was read for a while instead of make you
supper. Is that a crime?"

"Punishable by kissing."

"I suppose you're going to be one of those guys that
wants his woman barefoot and pregnant in the kitchen all the
time."

His eyelids lowered. "I'd like to try."

"Try what?"

He slid his hand higher up her thigh. "Making you pregnant."

She blushed. "You're changing the subject."

"You brought it up."

By her stiffness, he wondered if the abrupt change from rare touches to his constant caresses kept her off-kilter. Although she had seemed to crave his touch before marriage, maybe Brenna wasn't quite sure how to handle the strength of his sexual drive.

Despite his best rationale, her cooler attitude since the honeymoon made him insecure.

Brenna held out her hand. "Can I have my book back?"

"Nope. Not until we kiss and make up."

She puckered her lips and made a kissing sound. "Okay, now can I have my book back?"

Mitch frowned. "Brenna." The tone of his voice made him feel more like he was her father than her husband. "I don't want you to read any more this evening."

"You can't be serious."

"I am. I need to know if you're willing to make the decision to be strong enough when life is tough. I need to know that you can stay with me mentally."

"It was just a long day, not a life crisis."

"You have to form habits now for when it does get hard."

The last traces of the imaginary story world fled from her eyes, replaced with painful awareness. "I'm s...sorry. I'm not p...perfect..."

Her stuttering stung him. He wanted to pull her close and take it all back. "I don't expect you to be. You saw yesterday how imperfect I can be too."

"I'll fix you supper every night."

"That wasn't what I meant."

"And I'll meet you at the door with a kiss every time you come home from work."

"Brenna, I don't want you doing a list of things because you think I require it. I want you to do those things out of love – the way you do things for your mom."

"I do it for her because she needs me."

"I need you too."

"Not the way she does."

Mitch tucked her hair behind her ear. "Different yes, but not any less. Actually, more."

"But I need to help her," she insisted. "I need to be needed."

"Not if it's going to take a toll on your own emotions."

"Mitch, you can't be saying that I shouldn't go over to help my mother!"

"No, I'm not. But maybe you shouldn't go every day. Maybe you should get a job – try something new that you've never tried before – get out in public more. I don't want you to withdraw."

"You think I'm just like her."

"No, but you are similar. I want what's best for you, Brenna. I won't be like your father and sit back and allow you to hide."

She put up her chin. "I'm not always hiding when I'm reading. Most of the time, it's for the sheer pleasure of it."

"But tonight?"

She held up her hand in surrender.

"It's not that I don't want you to read, darling. I don't want you to use it as a solution."

"I'm s…sorry," she said again, her voice small.

"Don't look at me like that, Brenna, like I'm this mean ogre. I love you. You know that, right?"

"Yes."

"So, now can we kiss and make up?"

"I guess." She scooted closer to him.

He took her face in his hands. "And then can we go to the bedroom and do a little more making up?"

"How about we get some supper?" she hedged.

"I already ate." He slid his hands from her face, down her throat, and to her shoulders.

"I didn't."

"Then how about after you eat?"

She smiled timidly. "Do you really want to?"

He kissed her.

Every light in the upstairs duplex was on when Nick climbed the stairs. He could hear the stereo bass thumping through the wooden slats under his feet.

No one answered his first knock so he knocked louder. Marc opened the door.

"Nick! You're home." He stepped back to let Nick in. "We're having a party."

Nick looked around. Men from his Bible study gathered in groups around the couch and dining room table, holding cups and plates of food.

"Do you like the music?" Marc had to raise his voice.

Nick nodded. A catchy drum rhythm underlined the vocals.

"It's my band," Marc explained. "We cut our first CD. That's why everyone is here – to celebrate."

"Congratulations. I didn't know you played in a band." Nick shifted the old suitcase from one hand to the other; unsure whether or not Les would welcome him back.

"For several years now. I don't just play for worship team. You shouldn't either. You're good enough to join the symphony or teach or something, you know."

Nick did know. For months now, the Sunday morning repertoire had failed to satisfy him.

Les came out of the kitchen with a 2-Liter of soda. He looked surprised when he saw Nick but he smiled. "You came home early," he said, as though he had known all along when Nick planned on returning. "Did you miss me?"

"Yeah." Nick had missed more than Les's company. He had missed Les's approval and affirmation – the very things he had been looking for in his trip back to Western Kansas where he only found condemnation.

"Go put that away and come help us celebrate Marc's CD," Les said, pointing down the hall. He lowered his voice. "I'm glad you're back."

Nick lowered his own voice to match. "I wasn't sure if you would let me back in."

Les slung his arm around Nick and walked him to the hall. Nick knew the gesture made all look well to their houseguests.

"Didn't you trust me, Nick? I've had too many relationships fall through. I don't want that to happen with you. I need this. I need you."

"Why?"

Les sat down on the bed. "One of my stepfathers was always telling me how unreliable I was, how much he thought I didn't care about my mom or our family. I know now that he was just trying to control me but sometimes I think he was right. I can't seem to keep anyone close."

"Maybe it's because you try to control too."

Les was silent.

"Not in a bad way. You mean well. Maybe you don't even know you're doing it. It's just that I wanted to find my own place and well, you talked me into staying here. I wanted to go to college but you've always told me how much you need me full-time. I really want to do more with my piano and you keep telling me that God is using me in worship and discourage me from playing anything secular. But classical music is what I love playing most of all. I feel closer to God when I play Gershwin and Schumann than the same 1-4-5 chord repetitions of praise music."

"You play hymns."

"Yes. But hymns are predictable too – always the same harmonization. They don't challenge."

Les ran his fingers through his thinning hair. "You think I'm overbearing?"

"No. Well, maybe some. I'm just used to doing everything on my own, making my own decisions, taking care of myself – at least until I moved down here. I want things to work out between us; I just need more space. I don't want to feel stuck."

"It's true. I'm overbearing."

"No." Nick felt awful at the sight of Les sitting so dejectedly. "I just need you to be you, not try to be my father."

He hadn't realized it until he had said it, but it was true. Les had been a father figure to him, the older man who offered him acceptance. From the time Nick had met Les, Les had reminded him of Russell – the only man who represented a real father to him. The pastor from that church had been right. Nick was looking for a father's love. Maybe that's why Nick had gotten so angry with him.

"I love you." The Voice whispered in Nick's heart with the same tenderness and strength as it had when Nick had first prayed. The Father-God.

Nick hadn't felt God's presence so strongly since the beginning of his Christian walk. Maybe no Christian ever did. Maybe the initial experience of salvation was the closest one ever got to God. But when he spent time with Anya, he could see the same Spirit within her, even as she rebuked him.

"Come back to Me. Let Me be your Father."

Come back? He had never left, had he?

"I wasn't trying to be your father," said Les.

"I know."

"I'll try to do better. I really will."

But from the confusion on Les's face, Nick doubted if Les even knew how. Nick excused himself to the bathroom where he sat on the edge of the tub until his stomach settled down enough to join the party.

Nick shifted his weight awkwardly as he stood in the crowded foyer at the church. Les had stayed home nursing a sore throat so Nick had come alone. He didn't like feeling out of place without Les. He didn't like to think that he had become so dependent on Les.

But true to his word, Les had tried to back off and give Nick space. He helped Nick look up classes offered at the college in music theory. Nick was anxious to sign up but it was the middle of the second semester. He would have to wait for summer courses. Les had also made a point of giving Nick a raise so that he could save more for school. But as Nick's boss, Les still controlled his schedule. Nick knew his resentment wasn't fair. What else was Les supposed to do?

When Nick mentioned finding a different job so that they wouldn't have the boss-employee connection undermining their partnership, Les had warned him of his lack of training and schooling.

"You won't make as much money anywhere else as you do working for me," he said. "And you need to save up."

Nick knew it was true. But he felt cornered.

Nick tried to read his Bible during the hour after Les left early for work and Marc still slept but everything he read seemed to point him to Anya's words.

"Some of the people Paul spoke to were just like you and they changed... You can't claim ignorance if you haven't studied it out for yourself... Are you confident before God that you are right?"

A burst of laughter came from the group in the foyer. Nick edged his way past. He wished he had kept the information

Anya had given him. Maybe the pastor from that church he and Les had done tile work for could help.

He descended the front steps of the church, feeling the stiffness in his knees. The flu symptoms had not gone away or gotten any worse since he had returned. Nick knew his body probably wasn't sick at all – just the duress and hurt eating away at him – but he couldn't shake the deep-seated fear that God was judging him for his deeds.

Nick sat down in front of a computer at the library. He had told Les that he was going to the church to practice. He hadn't lied. He would go the church, but the bulk of his time would be spent here at the library. He didn't trust using Les's computer to look up the information he sought without Les finding out.

At the words "going straight", a host of sites popped up, some clearly skeptical of the whole concept. Others claimed the infallibility of their programs. Nick clicked on one that sounded reasonably encouraging without making false claims.

What he read made his skin prickle – testimonials so similar to his own life, the people writing could have grown up alongside him.

A man sat down at the computer beside him. Nick closed out the screen so that the newcomer would not see what he had been researching.

"Hello," said the man, breaking the unspoken city rule that you don't speak to strangers in settings such as this. "You know, you look familiar to me."

Nick turned. It was the pastor, the one from the church where he and Les had tiled the entryway.

"Yes. I know you. You're the tile worker. Kenneth Brooks," the man said, holding out his hand. "I'm sorry I offended you that day."

"Nick Pierce," Nick answered, allowing the man a shake. "And I thought I offended you."

"Come again?"

"I thought I offended you, not the other way around."

"How so?"

"With being who, or what, I am."

"Sinners don't offend me, Nick. We all are born sinners and would continue to be without God's forgiveness and power to overcome. Have you thought about what we talked about?"

"We didn't talk," Nick wanted to say. "You fired questions at me without listening for any answers before you labeled me." But the man's words and Anya's words had led him to the website he had just read. Nick felt his abdomen cramping, the same feeling he had felt on the night he had finally prayed and told God that he would serve him as a son serves a good Father. Was this a chance meeting with Pastor Brooks or was it an event orchestrated by the hand of God?

"Would you gloat if I said yes?"

The pastor grinned and pushed up his ever-errant glasses. "Maybe a little. What have you thought about?"

"Actually, I was reading about some stuff just now."

"Like what?"

"Some testimonials of people who left the gay lifestyle."

"What did you think?"

"I don't quite know if change for me is possible."

"Do you want to change?"

"I'm not sure. How can I expect to change who I've always been?"

"You told me that you consider yourself to be a Christian."

"Yes."

"When we become Christians, we die to the old man and become a new creation. As Paul says, we are no longer slaves to sin but slaves to righteousness. We have power from God to overcome the sin nature within us."

"So I should be able to change just like that?"

"Oh no. Dying to self is very difficult. It takes a lifetime of growth by reading God's Word and obeying the Holy Spirit."

Nick digested the words.

"Dad, I found the book I need." A teenage girl came up behind them. "Are you ready to go?"

"Can you wait at that table over there for a minute or two? Then I'll be ready to go."

"All right." The girl withdrew.

"My daughter. I brought her by to find a book for her science project."

"I think God sent you."

"He's done stranger things. I'd like to continue our conversation sometime, if you'd like."

"Maybe." Nick had a lot to consider. He wasn't quite sure how he would do any real thinking while sharing Les's bed.

"Well, you know where to find me. Feel free to stop by anytime." Kenneth Brooks made one last attempt at his sliding glasses and left the building arm and arm with his daughter. Nick watched them leave, jealous that the girl had a man in her life, a father who cared.

Nick went back to the duplex. Les met him at the door.

"Where have you been?"

"What do you mean?"

"I called the church three times looking for you and every time, Pastor Jeff said you hadn't showed up yet."

Nick stifled his resentment of Les's checking up on him. "I went to the library. I was going to stop by there first and then go to the church. I just forgot about going to the church."

Les looked at him strangely. "That isn't like you, Nick – forgetting about your music."

"I know."

"What is going on with you anyway? Are you still doubting my feelings for you? Is that it?"

Nick took a deep breath. "No."

"Then do you doubt your own feelings?"

"No. I still care about you, Les. I just..."

"Tell him, Nick. He needs to hear the truth." Nick knew that Voice. Could he tell Les his hesitations, his guilt?

"I just don't know if I can do this anymore. I don't know if I can keep living as a gay and a Christian. I can't buy the misinterpretation stuff anymore. The more I study the Word of God, the more I know it doesn't add up."

When Les finally spoke, his voice was hard. "So what it comes down to is that everything I've told you, everything I've taught you, you don't believe. You don't trust me."

"I trust the Word of God," Nick said quietly. "At this point, I can't trust anything else, not even myself."

"You're letting the enemy win, Nick."

"No, Les. I think you are." Nick couldn't hide the tears that seeped into his eyes. "I want to get my things. I have to leave."

Les swept his arm angrily, encompassing the duplex. "Fine. Do what you have to. Just don't take anything that doesn't belong to you."

"I wouldn't do that."

Les stomped to the door. "I'm going out. Be gone before I get back. Oh, and by the way, Nick, you're fired."

Chapter 23

Nick rolled over on the motel bed, bunching the covers under his chest for support as he read from Second Timothy. "For the time will come when men will not put up with sound doctrine. Instead, to suit their own desires, they will gather around them a great number of teachers to say what their itching ears want to hear. They will turn their ears away from the truth and turn aside to myths."

Nick winced. He had done exactly that.

"But you, keep your head in all situations, endure hardship, do the work of an evangelist, discharge all the duties of your ministry."

Ministry? What kind of ministry could God call him to after the horrible choices he had made? Nick lowered his head to his arms.

He didn't know what he would do. His money would not hold out long even with the cheap motel rates he got in this dump. He needed permanent housing soon but it seemed that every place he asked gave him the same answer. No openings until the end of May when college students cleared out. That was still a month away. And Nick had no income. College students held the jobs he applied for as well. "Come back in a month," he heard over and over.

When Nick went to a rival contracting company for a job, the owner politely told Nick no, he had heard that Nick was unreliable. Nick knew then that Les had called the owner out of spite. The dagger went deep.

He closed the Bible and laid it on the nightstand. He would go out again tomorrow. He would keep trying until he found a job and a place to live.

Something deep within him kept whispering for him to go to Anya's, but if he spent the last of his money on gas and she turned him away, he would be finished.

No, he would do this on his own. He would overcome his past sin and build a new life for himself – one that would please God at last. Anya couldn't be his salvation. Somehow he would manage. If only he weren't so tired.

Nick got up and went to the bathroom to brush his teeth. He looked at the note cards he had stuck to the bathroom mirror, bits and pieces taken from Colossians 3 that he found particularly encouraging. "Set your mind on things above, not on earthly things. For you died, and your life is now hidden with Christ in God... Put to death, therefore, whatever belongs to your earthly nature... You used to walk in these ways, in the life you once lived. But now you must rid yourselves of all such things... Put on the new self, which is being renewed in knowledge in the image of its Creator."

Nick spat his toothpaste into the sink and grimaced into the mirror. The dim lighting gave his skin a yellowish tint. He looked closer. Even the whites of his eyes looked yellow. He hadn't noticed it in here before. Maybe he just hadn't paid attention. But he couldn't blame poor lighting on the dark circles under his eyes. He hadn't slept well in weeks and his body cried out for naps during the day. The headaches and nausea that had started on his trip to Western Kansas still plagued him along with feeling achy and hot.

Nick wondered if he should go to a doctor but he didn't have health insurance now that he wasn't on Les's payroll. Nick told himself the same thing he'd been saying for several weeks. He would be fine. He just needed time to rest and get whatever it was out of his system. But the ever-anxious thought niggled at him – God's judgment. He had heard the rhetoric of the fundamentalists. He knew what they said of AIDS. Nick didn't know enough about the disease to even know if he had any of the symptoms but the worry ate at him anyway.

After taking several Tylenol, he crawled in bed and pulled the covers around his shoulders. It was still early enough in the evening for the sun to break through around the edges of the heavy window drapes but he didn't trust himself to watch television. The motel offered reduced rates on porn movies and Nick already fought the compulsion to rent one. It was easier to keep the policy of never turning the screen on.

The answering machine picked up her call - again. Anya sighed. Either Les and Nick had been away for quite some time or they were ignoring her name on caller ID. As she listened to Les's voice telling her to leave her name and number, Les suddenly picked up.

"Hello?" He sounded brusque. He was probably getting tired of all her messages. Anya thought of the persistent widow in the parable Jesus told. She certainly fit the bill.

"Hello, Les. This is Anya Martin. I met you some time ago."

"I know who you are."

"How are you?" She said it out of habit and winced. Les would not appreciate polite small talk with her.

"What do you need, lady?"

"Is, would Nick happen to be there?"

"No."

"Could you have him call me when he gets in?"

"No."

"Then perhaps you can tell me when he'll be in and I might call back."

"Nick doesn't live here anymore."

Anya sucked in her breath. That was news. "Do you know where I might reach him?"

"Not a clue."

"A cell phone or address or anything?"

"If Nick wants to talk to you, he'll call you."

"What if he wanted to and couldn't?"

"Nick's a big boy. He'll be fine. Go be someone else's grandma." Les hung up.

Anya wrung her hands. She had worried about Nick ever since their last exchange. She wanted to let him see how deeply she loved him no matter how he chose to live his life, that he would always be a son to her - but he had left so abruptly. She never should have confronted him so strongly. She should have known he would tire of her sermons.

No. She shook her head. Her love for him had made it impossible for her to remain silent about the truth. And now her love for him would keep her looking and praying.

"May I help you?" The church secretary spoke without looking up as she wrote a note and circled it with flourish.

Nick leaned against the front of her desk for support. His joints and head ached worse today despite the increased dosage of Tylenol he was taking every few hours. "I'm here to see Pastor Brooks. He said I could come anytime."

"He's in a meeting right now. Do you want to wait or come back later?" She smacked several sheets of paper together on the desktop to align the edges and slammed the corners under the stapler. Nick winced in sympathy for the paper.

"How long do you think he'll be?"

"Fifteen minutes, maybe twenty."

"I'll wait."

"Make yourself comfortable." She twirled her chair around to her computer screen.

Nick sank down onto a chair and leaned his head against the wall. He didn't really know why he was here - unless the pastor could miraculously give him a job, a house, or healing. Any one of the three would do. Nick closed his eyes and listened to the flurry of pecks on the keyboard.

The inner office door opened and a stranger walked out, followed by Kenneth Brooks.

"Nick Pierce. What a surprise!" The pastor held out his hand.

Nick stood quickly but a surge of nausea and dizziness hit him. He swayed as blackness filled his peripheral vision.

"Nick? Are you all right?" The words echoed as though from a far distance and Nick felt himself falling. His last sight was that of the secretary standing behind her desk and looking at him at last, with her mouth hanging open and her hand reaching out to him.

Nick gripped fistfuls of thin blanket into bunches at his sides. He lay flat on his back on a narrow table in the emergency room, surrounded by strange equipment and a pale green curtain. He couldn't remember getting here but he could remember someone sticking his arm for a vial of blood.

How would he pay for all this?

The curtain slid aside. "Mr. Pierce, I'm glad to see you're awake. I need to ask you a few questions," said a man whom Nick assumed to be a doctor.

"What's wrong with me?"

"We can't know for sure yet. We did take a blood sample to run some tests."

"What kind of tests?"

"Liver function tests."

"Why?"

"You may have noticed your skin and eyes looking more yellow than normal. That's a sign of jaundice, which indicates an unhealthy liver. We want to do the tests to see if your liver is functioning normally."

Was that why he had felt so tender in his abdomen? Something was wrong with his liver?

"Are you a drinker?"

"What?"

"Do you drink alcohol?"

"No. Never."

"Have you noticed anything different about your health lately, say in the last few weeks?"

"I've been tired, kind of sick to my stomach. I get headaches but Tylenol helps."

"How many were you taking?"

"Three or four."

"At a time?"

"Yes."

"How many times a day?"

"Every four or five hours, I guess."

The doctor frowned. "Tylenol is acetaminophen, which can cause liver damage. With your liver already compromised by the virus, you'll need to stick to aspirin."

"I didn't know."

"Now you do. Are you on any other medications? Antibiotics?"

"No."

"Have your stools been off color?"

Nick blinked in confusion.

"Your bowel movements. Have they been lighter colored, like clay?"

"Maybe."

"Blood in your stools?"

"Some."

The doctor looked at him sharply and made a notation on his clipboard. "Has your urine been dark?"

"Yes. But I probably just wasn't drinking enough."

"You did have slight dehydration when you came in but the dark urine can be a sign of your liver not working properly, not necessarily how much fluid intake you have. We've been giving you Saline solution for several hours now so you're probably no longer dehydrated."

Nick looked at the partially empty plastic bag hanging from the IV pole next to him. He hadn't even noticed the line going into his wrist.

"We're going to need to admit you into the hospital for observation and tests."

Nick rolled his head back and forth on the pillow. "I can't stay overnight," he said, hating the hoarseness in his voice. "I don't have insurance."

"That's the last thing you need to worry about right now." The doctor patted his arm. "Right now you have some possibly serious health issues that need to be taken care of. Liver damage can lead to liver failure and I don't mean to scare you, Mr. Pierce, but could also cause death. We'll make the finances work out the best we can for you."

Nick's muscles tensed. So he didn't have AIDS, as he'd feared in the darkest parts of his soul, but he could still be dying. God could still be giving him the verdict of death for his sin. Nick tightened his fists on the blanket.

"I'm ordering an ultrasound as well. The technicians are off work for tonight but they can get that done first thing in the morning."

"I thought ultrasounds were for pregnant women."

The doctor smiled briefly. "An ultrasound is simply a 3-D picture of anything on the inside. We need to see the extent of liver damage, if any. We'll hope for the best. Between the liver function tests and the ultrasound, we'll have a clear idea of what's going on and how to begin treatment. Someone will come in a few minutes with admittance paperwork for you to sign. Lie still and rest."

The green curtain had not stopped swaying from the doctor's departure before Kenneth Brooks entered.

"Hello, Nick. It's good to see you awake." His voice was hushed.

"I'm sorry I caused you trouble, Pastor Brooks."

The pastor shook his head. "I'm glad you weren't alone when you collapsed. And call me Kenneth."

Nick thought of the barren motel room and chills covered his arms. What if he had been alone? How long would it have been before anyone missed him or found him? Would he have died?

"Is there anyone I can contact for you? Can I call your... er, boss? Les – that's his name, right?"

Nick squinted at the pastor. Surely he wouldn't be offering to call the man who - inasmuch as he knew - was still Nick's lover?

"No, there's no one," he said, turning his face away. When he closed his eyes, he saw Anya's face.

Nick stared at the jell-o and clear broth on his breakfast tray. His eyes felt gritty from lack of sleep. Whoever said hospitals were places where people got well? If the staff continued to wake him up, he would never get rest. And if this doctor kept slamming horrible diagnoses on him, he would never survive.

Nick sobered. Survival. He'd always taken it for granted. Only a few minutes ago he had been told that his liver was failing – to the point that they had advised him to go on the waiting list for a transplant. All because of some untreated viral infection called Hepatitis.

He picked up his spoon and stared at the inverted reflection. He wasn't even 21 yet and he was dying. They hadn't said it, but he knew. And he deserved it. From the questions the doctor had asked about his sexual life or use of needles, Nick could only surmise that he'd somehow picked up the virus from Les. He certainly hadn't ever gotten a tattoo or shot up with drugs.

Only a few nights ago, Nick had determined in the motel room to make his life right without anyone's help – to prove to

God that he could make himself worthy. But God was having
the final say here. Nick would never be worthy. He was going
to hell. His father had been right. God didn't want a pervert for
a son any more than J.D. had.

"Nick?" Les stood at the foot of the bed, his face pale.

Nick laid down the spoon and pushed away the tray.

"Some guy named Kenneth Brooks called me and said
you were here." Les walked closer and put his hands on the
footboard. "He said you were diagnosed with Hepatitis?"

Nick swallowed. Les looked like Russell to him,
standing there with concern, real concern. He felt a stirring of
attraction and fought it.

"Nick, I am so sorry." Les whispered the words.

"What are you sorry about? I made the choice to leave."
Nick hid under anger.

"Not that." Les shook his head. "For you being sick.
It's my fault."

"What do you mean, it's your fault?"

"I'm a carrier."

The words slammed into Nick. He couldn't speak,
couldn't breathe. Finally he asked, "How long have you known
this?"

"For a while."

"Since you knew me?"

Les looked down. "Yes."

"And you didn't tell me?"

"I didn't want to scare you off."

"No, you just let me get sick instead." Nick felt rage
swelling up inside him, pounding in his temples.

"I never meant to, Nick. Most people don't get as sick
as you."

"My liver is over 90 percent destroyed. Did you know
that?"

The whites of Les's eyes showed all the way around his pupils. "No."

"Did they tell you my only hope of survival is a transplant?"

"Nick, don't make yourself upset." Les put his hand onto Nick's foot. "You'll make yourself worse."

Nick laughed. "Worse? Very funny."

Les removed his hand.

"You didn't make me sick anyway, Les. God did. He's having His judgment on me."

"Because of us? That's not true. God doesn't..."

Nick violently threw his hands toward Les. "I don't want to listen to your lies anymore. Get out, Les. Just leave."

Les put his hands to his ears to block out the hospital noises as he hurried down the corridor – away from Nick. He had seen too many friends in hospital beds, been to too many funerals, and what was happening to Nick was closer to him than any of those. Why was his community so stricken with sicknesses and diseases? Was Nick right? Was God meting out judgment?

Les slammed his hands on the bar to open the door and escape the hospital. He could hardly bear to admit it, but no matter how many relationships he sought and nurtured, none had filled the space inside him – the emptiness of never having a father's or stepfather's approval.

Nick had questioned him unlike any of his lovers in the past – had questioned his logic, his reasoning, his faith. It shook Les. He believed that everything happened for a purpose, whether good or bad. So, what was the purpose of this? What was he to do? What was he to learn? Les looked up at the gray skies as he headed across the parking lot. Was God trying to tell him something?

Karl sat beside J.D. on the narrow cot in J.D.'s cell so they could look at a horse sale catalog together. The closeness made J.D. nervous. He hoped none of the guards would think anything funny about his sitting side by side with another man. People talked. They said things like, "the apple don't fall far from the tree" and "he's just like his daddy".

"Why do you think he wants a life like that?" Karl had asked J.D. after Nick's visit. The way he looked at J.D. made him squirm.

"He's a sick pervert."

But Karl knew about J.D.'s addictions – both to alcohol and pornography. Not much had been left secret after his trial.

"So are you," Karl said. J.D. would have hit him if the guard hadn't watched. But Karl hadn't meant he thought J.D. was gay. He said that all sexual sin was sin, whether it was lust from a magazine or intercourse outside of marriage.

J.D. didn't agree. The kid was warped and twisted in ways that disgusted him. He was ashamed to have anyone know about his son.

Karl flipped the sale catalog shut. "Think I should go to the sale?"

"Wouldn't hurt."

Karl rubbed his nose, a precursor to something he needed to say but didn't want to. J.D. had learned a lot about Karl during his visits – more than all those years of having Karl as his boss.

"Mom's been trying to call Nick."

J.D. stood up. "I told you I don't want to talk about him."

"He's not living with Les anymore."

J.D. turned his back on Karl and stared at the cinder block wall.

"Mom wasn't able to get a phone number or address or anything. We're hoping he contacts us soon so we know where he is and that he's okay."

So the kid had gone missing. Well, not missing, really. Just vanished, like Julienne. The news should have given him the freedom to write the boy off but instead J.D. felt worry in his gut. For all the kid's independence, there was something fragile about him. Maybe that fragileness had been what irked J.D. most about the boy.

He didn't need to lose sleep over it. Anya Martin would do everything in her power to find Nick. She would fuss over anything, that one. Like a mother hen, she was. He half expected her to cluck.

Brenna left her mother and Sylvia folding warm towels straight from the dryer. She bounded down the front steps, glad to not be needed, glad to go home with time to fix a special meal for Mitch.

Sylvia had become more than a counselor since coming here. She had become Mrs. William's friend. The two went shopping together, cooked together, talked and even laughed together. The change amazed Brenna. She knew full well that her mother still had down spells but new medications and a fledgling social life were bringing her wholeness. More than once, Brenna had walked into conversations between her mother and Sylvia about God and she could only pray that complete wholeness would take place.

"Hey, Brenna." Her father walked toward her from one of the outbuildings.

"Hi Dad." She boldly kissed his cheek, filled with outpourings of affection that she had held back out of fear for so many years. He blushed and pulled away, same as he always did, but she knew he liked it. "How is your day going?"

"Can't complain." He never did.

"You and Mom have a great trip to the mountains tomorrow."

"Hope the snow's melted enough," he said. Brenna knew the farmer in him made him always wonder about the weather. "Too bad you can't come."

"Mitch and I will be busy moving the rest of his tools into his new building."

"I hope that repair shop works out for him."

"Oh it will, Dad. Mitch already has a good reputation and more business than he can handle."

"And you? Are you going to enjoy working in the office?"

Brenna thought about the office area Mitch had built onto the side of his new metal building. She had already moved in a desk and two file cabinets. She had taken accounting in high school and even though math had never been her strongest asset, she was eager to organize Mitch's wadded papers and develop her own system for sending out bills and doing the bookwork. "I'm going to love working in the same building as Mitch," she said.

Her father just shook his head. Brenna knew he thought she and Mitch were crazy about each other. And they were, more now than on their wedding day. According to Anya, it would only get better.

"Well, I'd better get busy if I want to finish everything before our trip," said her father.

"Tell Bradley I miss him. And tell him he needs to come home sometime this summer, even if he says the mountains are better than Kansas."

"Maybe they are," said her father. "Your mother seems to like them."

"Yes, she does, doesn't she?" Brenna smiled at the underlying pleasure on her father's face that seemed to say, "At last, I can do something for her that she will enjoy."

Les slipped into Room 209 where Nick lay with his head turned sideways on the pillow. Les sank onto the chair beside the bed to watch Nick sleep. He folded his hands under his chin and resisted the impulse to touch Nick's hand. The last thing he needed was for Nick to wake.

He didn't really know why he had come – maybe to pray, maybe to say goodbye to another attempt at love. But he couldn't pray. He didn't seem to remember how. He sat for a long time, watching the shadows from the window dance across Nick's bed sheet.

As he turned to go, he bumped into the bedside tray. A paper cup of water fell over. Les snatched it up and checked over his shoulder to see if Nick had slept through the noise. Nick didn't move. Les grabbed a wad of Kleenex from the box on the tray and dabbed at a stack of papers on the tray that had gotten wet. The papers were sticking together so he spread them out to dry. Then he saw the inscription at the top of each page. "Dear Mrs. Martin…"

Nick had written to Mrs. Martin, not to him. The dates showed that Nick had written a letter each day that he had been in the hospital. Les wondered why they hadn't been sent. Maybe the staff was too busy to take care of it for him.

Les knew he should offer to mail the letters but Nick had been the one to walk out. He didn't owe him anything. Les left the letters where they lay.

Chapter 24

"Mrs. Martin's here to visit you."

"Me?" J.D. looked up from the cot in surprise as Anya stepped into the hallway between the cells. She shivered as the gate clanged shut behind her. She had only been here once before – when the twins came to the jail on a Kindergarten field trip. There hadn't been any prisoners on that visit and they hadn't been locked in.

"Could we have some privacy, Ron?" she asked. The guard nodded and stepped away.

J.D. stood up and scratched his neck, apparently willing to let her speak first.

Anya hadn't seen J.D. since his incarceration but she figured he wouldn't appreciate small talk. "I got a phone call today. We know where Nick is."

J.D. raised his eyebrows. Anya wasn't sure if that meant to go on or that he didn't care. She rubbed her hands over the flowered pattern on her skirt. "He's in a hospital at Wichita. He's very sick. Apparently he needs a liver transplant."

"A transplant?"

"His liver failed due to some sort of infection."

"AIDS?"

"No."

"An STD?"

"Hepatitis."

"Same thing."

J.D. scratched his neck again. "His liver, huh?"

When Anya nodded, J.D. actually laughed.

"There's irony. I drink for decades and my liver is fine."

Anya didn't smile. Every bit of her wanted to jump in her car and drive to Nick as fast as she could but J.D. was his father. He deserved to know before she left.

"Did the kid finally call?"

"No." Anya hesitated. How much did J.D. know? "A man named Les Howland called."

"The boyfriend?" J.D. narrowed his eyes.

"They aren't together anymore. Les called because he said we should know what was going on." Anya didn't add that Les had seemed less than happy about calling even though she gathered that Nick didn't know about it.

"Where was he all this time?"

"Staying in a motel. He's been in the hospital close to a week."

"Can he leave the hospital?"

"They might release him in the next few days. But to be quite honest, I don't know if he has anywhere to go. I wouldn't think a motel would be the best thing for him if his health is precarious."

J.D. frowned. "You bringing him here?"

"If I can."

J.D. looked straight at her. "I ain't been no kind of father to him."

"I think now is a good time to start."

After another silence, J.D. spoke. "Don't know how I'm supposed to do that in here."

"J.D., you're the only family he has."

"Not sure I want to be. He deserves being sick."

Anya took a deep breath. "Did you deserve your jail sentence?"

J.D.'s eyes skittered away.

"We all deserve what we get when it comes to consequences for sin. Your son needs you, J.D. Please make things right with him."

Nick lay on his side and stared at the wall. His gown hung limp on his body. The blankets could not hide the jutting of his hip. The nurse had told him he had lost over 20 pounds.

She was getting mad at him, too, every time he sent back his food tray untouched.

"Nick?"

"I'm not eating," he said. "Take it away."

"It's not the nurse."

He rolled over. Anya had pushed open the wide door to his room. He blinked. She was still there.

"Les called me," she said. Her lips trembled. "I came right away."

"You shouldn't have." He turned back to the wall.

"I love you, Nick. I had to come."

He fiddled with the tape that held his IV line in place on the back of his hand. "You shouldn't."

"Shouldn't love you?" Her voice was soft, almost as soft as her footsteps and the touch of her hand on his back. The contact broke his reserves and he felt tears leak onto his cheeks.

"I'm dying, Anya," he gasped. "I'm dying and going to hell."

Her weight bowed the bed as she sat next to him and rubbed his back in little circles as if he were a young boy again.

"I deserve it. I'm unlovable. I can't change. I'm hopeless."

"Is that what you think?" She tugged on his shoulder, as though to encourage him to twist and face her.

"I want to die. I'm ready to die."

"Oh, no, you're not," she said. "People live with liver failure all the time. This is not going to beat you."

"God is beating me."

"If God beats you in this, what will He win?"

Nick fell silent.

"He doesn't win your soul if you said you were going to hell. Do you think He wants that?"

"I deserve it," he said again.

"We all do, Nick. That's why Jesus' blood is called grace."

She was quiet for a moment. He tried to control the sobs that wanted to heave his body.

"Can I get you a tissue?"

"On the bedside tray," he said, subdued.

He heard her rustle around for the tissues and pause.

"Nick? What are these?" she asked.

Too late, he remembered – the letters. Some clumsy night-shift aid had spilled water all over them and laid them out to dry. Nick hadn't bothered to restack them.

"You wrote all these letters to me?"

He wiped his cheeks with his palms.

She exhaled. "Oh, Nick. May I read them?"

"Maybe later." He accepted a wad of tissues from her and blew his nose.

"Hello, Nick." Kenneth Brooks came in, looking at Anya with curiosity. "Looks like you have company. I'm not interrupting, am I?"

"No, it's fine." Nick hoped his eyes weren't as red as they felt. "Anya Martin was my neighbor in Western Kansas."

"Nice to meet you, Mrs. Martin. I'm Pastor Kenneth Brooks."

"The guy who saved my life," Nick added. He couldn't hide the irony. Kenneth saved his life – a life he no longer wanted saved.

Pastor Brooks pushed up his glasses several times. "I didn't do anything. You just happened to be in the church when you got sick."

Anya looked between the two. "What church?"

When he told her, Nick saw the relief on her face. He wondered if he would ever be free from the speculations of others any time a man was involved in his life. He wanted to explain the role of this man to Anya but some nasty place inside him didn't want to admit that he was changing. He wanted to test Anya's love up against his own ugliness. Would she love him no matter what he was?

"I brought your street clothes." Pastor Brooks held up a Wal-Mart bag. "The nurse at the station said that you can go ahead and get dressed."

"Dressed? Are they letting me go?" He was ready to die and they were letting him go?

Even Anya looked unsure. "Will he be okay?"

"As long as he follows the dietary instructions closely and gets some physical exercise, he should be fine – at least as fine as he can be until after the transplant."

"And emotionally?" Anya lowered her voice.

"Getting him out of here and into as normal a life as possible is best. Give him a purpose to beat the blues."

Nick resented their talking about him as if he wasn't there. "A normal life? How can I have that? I have no home, no job, no money…"

"You'll come home with me," said Anya. "You can work for Karl or Mitch. And as for money, God will provide."

Nick sat up, weak and shaky. He had been having nightmares each night about seeing his own corpse; he was so sure that he was dying. As Kenneth Brooks helped him stand and walked him to the bathroom to change, he felt like a child learning to walk again. He felt… resurrected.

"I brought someone to see you," Karl said when the guard escorted them into the visitation room.

J.D. looked up from the table. Nick wished he could hide. Why had he let them talk him into coming? He still felt the sting of his father's loathing from that first jail visit, still heard the hateful words. "You're no son of mine… I always figured I would've done the worst possible job if my kid turned out to be a fag…"

J.D. stood and tucked his thumbs into his belt loops. "Hey."

"Nick is living with Mom for a while," said Karl.

J.D. eyed Nick. "They said you got sick, son."

So they were back to "son" now?

"That's what they tell me."

"So you're waiting for a transplant?"

"Yeah."

"How long?"

"Don't know. Anywhere from a couple of weeks to a couple of years. They have to find a match for my blood type, age and the liver size."

"How do you live without a liver?"

Nick grimaced. "You have to watch what you eat." He thought of the proteins he had to count and the saltshaker Anya had removed from her table.

"No more liver and onions?" J.D. actually laughed. Nick wasn't sure if the joke was intended cruelly or not.

"For most people, that would be cause for rejoicing," said Karl. "Should we sit down?"

J.D. took the seat across from them. He leaned his elbows on the table. "You feeling okay now?"

Nick crossed his legs then uncrossed them, nervous of what his father would think of the feminine pose. "I'm all right." No sense telling of the pervasive tiredness, achy joints, and the swollen midsection he hid by keeping his shirt untucked.

"You don't look all right."

Karl patted Nick's shoulder. "He'll gain his weight back soon if Mom has anything to do with it."

Nick looked down. No sense telling of his digestion problems and bloody vomiting either.

"That's true," J.D. agreed. "She'd solve world hunger if she could bake enough cookies."

Karl laughed. "She would at that. What was your mom like, J.D.? I don't think I've ever heard you talking about growing up."

J.D. spread his hands flat on the tabletop. "Don't talk about it much." He glanced up at Nick. "My mom - your grandma - was real sweet. She treated us fine. But she died when I was seven, you know. Then Dad took off and my big sister raised us. Guess she resented us cause she weren't nothing like Mom had been."

Nick sat up straighter. He had never stopped to think about his father's childhood; he had been so busy feeling sorry for himself about his own.

J.D. shrugged. "I dropped out of school when a rancher offered me a job. Moved out to his bunkhouse. Didn't regret leaving."

"How many brothers and sisters do you have?"

"Four. Two brothers. Two sisters."

He had aunts and uncles and probably cousins – more family that belonged to him.

"Where do they live?" asked Karl.

"Don't know. Never went back to visit much after the first couple of years. Last I knew, most of them was still in Wyoming." J.D. slapped his hands on the table. "That was all a long time ago. Don't really like to think about it much."

Karl leaned back in his chair. "My mom died when I was twelve. A kid doesn't get over something like that. I even had the best of circumstances with Dad marrying Anya. But I still miss my mom."

"I never knew mine." Nick blushed as both men's eyes turned on him.

"You don't remember Julienne?" asked J.D.

Nick shook his head. "Grandma Bates said I was three, but I guess she didn't take care of me much before that. I don't remember anything."

J.D. cleared his throat. "She was real pretty. You look like her, sorta."

Nick glared at his father.

"I didn't mean it bad."

"Why did you tell Karl you'd like to see me today?"

"Because I wanted to."

"Why?"

J.D. shifted his weight. "I don't have nobody left, Nick. You're my son and…"

"Tell him, J.D." Karl lowered his chair back on all four legs and leaned forward. "Tell him what you told me."

J.D. traced little circles on the table with shaking fingers. "Don't know as I can say it."

Nick held his breath.

J.D.'s eyes pleaded with Karl. "You say it for me."

Karl shook his head. "That's your job. You're his father."

When J.D.'s eyes came back to him, miserable and begging, Nick knew. He knew what his father wanted to say. He also knew he had a choice. Would he allow the words or turn away? Russell's Father-God wanted to say the same thing to him. If Nick made the choice to reject his father, he'd be rejecting the Father-God's words as well. Nick swallowed. Could he forgive the man who hurt him and neglected him? Could he accept the life God had given him? Could he believe, really believe that the words were true?

Nick reached across the table and put his hands over his father's. "You can tell me, Dad."

"I… I love you."

Several months later, Nick felt the vibration of the cell phone in his pocket during church. Nick carried the cell phone with him at all times except for when he plugged it in the wall at Anya's house to charge. He had only given the phone number to the surgical unit at Wichita. There could only be one reason for the call. Still, he feared that it couldn't be - not this soon. He had prepared himself to wait for years.

Nick held up crossed fingers as he squeezed past Anya's knees and into the aisle. Mitch and Brenna watched him from the back pew as he let himself out into the foyer.

Nick had worked for Mitch these last few months – as much as his health would allow. At first, Mitch intimidated him, always covered in grease with some foreign tool in his hand. The maleness of the repair shop confused Nick and he braced himself for more teasing from Mitch but none came. If anything, he and Mitch had formed a shaky sort of friendship. Brenna told him Mitch appreciated Nick's ability to learn quickly.

"Maybe it's those piano fingers of his," Mitch said. "He can operate on those engines pretty well for someone who's never had any experience."

The rest of the time, Nick played Anya's piano. He pushed his abilities harder than ever before. If he made it through this health crisis, maybe he could get a music scholarship.

The sanctuary door closed behind him and muffled the sound of the sermon. Nick opened the text message. His heart stopped for a long moment then pounded. He went back to Anya and knelt in the aisle beside her and held up the phone so she could read the message.

They had found a match.

Epilogue

Nick weighted the envelope with gravel from the drive that went through the center of the cemetery. He could recite the letter inside by heart.

"Dear Mrs. Martin, thank you for standing by me and in prayer for me for so many years. You loved me when I was most unlovable. You mentored me when I most needed someone to care..."

Along with the letter, he had folded a sheet of music, a classical music piece he had written in her memory and soon to be performed by the Wichita Symphony. He could almost hear the strains of the song on the Kansas wind, that same wind that had slashed past the gravestones on the day of Russell's funeral. He was sorry to have missed her service – this saint who had meant so much to him. But he had been in Europe - on tour with a small and relatively unknown orchestra made up of men and women who each had a unique testimony of freedom and forgiveness to share in between numbers at the concerts. Every time he spoke of his past, Nick could only pray that his story resonated with someone in the audience struggling with the silent agonies he once had.

Nick studied the marbled stone above the graves. Two decades had passed since the date underneath Russell's name yet Nick's memories of that summer when he was twelve seemed fresh and close. He had learned God's goodness that summer. He would never forget.

The date of Anya's death was freshly edged in the rock. Nick bowed his head. He had known the last time he visited her that she would not be on earth much longer. She had been as eager to feed him as ever, even though the only thing she could find was stale graham crackers. That day, she told him she was dreaming about Jesus and Russell nearly every night.

Nick put his hand to his midsection and thought of the new liver inside him – the organ that gave him the life and energy and cleansing that he needed. The blood of Christ had given him cleansing as well, taking a boy so hurt and unwanted and giving him life.

Nick tucked his hands in his pockets and walked back to the car parked at the edge of the cemetery. Mitch and Brenna waited in the car to give him time alone, even though Mitch had a greater right to grieve than Nick. Nick also knew they would wait until he was ready to smile and laugh again before they regaled him with tales of their children's exploits.

Perhaps this time he would regale them with a few tales of his own, how God had saved him and redeemed him. It didn't matter that they knew his story forwards and backwards or that Nick still couldn't get through it without a lump in his throat. He never tired of telling it, not with words or with the music that flowed from his fingers in praise to his Father, the Father-God.